P9-DYY-394

Praise for *The Sound of Stars*

"*The Sound of Stars* is a stunning exploration of the comforts that make us human and the horrors that challenge our humanity."
—K. Ancrum, author of *The Wicker King*

"*The Sound of Stars* is a marvelous genre-bending debut."
—*The Nerd Daily*

"This book has everything! Aliens set on conquering earth! A determined heroine with a hidden stash of books! And the power of music and stories to give those with every reason to hate the power to love. Who could want anything more?"
—Joelle Charbonneau, *New York Times* bestselling author of *The Testing* and *Verify*

"Dow paints a moving picture of two young people's defiance and the power of song and story to combat despair."
—*Publishers Weekly*

"A promising debut that begs for a sequel."
—*Kirkus Reviews*

"This book has everything – from two charming and endearing characters who are impossible not to root for, an adorable romance, all the way to a grand adventure that is as high stakes as you can possibly get. It's an absolute must-read for everyone."
—*Book Riot*

"Dow's debut is a testament to hope and the power of art."
—*BuzzFeed*

**Books by Alechia Dow
available from Inkyard Press**

The Sound of Stars
The Kindred

THE
SOUND
OF
STARS

ALECHIA DOW

inkyard
PRESS

If you purchased this book without a cover you should be aware that this book is stolen property. It was reported as "unsold and destroyed" to the publisher, and neither the author nor the publisher has received any payment for this "stripped book."

Recycling programs for this product may not exist in your area.

ISBN-13: 978-1-335-40669-9

The Sound of Stars

First published in 2020. This edition published in 2021.

Copyright © 2020 by Alechia Dow

All rights reserved. No part of this book may be used or reproduced in any manner whatsoever without written permission except in the case of brief quotations embodied in critical articles and reviews.

This is a work of fiction. Names, characters, places and incidents are either the product of the author's imagination or are used fictitiously. Any resemblance to actual persons, living or dead, businesses, companies, events or locales is entirely coincidental.

This edition published by arrangement with Harlequin Books S.A.

For questions and comments about the quality of this book, please contact us at CustomerService@Harlequin.com.

Inkyard Press
22 Adelaide St. West, 41st Floor
Toronto, Ontario M5H 4E3, Canada
www.InkyardPress.com

Printed in U.S.A.

To the dreamers, readers, librarians and music makers—even if you only sound good in the shower. And to Liv, you're the stars in my eyes.

PROLOGUE

The invasion came when we were too distracted raging against our governments to notice. Terror had a face and we elected it, my mom said. We were more divided than ever, and that division made our defeat easy.

One moment we were screaming at each other—fingers pointed at the bigotry, the chaos, the hatred—and the next our gaze lifted to the chrome spaceships hovering behind the clouds. No one knew what to do. There was panic; there was fear. Anyone who could left the city and headed for their second homes or their families out-of-state.

Not us, though. We had nowhere to go, no option but to stay behind, locked inside our apartment, waiting for the news to tell us what was happening. For days, the reports told us nothing other than what we already knew; there was now incontrovertible proof we weren't alone in the universe.

News was hard to come by. There were whispered rumors, nothing confirmed, nothing that inspired confidence in Mom or Dad, who already expected the worst. We didn't dare leave our apartment building till something concrete reached our ears. It never did.

Other than speculation, there was no official communication that first week. The White House was silent. It was as if they invited chaos by not releasing a statement, by not acknowledging the truth or establishing a plan. All we could do was sit on our couch and wait. That was the longest week of our lives.

And then, one night, the sky lit up a brilliant orange, brighter than the sun. The explosion that followed shook our walls and pierced our eyes. *We hit the aliens*, the radio blasted across the block. Three massive ships were hit; one in the US, struck over New York, crashed onto the California coast! *We destroyed them*, people shouted in the streets. Had we won? Was it over?

And then they struck back.

Army bases were their first targets. But there was still hope, the news reports said. We still had our national guard. We didn't need jets and planes. We needed troops on the ground. They were mobilized just before the invasion.

Major cities across the world were overrun within days. The battles raged just outside our walls. The Ilori—we learned their name and their abilities—didn't use bombs. Didn't need weapons. They marched in black armor and masks and used their hands. They hunted by sound; they could hear our hearts beating, our inhales of breath. They could use their minds to destroy ours. And yet, after taking out the leaders, they didn't. These seemingly invincible creatures responded only to our attacks. Whatever their goal, it didn't involve annihilation— not that that made a difference.

There were losses on both sides; more of us than them, but enough of them to make humans feel like we stood a chance.

Every dead Ilori was taken and analyzed. I still remember the way people cheered in their homes as breaking news reports filmed, not from news stations, but from hospitals within protected bunkers. Scientists had found a way to kill the Ilori. They weren't indestructible. Underneath their armor they looked like us. They had eyes, ears, lips, hair and skin, which meant they could bleed. Their blood was as red as our own. Yet, killing them was difficult. If you were lucky enough to outnumber them ten to one, you might be able to overpower them, maybe even shut them down.

Electricity…that was their source of power, we were told excitedly. They need it to survive. I chuckle thinking of it now; how we thought, because we found their weakness, we'd win. How our soldiers switched out their guns for electrical weapons, and we thought we had a chance.

We were wrong.

PART ONE

THE CENTER

Up in the Stars Podcast

Transcript of the Interview with Allister Daniels and Cecil Wright by Mandy LaHoya.

Mandy: Hey, it's your host, Mandy LaHoya of the Starry Eyed podcast, *Up in the Stars*! And guys, I'm beyond excited. This week's fast and fresh interview is the biggest of my career and it's everything I've ever wanted. Today I'm here with Allister Daniels and Cecil Wright of the Starry Eyed! Can you even believe? Not only is it super rare you'd get to speak to one of them, but the two of them together—

Cecil: *(inaudible)*—not *my* fault. That's all on Allister.

Allister: My apologies for Cecil, Mandy. He forgets the world doesn't revolve around him. We're very happy to be here, please continue.

Mandy: *(giggles)* Right! It's not only rare that the two of you are together for this interview, but you usually disappear before a release. So, we're really surprised and lucky to have you on here! Anyway, let's dig in. First question: What inspired your new album, *The Sound of Stars*?

Allister: *The Sound of Stars* is about love and… annihilation. I put my heart, my everything, into these lyrics. And Cecil, Rupert, Whisper—they're truly brilliant—found the perfect harmonies to make this our best album.

Cecil: That's kind, Allister. The thing about Allister's lyrics is that he—he really has a story in mind, and every track tells an important piece of it. He's extraordinarily talented—

Allister: Thank you, Cecil. I wasn't expecting that.

Cecil: And difficult…just a phenomenally difficult person. But yes, *The Sound of Stars* is about love during conflict. Bridges during division. It's our present, our past and, we believe, our future.

Mandy: That sounds amazing and intense, and I can't wait to listen! But you said you put your heart into this, Allister—why? Why does this album mean so much to you?

Allister: *(clears throat)* Because…it might inspire our fans, our listeners, to save the world, to save each other, to…find hope. And we need hope more than ever right now. The only way we'll survive is if we build connections through passion. Through love.

Mandy: That's beautiful. And I know your music will change the world, it has definitely changed mine.

Cecil: *(laughs)* Don't encourage his vanity, Mandy. I promise you, he has a big enough ego as is. Ow!

Allister: Thank you, Mandy. It means a lot to us that our music reaches and resonates with so many people. And we'd love to share *The Sound of Stars* with you today, if you're up for it?

Mandy: Heck yeah! Let's do it!

CHAPTER 1

"I have had all this hanging on my mind, without being at liberty to speak of it to a single creature…"

Elinor Dashwood, *Sense and Sensibility*, Jane Austen

JANELLE

I blame the Starry Eyed for the risks I take. Allister Daniels, the lead singer, once said that life's short, but it's the longest thing you'll ever do, so give more than you take and be kind. I guess that meant a lot to me, because here I am, giving and being kind… And it's probably gonna be my downfall.

It's that thought that sticks with me as I stop to tie my shoe, slipping a scrap of crumpled paper into my sock before standing. *Easy*, all part of the routine; collect a note from the edge of the trash can in the back corner, hide it and read it when I get home. I wonder what my patron wants this time. Mysteries are always popular, so's military nonfiction for those looking for hope. But it's about time everyone understands that there is no hope. This is it.

It's warm in here; half the building is sweating in this makeshift gym while human guards look on with boredom. I swipe the beads of sweat lingering at the base of my hat and blow air through my teeth. Sometimes we go into the courtyard, but it's winter now and the Ilori don't trust us to take care of ourselves. Still, I'd rather be cold than in here, overheating. So I guess I'd prove their point.

The lights blink, telling us we have a few more minutes before we're to go back to our own apartments.

"Janelle," a whisper comes from the crowd behind me. I slow down, allowing whoever it is to catch up to me.

"I loved it. Thank you."

I don't turn around but recognize the voice. Marcus from the eighth floor. He borrowed one of my dad's books, *Watchmen*. My dad is—*was*—a big fan of graphic novels, while my mom loved romance and classics. As for me, I like everything, especially YA where girls kick ass and boys don't get in their way. Most of my patrons go for my books, but every so often, I get a request that has me looking beyond my stuff. And I'll do it, every time, if it means a story can change someone's outlook, if even just for a day.

Stories do that for me.

When recreation time's over, we shuffle our way back into the hallway and up the stairs, where the air is immediately less stale. I should be grateful that we're all locked in here, that we're alive. That we're clothed, fed, sheltered and the Ilori don't seem to want to kill us…until we break their precious rules. But freedom might be better than survival.

Back at my apartment, I snatch the book request from my shoe.

Something with dark humor, please. Jack 3B

My mind's already roving through possibilities when a knock on the door has me frozen in panic. It's too soon to expect anyone. The numbers rise to the surface of my mind, threatening to overtake my world for a few minutes before I can be a functioning, normal person again. But there's no time for that right now, and I can't keep panicking like this. I gulp and open our beige door, my heart pounding.

Zoe Landson stands before me, an uneasy pout on her lips. "I know this is wrong, but I really need a book."

"You shouldn't be here." My gaze darts up and down the hallway, making sure there are no guards around to bust us. We're lucky everyone important is either prepping dinner or upstairs.

Zoe's gaze locks on mine. "I know, but—"

"This isn't how I operate." I pull her inside and flick off the lights, washing us in shadows. I never do library business in the apartment. "There's a system. First, we establish contact through passed notes. That's half a transgression if caught. This—" I point to her in my apartment "—is a whole one."

The rules of social transgressions are pretty easy: Speaking in private places? Half a transgression if it's innocent, i.e. not plotting to attack or something. If it's about contraband and making plans to engage in illegal activity? That's one transgression, and you get only two until you're executed. Lying won't work with *them*. The Ilori have ways of finding out whatever you try to hide. They're powerful, especially if they think you're planning their demise.

"Then I vet you. I find your secrets and I test your loyalty." What I don't say is that I rely heavily on Alice for that—she finds the dirt on everyone. It's her talent and my secret weapon. "Then, and only then, can we discuss books."

Zoe squints at me through the moonlight that shines in

from the bare living room window down the hall and across from the kitchen. She's a year younger than me, and although we both are—*were*—outsiders in this building, we were never close. My parents inherited this apartment, and her dad was the repairman slash janitor. We stuck out, and probably would have stuck out even more if we became friends. "I'm sorry, Ellie. But I really need a book."

I shake my head, nostrils flaring. "You broke my rules."

"Please. You don't know what it's like over there." She motions to the door, across the hall to her apartment. "My dad's all I got and he's—"

"How do I know you won't toss me to a Kill Squad to cover your own ass?"

I clench my jaw, the words harshly whispered. Honestly, I doubt Zoe's gonna do that, but I vet people just in case. I like my rules and process. "You don't come here outside of socialization hours, and we never talk about the library. You slip me notes like everyone else. And you don't give them a reason to suspect either of us. This system works—and it has for a year, but it only works when people follow it."

A tear tumbles down her cheek, catching the light. Her bottom lip trembles.

Just say no. Don't do it. Why risk yourself? These are the things that run through my mind before I once again decide my role as librarian is more important than my life. Yeah, she came to my apartment, potentially exposing me, and yeah, I'm terrified of punishment. But a part of me likes the challenge. And another part of me, the foolish one, still holds on to the words of Allister Daniels.

Give more than you take. Be kind.

I lower my voice. No one's around to overhear us, but better safe than sorry. "What are we talking?"

"Really?" Her eyes widen, but I keep my face blank, impatient. "Paranormal, please?"

I nod. "Don't come back here again. Follow the rules, or you're off the list. Got it?"

"Thank you, thank you." Zoe goes to hug me, but I inch backward. We aren't friends like that.

I give her a polite smile that probably comes off as more of a grimace. I ease the door open, allowing her to peek out first. Satisfied, she bolts across the hall. I don't wait to hear her door close before I shut mine. That was close.

Too close.

My breathing finally slows just as the doorknob bumps into my back. I scoot aside to let my mom in, shoving Jack's note underneath my hat. "Janelle, what are you doing? Why are the lights off? Are they here?"

There's frenzy in her jerky motions, and her loose bun loses a few strands of matted dark brown curls. When was the last time she showered? I take in her blue scrubs, which hang off her diminished frame.

"Mom, everything's okay. I was just walking around the apartment. Getting exercise." I hate lying to her, but her eyes are far-off already anyway. She's been mentally checking out more and more. I sit her down at the kitchen table.

When Dad stomps inside and takes a seat, barely glancing at us, Mom pushes her chair as far away from him as she can. I remember how they used to laugh about silly things and get lost in their own little world of love. Now, they're both lost, just in very different worlds. And the love seems nonexistent.

Minutes pass in silence until I answer the door for dinner. There's a polite smile on my face as I accept the trays and thank one of our elderly neighbors, but I can't help recoiling at tonight's meal. For the fourth time this week, we're given hard crackers smeared with a tasteless protein spread. The canned peaches are new, though.

After setting the food down, I hand Mom a paper napkin, although she barely ever eats enough to make a mess. I know I shouldn't ask anymore, that I should keep quiet and let everyone be, but I miss talking to them. "How was... Was it a good day?"

Mom shoots me a look as she pushes her untouched plate toward me. She's reluctantly lucid and terse. "There are no good days."

I take her portion of peaches and eye Dad, wondering if I should even try to reach him. He's stoic, and survives only to serve *them*. His humanity, if he still has it, is dwindling away. In the beginning, he used to hug me fiercely and tell me that knowing I'm still here got him through dark days.

And yet, the days are darker than ever, and I'm not certain he even remembers my name. The anger at how unfair it all is keeps my mouth shut.

After he inhales his food, he marches off to bed, leaving Mom and me to go through our usual motions. I clean up. She sneaks around the house to her various stashes of alcohol, drinks enough to dull her pain and stumbles to the guest room. I wait in my bedroom until their snores echo down the hall before I make my move.

Twenty-three steps from my room to the kitchen. From there, fifteen steps to the door. *Easy peasy*, I tell myself.

But I can't hear my footsteps over the incessant pounding of my heart.

I'm breaking more rules than usual tonight: out of bed past curfew, out of domicile past curfew—yes, those are two separate things—fraternization outside of socialization hours... The list goes on. If I get caught, and it's a sympathetic human guard whose injection hasn't kicked in today, it'll be just a half a transgression. But if they find out I'm going to my contra-band library in the basement, I'll be up for execution.

It's that last part that gives me chills.

Breathe in, breathe out. Listen.

No one's here. The stairs are deserted. I know the guards' schedules and plan accordingly, but plans sometimes go awry.

I gotta believe it's worth it.

A book can change someone's world. Especially Zoe's. Her dad, the building's repairman, and my dad, are part of the half-solutions program, a monthly mood-enhancing vaccine that turns humans into obedient Ilori servants. But at least I've somewhat got my mom. Zoe has no one, and she's been pull-ing her hair out of loneliness, boredom and probably terror. Fear makes folks reckless enough to risk their lives. I get it.

Down just the two flights of stairs. That's it. Take another breath and wait.

I swallow before pushing myself off the wall and down the stairs to the basement. One glance around, and I pluck the key I keep hidden under my purple beanie. There's not too much light, but I know this door well enough. I touch the edges of the lock and slide the key in. One quick twist, and I swing the door open.

Once I've closed it behind me, my shoulders finally un-hunch. I'm in.

Our family storage unit is the first door on the right with a broken padlock. The Ilori broke it the moment they seized control of the building, although they never searched it hard. I'm grateful for that.

Everything's smooth sailing now, but still my gaze flicks down the hall to the boarded basement hatch. A painful mem-ory I try to block out slams into my mind and heart until I gasp and let it claim me.

I was fifteen when they took over. I'd been looking out

our living room window, rocking back and forth, mourning. Another execution had happened less than an hour before. It wasn't the first, but it was the first time a teenager was killed. Alice cried on my shoulder—she'd gone to school with him—while I looked on. My eyes were open, but my mind was closed. Our situation had become real.

None of us would be spared.

I'd seen a mother and child run toward our building, to the basement hatch. My emotions were raw, and I knew they'd either get taken in or killed. I ran from the apartment, down the stairs just as the shift changed, a lucky break for me. I went to the basement and hurried toward the hatch. It required a key. I didn't have the key. I tried my own, but it didn't work.

"Please, let us in," her voice called from outside. "Please. I have a little girl."

"I'm trying," I answered through the door. "I'm trying."

I pulled, I scratched, searched for something—anything—that would fit in the lock, that would open this door to hell and offer her purgatory. Tears streamed down my face, and I muttered, counted my numbers, hummed a song, recited a quote from a book...but nothing opened that door.

And then I heard his voice. "I told you not to leave. I told you..."

"You hit me, you—" The woman's voice wavered.

"I love you... Stay with me. I can save you, I can—"

Her panic seeped through the door. "I want to be safe. I'd choose the Ilori over you. They have food and heat."

And then she screamed.

The little girl yelled for her mommy. I grabbed a book and hit the lock over and over and over, drowning out the shouts and the sounds. It clattered to the ground, and I opened the hatch. There was a pool of blood, but the woman and the little girl were gone. So was he. I closed the doors and ran back to my room, where I sobbed and told myself over and over that it wasn't my fault, that they were okay…even though it was impossible. There's no way our stories have happy endings anymore.

A few days later, I began lending out books.

I push that memory aside, like always, as I hit the flashlight on a few times to make it work. The agony in my chest subsides as I remind myself that I can't have an emotional breakdown right now. I was helpless, too weak to stop whatever happened to that woman. Too slow. But now I can help people. *Some* people. Patrons.

My flashlight flickers on. I'm out of batteries, so I don't waste too much time collecting the books.

The space is tiny and tight, and a great hiding spot. I sidestep random old furniture my parents moved down here when Mom wanted new decor. I weave past the midnight blue ottoman my dad used to prop his feet on while reading the newspaper in Brooklyn. He'd kick the ottoman away in anger and comment about another senseless hate crime, or nuclear tensions rising, or climate change, or our morally corrupt politicians. My dad refused to throw it away when my mom said the color didn't match our new couch. Sometimes I go down here just to be reminded of our other life. And him.

My hip brushes against one of my great-aunt's old table lamps. And then my eyes flash to the floor. The matching lamp is scattered in ceramic pieces. That's not right. My body tenses as I maneuver around the shards to the old mattress.

Breathe in, breathe out. A broken lamp doesn't mean anything.

I tug on the ripped fabric, lifting the flap I cut, and let a sigh loose. My books are still inside. Thank goodness.

My gaze roams over the titles before I pull out my old, tattered copy of *Twilight* and then, because I really am committed to being kind, the first book in *The Dark Artifices* series. Zoe will love these. Then I grab *The Hitchhiker's Guide to the Galaxy* for Jack. I'm about to replace the covering when a gap in the shelf catches my attention. How many books are checked out?

Seven.

I scan the stack. Then why are there eight holes?

No. Am I losing it? *Think, Ellie.*

I remember every interaction I've had regarding the library. In the last few days, I've lent seven books to four patrons. I count again. Fifty-two books. *Only* fifty-two books. I'm going to hyperventilate. Oh damn. Numbers roll off my tongue as I try to keep it together.

But who could've taken it? Which book? Another scan and I know. *The Hate U Give.* I stood in line with my dad to get Angie Thomas's autograph at the Strand.

Why would someone take it? If it was *them*, I would know by now, right? A small, mirthless laugh escapes me. If it was *them*, I'd be swinging by my neck in front of everyone already. Did I misplace it? A shudder rolls through me. No.

Who took it?

My eyes flick toward the corner, where, for a second, I think I see movement. There's this sudden sensation that maybe I'm not alone. But that's ridiculous. This space is too small for someone to hide. I stamp down the thought before the realization hits me. My name is on that book. The what-ifs strike.

What if my mom took it? No. She's never down here, and she doesn't know about the library.

What if it's someone who hates me and wants leverage? I make a list, but it doesn't take long. There's only one person who hates me enough to want to see me dead: Mr. Hughes, a neighbor with a serious chip on his shoulder. But when would he have had the time?

What if it's somewhere out there, waiting to be found? Already, I can feel the rope tightening around my neck.

This book is going to get me killed.

CHAPTER 2

* ✦ +

"Raspberry Beret"
—Prince

MORR1S
ONE HOUR AGO

Stage three is complete, M0Rr1S says into Il-0CoM, the internal Ilori communication system, as he sets his tools carefully on the marble counter of the makeshift laboratory. The liquid formula has taken nearly two years to perfect, and he is confident it will do exactly as true Ilori leadership expect. He leans back in the chair, closing his eyes. His shoulders tighten at his neck as he prepares for the conversations and orders that'll stream into his mind.

Satisfactory. Distribution Services are on standby. Several voices say in unison. M0Rr1S cringes. His charge is low, which makes his head hurt, and their intrusion exacerbates the pain. He has been on Earth for only three days and has had no chance to rest.

Finally. A true Ilori commander speaks with condescending authority. *It has taken you too long. We have given you thousands of scans and samples of blood. We let you create costly projections to determine how their minds react not only to the behavioral vaccines, but also to artistic stimuli provided by their human art. We have never fully understood why that was necessary or why you've rejected human experimentation.*

M0Rr1S responds carefully. *Live experimentation is wrong and would not yield consistent results.*

Take care with your words, 1lv, the commander says pointedly.

M0Rr1S straightens, panic threading through his gut. He may carry the 1lv name, but he is still labmade. Still expected to be obedient to his superior. *My apologies. I meant only that their minds are stronger when they're in control of their personal autonomy. To force beings—*

This conversation is useless, another chimes in.

Correct, a labmade from another faction states. *Earth's preparations are thirty-three rotations away from completion. We are engineering the atmosphere for upper leadership arrival, and Habitation requires twenty-one rotations to cleanse the surface. The humans are the last, small piece.*

M0Rr1S must convert the time. He hasn't seen much of Earth's one sun to calculate the rotations, unlike home where there are three. For Ilori, one full rotation equals eight human hours. Three rotations are one day. Thirty-three is eleven days. Twenty-one is seven. Only seven. They are moving fast now.

Begin testing tomorrow. Distribution labmades are charged and waiting with your list of ingredients. A true Ilori voice leisurely cuts through the others. The owner is in one of the fourteen carrierships hovering somewhere above the atmosphere. Maybe even the same one M0Rr1S lived in while creating the vaccine. Only instead of working, the true Ilori bask in luxury, drinking photosynthesis teas while surrounded by simulations of their origin planet. They cannot enter Earth while the air is so polluted, the landscape so unclean. It would kill them.

Unlike M0Rr1S.

Their species is comprised of two races, and M0Rr1S hears reminders of that fact every time one of them interrupts with a dictatorial tone. The true Ilori, immortal beings with a violet sheen—called their shell—clinging to their energy form, develop the majority of the universe's technology and advancement. They are wealthy and prone to sustaining that wealth by colonizing worlds for their needs, and sometimes pleasure. When they realized how much work and danger it was to invade and take control of entire planets, they created a new race, the labmade Ilori, to do it for them. Labmades are modeled after the dominating life force that controls the planet the true Ilori want to colonize. They are conditioned to serve, to eschew emotions like their masters and to operate the new colonies for true Ilori usage and profit.

The labmades on Earth were created to look human. To maintain Earth for the true Ilori and make their new colony a truly immersive experience. Even so, M0Rr1S feels out of place.

He misses home. If he shuts out the voices and the images of the sad world around him, he can imagine the tall trees climbing into the cerulean sky, his family estate nestled between the thick trunks atop the capital city. There are no walls there, unlike here. Home is open, allowing air to come and go, while the thick, massive leaves provide shade from the three suns that set and rise every eight hours, or rotation.

And the food. He almost salivates thinking of fresh, juicy stardust berries and the sap-infused hofis plucked from within the bark of breeding trees.

It seems no one on Earth is pleased with the current arrangement. The humans are hungry for freedom, and M0Rr1S is hungry for home. But there is no more home. Not after this.

Commander M0Rr1S, we will be contacting you before the first round of treatment. Upon successful implementation, you will be directed to extraction protocol. Understood?

Yes, M0Rr1S responds to the true Ilori. *Thank you, Acquisitions Command. Permission to sign out for temporary energy relief.*

Granted.

He clicks off the small metal switch located on the panel running along the left side of his jaw.

The sudden silence is most welcome, but across his small office the door opens, requiring more of his attention. He is both lonely and never alone.

AvR0la enters, and M0Rr1S relaxes. "Congratulations, sir." Their tone is purposely blank.

"Avi," M0Rr1S huffs. His mouth twists with the Ilori dialect from their origin planet. To a human, their language might resemble something akin to a mathematical equation, and it sounds like one, as well. "We were grown in the same lab. You do not need to call me sir."

AvR0la punches a few keys on the panel, their breaths coming in tiny spurts. They have been on Earth longer than M0Rr1S and they have not yet adjusted. AvR0la has been his personal assistant and companion since youth. They are nonbinary, efficient and far more sensible than he. Their pale blond hair is pulled back into a severe bun, and their green eyes shimmer in the reflection they cast in the window. "Not all of us are granted permission to sign off Il-0CoM, sir."

M0Rr1S never forgets that; it's just that sometimes he wishes it weren't so. They are both labmades, yes, but unlike AvR0la, M0Rr1S was not created expressly for this invasion. Genetic material from the highest-born family within the Ilori empire lies inside him. This has allowed him certain freedoms—and abilities—his peers will never have.

But he aspires to openly be friends with AvR0la, however

frowned upon that would be. Labmades, most created only for colonization missions, are lesser than their true Ilori masters. Regardless of their inclinations, they are not supposed to form connections or feel. Only serve.

"Surveillance will be down, as scheduled and requested, tomorrow night in our current location, Center 11408-H, sir."

On unsteady legs, M0Rr1S wanders to the window and raises the shades. "Explain to me why we have scheduled downtimes?" The jagged skyline of deserted skyscrapers and veliopter cranes, solar-powered machinery used to demolish large structures and excavate natural surfaces, stares back at him as the sole sun sets. The stars peek through, but they aren't bright, not like back home.

Ilori have taken this world, yet the cost has been great. Not only for the humans. Currency and the lives of many labmades were lost making this planet suitable for true Ilori needs. And M0Rr1S has a role to play in that; he is the head scientist in charge of the final stage of acquisition and the commander always concerned about the bottom line, interested in every detail. *Play your role.*

"You approved of humans having unmonitored recesses within this quadrant, as it is one of the last origin quadrants still in lockdown. You said, sir, that when humans believe they have a modicum of freedom, they are less likely to revolt. And that we need their compliance until their permanent housing has been allocated and the vaccine is effective. I have made sure to keep these evenings scheduled. No one has questioned my authority, and our fellow labmades need the respite."

"Thank you." M0Rr1S cannot quite recall saying that, but it does align with his, with their, ideals.

And AvR0la is correct. There are so few origin quadrants—designated sections of land where humans originated and still inhabit—left. While other commanders across the world moved humans into housing reconfigured specifically by Habitation Services for the species, this land, New York, M0Rr1S recalls, was too heavily populated to clear quickly. Thus, it had been determined by true Ilori leadership that the humans with the necessary requirements would remain here until the vaccine could be effective, forced against their will—and against M0Rr1S's wishes—to be the first testing quadrant. As true Ilori waited impatiently for him to complete the formula, it has become the most guarded, most policed, most volatile quadrant. Humankind stands on the edge of rebellion without their freedom.

It is fortunate, then, that AvR0la was able to give those commands in his stead. This is the first time in months, possibly a year, that he has had free time to wonder about what has been happening in this quadrant. Although he communicated with Avi regularly, he was under constant surveillance by true Ilori above, performing at full capacity. His focus was divided unevenly.

M0Rr1S turns to AvR0la, exhaustion in his very bones. "What do the humans do on these surveillance intermissions?"

AvR0la shifts against the doorway. "The humans engage in what they call a party. They fornicate, converse, listen to music—"

"Music. Where do they get it?" M0Rr1S tries to sound less excited. He has to approach this and all things in a calm, detached manner. It is the Ilori way. But this center has music, and he has struggled to accumulate more since true Ilori allowed him to experiment with the media.

Music is human expression. Human expression is dangerous and leads to free thinking. Revolt. Death. And so true Ilori leadership has banned it, much to M0Rr1S's dismay.

"We don't know, sir. We've done sweeps, but we have not found where they are keeping their illegal collections. Admittedly, most sweeps are done by our altered, mood-enhanced humans from the half-solutions program, and we cannot be certain of their diligence."

M0Rr1S turns to AvR0la. "Has that aided in fewer human executions?"

"I was ordered to withhold those details from you, as it would contradict your command." AvR0la's words are measured for Il-0CoM. They know M0Rr1S has a revolutionary view of human treatment that would make him a target for true Ilori derision. M0Rr1S awaits the answer AvR0la reluctantly gives. "Executions have declined, but they still happen too often. Our quadrant alone has had the most executions globally."

He keeps the anger from his voice. "Why is that?"

"Sir, as you have been isolated in medical services above, true Ilori command—specifically your familial code—has stepped in to evaluate effective management of the human population here."

Not his father or his mother. Both would surely be too busy, too important for something so trivial. But his brother. Brixton. Of course, he would condemn humans to death. He would surmise that there are enough humans to spare, and a message must be sent to those who remain.

It is also a personal message for M0Rr1S; his command means nothing to the true Ilori. He will never be free and will always be lesser, not only for his labmade origins, but for his desire to feel.

"It is good, then, that our quadrant will be the first to be tested," M0Rr1S admits. "We need to stop killing the humans—our success depends on it. And the formula will work, I know it will. How long must we wait for production?" He sighs with an air of impatience, but it covers his despair. He doesn't want to leave, not just yet. Not without the music.

"They've said your vaccine shall be tested in this center within the next six rotations. If successful, completion is projected in nine. Globally in twelve."

"Fast, but good." M0Rr1S straightens his back. "The parties, where do they happen? I believe I will be able to locate the contraband materials, and perhaps prevent further…punishment for the humans. Will you connect to my drive and send the building plans to me? I have not explored beyond the labs."

AvR0la smirks but keeps the humor from their tone. "Of course, sir. When do you need them?"

"I'm free now." A weight seems to lift from his shoulders as he utters those words. "The freest I've been since I was brought here."

"That is good, sir." Their tone cracks a little before they correct themself. They have never been free. "I will send the plans."

They leave M0Rr1S to solitude once more. He thinks of AvR0la as family. Real family. They are direct, quiet, loyal and never question him, although they should. One word from AvR0la could have doomed M0Rr1S before he ever got the chance to prove himself or attempt this mission.

A mission that has named him the youngest commander in Ilori history. One most believe he was assigned only because of his familial code.

When the labmades survived the landing less than two years ago, their bodies adjusted to Earth, the air and the food just as they were designed to do. Some true Ilori had cheered, as if they were not certain their experimentations would work until the labmades entered this new atmosphere. M0Rr1S hadn't realized until then just how expendable his race was to the true Ilori. He'd known he would always be considered their lesser regardless of rank, that the labmades would never be considered equal no matter how hard they worked, but that moment was when he'd understood that the true Ilori did not value his kind.

That understanding grounded him further. He'd taken the lead on human services: from the half-solutions program to the vaccine. He became the face of Ilori innovation, earning a promotion from the Chancellor of Acquisitions. He did it all without live experimentation in isolation on a carriership above.

The isolation that has doomed this center's human population.

His gaze catches on the only buildings lit up in his designated quadrant. The last centers. Humans that fit their desired specifications—those between the ages of sixteen to fifty with strong immune systems, most compatible with, and most likely to survive, the vaccine. However, some will still be moved to human housing, where they have more freedom, less restrictions, better access to food and medicine. Especially the elders, a requirement created by true Ilori who value age above all else. Already young children, babies and those expecting or nursing babies, and those incapable of giving consent, have been moved. It is important that humans do not perish, only their freedom.

Once the last of the humans still in hiding and battling in caves fall, the true Ilori will finally have their controlled vacation destination.

Earth; a planet of lush landscapes, oceans brimming with natural wildlife, and seasons beyond imagination. A new destination. A new escape from the mundane. Earth; a new Ilori colony.

M0Rr1S imagines another advertisement, this one more enticing.

Live and breathe like the humans. Leave your shell behind and experience life in this world through the eyes and body of a native. Embark upon a new adventure.

The ads will circulate universally, and the profits made from rich tourists will more than make up for the costs of creating custom labmades to blend in to each new colony. There are endless possibilities. They could expand, market to other worlds, to other species wishing for exciting getaways.

M0Rr1S entertains the thought of more newly acquired Ilori colonies. There are many already, and several scheduled for acquisition after Earth. If he were true, if his mom hadn't raised him, he might feel as if this were his right. He'd study advertising and care nothing about the lives destroyed during colonization.

But he is not true, and like all labmades, his life is not his own to determine. It never will be. The humans will now be the same. It's unfair, M0Rr1S knows, to take a world from beings with limited technology and understanding of the universe, as if the Ilori are entitled to their bodies, homes, their nature, and then use it all for profit... It can only be wrong. Just as it is wrong to create beings to serve others. And yet he must help his masters do both.

He will play that role; too much depends on his abilities and knowledge.

On the second from the top floor of this center, M0Rr1S's focus returns to the world outside the window, where the final traces of humanity are being stripped away. The veliopters tear down the deserted skyscrapers and buildings, dig up the cement until they strike dirt, and then they fertilize.

AvR0la knocks again, startling him.

"Sir, the plans should be in your incoming mail. Will you require anything else?" M0Rr1S regards AvR0la for the thousandth time. It is easy to mistake them as cold, impersonal. But he knows that AvR0la prefers precision, dislikes attention and has an unflappable, militaristic nature that comes from being the top of their class at academy. They are the perfect Ilori, unlike M0Rr1S.

"No, that is all. Thank you, AvR0la. What G00287 granteth—"

"—the Ilori taketh." AvR0la's lips quirk before they nod.

M0Rr1S grasps the back of his chair and unwraps the black jacket there. According to AvR0la, it is uncomfortably chilly in the lower half of the building. His origin planet is warm, and this cold seeps into his bones and makes him homesick.

He pushes the third button on his panel, accessing his main menu. It pops up over his left eye, where the in-box flashes once, alerting him to a document. Using focused thought, he opens the plans for the center he has lived in for three days but knows nothing about.

He stares at the levels below the surface, marked as uninhabited. This, he decides, must be the place. Wherever humans store their possessions not in use, there are things surely worth finding.

As he strides through the sterile white laboratory rooms that once served as human doctors' offices illuminated by bright fluorescents overhead, he purposely avoids the humans sitting behind tables, completing their manual labor on projected screens. It is his fault that their skin is sallow and reeks of chemicals, that they're exhausted, staring at mathematical formulas on screens that are too wide for them to fully grasp without difficulty.

True Ilori have declared that a purposeful human is a good human. They must be kept busy, or they'll have time and energy to rebel. In a building of approximately twenty-five hundred occupants, like this one, rebellion could mean failure.

He nods in the direction of those that greet him and follows the blueprints to an unadorned cement stairway. His time is short but he prefers to move down the stairs instead of using the elevator.

When he reaches the end of the stairs at the bottommost floor, he is met by a locked door. He closes his eyes and pushes the lock with his mind, eliciting a small pop as it swings away from him.

It's even colder down here.

On his panel, he switches his built-in lenses to night vision. He enters the darkness, breathes in the dust and mustiness. He likes these smells. They are new, different. He had always hoped to explore places like this. Below the ground, damp and cold, finding something hidden. Having a small adventure.

And that is what he plans on doing now. Searching. Undisturbed. He doesn't want to hang some poor human for hoarding contraband music; he wants only to keep it for himself. His collection is small but growing, and he'd like it to be large enough to fill an individual transportation pod when he travels elsewhere in the galaxy—assuming he is granted that privacy. If he has any luck, he will find intact hard drives with large music files.

Before computers were destroyed, humans kept all sorts of personal items, including music, on these plastic little boxes with USB cords or small sticks he'd been told. Apparently, they imported most of their music into the "cloud," but Ilori command shut that down after the initial invasion. They directed electricity away from large, global servers for their more advanced needs.

Thus, he must look for the physical remnants. So far, the only computers given to him have been old, and most, if not corrupted, had very little music. It was difficult to gain access to them; true Ilori didn't see the value of allowing M0Rr1S to analyze human technology or art for the purpose of the vaccine. Here, he can get them himself.

If he were caught searching, he could claim it was necessary to understand behavior for the vaccine. They would not doubt his name over a flimsy excuse. But if they truly knew why he was searching, that he was collecting music, he could be punished. Maybe executed. And yet, he cannot bring himself to burn such beautiful treasure, no matter the cost.

He stands in front of twenty storage units lined against the walls with slotted wooden doors. Inside them are personal belongings that will either go with the humans to new housing or will be left behind. Nothing of value, an Ilori would say. His eyes flick toward the first door on the right.

The lock is already broken, so he opens the rickety wooden door, and his spirit lifts. Mattresses and tables, lamps and toys.

A trove. He shifts things around, expecting dust, but there is none. This room is used, and used often. But for what?

A lamp shatters on the floor, and he jumps in fright before laughing with little humor. If they could hear him laugh, they would wonder if he was malfunctioning.

We do not laugh, for we do not feel joy. We do not cry, for we do not feel sorrow. We survive without weakness.

He thinks of his father's words, echoing in their chamber every morning. *There are no feelings, child. You are weak. You are a disappointment to the 1lv name.* Father is right. He is weak, and he will—disappoint him.

That brings M0Rr1S something akin to joy.

A glittery substance catches his eye. He turns his head and narrows his gaze on the mattress. *Clever human.* He strides over and reaches for the corner before gently peeling back the fabric. His eyes widen. Books. Many, many books. Who would be rebellious enough to keep these? In this center, this counts as two transgressions—instant death.

True Ilori leadership commanded labmades to ban all human art and execute any human in possession of it globally, but especially here where the humans outnumber the Ilori seven to one.

They stated that humans use books as a means of covert communication. That the books themselves could create codes, for coordinated attacks, that the labmades couldn't crack until it was too late. They cited that some of the early failures in Ilori-run centers were because of human art. And there was no way to disprove this. Especially when many Ilori perished in those battles.

As for music, leadership banned that from the very beginning. It interfered with their hearing, making ambushes by the humans too easy. Most was confiscated and destroyed in centers like these, but humans, M0Rr1S knows through study, cherish their art. They hid it in any way they could or down-loaded it onto tech devices they can't even access anymore.

His focus flicks back to the books. He longs to touch their jackets, to run his fingers across the words there. And he does. He can read human languages, but he is not allowed to, much like he is not allowed to listen to human music. The Ilori have their own stories and music, but they are mostly propaganda about the greatness of their kind. He much prefers the sounds and consonants of the human languages when spoken and sung, but he is afraid of getting caught. A book cannot be downloaded onto his system in such a physical form, yet music, in the right form, is untraceable.

The true Ilori say there is nothing to gain from reading human texts or appreciating their art. That the knowledge labmades possess should be acquired only through Ilori teach-ings. The true Ilori do not just desire superiority, they want full control over labmades. Yet, as his fingers run down the spines of the books, a part of him finds joy in their presence. And a desire to know what stories lay inside.

He flips through them, putting each back in its place as he goes. No underlined phrases or notes fall out—no, these books are not harbingers of revolt, like command has warned. Death will not find their owner for this, not on his account anyway.

The door clicks, and he wonders if he should hide or stand his ground, scare the poor human to death. The former suits him, and he hits a button on his wristband, creating a shadow where his body once stood. He squeezes into the one empty corner before he realizes he is still holding a book in his hand, lost in the shadow with him.

The door opens, and a human comes inside—a girl, based on the identification code on the collar of her blue top. JQB-305-7-21. The numbers tell him not only who she is, but state her personal frequency marker, a way to send messages to her mind.

She regards the broken lamp, her eyes assessing. She strides to the mattress, stepping into the dim light of her flashlight and avoiding the broken glass, before she pulls back the fabric.

He hears her counting, just under her breath. Her fluffy, curly hair spills out of a purple knit hat.

She counts the books again. She must have realized one is missing and is panicking. If he comes out of the shadows now, it'll cause a commotion. And he'll be expected to kill her. If he doesn't kill her, then he might start a chain of events that will eventually lead to more death. He doesn't want to kill her. He has to put the book back.

Her gaze shifts to the corner and, for a moment, it's like she's staring through the darkness right at him.

She is fascinating.

He wants to know why this human girl is keeping books in a mattress when the cost could be her life. He respects her strength. Would he do the same for music?

Suddenly, the book feels glued to the palm of his hand.

M0Rr1S can't just put it back and forget about it. He has to meet her, talk to her, ask her. Why does she rebel? What do these books mean to her? Do they make her feel less alone, like music makes him feel?

A song pops into his mind, one of the first he ever downloaded from a confiscated phone. "Raspberry Beret," by a musician called Prince. He doesn't know why she reminds him of this song. The purple hat, maybe, the captivating beauty… He wonders if she likes music, too, or as much as he does.

A voice whispers in the back of his head that she's human; they're from different worlds…

Maybe that's why he decides to keep the book for now.

CHAPTER 3

"Nowadays people know the price of everything and the value of nothing."

—Oscar Wilde

JANELLE

"It's basic math." I adjust my glasses on the bridge of my nose. We're lined up outside the former "residents' retreat" room, waiting to be let in. It used to be a nice space, with oversize couches and armchairs, televisions, a small library of books neighbors donated and a pool table. Only the armchairs remain, stationed in front of large dining tables with whatever today's lesson will be laid on top.

Before the invasion, this was a normal, luxurious Upper East Side apartment building, reflecting the successful and rich New Yorkers it housed. It was right off Museum Mile, a stone's throw from the Met, Central Park and the Eighty-Sixth Street subway stop. Beautiful and tall, with plants erupting from balconies, a flawless green awning and a white polished front without a smudge of dirt. It had the best views in the city.

Now it's a prison.

The empty rooms, freed up from neighbors who left for somewhere else or had children and were moved elsewhere, have transitioned into living spaces for the Ilori guards or folks bussed in from other buildings that the Ilori deemed unacceptable. The penthouses were converted to apartments, offices, or left as medical labs, while the gym was gutted and left bare so that we could use it as a lap room, keeping our muscles from atrophying. Like cattle.

The floors are stained from things it's best not to think about, and the pocked walls tell stories of struggles and death. Of fights between humans trapped inside, who let their anger and frustration tear each other apart. The worst part, though, is the chemical odor that clings to the surfaces and makes our skin itch. I doubt it's lethal, just a by-product of whatever's upstairs.

I sniff, turning to Alice, whose perfect pink lips settle into a frown. She pulls at the strands of her long, dirty blond ponytail, while her dark brown eyes bore into mine.

"I haven't done math in forever." Alice leans closer.

"We haven't done anything important in forever," I grumble. We still go to a form of school, but mostly we sit around learning things we already know while doing pointless tasks. I remember someone saying once that idle hands make idle minds; but from what I've learned in the last two years, it depends on what you're doing with your hands.

"True, but if it's basic math, how come I don't understand it?"

I don't bother suggesting that perhaps Alice doesn't understand because she's not paying attention. That she's only half listening. I can tell by the way her gaze keeps darting down the hallway and pausing on Jackson Hughes. But I don't let it get to me. I have bigger things to do than analyze our friendship. We're friends, and nothing will change that, even if we didn't become close until we were imprisoned together.

"Zoe Landson needed some paranormal. I gave her two. Jack Gibbs requested one dark humor, I dropped that in the broom closet this morning. A few days ago, Josh Farrow asked to borrow nonfiction military books. There was only one book that fit the bill. Heather Robard wanted to borrow one book on music composition and another on fairy tales. That's seven books checked out."

Alice huffs and brings her fingers up to count them. "Yeah, that's...seven books. Okay. So, what's the problem again?"

"The problem, *again*, is that eight books are gone."

"I don't understand." Alice shakes her head, while Jackson winks at her from down the hall. "You have a log."

I fight the urge to roll my eyes. Over a week ago, I told her that my log was gone. "I got rid of the log. I've got a good memory—and I never should've kept records in the first place. It's only sixty books. The problem is the missing book."

"Okay, but so what? Even if someone found it, how would they know it was yours?"

"The book's got my name on it." Truth is, quite a few of them do, which is pretty careless on my part. I scribbled out most of the labels when I started lending them, but there're a few I had autographed that I just couldn't efface.

"Damn it, Janelle!" Alice's voice falls to a whisper, her undivided attention now on me. "Why do you do this? Why even have a library?"

This time I do roll my eyes. "I love books. And I want to help people. The Ilori don't get to tell us how we can live before we die."

"It's so dangerous."

She's right. After the Great Death—that's my name for it, everyone else calls it the Purge or whatever—*they* took our electronics; computers, phones, anything that needed to be charged. That hurt, but not as much as when they took the things that made life nearly bearable. Books, instruments and art…everything they found was collected, taken outside and burned in the courtyard. I remember smoke clouding the sky, and not just from our building.

But they didn't find my stash. Some belonged to my mother, once an English Literature professor at Columbia, and some came from my father, once a librarian in Brooklyn. Most were my own. Others I stole from piles of trash people were throwing away while we still had the chance. And I hid them in storage, knowing that that choice could end my life.

They don't get to tell us how to live before we die.

Alice angles closer as if to comfort me. If she gets too close, the guards will break us apart. They don't care about us talking quietly, but contact? They'll punish us for that. Getting in trouble now is a death sentence later.

"I know it's dangerous." It's why she and I vet each potential borrower, learn everything we can about them till we believed they won't toss me to the Ilori. If we were allowed our Kindles, I could've found a simpler way to share my books, a safer one, too. But when the Ilori came to confiscate our electrical items, I hid my Kindle but forgot to hide my charger with it. We still have electricity, yet no internet. I tried to create a charger from spare wires using my own instincts, and nearly succeeded, until it burst into flames.

That was devastating. But I reminded myself that I still had the books I cherished most. The ones I waited in line at bookstores to get on release day, and had signed by the authors who created the worlds I lived in and loved.

I couldn't keep them to myself forever. The idea of bringing stories to those in need outweighs my fear. Makes me a rebel. If I die for it…there are worse things to die for. Better things, too. And in my heart, I know I'm doing the right thing. My patrons rely on me to give them literary escapes. Still, I don't want to die today because someone took a book and exposed me.

They've killed people for less.

"What are you going to do?"

"I have to… I haven't decided yet. I could wait, hope it turns up. Or I could interrogate the last three people who came to my library."

Alice tilts her head. "You need my help, don't you?"

I messed up. That's not something I usually want to admit, even to a friend. I don't want anyone to think I'm weak or fighting a growing sadness. Even though I am.

"You're better at people than me." I brush a loose curl behind my ear and adjust my standard black glasses once more. What I don't say is that, while I like my patrons enough to risk my life for them, I generally dislike everyone else. They've made their judgments of me pretty clear since the beginning, and I'm not ready to forgive them.

"You mean I'm capable of getting answers without offending or insulting someone?"

"That's what I said, didn't I?" I raise my eyebrows at her.

"You know, you could be better at people if you put in a little more effort."

"I put all my effort into running the library. I help the only way I can. I don't sneak off to underground parties to kiss people."

"Janelle, you're cute, you know."

"I'm not cute." I narrow my eyes at her. "I'm serious. And I'll be in *very* serious trouble if I don't find that book. I'm asking you, Alice Dresden, my only friend in this sad, cruel, gray world, for help. Will you help me?"

Drama works with her, and it's all true.

"Of course, I'll help you. But on one condition. You have to come with me to Jackson's underground party tonight."

"But I'm busy," I whine.

"Look, I do for you, you do for me. If we get caught, who would believe Janelle Baker would associate with anyone or anything so scandalous? You know how the old folks are, they'll be like, 'no, please don't kill our kids, Janelle was there, which means no one was doing anything wrong!' It'll only be your first transgression anyway."

A guard passes by us, and we quiet until they're out of earshot.

"That's exactly why I don't go places," I whisper. "If I ever get caught with the library, I want them to think I'm a saint, never a step out of line. I might live a little longer."

"You have to live a little more while you can. Doesn't your mom tell you that?"

My mom is a bad influence. She spends her days drunk, even though alcohol is illegal and hard to come by. She's bartered away most of our silverware, all of her fancy dinnerware and every last designer dress in her closet for her precious supply.

In the beginning, she loved to break the rules. If she'd known before she lost herself to desperation that I ran a library, she would have been proud of me. If she knew I'd been invited to an underground party, she'd pick out my clothes and scrounge up some makeup. But now? She either scowls, mumbles nonsense and/or drunkenly cowers in a corner.

"I'll go for an hour."

"Two." She holds her head high, like an unimpressed swan.

"One and a half."

"Deal." She smirks.

And I smile back before the sirens blast overhead, reminding us that we're here. That we aren't safe, not really. We fall to our knees then lie facedown on the checkered floor with our hands by our sides.

I take deep breaths, trying to keep my cool as stomping boots approach. Count, sense and relax. 5-4-3-2-1. If they can read minds, all they'll hear are my numbers. 5-4-3-2-1.

Five, Alice, whose eyes lock on mine. She smells like…like jasmine and grapefruit, her favorite perfume. Are they here for me? Already? Four, I count, *blue shoes that tap on the linoleum.*

I'm going to die, I know it.

Three, fingers flat against the cold, unyielding floor.

They'll melt my mind until I'm gone. My eyes will bulge out at my peers as my soul disintegrates. Just like I saw it on TV before our world was taken over.

Two. The anxiety is at its peak now. Will it hurt? *Two.* I can't… I can't find something else. *Two, two…*

I stop counting and suck in a breath. Whoever they're coming for has done something bad. Eight pairs of black boots pass inches from my face. *Two, a Kill Squad.*

Screams echo down the hall. The voice is familiar. But I can't quite place it. Alice's hand brushes mine, telling me she's here, we're here, we're not going anywhere. We're in this together, she and I. I could cry thinking of how lucky I am to have a friend. I feel bad for thinking she isn't capable of paying attention when boys are around.

Standard blue tennis sneakers are dragged past us, and I look up to see bright red hair I recognize instantly.

One, Erica Schulman. Second transgression. I remember hearing about her first transgression: she tried to build a radio to communicate with any free humans. But she failed. What could she have done now?

Alice mouths the word *bomb.* My eyebrows lift. I wouldn't have expected that from Erica. But then, all I know about her is that she's a year older than Alice and me and planned on becoming an engineer like her mom. She was good at science, but her projects tended to be about solar ovens and baking bread, not bomb making.

The loudspeakers boom overheard. "You are all ordered outside for an execution."

Outside? Nine out of ten executions are spoken of, never seen. The Ilori can use their minds to crack ours into a million pieces. But when they want to make a point...they hang someone from the seventh-floor balcony.

Alice and I get to our feet. We don't bother talking, just shoot fearful glances at each other as we follow the others down the hallway, bypassing a group of soldiers dressed all in black, with black masks so that we'll never know their faces. We know they're human; the Ilori move fluidly, otherworldly, while humans are clumsy in comparison. My own father might be among them.

We step through the glass doors into the enclosed courtyard, the air biting and brisk. Normally the Ilori want us to stay warm, but the announcement didn't say we had a few minutes to collect coats. I saw someone make that mistake before, and the beating wasn't worth it. Better to be cold than bloody.

We take our places in the back and I greedily inhale the fresh air. Alice bumps elbows with her crush, Jackson, and my pulse pounds in my ears before I reluctantly stand beside Monica Lehrman. Tears stream down her face, and I want to snap at her, tell her to save it for later so that she doesn't draw attention to us. But it's not my place to tell her when she can be sad with our lot in life. Just because some of us have accepted it doesn't mean it's acceptable.

Our heads all whip up toward the same spot on the over-size balcony that's missing a protective fence. Erica screams, begs for help. She tells us all that she's innocent. But innocence means nothing when the Kill Squad comes.

"Human F.S-1-A-11-B has been found guilty of building a technological weapon. The punishment is death."

Erica bellows, her eyes searching for someone among us. Beside me, Monica bursts into fresh tears, and I find myself wrapping an arm around her shoulders. Monica once started a petition to have me removed from our performance arts summer camp, because she thought my presence was proof of affirmative action, not based on merit. I try not to hold that against her as I console her. It's uncomfortable, but I know it's what people do, even when they loathe the other person. We're supposed to be there for each other now. Or at least appear to be.

A soldier above us ties a noose around Erica's neck and flaming bright red hair. There's no warning, no final words when she's pushed off the edge. Her neck snaps when she reaches the end of the rope. *Lucky.* Her blue sneakers touch the brick building while she swings gently in the cool breeze.

Goodbye, Erica Schulman.

Alice pulls me to her side and brings her lips to my ear. "That could be you."

"It won't be."

My mind travels to that woman and her daughter outside the basement. I can still hear her screams, remember the blood. I won't stand by and do nothing anymore. My library is too important.

"I can't lose you," Alice says, her voice raw. "Please, Ellie."

We're in our own bubble, lost in the crowd staring up at a dead girl who dared to do science in a time where math, science, creativity, books and art are illegal. They want us numb and hopeless; it's easier to roll over us that way. They want us beaten and broken, too scared to rebel.

But they don't know that rebels are made in the worst of circumstances, and even death can't stop them.

Us.

CHAPTER 4

"As"
—Stevie Wonder

MORR1S

M0Rr1S paces with his fists by his sides. The fear spiraling through the humans makes his stomach churn. His black boots stomp on the white tiled floor. Another execution.

"They will lose the will to survive. Is that not more dangerous? Is that not more likely to result in revolt?" His voice echoes across the lab. The teams of Ilori, minus their half-solution helpers, stand before him. There aren't many left. That is why they needed to modify some humans early. If the humans knew how few there were… "Why was I not consulted?"

"We were told not to disturb you, sir, by command." A timid labmade with a fourth colony accent and black hair cowers as if she has to fear him. For a moment, he is uneasy being regarded in such a way. But then, he considers, perhaps she is not afraid. Perhaps it is that he is expressing emotion. Openly defying the rules. Her gaze slides to AvR0la's before settling back on him.

M0Rr1S quickly straightens and exhales the anger. It would not do well to have any more attention on him. How many true Ilori are listening through Il-0CoM? "My apologies. My charge is low, and I haven't had the time to connect."

AvR0la steps closer to M0Rr1S, covering for his outburst. "As per true Ilori leadership, we are entering the final stages of acquisitions. The vaccine will be tested. Until then, please confer with our commander before human penalizations."

There's a collective nod, but M0Rr1S doubts any will trust his judgment. Not when they've been directed by true Ilori via Il-0CoM all this time. They don't consider him a leader, and why should they? He's too young. Too emotional. He hasn't been here long enough to have earned their respect. They tolerate him only for his name.

"You are dismissed." M0Rr1S stalks toward the elevator with AvR0la following as the labmades scurry back to whatever assignment they'd been given. The sun rises, sending beams of light bouncing off the white interiors. Even the warmth doesn't elevate his mood.

This day has just begun and already it is not going in his favor.

Inside the elevator as the doors close, M0Rr1S sends an invitation to connect to AvR0la. Once they accept, he disengages their Il-0CoM by patching into their system and gently overriding the codes. Using as little energy as he can spare, he then connects to the mechanics around him, pausing the cords and electricity that would bring them to their destination.

They have two minutes at most.

AvR0la's shoulders sag. "How was your search?"

"I found a book." He doesn't mention the human girl he took it from, or that he wants to see her again. Or that instead of searching through the storage, he sat down and read the book, cover to cover. It took up most of his night. He didn't accept calls from Il-0CoM either, which surely had been noticed. "That was close."

"Too close," AvR0la agrees. "When you let your emotions show, they do not know how to respond. I cannot always distract them from your impulsiveness."

"I'm sorry." M0Rr1S runs a hand through his hair. It has grown since they arrived, but he doesn't want to cut it. It makes him look unique. More human.

"Leadership will contact you soon. When the vaccines are administered worldwide, barring issues, you will be expected in the central carriership. Have you—"

"Avi, can we discuss something else for the short time we have?" M0Rr1S exhales, letting his head fall back on the metal wall. "For instance, I've learned that human stories have parallels to our way of life, and yet they found a way to fight back."

AvR0la turns to regard him. "What do you mean?"

"The book was about a human with brown skin, which meant they were viewed as lesser than those with pale skin. Similar to how the labmades are viewed by the true Ilori." He is excited to share this...this feeling he has bottled up deep inside himself since reading. "The human girl witnesses her friend die unfairly, and decides to fight for justice and equality by speaking the truth. It is very powerful."

The elevator shifts in the beat of silence. He cannot hold it much longer, and already his charge is blinking at 10 percent over his left eye.

"Speaking our truth will only get us killed. You know this. Just as you know that reading their books is forbidden. We kill the humans here for it, what makes you think they won't kill you, too?" AvR0la's eyes lock on his. "You are too important to make mistakes. If you fail, they will pry, and then kill you."

"If I fail, what was the point of my life?" The question leaves his lips before he can think better of it. The power slips from his hold, and the elevator begins its ascent to the penthouses on the top floor.

"We all have a purpose." AvR0la's words are edged with anger. "Do not forget yours. Do not forget what is at stake."

M0Rr1S doesn't respond. They are right. As always.

Just before the door opens and M0Rr1S must engage their Il-0CoM, AvR0la's face softens. "I wish I could have read that book. To feel as these humans do… How did the story end?"

"With hope."

The corners of their lips lift as Il-0CoM pings back to life within their mind. The moment is gone, and yet it was a good one that M0Rr1S will cherish.

AvR0la heads the opposite direction to their next assignment, while M0Rr1S must go to his private quarters to charge. Thankfully it is just the two of them at this level, which gives him much desired privacy.

He was given the highest apartment in the human center upon arrival. A sign of respect.

The kitchen is stocked with Ilori food designed for labmades; electrolyte loaves sprinkled with freeze-dried krulbs, globuli protein bars in various flavors and steamed bonji meat wrapped in donderaa leaves from his origin planet—his favorite. This space has been redesigned as permanent housing for labmades when their mission is complete. There are plush white carpets and solid white, unadorned walls. The Ilori love white. A window, taking up the entire far wall, has a view of a large natural reserve across the street. The bed, an exorbitant human structure, stands in the center of the room, although it is only for comfort and leisure activities.

Ilori don't require sleep if they're charged, and as such, the bed is the perfect place to listen to music. He sinks into the mattress and runs his fingers over the panel that stretches from behind his left ear to his jaw. It has six buttons; one for eye brightening, to see in dark places, another for uploads where he keeps documents, recordings, memories and files, a small button for translation, one for data display such as relevant information and charge percentage, the fourth for recording present or past memories, and lastly, the power button, which requires three on-screen prompts, asking if he is certain he wishes to shut down. Beneath the buttons are two inputs, one for a charge, and one that can accept most cables, even Earth-created ones like USB cords. And then there's the switch for Il-0CoM, at the top. Closest to his mind. Very few select models have this option.

He keeps that off as he inserts the charging cable into the correct slot. He changes the charging speed to the slowest possible—too fast and he'll be wired.

Once the pace is set, he sorts through the uploads folder, finding just the right thing to cure his uneasiness.

David Bowie. M0Rr1S has acquired two of Bowie's albums, and since then, he has let the musician play softly in his mind whenever he has privacy. It's not his favorite way to listen to music, but it is the safest way. When he leaves Earth with all the various formats and devices containing music files, he will be able to give them a proper play in his pod, out loud, so that he can feel the beats with his body. Maybe even sing along. But for now, he is content for just his mind to hear about Ziggy Stardust, who could play a guitar.

He taps another button on his panel, making the time appear before his left eye. In another few hours, he'll be in a conference call with leadership, and he'll be expected to be on his best behavior. Already, his body tenses up.

The charge icon appears on his main menu, alerting him he's at 13 percent charge. He is supposed to charge every day to maintain health and abilities, but sometimes he delays it almost to the point of having to dip into his reserves of energy. The stronger the charge, the louder Il-0CoM. He prefers to hover around 50 or 60 percent, that way he doesn't feel like electricity is constantly streaming through his body, making him twitchy. He feels less labmade, less Ilori.

M0Rr1S closes his eyes, running his hands over the soft material of the blanket. Another human addition made for warmth and comfort. His fingers catch on the book he read the night before. How could something so thick and cool to touch be so personal and important?

He pulls it toward him, and the book flaps open to the first page. There, his eyes catch on a note written in pen. Could it be instructions for an attack? Could the true Ilori be right?

But no. It says only a few words before it ends with a signature. It doesn't seem to make plans or hide a complex code. *To Janelle…*he reads.

That must be the girl with the purple hat, the raspberry beret.

Janelle. He says the name again, aloud.

Tonight, he decides. Tonight, he'll meet her.

THE STARRY EYED: "FAIRY-TALE GIRL"

The Sound of Stars
Written by: Cecil Wright, Allister Daniels, Rupert Montague,
Whisper Landsome

> *Far from the center, two worlds collide*
> *Soon they'll find each other among the divide*
> *She fixes her purple crown*
> *While he tells his big lies*
> *Secrets cloud their darkening skies*
>
> *Fairy-tale girl, don't give up now*
> *The story's not over yet, you can't take your bow*
> *This is just the beginning, darling, don't you see?*
> *The world's in disarray, but it won't always be*

Sow those seeds and dare to rebel
Keep your tales and songs hidden well
Travel beyond but beware the cost
One misstep and all will be lost

The world is ours, but how long can it last?
Take your fall forward, but don't drop too fast
Use your numbers, take back your control
You think you know now, but what is your goal?

Fairy-tale girl with stars in your eyes
Use those stories to see through his lies
You only have now, it's just you and he
The world is theirs now, but it won't always be

Don't!
No, don't!
Don't ever!
You can never give up

CHAPTER 5

·———✗—✦

"There is always more misery among the lower classes than there is humanity in the higher."

—Victor Hugo, *Les Misérables*

JANELLE

Someone sobs loudly somewhere in the building as I stare at a picture of Mom and me, smiling with a group of women in pink hats.

We stopped for chocolate doughnuts on Independence Avenue on our way to the Washington Monument. She was telling me about my grandparents and great grandparents, and how they marched on this very road with Martin Luther King, Jr., when a group of ladies asked to take pictures with us and our signs. After that, we walked together to make a wave so tall that we could wash those streets with our anger. And yet, everyone was so nice and friendly.

Weeks later, we were holding signs in Union Square, protesting police brutality. No one was wearing bright, happy colors, and this time the faces standing beside us weren't all shades under the rainbow. They were black like ours. And they were tired. Like us.

Another few months passed before the world fell apart. Invasion. Humans fought back in the streets, fields, the air... and lost. It was over too soon to really know what happened. For most of us, we'd heard only rumors before the occupation began. They seemed reluctant to kill us, but they could be keeping us alive for something worse than death. It was that ignorance—and that mom and daughter disappearing—that compelled me to start my library. I needed to find and provide my own kind of answers.

I settle back on my bed and exhale. The first bars of a Starry Eyed song have just come to mind when a thump in the hallway has me sitting up.

"Janelle." My mom is whispering outside my door. It's late, and she could get in trouble with Dad if she speaks too loud.

I shove the picture under my pillow before I open my door just slightly.

"Can you hide this in here?" She holds up a flask.

"Mom." It's all I can say. I weigh the options in my head. If she gets caught with it, it'll be her second transgression. Death. If I get caught with it. It'll be my first. Unless that damn book gets out. Although, to be fair, that would be two transgressions at once. So, what the hell? I take the flask with a nod.

"Thank you, baby." Her words are slurred and she kisses my cheek. "They're coming. They never leave us alone. The world's theirs now. Don't tell your father, okay? Don't tell him, we can't trust him. I'm scared." Her gaze shifts away from me and she steps back, not really seeing me anymore. She disappears down the dark hall, and I close the door. She'll sleep across the hall from my dad, who isn't really my dad anymore.

Not that he looks any different.

I got my careful defiance, dark skin and thick, wild curls from him. But my introversion, freckles and big, brown eyes come from Mom. She's mixed, and I suppose I am, too. Dad isn't, though. He's black, nothing else. Mom says that was why he had the hang-ups he did; all his life he was feared for no reason at all. Treated poorly for no reason at all.

When they came for us, he thought he might have a chance to negotiate. He was outspoken, clever and, honestly, he could have run for office with his ability to reach people. And he did. Just not the Ilori.

There was a bigger threat in town now than a smart black man; guns were pointed in a different direction. The same people who imprisoned people like him, killed them or judged them, were the people who looked to him to save us all. There was power in it, Mom said, and power does bad things to good people.

The neighbors asked Dad to negotiate with the Ilori, advocate for our rights, but when he stepped over the line to argue against stronger punishments for those who assaulted guards—people Dad didn't know or care about before—the Ilori got fed up. They took the troublemakers, anyone who didn't look like they'd step aside easily, and gave them a vaccine. The half-solutions program, they called it. Some responded "well," becoming temporary half-shells of themselves, and some didn't, either dying or running away.

Dad is one of the shells. He's still in there, yet, there is this other…thing, too. Something foreign, willing to kill. He gets his injection monthly, but every few days, he peeks through, each time shorter than the last. He didn't sell out my mom and her drinking the first time, or stop me when I concealed a book under my jacket when they came to round up the books and burn them. But I won't risk telling him about the library.

This is the world we live in now, where we can't trust our own fathers, and where our mothers spiral out of control.

This is what the Ilori have done to us.

I slide the flask into the hiding spot of my beloved copies of *Harriet the Spy*, *Matilda*, *Corduroy*, and *Amari and the Night Brothers*, behind my bed in a loose wooden wall panel. This room has been searched nothing short of seventeen times, and not once has someone stumbled upon it. I doubt they care too much about finding things anymore, but they want to appear as if they do. If they did care, they'd have found my library, and I'd be dead.

I sigh, pacing around my once colorful room. The walls are blank; all of my Starry Eyed posters were torn down; there's no color, no joy; only bleached bedsheets and graying linen. I remember when people would say they don't see color, and I'd laugh. Did that mean they couldn't see me? Was that supposed to make me feel good, equal?

But now they have no choice. My family's color is probably the most interesting, most vibrant shade of skin in our Upper East Side apartment building. While they're pale from the lack of sun, I stay brown as if the sun lives within me.

Our skin still angers some folks, but the Ilori don't care at all, which is nice. They just see me as another human, equal to all other humans. Taking up space and eating food until whatever happens, happens.

I stop, scrunching up my lips as I keep myself from punching the wall.

How could I have lost that book? Signed and autographed with my name above the dedication. Suddenly all my reasons to start a library and trust people seem ignorant and naive. I'm going to die for giving more than I take, for being kind.

The worst part is, I used to be smarter than this.

Dad's mantra echoes in the back of my mind. *Never tell them how smart you are. Work harder, speak softer, let them underestimate you.* For years he told me that, and I tried, no matter how confusing and angry that made me feel. I became quiet and unsure. And that's gotta be the reason I'm in this predicament.

Well, that, and my poor interpersonal skills. I learned everything from socializing to surviving from books. Characters, with their twisty plots and drama, were better than reality. Humanity's better in stories. That's why I saved as many books as I could, basically saving the humanity worth saving.

First, I read them on my own. I didn't share; I didn't trust anyone.

But then Alice caught me.

We knew each other before the Ilori came, we lived in the same building. We'd wait in the lobby in the morning together. She would wait for her taxi to take her to school, and I'd wait for Dad to take me on the subway. She was always on her phone or meeting with her popular friends, but sometimes she'd look up and smile. Sometimes I'd smile back.

When the Ilori came, we were forced together. Two terrified people desperate for friendship.

One day, I had a book hidden in a flap of my sweater. It was well hidden, or so I thought. Alice cornered me in the bathroom.

"You have a book?"

I held my breath, eyeing the bathroom stalls and corners of the ceiling. I nodded.

"Can I see it?"

"Too dangerous," I muttered.

"Please?"

I sighed and took it from my pocket. I opened it and brought it before her. "Look inside."

Her gaze fell to the illustration and widened in wonder. "What is it? I mean what's it about?"

"Dragons."

Her breath caught. "Can I borrow it?"

"No. They'll kill you if they find it."

"Janelle, if I don't read it, I'll die a worse death. Come on, I love dragons. Please?"

I gave it to her and told her to call me Ellie. Three days later, she handed it back, asking for another. Soon, she'd told a person, who'd told a person, and so on. And she had the nerve to ask me why I started the library in the first place, when it was just as much her fault as it is mine now. Only thing is, for her, being part of the library would be a single transgression.

I snort, wondering if my dad will cry when they hang me. Or if he'll be the one to put the noose around my neck.

I push that thought away. Who does that help?

Then I realize it's quiet, so quiet. That means it's time to go to the underground party, as promised. I could find my mom's hidden makeup stash and attempt to do my face myself, or I could go as I am. I glance down. I look all right.

Creeping through our apartment is easy. The space is laid out like an oversize plus sign; a small entrance where our shabby coats hang leading to the kitchen, the living room across from it, bisected by a hallway with two bedrooms and a bathroom on one side, my bedroom and bathroom on the other. There's no way Dad can hear me over his snoring. I make it to the front door and take a deep breath.

It's ten at night; the patrols should be on. But they aren't... not when the parties happen. Even the cameras are off. I've always figured it's because people successfully bribe the human guards—the Ilori guards are scarce, almost nonexistent at night. Alice and I have asked but never found out. We just accept it. The lack of watchful eyes helps me with my library, and provides Alice with the opportunity to dig up dirt on potential patrons.

If all that weren't weird, we hardly ever see the Ilori on

night patrols. It's like night falls and they disappear into the shadows, leaving only half-solution guards in their place. Some of the guards are as loyal to the Ilori as my dad, but some are not. I rely on those ones to get away with breaking the rules.

With that in mind, I shut the front door behind me and peek around the corner. I grimace as I slip down the hallway, making so much effort to get somewhere I don't even want to be.

I creep down the stairs.

When the Ilori took over our building, my parents and I cowered in our apartment, unsure of what to do. After a few days of nothing but fearful whispers, the Ilori rounded up the adults. Mom and Dad left while I remained pacing in our living room.

A few hours later, they stumbled through our door with wide eyes and sat me down.

"Ellie, you'll be going downstairs every day. There'll be school for you and the other older kids to complete. They're going to keep you busy so you can't fight back." My dad spoke calmly, but there was a waver in his voice. Nerves.

"What about you and Mom?" I sat on the edge of my seat, the reality of our loss of freedom setting in.

"They'll be taking me upstairs tonight to talk about that."

I wanted to press more, to ask him if he was scared, but I could tell by the way he kept looking away that he didn't want to talk about it. "Your mom volunteered to work upstairs with the Ilori during the day."

"Why?" I turned to Mom. "What will you do up there?"

"I'll learn what's going on." That's all she said. As if it was no big deal, not worth discussing. But she had that same shell-shocked look as Dad. They withheld the truth because they were protecting me, or they were too afraid themselves.

Since then, Dad got vaccinated and put on patrols with other guards and Ilori. Mom? I'm not sure some days. All I know is that she cries most nights and drinks every chance she gets. Her mind is addled, and she has irrational fears that can be appeased only by a sip, she says. Just a sip.

I have a lot of ideas about what she and other adults are doing up there, but nothing concrete. I know sometimes they work with chemicals, because they come back with impressions of masks on their faces, and some parents talk to their kids about it. But I don't push my mom to tell me. What if it makes it worse for her?

In the beginning, I asked her if she was afraid. She replied, *I'm afraid every day. But I have you, and you keep me together. As long as I have you, I'll keep holding on.*

Guilt floods me as I descend to the final floor. If I die for my library, I'm killing her, too.

I knock once on the door and wait for a prompt. The response is always the same. The grate opens and a mouth appears.

"We are the descendants of poets and prophets." The voice is deep, mature.

"We are the keepers of time and tales," I respond.

"When the story ends."

"We die." We answer together.

They open the door and give me a small grin. Their name's Angel, an enby from the ninth floor. They're maybe three years older than me, blond, skinny as a rail, with blue eyes that dart back and forth like they're expecting something, but that might just be their normal expression. I follow them down the dark hall to the former laundry room, my suddenly sweaty hands sticking to my sides, as we approach the music, light but audible. It's some classical music, most likely from a record player. It's only classical or oldies now, since none of us had physical versions of more recent music. I have a soft spot for cheesy lyrics and addictive hooks, but I enjoy classical music.

I used to play the cello. I started when I was nine. My mom

said she just knew I was meant to play, and one day, I came home and found one in our living room, leaning against a chair. Two years ago, it was confiscated and burned outside in the courtyard. I was fifteen, and we had just lost control of Earth. The strings popped and the wood blistered. I try not to remember it. My heart breaks when I think about all we lost in the ashes of our dwindling human existence.

Soon, the Ilori will cure us of our humanity.

Another vaccine. It won't be like the half-solutions program, although same principle. They've been up in the sky perfecting it, making it more powerful and potent. They're going to take away our minds. Just like they did with Dad, only somehow worse.

I asked my mom about it before she lost herself.

"It's true," she said. "They're creating a new vaccine. They promised there'd be no deaths. That it'll be safe. Painless."

She refused to answer my other questions, saying only that "knowledge is a burden."

But I've overheard conversations in the cafeteria and gym, and formed my own conclusions.

Our building contains one of the biggest human populations left in Manhattan. That I know for certain. Once, in May of last year I think, there was a bus that stopped in front of our building. I peered down at it from my living room window. Families stumbled out carrying small garbage bags of their things. None of them cried; they looked…numb. They moved into the empty apartments and adjusted to life here. A few days passed before we all knew the rumors they brought with them; the Ilori were consolidating the humans. Moving most like the elderly and parents with babies to permanent housing, and keeping everyone else here.

The biggest rumor: they need us alive. At least, some of us.

And because of this, we started to break the rules. There

can't be much time left before the vaccine. Erica Schulman knew it, Alice knows it. My mom drinks to it, and my dad kills for it. Our time is running out. That's why we party and I hand out books to those I find trustworthy. It's my hill that I'll die on. If, of course, I can choose to die instead of losing myself like Dad and Mom.

Angel pats my arm, bringing me back, before they stalk down the long hallway again. I hum "Fairy-tale Girl" by the Starry Eyed to soothe my nerves while I look around.

"You're Janelle, right?" The boy's eyes are blue in the candlelight, and he smells like beer.

I nod, gulping, my poor throat suddenly dry. My gaze searches for Alice. "And you?" But I know his name, I'm just trying to be polite.

"Dallas." His eyes take in my curves and hair, my breasts. Before the invasion, I remember Alice telling me that Dallas had a thing for black girls. Gross.

I step back. I'm not desperate. In fact, since I'd rather die instead of becoming a zombie like Dad, I'd rather die a virgin, too. The idea of doing something intimate, of being naked, being touched, held…by a stranger like Dallas, gives me goose bumps and turns my stomach. I know I'm ace, or at least on the spectrum of that, but still, a voice in me whispers: *You're going to die anyway, why not try something new?*

I ignore that voice. "Have you seen Alice?"

He turns away. "Alice is in Wonderland." He cocks his head, and I follow the direction to where Alice is on Jackson Hughes's lap, kissing him like her life depends on it and grinding as if her body requires it. I shrug. I can wait.

"We can join them?"

I make a face and shake my head, moving away from him. He doesn't seem all that disappointed either; a moment later, he's crossing the room and picking on a new girl. At least Dallas has seen me and can tell Alice I was here. But I need to ask her if she's spoken to her friends. If she has any leads on the missing book.

I take a seat on the floor close to the music. I glance at Alice and Jackson quick before my gaze falls to the scuffed linoleum.

I don't love the idea of Alice and Jackson together. He's sorta the worst, and his father hates my family. I would have cautioned her to stay away from him, but Alice does what she wants. For better or worse.

My eyes close as my head falls back against the wall. The music is nice, and maybe I won't mind getting out of my room and head for a bit.

As soon as that thought creeps into my mind, a voice joins it. *Come here*, it says warmly.

The air freezes in my lungs.

I gulp like a fish out of water, my head whipping around to find who's talking to me. One of them is here, at this party. Calling me. Calling me where?

Come here. To your library.

The voice is quiet but demanding. My gaze flits to the others as they dance, laugh, kiss... They don't know there's an Ilori in my mind, about to wreck my life or end it.

Calm, human, calm.

It has to be a strong one if it can speak into my mind, right? Or can they all do this? We know some of them use this ability, that they can destroy us from the inside out, or take whatever they want from the farthest reaches of a human's mind. I even know some of my neighbors experienced it briefly. I just never expected or wanted to have the experience.

Come to me.

I have to go. Even if it kills me. The voice is insistent. If I don't do what it asks... I don't know what will happen.

Oh God.

No one notices me internally panicking. I leave before I

can even make eye contact with Alice, but then it probably doesn't matter anymore. One of them is here, one of them knows. I'm walking toward my own death.

As if in answer to the voice, my knees buckle and a strange calmness settles over me. I'm not sure if I feel relief because the future is bleak and I don't want to live it anyway, or if I'm simply afraid.

Maybe both.

Silence greets me as I take the flight of stairs down into the storage basement.

Come here.

I unlock the door and follow the light the Ilori must have left on for me. Beads of sweat prickle along my hairline as I cross through the hall to the storage unit.

My hands are shaky as I swing the door open. And there it is. It waits for me, leaning against a broken desk, facing the door.

When they first arrived, we didn't know what to expect; green-skinned creatures like we'd seen in movies or something else entirely. But behind their metallic battle armor, they look like us. They have the same anatomy as us. They could pass for human, if you ignore the silver panels backlit with blue light that extend from behind their right ears to their jaws, and their otherworldly glow of optimal health. Beyond that, they come in all shapes, sizes, skin tones…like us.

This one looks a little distracted, probably communicating with other Ilori using their minds. The Hive. I remember scientists explaining it on TV, pointing at this one little switch on the panel of a dead alien and saying, "This is something we've never seen before. A hive-mind mentality."

It looks at me through its long eyelashes, hazel eyes seeming to pierce through me. Black hair curls around the sides of its face, and its skin glows in the minimal light of the storage room. It's darker than olive-skinned but lighter than black. If it were human, I would guess it's Latinx, but that's just my attempt to label it, make it familiar somehow. It's beautiful. Alluring.

Dangerous.

"Please come in." Its accent is nothing like any human one either. Its words are staccato and precise. "I apologize for entering your mind without consent. I hope you can forgive me."

My gaze darts around the small space. It's alone.

"My name is—" It sounds like beeps and clicks. "I suppose to humans, that doesn't sound like much. I've noticed that when written using your language, it could sound like Morris. Please call me Morris."

I can't say anything.

"I must ask you to close the door."

I stumble slightly as I comply.

"I have your book."

My gaze shoots up and my heart feels like it could stop any moment. Most likely it will.

"I put it back inside the mattress." It stares at me hopefully. "I'm not going to hurt you. I will not speak of your library to the others. I've come to ask for help."

I step back into the door. "I... I don't—"

"Calm, human. Calm." It steps closer. "I will not hurt you. Not you. Not anyone." It looks away, back to the library. "Do you love books? I'm afraid I haven't had enough time to read them. But I read the one I took. I liked it very much..." It rubs its arm, as if it's uncomfortable or cold or uncertain. "You like books. We have books in Ilori. Not stories like these."

"I didn't mean to...to keep these. I know they are illegal, I know that. I—I just, I love them." My mind works to formulate something, anything to absolve my sins.

It smiles. "Do not worry. Please do not worry. You have learned that we are enemies, yet I will not hurt you. Your secret is safe with me."

I begin to shake. Suddenly, it catches my hand and keeps my feet planted on the floor. My heart hammers in my chest. I may pass out. And then the most amazing and weird thing happens.

"Raspberry beret," it sings, wobbly, and the words sound foreign on its tongue, but its voice is beautiful, and I find myself calming. I half smile despite myself.

"I like music. I like the way the sounds come together and make something so…" It laughs. "I do not know the word for it."

"Harmonious?" I suggest, trying to swallow my nerves.

"Yes, that's it!" Its smile is forced, maybe a new effort, but it tries. "Let's start this again. My name is Morris, I am male and a commander in the Ilori Acquisitions Force. I have a deep appreciation of music. And you are Janelle."

"How did you— Did you read my mind?" I blurt through quick breaths.

"The Ilori cannot read human minds." He crosses and then immediately uncrosses his arms awkwardly. "I suppose it's like a radio. Once I know your frequency—" he points to the identification number on my chest "—I can send messages to it. I cannot receive messages back."

I gulp, surprised he's telling me this. "But you can kill us with your minds."

"We can move energy and electricity." Morris shrugs. "If you remove the electricity from a living being, they die. I suppose it's like unplugging a computer from the output."

I don't know what to make of that, so I store it away for later and swallow the lump in my throat. "My name is Janelle Baker, I'm female, I have an appreciation for books and I'm about to die for it."

Morris shakes his head. "No harm will befall you for this, Janelle. I don't—I can't see any more death." He winces. "You humans, we need you. And you will not die…your mind will merely cease to function." He stares at me, as if he thinks these words will help me understand my situation better. But they don't. "Do you know why they made us take away books?"

Books speak to the human condition? They give people an escape from their lives? They give people something worth fighting for? I don't know, not really, so I shrug.

"Ilori leadership say your people used books to communicate and coordinate attacks. It is true that humans did plan some successful attacks that killed hundreds of my kind…" He looks away, as if collecting himself. "But I've read your book. I did not see plans of revolution hidden inside. And it is not only books they forbade, but art, music, expression. They want to control you, but I have no desire to do that. I do my job only so that I may…go home with honor."

"I don't care about why you banned books and music. You've killed a lot of humans—*my* kind. You continue to kill us. There's no honor in that."

"I did not kill anyone, Janelle. If I did not come here, someone else would have. I do not control the Acquisitions Force, nor my planet. Unrecognized fear manifests in callousness." He rubs his arm, glancing away. "I do not wish to kill anyone."

My anger rises, and I know I shouldn't say anything. But I have to. "That doesn't mean people haven't died because of your job."

"It is not that simple." He makes a small noise, his eyes locking with mine. "There are many reasons why your world has fallen. However, I'm afraid you lack the knowledge to understand them. It is not your fault. You are only human, and therefore limited."

I roll my eyes, and if he kills me for that, I stand by it. "Humans are smart. Just because—"

"I think that is a discussion for another time," he cuts in.

"What I need from you is help. And I chose you because you could be killed for these books you possess."

"You're *blackmailing* me?"

His brows knit together. "What is blackmail?"

"You know something that if other people know could hurt me, and so you think I have to do what you want."

"I do not want to force you to do anything." He exhales. "I am asking because I think you understand. Because these books could kill you, and music could kill me. We are both in precarious positions."

I snort. I know I should be more respectful to him, but I'm so tired of it all. "What do you want?"

"I believe that if you were able to collect all of these books, you might be able to find music for me. No one has turned you in, and no one has come for you—people must trust you. I need to collect all the music from this building in two days, if possible. I'll provide you with opportunities, but it will require a bit of investigative work from you. It's just that... music is..." He sighs, staring up at the ceiling as if searching for words. "Everything to me."

I exhale. I do understand. I feel the same about books. But am I supposed to sneak through apartments in search of be-loved vinyl, iPods, phones, USB sticks or external hard drives buried underneath floorboards for an alien? It's dangerous, risky and illegal. "Is that all?"

He nods with another alien smile. "Yes."

I rock back on my heels. "What would stop me from tell-ing the other Ilori that you love music? Do you think they will let me live for selling you out?"

Morris's eyes flash, and in them, I see doubt. "If you don't—" I take notice of the more informal language as his words come faster "—wish to help me, then there's no point in continuing the conversation. I will not 'blackmail' you, as you say. I just thought that you and I, we appreciate art and we have limited time. We could help each other."

"You're asking me to risk my life to get you music. I understand, but I'm the one they'll kill if I get caught. Not you." I won't be cowed into risking myself further. Not for an alien. Not without something in return.

"They would kill me, too, Janelle. Your life has more value than mine." His voice cracks a little as he looks at the floor.

"Yeah, right," I scoff. "I've never seen an Ilori get hanged. You're one of them. You're a commander, you're in charge."

"I assure you, I am not." Morris shakes his head, and for a second, I could almost think he's human. "They don't hang my kind. They have other ways."

If he's lying to me, I can't tell. But there's something about the way he says it, and the way his eyes crinkle at the edges, making him look tired and defeated, that makes me want to believe him. Why would he lie? He could be appealing to my humanity, gaining my sympathy so that I'll get him music. Yet once he has it, if what he says is true, they could kill him for it. What's the end result for him? Getting music, or fooling a human? Either I'm being manipulated, or he's telling the truth.

"I know you do not believe me, and I want to earn your trust." Morris suddenly holds his head high, straightening his back. "I'll protect you. I'll protect your family. I can't guarantee their safety, but I can try."

The thought of him saving my family, maybe Alice and even her family…that's too good to pass up. Even if he is manipulating me, which still seems off. "Okay."

Morris beams. "Oh, this brings me such joy." His tone is far more exuberant than I would expect of an Ilori.

"I thought your species isn't big on emotions?" That's what the television reports said. They don't feel. There is no compassion. If you see an Ilori, run. Morris might have sung to me, but I can't unlearn what I've heard.

He frowns. "We aren't supposed to be."

I don't have time to unpack that, so I move on. "What happens in two days?"

Morris fidgets with the cloth on the mattress. "The vaccine. Those with the necessary specifications in this quadrant will receive it."

"Necessary specifications?" My eyebrows lift.

"Blood is like a map. It can tell the history of a person, their strength. If they can survive a procedure. As you are here, you meet the criteria."

"Great, I guess I have strong blood." I snort. "So, you want me to find music for you, and you won't let them kill me. I give you the music, and then I'll die anyway?"

"I will protect you." He's quiet for a moment. "I'll…move you and your family somewhere safe." He rubs his hands together. "I can do this."

"How can I trust you to protect us if you're just as powerless as I am?"

I'm not just as powerless as you. His voice whispers into my mind. "When an Ilori makes a promise, they keep that promise."

"You didn't promise me anything."

Morris regards me closely now and nods. "You are right. We are risking much, both of us. I promise you, I'll keep you from the vaccine as long as I can. I will move you. I will… find a way." His chin dips in conviction.

If he can save everyone who matters to me and keep me from death a little longer, I'll do it. "Deal. But no more talking in my mind without permission."

"Deal." Morris smiles, and it almost looks human this time. "You will not regret this, Janelle Baker." The way he says my name would have made me laugh, if I weren't so tired and scared.

"Just call me Ellie."

"Ellie," he says, his fingers tracing a book inside the mattress. "Why do you do this?"

"Books make me feel like...myself. I want others to feel the same." I have a million more reasons, and I won't explain them now. Not to him. "Why do you like music?"

"Music makes me feel." His answer is soft but rings with his truth. "I like feeling."

I nod, silent. He's my enemy, but he sang to me. He might cast me aside and let me die, but he admits to weakness. He's done something, in this brief introduction, that I would never have expected; he put a face to the Ilori and, in doing so, he's made me doubt, even just a little, what I think I know about them.

"You are an interesting human, Ellie."

"Have you ever met a human before, Morris?"

He exhales, gaze falling to the floor. "No. I—I've been on Earth for only three days." For a moment I think he's going to say more, but he doesn't.

I back away and open the door. I won't engage, because there's nothing I can say without unleashing my bottled-up anger. "I'll get the music."

"See you soon, Ellie."

Back in my room, my thoughts are jumbled, and my heart's still racing. He didn't ask, but that was the first time I ever spoke with an Ilori, the first time one has ever looked me in the eyes. And it wasn't what I expected. It wasn't like the news reports, or the horror stories circulating around the building. I can almost believe that Morris isn't going to kill me.

Almost.

CHAPTER 6

"Landslide"
—Fleetwood Mac

MORRIS

A sigh escapes through his teeth, and he turns off the music. Time's up. A new day begins. He pours a glass of calef juice, imported from home. But he drinks it from a human glass, which makes it thrilling.

Home is so far away. He wonders if his mother misses him or is afraid for him, or if his father thinks better of him now. He laughs, surprising himself. *Never.* His mind drifts to Janelle—Ellie—while he settles at the table and drinks.

He…he finds himself wanting to talk to her again. Be friends, maybe. But their arrangement is dangerous. Will she get him music? Can he keep her and her family alive? Could she ever forgive him for who and what he is? Many questions with few answers. He was not granted the ability to see the future—such abilities don't exist, anyway. Not for Ilori. Although, it would be most welcome at this particular moment and time.

A lyric strikes him, and like all music he enjoys, he lets it pass through his lips in a melody that brings him comfort and warmth. Fleetwood Mac. A strange name, but the music is nice. He sings along, unsure of the words but lost in the emotions that it pulls from him. Will Ellie be his "Landslide"? The final piece that brings him down and leaves him vulnerable to Il-0CoM?

Having the communication system in his mind is unsettling. One slip-up could be his doom. Yet, if he wants to, even so far away, he could send an invitation to connect to his mother. She could comfort him and tell him it'll be okay. He could tell her that he's safe and fulfilling the role she requested of him. But he's not in the mood to fake confidence.

She's the reason he's here. She's the reason he was raised to feel, and to follow those feelings.

M0Rr1S closes his eyes before flipping the switch. Il-0CoM starts like static until it becomes sharp. Names float around, identifying the speakers, as he enters the conversation.

How are we on the vaccine?

We have troubles with human forces in the drylands.

Do we bomb them?

Do not destroy the land. We will find a solution. They cannot hide in their caves much longer. They will need food. They will need air.

Weak.

He does not recognize all the voices speaking in circles inside his mind. If he could focus on just one voice, he might, but it is too overwhelming.

These human cars are efficient. With tinkering, we could make them more ecological. We must reduce the emissions, and bring the CO_2 levels down. All commanders are to use cars while our transport veliopters should be used sparingly.

Humans. Unwise. Destroying such a world.

It is not only the humans that inhabit this world. Andarrans are

scattered along the West Coast of what was called the United States.
It is said they—

We have a peace treaty with the Andarrans, a general insists.
They may live wherever they like. As long as they do not burden us
with their insight of time. Or stand in our path.

The Andarrans, more voices mutter.

Expressionists.

Too much knowledge of the universe.

M0Rr1S wonders how there could ever be "too much
knowledge" about the universe, as it is unending and constantly changing, but he doesn't say so.

The Andarrans, a true Ilori says, *are innocuous and have never*
engaged in war, but their leaders are ancient. They rule by their emo-
tions. In this regard, we must always exercise caution with them.

Let us discuss more pertinent topics, another true Ilori huffs. *Is*
all of Earth salvageable?

Certainly, a labmade from Habitation chimes in. *We have*
also allocated and utilized land conducive to human housing. We have
built solid structures, reconfigured their outdated heating and cooling
systems, created more natural environments, not only for local wild-
life, but for farmlands that produce nutritional foods for humans' im-
proved health, given them synthetic clothing that should increase their
comfort and created access to advanced medicine, education and assis-
tance. Why, it is our belief that we have improved the quality of life
for 63 percent of the human population. They pause as unwanted
excitement has begun threading through their words. *The hu-*
mans may even be content in time.

That would be ideal, another labmade says.

However nice the permanent housing, M0Rr1S knows
freedom and choice would lead to further contentment, but
doesn't say as much.

That was never our objective, a true Ilori states plainly. *The hu-*
mans are a product we need. Their contentment and treatment mean
nothing to us.

The contentment of humans, not just those that will be used as husks, is necessary to avoid rebellion. We have the resources. It would be shortsighted, sir, not to consider their permanent treatment, another labmade says, and M0Rr1S wishes they hadn't. Their name vanishes from Il-0CoM a second later. They were either booted out, or shut down to face penalization. Some true Ilori, especially the older ones, don't care to be corrected and will not hesitate to end a labmade life when disrespected. Further proof that true Ilori feel, yet no one is allowed to say so.

Commander M0Rr1S, how is your quadrant of Earth coming? One of the last origin quadrants, yes?

The congested metropolis was too difficult to move altogether into housing, someone answers on his behalf.

Commander M0Rr1S, today is vaccine testing, correct?

He debates not answering, but they are aware he is connected, logged in. If he does not, it will be just as suspicious. *Vaccine testing will begin shortly. We separated those with the required specifications from those without and moved them into housing in the north of the hemisphere. The entirety left within my quadrant will be tested. From there, the vaccine will be produced and utilized on those within housing at Command's discretion. My work here is nearly complete.* It's true; Manhattan was once so densely populated that finding humans was easy. From there, they were locked down in their buildings and separated to await the vaccine. Only a few buildings remain in his area. Thirteen in total. *But as I've stated before, and shall state again, we must cease killing humans for transgressions. We are losing our most viable husks.* M0Rr1S sits up, hoping his words will be considered.

A chatter breaks out that causes M0Rr1S to rub his temples.

As you can hear, Commander, there is dispute on how best to handle our human problem.

Our true Ilori masters are skeptical about the harvesting process.

There is…an element of unnecessary emotion among you labmades. You find it difficult to kill those you were created to imitate. You may even feel guilt over the humans. However, we, your masters, find that eliminating human threat is best for control, especially in your locked-down facilities.

M0Rr1S wants to argue, but he must choose his words carefully. One slip... *I am commander of this quadrant, yet my authority has been overridden. There are still executions without my say.* He tries to keep the slight edge from his voice.

If your authority is being overridden, the orders come from higher up. This will hardly be a problem once the vaccine is administered.

Hardly a problem indeed. When they are quarantined in permanent housing, they can grow more. And there are still many of them.

M0Rr1S shakes his head as his concern is overlooked once again. He is commander in title only. No labmade has ever been in complete control. True Ilori monitor them and involve themselves in every situation. That is why M0Rr1S keeps Il-0CoM off more often than not, why he has trained to keep his thoughts and memory private.

Commander M0Rr1S, when your centers are vaccinated, your pod will be awaiting you outside the metropolis. Area L1B-72-Gr-S. When you arrive, your passcode will be given, and you can upload your memory onto the main system.

M0Rr1S sits back, taking another sip of his juice. He must keep the eagerness from his thoughts. *Thank you.*

Pleased to leave, Commander? You were on Earth but a few rotations. A snicker accompanies the question.

He must be thoughtful. "I desire to serve my empire with a new task."

A new task?

If you desire to be useful, Commander, perhaps you can find a solution for the humans currently engaged in warfare against us. That would be most helpful. We can adjust your extraction so that you can apply your usefulness there. Let us know at your convenience.

Have you ever been engaged in war, Commander? A voice far away cuts through the discussion with a hint of superiority. Another commander who didn't need their family name to acquire the position, most likely.

He is young. Inexperienced. Another adds. Brixton. He knows that voice better than anyone.

Captain Brixton, a pleasure for you to join us, M0Rr1S lies. There is no pleasure derived from exchanging words with Brixton, but feeling the way he does only proves he is not equal to him. So, he must lie, pretend to be made of stone, impenetrable. *We do not feel.*

Commander M0Rr1S. I assure you, the pleasure is all mine. Brixton's words are as flat as expected. His older brother is as stoic as an Ilori is meant to be, as Father expects them to be.

M0Rr1S looks for the right words, grasping to say something, but AvR0la interrupts. *Ah, there you are, sir. We are to begin testing the vaccine on a select group today.*

His shoulders sag in relief. Saved. And then he remembers what this means. *Thank you, AvR0la. What G00287 granteth—*

The Ilori taketh, Il-0CoM answers in unison.

He does not switch the feed off yet, but he lets the voices fade till they're mild background chatter.

The vaccine. He wonders if Janelle knows the subjects. The answer is immediate. She's been trapped in this building possibly since Ilori took control. There are a thousand of them, but they all must know each other. And undoubtedly, her mother will be among the first wave of vaccinations.

M0Rr1S ducks into the commode to splash his face with water. He wraps his black jacket around himself and straightens his title dangling on his chest. The door opens at his command, and he takes the elevator down to the testing floor, two stories beneath his apartment.

He places his hand on a screen panel, and a door opens to the white hallway and bright lights. AvR0la awaits him by the first room. They look somber, and their gaze darts to the inhabitants inside.

M0Rr1S leans in close to AvR0la. "There are three humans that need to be kept from testing. I believe they live in domicile 2H. They have a daughter, JQB-305-7-21. Are any being tested now?"

"Will check the records, sir." AvR0la glances upward at their optic screen, rushing through files. "The elder female is scheduled for tomorrow."

"Cancel the directive. Keep that family away from vaccinations until I determine what to do with them."

"Yes, sir." AvR0La doesn't question his orders. "It is time." They hold their hand out, inviting him to enter the small office first.

Where once there were tables and screens, there are cushioned beds with humans strapped to them. The first sound to reach M0Rr1S's ears is that of sobbing. Despite his desire, M0Rr1S can't do anything for them. His oversight is necessary, while true Ilori will listen in from afar. They step inside the small space, an Ilori doctor standing in the back, monitoring the humans' vitals.

M0Rr1S never explicitly studied humans, but he does know some things about them, after all, Earth-mission labmades were designed in their image. While they share most common features, human behavior is different. Behavior comes from surroundings. Labmade Ilori are expected to let facts and true Ilori dictate their expressions. Humans feel and express everything, sometimes regardless of facts. It is why they are so fascinating.

"Commander." AvR0la is looking at him with curiosity. "Have you heard the question?"

"No, my apologies. I was reflecting."

"Of course, sir. Shall we do the vaccine in blocks of ten patients and monitor their behavior for a day or shall we do them all today?"

He knows what he is expected to say. Three faces stare at him while he decides. One is AvR0la, who will not question his decision. Another is a doctor, who is communicating via Il-0CoM. The last is the patient on the table, a mask over her mouth. Her eyes are frantic, but she is paralyzed. He needn't worry about her. Yet, he does. "Test all prepared subjects today."

The doctor nods in M0Rr1S's direction. "Simultaneous inoculation. I will communicate your orders to the others on standby down the corridor." The other rooms down the hall.

"We will keep a few spares for later." M0Rr1S nods to AvR0la. "We haven't time to waste. We will monitor their behavior, and, assuming it proves satisfactory, we will administer the vaccines to the next group tomorrow and the youth the following day. Across all buildings."

The doctor's face goes slack as he engages in Il-0CoM. This was the correct answer, they all know that now. The doctor gives him a slight, insulting bow. The vaccine is administered into the patient's neck through a metal-tubed stunner. The effects are instant. They monitor her as her blood pressure plummets but her heartbeat stabilizes. Her brain activity ceases, and her breathing becomes rhythmic and slow.

The doctor regards her. "I believe the vaccine is satisfactory. Well-done, Commander."

"And her consciousness?" M0Rr1S steps closer, searching for a spark of understanding in the human's eyes. And then wishes he hadn't asked that; he knows it worked. The formula was tested on all of his projections, and never failed once. Asking was illogical. He hopes that his mistake will be overlooked.

"That test will take several hours." The doctor checks her eyes, her chest, but the patient has that same glazed look as before.

"It is of no importance," M0Rr1S offers.

The doctor ignores him. "There are no casualties. All reported the same results. I will have more information for you later, Commander."

"Thank you." He turns to AvR0la. "I want to check on

the human production below. Keep an eye on the doctor."
He stands back as he clicks Il-0CoM off.

When he enters the room, he can't help but search among
the younger humans for her. Their clothes lack vibrancy, their
faces are drawn and tired as they sort through millions of
flower and vegetable seeds all mixed together. They've been
tasked with separating them into piles after running each one
under individual scanners. A lesson in botany. It's a silly thing
to do, but a human desires purpose.

He spots her at a table with another girl. She barely looks
up at him, meeting his eyes once before she continues sorting
through her pile. Her shoulders are hunched, and she averts
her gaze. *Discomfort.* She finds his presence discomforting.

It is a shame that this is the feeling he inspires in her. From the
moment she entered his life, or he entered hers, she has inspired
music and literature, pretty words and sounds in him. Part of him
wishes he could read her mind. He wouldn't want to pry, though.

Prying involves skilled precision while stripping away pieces
of memory like codes, and peeking inside, scouring for whatever he so desires. Skilled Ilori use it against one another on
true Ilori command, and it is painful for the pried, energy
draining for the prier. No, he just wants to know Ellie, and
for her to trust him. Her hands shake, and he can feel her
nerves across the room.

May I, Ellie? he asks into her mind.

She looks up at him, only briefly, and then nods once.

He sings Fleetwood Mac gently into their connection, trying not to hurt or scare her. They could punish him for this,
say he's breaking protocol, defective…yet, here he is, singing
to her, hoping he can enjoy her presence longer than a day or
two. That they'll both be alive for another day or two. Because despite their circumstances and the danger, he is drawn

to her. The books, the wild willfulness, her beautiful eyes. He's breaking the rules for music, and now for her.

She looks at him, her shoulders unhunching and, for a moment, he thinks she might smile. Then the girl next to her interrupts their moment.

"When they came here, tell me you didn't think they would be green with bug eyes and round fingers?" she asks, not waiting for a response before continuing. "But they aren't. They're like healthier versions of us. Scary, but beautiful, even with those electronic panel things and the way they stare at you. That one over there—" her head nods in the direction of M0Rr1S "—reminds me of Allister Daniels, you know, from the Starry Eyed? Just as pretty. If he wasn't an Ilori, I would date him. Hell, I'd do more than date him. Wouldn't you?"

Ellie shrugs.

M0Rr1S frowns. She wouldn't date him? Why not?

What is dating?

"Why's he staring at you?"

Ellie shrugs once more.

"I'm sorry about the party, if that's what you're mad about. I got caught up in the moment." The girl's head leans closer to Ellie's. In that moment, Ellie's countenance transforms into myriad different emotions, reminding him how perfectly human she is. There is surprise. Confusion. Anger. Concern. Affection.

"Don't worry about that, Alice. I found the book."

"Really? Where?"

"I—I found it where it was supposed to be. I miscalculated."

The girl named Alice makes a small noise. "That is the first time you've ever admitted to a mistake."

"Well it doesn't happen often." The corners of Ellie's lips rise into a smirk or a grin. M0Rr1S doesn't know which. He will practice it in the mirror later, that may make her more comfortable with him.

"Seriously, he's still looking at you," Alice whispers. She doesn't realize that the Ilori can hear human whispers. True Ilori desired to make communication a transgression, but they would have lost the entire human stock if they had. And, they found, when quiet was enforced upon the humans, their productivity and health suffered. Communication was preferable over revolution.

"He's probably connected to their Hive thing. Remember? He's not really seeing me or us. Like the rest of them." She waves a dismissive hand.

M0Rr1S glances around at the other three labmades, and wonders if it's true—if they are all connected to Il-0CoM to avoid watching the humans perform the mundane tasks they were set. One labmade catches his gaze and dips her head quick, fist over heart. He returns the salute, although it is dangerous, before returning his attention to Ellie.

"I don't know. I think he likes you."

Ellie lets out a long breath. "They took control of our world and murdered a ton of humans. They killed Erica yesterday, Alice. Even if they could feel, I doubt they'd waste their energy on worthless shit like *liking* one of us. I hope they'd feel guilt."

Alice is quiet. "Jackson didn't even look at me today. Do you think he still likes me?"

"Probably." Ellie straightens, thoughtful. "Wait, sorry to change the subject, but do you think Jackson can let me borrow his father's collection of…" She glances around, her voice falling to a whisper. "Tunes?"

Tunes? Is that another word for music? *Clever.*

Alice tilts her head, considering. "You'll have to ask him yourself. I don't know where I stand with him."

"You do know where I stand with Jackson's dad, though."

There's a sharpness in Ellie's tone, but her friend doesn't appear to be listening.

Alice heaves a sigh. "Do you think the Ilori are good in bed?"

Ellie stops and stares openmouthed at Alice, and her next words come out in a quiet hiss. "They. Do. Not. Feel. Alice."

M0Rr1S turns away. He doesn't understand the question, and he dislikes seeing Ellie uncomfortable. He waves a hand, and all the seeds sort themselves across the tables, eliciting startled gasps and weary expressions. He approaches the nearest Ilori guard. There are three in this room, twelve in the center completely; their numbers are spread dangerously thin.

M0Rr1S doesn't switch on Il-0CoM but instead lets his voice drop into the deep timbre of Ilori. "The humans need some exercise. They grow weak. We need their muscles to be in shape for transplantation."

"Yes, sir. We will do so now." Seconds later, the command to stop and gather for exercise is crackling out of the loudspeakers above in broken English.

"Give them time to collect their coats. It is cold outside, and this does not benefit their movements."

"Yes, sir."

As the humans disperse, M0Rr1S connects to Janelle's mind once more.

Now is your chance to find the music. I will keep you safe, but you must go now. Meet me tonight in your library, same time.

She nods and follows everyone up the stairs to their apartments. He assumes she'll wait as the others grab their coats and go outside before beginning the search. He hopes she'll be careful. Yet, M0Rr1S switches on Il-0CoM to keep Ellie off any stray Ilori's radar, just in case.

CHAPTER 7

"I am no bird; and no net ensnares me: I am a free human being with an independent will."

— Charlotte Brontë, *Jane Eyre*

JANELLE

I sort through the floorboards of the living room underneath the corner patch of our once-fluffy maroon rug. When the Ilori came, Dad removed one small plank and hid our most precious items beneath. I've taken and saved all the books, but I remember a vinyl of something or another. Mom hid it. I remember her saying it had the song she and Dad listened to on their first date.

I shift through documents: our birth certificates, passports, money, pictures, jewelry, drawings I did when I was a child, and tons of little things and cards that serve no purpose. But there at the bottom, I find it. Mom said there's nothing comparable to the sound of Billie Holiday. I slide the record out, but find three instead of one. Aretha Franklin, Jimi Hendrix and Billie. I shove them into an old sack and put everything else back. It feels wrong to steal these, but we have no record player, Dad isn't himself anymore and Mom has unraveled.

Sometimes I wish we'd stayed in Brooklyn. In my mind, if we'd been there, we would have fled when the Ilori came, Mom would be normal and Dad would be whole. We wouldn't have been stuck here with people who pretended to be our allies until they were confronted with their own privilege. Who called the police on me when I waited in the lobby for Dad to get his school bag, because I didn't look like I belonged there, or where they weren't "pleased" with the politics but it didn't really affect them, so they moved on. They *could* move on. The Upper East Side ruined my family.

I lock the door behind me, although there's no point—what can anyone steal and what would a lock do to stop the Ilori? I head to the next apartment. I'm about to knock when the door opens. It's Mrs. Turner, a friend of the aunt who left us this apartment. Her white hair wisps at her temples, and there are worry lines etched into every patch of her face. She's too old to be forced into guard work, and the Ilori have no reason to kill her.

"Janelle Baker, shouldn't you be outside with the others?"

I dip my head as I concoct a lie. "I'm…on a special mission, Mrs. Turner. I heard they're going to do a search tomorrow and…well. Um…"

"What is it, dear?" Mrs. Turner shoos me inside and gently closes the door behind us. She whispers softly, "Are you in trouble?"

"I'm afraid they're looking for contraband, and I don't want more people to die." It's not a lie, but it's not the whole truth either. "I don't want anyone to get caught."

"What can I do?" Her tone is kind and caring, and I hate myself for concerning her.

"Music, any music you have, hard drives, anything. I have a place to hide them, if you'd give it to me…"

She wraps me in a hug. "Oh honey, if you get caught with all of it, it'll be a double transgression. No one wants to lose you, too. So many deaths lately. Too many young people. You deserve better."

"I'm all right with taking risks, Mrs. Turner. I just—" I stare into her eyes, and I'm racked with sorrow for the dwindling number of days she has left. No one knows what the Ilori will do with the older humans. It's never been discussed. I wish she could've enjoyed the rest of her life free, but she lost her sons and grandchildren before the invasion. She doesn't know where they went, and I imagine they won't see each other again. "I just want to help."

"You really have a good place for them?" Her eyebrows lift until I give her a confident nod. "Can I have them back later? I can't play them anymore, but they mean something to me. There are pictures on them…"

I nod once more, and she sets off into the apartment, making little to no noise. When she returns, she hands me an old iPod and a few vinyl records. Morris better love these, because I just took away something precious from a gracious woman, and I'm certain she'll never get these back. I want to hug her and say I'm sorry. I want to tell her the truth, but the way she's looking at me…it breaks my heart.

"Thank you for trusting me with these. I'll return them when it's safe." The words nearly choke me. But I smile before gently sliding her belongings into the bag.

I go down the hall, knocking and entering when no one's

home, searching for music. After an hour, I've done four floors out of nineteen. I'm shifting the sack on my shoulder, full of maybe twenty old iPhones, a few iPods and flash drives, and fifteen vinyl records—including my own complete collection of the Starry Eyed—when people begin returning from the outside. I rush down to the basement to drop off my bag, then hurry up the stairs and into our apartment for dinner.

Men and women with health issues that prevent them from duties like Kill Squads or working upstairs with Mom deliver our food, same as clean linens and clothing. It's a bit like before; we always had our laundry sent out. We also ordered takeout whenever we were too lazy to cook, which was most days. Only now it's our neighbors. And we have no choice. Everyone serves a purpose. Tonight it's Mrs. Turner. She smiles, bent over her silver, rickety pushcart, and hands Dad two plates. She waves at me with a wink, causing a flip of nerves in my gut, before she wheels away down the hall. I took her music, I promised to bring it back. I'm lying for an alien.

Dad closes the door before he sets down the plates of food on the table. I pick up my tuna fish with vegetable paste on cracker bread. I wait for Dad to sit down before I tuck into the meal.

"How…was your day?" My dad surprises me with the question.

"Ahhh… Okay." I can't keep the shock from my voice. It's been over a month since he resurfaced. I was beginning to think he wouldn't. "You're really here?" The corner of his lips quirk.

I bolt out of my chair and take him in a big hug. Tears roll down my cheeks and for a moment, it's like the last two years didn't happen. A weight's been lifted.

"I don't have long." He says it like it pains him. "Already, I can feel it."

"Dad." I close my eyes as he wipes a stray tear from my cheek. "I miss you."

"You're the only reason I'm still here, Janelle. But it's so hard, honey. I don't know when—" And then his eyes glaze over. It was too short this time. His back stiffens, and I drop my arms. "What are you doing over here? Eat."

I push down the anger threatening to erupt from my mouth like lava that'd burn our prison till there's nothing left. There isn't anything left anyway. Not anymore. And that'd definitely be a transgression.

I take my seat and collect myself while attempting to eat. "Where's Mom?"

The cracker is brittle in my hand and breaks into jagged pieces while I try to bite it. If I didn't eat, Dad would tell someone, and I'd be force-fed. I wouldn't do that, though; I'm hungry. Self-preservation always wins out when it comes to food.

Books, not so much.

"Needed upstairs for the night." He eats small, dainty bites keeping the cracker together. There is nothing familiar in his gaze.

We get three slices of cracker bread each, an apple and a glass of vitamin juice, probably to keep us in top shape for the vaccine. Although, what if we don't all survive it?

No one talks about that. I wonder if the vaccine is ready—really ready.

From my minimal understanding of what happened around the world after the invasion, humans were rounded up and forced into new housing. But in big cities, they were sent into centers like ours. Imprisoned. Rumors were that the Ilori needed us, and Morris confirmed that. I used to think that meant they were going to use human bodies and organs for alien transplants. Our anatomy is the same, so it makes sense that maybe they need our organs for their people or something. But after seeing how the half-solutions program works—I mean, it's staring at me from across the table—I know we'll become an updated version of that.

Will we become servants like Dad and the other guards? What will they do with us? And there are a lot of us prisoners. I suppose that's why they kill us for transgressions; if what Morris said is true, if we communicated and coordinated attacks that actually worked, we might still have a chance of overwhelming them.

But we're weak now. They've turned our own people against us, like Dad, and some of us have begun to lose our minds, like Mom. This world started to take everything from us, but the Ilori finished the job. Humans were already stripping away our humanity before they came, but the Ilori created a vaccine to rid us of it completely.

Morris said it will work in two days. Time's running out.

After dinner, I pace in my room waiting for my dad to fall asleep. It takes forever, and all my thoughts and fears and anxieties flare up. What if this is a test? What if Morris is using me? I can't imagine why, but he could be. I should have told Alice, asked for her help.

It's late, and my mind can handle only so much. I back into the wall and take deep, calm breaths. If the books don't kill me, the anxiety will. I used to take medicine for it, and for my hypothyroidism, too, but it ran out months ago. Take deep breaths, sense and count everything around the room. 5-4-3-2-1.

Five, my yellow, threadbare blanket. I run my fingers on it. It feels scratchy, like sandpaper.

Four, my white mattress that pokes me in the back. It squeaks when I roll to my side in the night.

Three, my chair, light purple chevron. Soft and comfortable.

Two, my purple hat with a silk lining inside. It smells like...like coconut and argon oil, even though I ran out a long time ago.

One, my mirror, and my sad reflection staring back. Zero, I repeat as my breathing slows. *Zero. I'm going to be okay.* Slow and steady. *I'm going to be okay.*

No more time to waste.

I lace up my shoes and sneak out of my room, through the hall and down the stairs. The doors are unlocked when I arrive. In the storage unit, Morris is standing in front of me. He's trying to grin, maybe, but it looks weird.

"Ellie, I am so happy to see you."

I don't bother with pleasantries. "The sack behind you is full. I got through a few floors but there are more to go. I'm not sure I'll get it all done tomorrow."

Morris grabs hold of the bag. He opens it with a sense of childish wonder, and for a moment, I forget he's one of them, one of the enemies that destroyed my world and home and family. But then some part of me remembers...we made it easy for them to destroy us. If they hadn't come, we might have destroyed ourselves.

"Oh, Ellie. They're perfect. I don't have any of these yet." His fingers trace the lines of the records and he closes his eyes as if he can hear them already. "I really enjoy David Bowie, do you know him?" He is so gentle as he places the music back in the bag.

"Everyone's heard of David Bowie."

"What is your favorite song of his?" Morris smiles at me, encouraging me to see him as anything but a threat.

"'Life on Mars'?"

"Ahh, I have not heard that one yet. Maybe we can listen to it together sometime." He completely sidesteps the fact that I don't know my future, and that we can't do anything together. "My favorite is 'Golden Years.'"

I nod.

"What is your favorite band?"

I stop and think. My favorite band? When was the last time I listened to my favorite music? About two years ago, when the war started, before they took it away. "I love Beyoncé, and Rihanna. Of course, David Bowie, Queen and Prince, definitely. And I like classical music, you know like Bach, Tchaikovsky, Beethoven… But my favorite music of all time? The Starry Eyed. They incorporate orchestra and pop. It's so—" I stop myself, shoving the pieces back inside of me. *Too friendly, El.*

But Morris seems in awe of the words I spoke, and my animation. He's silent for a moment. "I am… I'm so sorry, Ellie."

"What?" My voice comes out high-pitched with surprise.

"I never thought humans were… If all are like you, then I grieve for what has befallen your world. I'm truly sorry."

My retort blurts from my lips with little thought. "They *are* all like me, and you should grieve. Everybody is either dead or dying or will be nothing soon because of you and your people."

Morris ignores that and eyes the shelves in the corner. "Why wouldn't you date me?"

I nearly choke on my gasp. *"What?"*

"Alice asked you if you would date something—someone—like me. You didn't seem interested. Why wouldn't you date me? And what is dating?"

"We have far bigger problems than dating, you know that, right?" I cross my arms.

"Please tell me, Ellie." He makes sad eyes at me, surprising me even more.

"You know. Dating—when two people spend time together, romantically."

"Oh…like getting a drink together? It's confusing, you

see, because dates are days. I didn't think it could mean more than that. And I wonder what humans would find romantic anyway." The corners of his lips lift as if in thought. "Is this a date?"

"No," I gasp. "That is not our situation at all."

"If we were in different circumstances, would we?" His fingers twitch by his sides, and he glances around. I wonder if he's nervous.

"I don't know," I admit. I mean, he's cute. He's got adorable qualities, actually. But at the end of the day, I can't imagine different circumstances; his people have killed, and are ruling, mine. Maybe *he* didn't kill anyone, but still.

He doesn't push me on that. "What do humans do on dates?"

"I can't tell you that. Never dated." I shrug.

"I believe, by your definition, I have dated before, with an Ilori, obviously. I didn't enjoy it, though."

Part of me wants to know why. Another part of me just wants to get out of here and enjoy the small amount of time I have left.

"It's hard to be yourself when you are different," he finishes and smiles again at me.

"Well, if that's all—"

"Would you be my friend?"

I heave an enraged shudder. "Ilori have killed people—"

"It wasn't our choice. We had hoped to negotiate. We—my kind—didn't wish to kill you. Your planet has begun warming at a dangerous rate. We've seen it with other planets, where the primary life force catalyzed an upset to natural occurrences."

"Global warming? You came here because of *global warming*?" I cock an eyebrow.

There's a pause before he answers. "Partly. We were planning on establishing a colony here while reversing the human impact on your world… I guess, like blackmail? But then you struck down three ships of emissaries. Bi1k0, H3L10 and IpS1L… Many Ilori were murdered…"

I open my mouth and close it and open it again. I'm a fish out of water, discussing things few humans will ever know. "But it's okay to *murder* humans?"

"Again, it was not our desire to kill you. *We've* only killed in self-defense. We used to, anyway. Until Command changed our orders." He shakes his head. "The true Ilori are opportunistic—they see a planet on the brink of danger, come in, take control, make it better, add it to their holdings and increase their empire."

Weird how he went from *we* to *they*. As if there are two types of Ilori.

"In all honesty, I must say this is my first mission and I haven't been here long. True Ilori decide our actions. All of this death, it was not sanctioned by us labmades. Or by me… Do you believe me?"

"I don't know the difference between what you are and what the rest of your kind is. I don't even need to know. But just yesterday a girl was hanged in front of this building." I raise my eyebrows at him, waiting for an explanation.

His voice becomes small. "There is no justification for it, and any answer I give will not change what you have seen. But I have never killed a human. I do not want to kill a human. It's important to me that you believe me."

"What does it matter, Morris? Why do you want me to believe you?" My confusion and anger are currently at war with each other.

"Because I like you. I want to be your friend." He's so earnest and eager for an answer that I find myself not caring about the ridiculousness of all this. I have nothing else. The only friend I have is Alice. And I've been lonely. Why should I care anymore?

"Sure, yeah, we can be friends. But keep your promise. Protect my mom and dad, and make sure Alice stays safe."

"I will not kill your mom and dad. However, I do believe your mom is upstairs, helping to administer the vaccine. I've made sure she will not receive it, but I don't know how long I can keep her from it."

"You said you'd save her, you said—" I turn my face away from him, struggling with my feelings. I suspected that she'd been doing medical work in the labs; she hasn't been the same for months. But still. I refuse to walk away from the dream of Mom and Dad being with me, as a family, before the end of all things. I brush away a tear. Maybe she *should* get it. Maybe then she won't feel pain or stress or anything anymore.

"I asked for help, but I'm unsure if it will be successful for long." He steps closer to me as if to comfort me. "I'm sorry. I know I promised to save them, and I want to. But if I do it now, do it openly, they could kill me, Ellie."

I close my eyes, remembering her face and the way she was before the war. "If she gets the vaccine, will she be gone?"

"Nothing is ever truly gone." He reaches for my hand, but I push him away.

I shake my head. "What does that mean?"

The light brightens on his panel, startling us both. Morris shifts on his feet before his eyes glaze over and his breathing becomes haggard. He's got that same robotic look as the others when they communicate in the Hive. I wonder who he's talking to. Who he asked for help. If any of this is real or not.

"I must go."

I hold the door open for him.

"Ellie, thank you for the music. Same time tomorrow night?"

He walks past me and stops, his face inches from mine.

"I'm sorry. But I promise you, one way or another, we will save her. And I am lucky to have your friendship." He touches my arm with the tips of his fingers, another attempt at comforting me, I think, and then leaves.

I take a few minutes to calm down before heading upstairs, where I fall into a dream-riddled sleep. In every dream Mom is screaming, and Morris smiles and calls me his friend, and I wonder if this is a dream or a nightmare.

The next morning, our task is to deconstruct broken cell phones as part of a technology lesson. Alice yammers on about me not joining her outside for exercise and how Jackson's ignoring her, while I'm sitting on a secret that could derail our entire way of life. The vaccine is here. The illusion we've created for ourselves, the one that this life is normal, is about to shatter into a million pieces. How did we even last this long without falling apart?

Truth is, I think it's part of the human condition. If someone keeps stripping away our things, rights, freedoms, then we'll hold on to what we know. That's what we've done. Sitting at our tables in the assembly room all day, talking about nothing important. Doing things to keep our fingers nimble.

Some things have stayed the same. The building's still full of movement and routines. But noticeably absent are the sounds of life from the world before. The sirens as firetrucks and ambulances rush off to put out fires and collect the fallen, the pained, the dead. The subways screeching on tracks and shaking the ground. People stopping to chat on street corners as the block blurs around them in business suits and strollers. Everyone always had somewhere to be outside these walls.

We can almost forget that life as our ears strain to catch something happy. A giggle echoing in a stairwell or light music in the underground parties. Little bits of hope that make us forget that our time is running out. Even as service crews come through the halls with their pushcarts of food, or amble through with big bags strapped across their backs, ready to collect our dirty clothes and dishes like we have another day or week. Or as we deconstruct in our assembly room, stopping at noon to eat some nutritiously disgusting lunch.

Every other day, I think about the lunch I'd grab from Pick A Bagel around the corner; a whole wheat bagel with garden vegetable cream cheese and a black-and-white cookie to balance it out. And then I remember, belatedly, that this does nothing to help me survive. So I manage to stamp down those feelings of longing and sadness until we get our allotted gym time. We do laps until evening. Then dinner, and lights-out.

We think this is normal. We consider it normal. Even when people are executed in front of us by a noose or a single Ilori, who could stare at a neighbor's head till their eyes rolled back and they were gone. Just gone.

For the second time, I wonder if maybe the vaccine is the better way to go.

I excuse myself to the bathroom and sob until the tears refuse to come anymore. I've grieved for my dad already, but the sting of knowing I could lose Mom is...too much to bear alone. I have a day left, and then Morris will either find a way to save me, or stick the syringe in my arm himself, laughing at me for believing he had any intention of honoring our deal.

How could I have been so foolish as to have trusted an Ilori? What if it's all a con?

My cheeks are dry by the time I step back into the cafeteria. Alice waits for me at the table, fingers drumming. "You should go ask Jackson about his sounds at the next break," she says. "And while you're there, can you ask him about Melanie? Are they together now? God, I'm pathetic."

"You're not." I squeeze her shoulder. "I hope I never made you feel that way. I know I can be judgmental sometimes."

She gives me a small smile while placing a small metal piece from a cell phone on the pile. "You can, yeah, but this time, I really *was* pathetic. We hooked up, and now he's, like, pretending I don't exist. I'm so ready for the world to end."

"It will."

She turns to me with raised eyebrows. "Do you know something?"

"No," I lie. "Only that it's going to happen at some point, right?"

"My mom and aunt didn't come home last night. I know what's happening, Ellie. I know you don't want me to panic. But I'm sorta over the whole thing. Aren't you? If they inject us, there's no pain, there's no more of this place." She waves her arms around, attracting attention. "I lived, you know? I had love for a little while, I kissed all the prettiest boys, and *some* of the prettiest girls." She winks at me, and my cheeks heat.

We never discussed it, and I never came out to her or my parents, but I did mention to them that gender didn't matter to me romantically. I only ever wanted to be with someone who has a good heart, good taste in books and music, and is kind. Alice is all of those things, and was my first crush, too. But things changed. The aliens came, and I never thought about it again. Now she's my friend.

I smile at her, not knowing what to say. Alice is youth and life and so… I would have been her friend even if we weren't trapped together at the end of humanity.

Her voice falls and strikes me with its rawness. "I wanted to kiss you so bad, but as I got to know you, I wanted something better. Friendship. Love. All of these people in here, they know they're dying." Everyone is staring at us now. "And they live like it. But you—you still live like there's a future. With your stories, and secrets and all that intelligence. That's why I'm still here, not hanging outside like Erica Schulman, or Thandi Philipps, or Edgar or Michael or..." She doesn't finish, nor does she bother to wipe away the tears sliding past her nose.

"I'm tired," she says, as guards begin to close in around us. "I'm okay with it all ending. I have no regrets."

She leans in and kisses me. Her tears stain my cheeks, but her eyes hold mine. I'm surprised, but I do love her, the same way she loves me. My best friend at the end of the world.

"Never stop rebelling," she whispers, before she's dragged away by two human guards and an Ilori who tells us all to get back to work. But I sit there, my bottom lip quivering, and a lump stuck in my throat as Alice is dragged to the door. An emotional outburst that disrupts our work and morale is only one transgression, and only a first transgression for her. She'll be locked in her apartment without dinner, but she'll be okay. *She'll be okay*, I say once more to myself. And I really hope she will be.

"Goodbye, Janelle Baker. The best damn person in here!" Her voice carries across the room as the guards struggle to open the doors. "Goodbye, Jackson Hughes. May your dick fall off!" And then she screams the lyrics to the Starry Eyed's "These Starry Dreams" as the doors close behind her.

I smile, blinking back tears. I swallow that lump in my throat. Always one for making a dramatic exit, despite our circumstances, Alice Dresden. Truly and utterly herself. Even in the darkest of places, she keeps on shining.

If I trust Morris, can he save her, too? The clock is ticking.

Morris shows up right before recreation time and asks, *May I?* I nod quick before he says briefly, *Same as yesterday.* His hazel eyes stare at me from across the room, encouraging.

After the speakers crackle alive, I'm off searching. I toss some things around in random apartments and rooms, and I shove others into the backpack with little thought or care. My mind is still on Alice. My backpack's full and I'm about to bring it to the basement when I catch Jackson coming back to his apartment. I know that he has a great music collection. But our families have a bad history.

"Jackson," I whisper.

"What's up, Ellie? You're not here to talk about Alice, right? Do you—" His eyebrows wag.

I gag a little, but focus. Maybe it's watching my best friend get dragged away, or the pressure of knowing the vaccine is real and happening, but I become reckless. And too impatient to lie. "No, I just… I want your—" my voice drops "—music. Can I have it?"

"What?" He shakes the dusty blond hair out of his eyes. "Why?"

"There's going to be a raid later, and I've got a good spot for it. I want to help save everyone, you know?" I look at the ground, kicking my feet at the carpet.

He shifts from foot to foot. As the seconds pass, I think he won't do it and he's just wasting my time. But then he lets loose a long exhale. "Yeah, you can have it. Hold on—"

He runs into his apartment just as his father appears at the other end of the hallway. My stomach flops. Mr. Hughes's gaze narrows on me, and anger and disgust roll off him in waves. I know what he's thinking.

When we moved into this building years before, Mr. Hughes was the CEO of some nonprofit downtown. He owned the top three floors of this building and was an active member of the housing board. His wife was a pediatrician and, at some point early on, she moved out but kept her doctor's office upstairs to visit with Jackson.

I remember my dad saying that he'd overheard Mrs. Hughes screaming at Mr. Hughes for a divorce, in part because of the way he treated our family. Dad said it tore Mr. Hughes up inside that we moved into his building, and that he worried we'd ruin its reputation. In the end, it ruined only his.

From the way he glowered at us each time we passed him in the halls, I think he considered my dad a thug and my mom a welfare queen. Didn't matter that my dad made good money and my mom had her doctorate. He questioned whether my parents could afford the place, even though we inherited our apartment and could pay the additional costs easily.

He was relentless with *I'm an ally, I'm a liberal.* And in the same breath, he'd mumble to our neighbors, *But we don't want this sort living here.*

No wonder his wife left him, Mom would say.

I never told my mom or my dad that most of the other residents were like Mr. Hughes. That while he was outspoken about it, the others would grip their purses a bit tighter when they saw me, or stare at the lapel of my school uniform with awe—the unasked question hanging between us. *How did she get in there?* Or they'd lift their chins and sniff, keeping their distance as if our presence would infect them. I didn't tell my parents any of that, because it meant the dream we'd given up so much for hadn't come true. It was better to lie and let them think it was only Mr. Hughes who made our transition difficult.

Mr. Hughes's wife died when the Ilori came and seized the medical offices. She resisted them, and Mr. Hughes somehow blamed us. If his wife hadn't left him, he said, she would never have been up there. She would have been downstairs with him, in their lavish condo with their son. Not trying to fix up soldiers to fight the invasion.

He was at our door telling us this, accusing us, as the Ilori took over. His finger landed on my dad's chest while tears streamed down his face and hatred blazed in his eyes. Mom and I stood beside Dad, unsure what to do other than tell him to quit it, to go back home. To leave us alone. But a crowd formed around us. They didn't care about what my dad did or didn't do. They didn't care about Mr. Hughes's poor dead wife. They cared about what would happen next.

They asked for help. And so my dad gave it to them. He tried to, anyway, before becoming what he is now.

He stops beside the door, silent. I can feel my anxiety uncoiling in my gut. "What do you want?" He crosses his arms, and mine grasp the sides of my backpack.

"I—um—came to talk to Jackson. I—" It doesn't matter what comes out of my mouth. I shouldn't have come here, and I'll pay for it. I messed up.

Jackson spares me from further lies as he comes out with a bag stuffed with linens covering their massive musical collection inside. "Dad, back off. She's joining the cleaning crew and asked for our linens, that's all."

"Seems about right." He smirks.

I grab the bag and run to the basement to drop off my loot before dinner. By the time I'm back in our apartment, my feet ache and my heart's still pounding. My dad's waiting at the table, his eyes locked on something beyond my sight.

"Dad, Mom's not safe upstairs. The vaccine…" I sit down opposite him and try to connect with him again, even though it's unlikely to happen two days in a row.

He doesn't look at me. "She'll serve a higher purpose."

There's a rapping on the door, and he goes to get the food. I sit back at the table, trying to understand how I can tell him in a way that whatever part is left of him will understand, that the love of his life won't be here anymore.

He sets down two trays of steamed vegetables, beef, rice

and oranges. There are two glasses full of grape juice. I can't help but feel this is our last meal. We've never eaten this well under Ilori occupation.

"Dad, Mom will be gone."

He takes a measured bite of rice. "Nothing is ever truly gone." My mind circles back to the way Morris said nearly the same thing, which means Dad's more Ilori now.

I tell myself it's over, that he'll never come back, as I shove food into my mouth, undignified and hurried. I don't even want to be around him, to look at him. He's not my father anymore. He's a shell of a once great man, a man who would read *Corduroy* to me every other night as a child, who took me to the library and let me fall in love with books.

When Mom's aunt died and left us this apartment, he was the one who quit his job—the job he loved—and moved us here without complaint. He took a school library position down the block even though they didn't welcome him here. He did that for us. He taught me to love, to feel safe and to be okay with who I am, even when the world seemed to be against me.

And he's nothing now. Same with Mom. The Ilori did this.

For a moment, I find myself hating Morris. I didn't vote for the unhinged leader who struck those ships without thought, who made us so vulnerable. I didn't sign up to lose my childhood. No one asked us.

I pluck the orange off the table and begin angrily peeling it. My dad glances at me, his fork hovering in midair. "Janelle…"

I pop an orange slice in my mouth.

"Janelle." His voice sounds stronger, more like him again. And I want to believe it's happening. That he's lucid and can be there for me. I need him more than ever.

But there's another knock on the door. The look of recognition disappears as he walks over and opens it. Dread sinks like a stone to the pit of my stomach.

A Kill Squad stomps inside.

I gulp air greedily. My fingers twitch on the table. I know what's happening. I know it's time.

They don't run; their movements are calm, prepared. They don't talk; they block the exit and gather around the kitchen. They don't carry guns—those aren't allowed anymore—but I have no doubt they'll hurt me if I do anything but comply. They're here for me. I couldn't escape them forever, I knew that. One way or another, I was going to get caught for something.

Fuck it, my brain says, *if I'm going to die, at least I had fun.*

Nothingness washes over me. Silence, peace, grayness. I'm prepared for this moment.

My dad stands aside as they surround me and lift me from the chair. I don't speak, I don't make a sound. I have nothing to say anyway. Maybe this was Morris's plan all along. Get all the music and books, and then throw me to the wolves. I won't falter, I won't cry. I'll die while I'm still me.

The intercom comes to life as I'm dragged down the hall.

"All humans are ordered to the courtyard to witness an execution."

My blue sneakers touch the stairs, but not of my own will. The guards won't let me walk. I wouldn't mind walking to my own death. I try to push them away so that I can, but they don't budge.

The door is open at the top of the stairs to the seventh-floor balcony. The air is cool, giving me the chills. The stars are blocked by ships in the sky and Ilori cranes that continue to destroy everything we humans have built.

I close my eyes, savoring the rush of fresh air. I haven't been outside in the nighttime for over a year. I forgot how much I love it. I greedily suck in the breeze drifting around me, letting it cool my lungs and wash over me. I feel so distant from the warm, scared girl who lived below. Now I'm the defiant, cold girl, standing before her death, and feeling a tiny bit proud of that.

I'm done fighting and holding on.

They escort me to the edge of the building, and all I can do is look down at everyone. I can make out my dad below. He stares up at me, but I doubt he knows who I am anymore, nor does he care. Then I notice Mr. Hughes. He sneers. He sold me out. I knew it. I was too reckless. Too emotional. At least his son has the decency to appear sad.

I see so many other faces, some I've known for years, some I've known for months. My patrons. I wish I could see Alice one more time, and my mom, too.

"Human JQB-305-7-21 has been accused of illegal activities and paraphernalia. The punishment is death."

My mind wanders to *A Tree Grows in Brooklyn*. The main character, Francie Nolan, stood on a roof and realized her dreams. Now I stand on a roof, not too far away from where she did, about to die for them.

The rope wraps around my neck, and I tilt my head back, searching for anything to give me a moment of solace. And there I find it—a star. The North Star. I'm not alone.

No one dies alone.

A lyric from "Fairy-tale Girl" pops into my mind. *"Take your fall forward, but don't drop too fast."*

Relief surges through me as I'm pushed into space.

CHAPTER 8

"Dreams"
—The Cranberries

MORR1S

The speakers interrupt M0Rr1S as he arranges the music and the books like puzzle pieces that can be hidden under a blanket in the car. He's going to transport Ellie to another center where she will be safe for a little while. AvR0la helped him secure transportation. It's all set.

He even snuck into Ellie's room while she was in the cafeteria and her father was on guard duty, to find anything she might have wanted to take with her. At first glance, the room was bare beyond furniture, but then he saw a flash of color behind the headboard of her bed. A photograph of Ellie and her mother. He plucked it from the wall, revealing a hidden crevice beneath, where a small pile of books and a few photographs sat. They must mean something to her if she kept them that close.

She's his friend—his only friend—in this desolate world. Ellie risks her life for stories, and M0Rr1S risks his position and plans for his love of songs. In this way, they understand each other. At least, he thinks he understands her. Perhaps they can listen to music together. Maybe she can tell him stories. He wonders what her laugh sounds like. *No.* He cannot become attached. What he is, what he must do, is dangerous. And his people have taken her world.

But he can't stop himself either. She is a friend.

When a voice from overhead explains that there will be an execution, M0Rr1S grimaces. Why do they do this? Why did no one consult him? This is the second one in days. Aren't they tired of killing? The vaccine is ready, why bother now?

The speakers crackle again, reminding him that a human will die. The panic hits him in the center of his stomach. What if it's Ellie?

He connects to Il–0CoM while bounding up the nearly twenty flights of stairs as fast as his abilities allow.

Human JQB-305-7-21, accused of illegal activities and paraphernalia.

M0Rr1S closes his eyes, remembering Ellie's uniform and the number and frequency stitched into the right collar. A weariness envelops him. It *is* Ellie.

He tries to remain calm. *We do not need to execute anyone. The vaccine is ready. Stop the execution. This is your commander.*

A true Ilori voice cuts in. *Maintain control until all are inoculated.*

Commander, an uprising now would be unwelcome, a general appointed by his father states with a hint of annoyance in his tone.

There are not enough Ilori troops within proximity. One incident may lead the path to many more.

We have a functioning vaccine now. A fourth of the population have responded well to it. Only one death from a heart defect. Many more are already primed from the half-solutions program. Only the younger humans are left. We want their obedience; our numbers are decreasing out west, and we have fallen behind schedule. This display is necessary.

Commander M0Rr1S, do you agree? The voice is from true Ilori command, lurking somewhere above him at this very moment.

M0Rr1S knows the answer he is supposed to give but he can't. They can't take Ellie. She is… She can't die. He promised.

He pushes through a crowd of guards wrapped in the darkness and chill of the night. He catches sight of Ellie just as she falls forward off the edge. He sprints across the rooftop, batting guards out of the way, and jumps.

Time slows.

The rope will catch her and her neck will snap.

He focuses on the threads of the rope, fractions of seconds ticking by as he focuses his mind and abilities, pulling string by string, thread by thread until the rope disintegrates and Ellie continues falling. But M0Rr1S plummets faster, breaking the laws of Earth's nature through sheer will and draining his charge, and scoops her from the air. He lands on his feet with her body draped in his arms. She stares up at him, swallowing air in short bursts, wide-eyed. He holds her tighter.

They will come for them.

The humans surround him, half in awe, half in confusion. There are no lights, and the Ilori are unsure what to do. This has never happened before. *Where should he go? What should he do?*

Run.

Ilori are fast, and M0Rr1S is especially capable. He doesn't wait to figure out a plan before bolting toward escape. He reaches his car, which he'd parked on the other side of the building to load his purloined music into it earlier. There are no guards here; he cleared them before the announcement. He settles her into the passenger seat.

She's silent, grasping her neck, as he pumps on the gas and speeds down the rocky, empty streets. Where should they go?

Out of the city. The Ilori cannot kill him; it's a crime. But they can kill Ellie, and he promised to save her. She begins coughing.

M0Rr1S lets one hand fall from the wheel and touches her neck. He cannot heal a human, but his touch will comfort her if he does it just right.

"Calm, Ellie, calm." He repeats until she starts taking deep breaths, the cough subsiding.

"Alice." Her voice cracks.

M0Rr1S understands what she wants. Her friend isn't safe. Maybe he can do something to help her. He sets the steering wheel on autopilot as he risks exposure by flipping the switch and connecting to AvR0la. They use their secure channel of Il-0CoM, which was to be used only in case of an emergency. A command rolls off his mind. "Human girl. I do not know her ID, named Alice. Find her. Save her."

AvR0la is silent for a moment, but he knows they're there. "Sir, your command has been rescinded. The passcode to the pod has been invalidated, your connection to various platforms terminated until Inquisition can determine your state of mind. Avoid Il-0CoM—even secured lines are open to inspection. There is nowhere safe now, you will be hunted. Go west, find an excuse, any that will involve you needing this human. Be creative. Lean into your name and position. Offer to help Acquisitions Force with the human problem however you can. Gain their trust. That may be the only way."

"I know you're displeased—"

"Disappointed, but all is not lost." AvR0la sounds resolute, as if this is only a small hitch in their plan. "The mission continues."

M0Rr1S's mind is plagued with concern despite AvR0la's
reassurances. He can't connect now, he can't upload or broadcast. He never considered creating a secondary plan if he failed
the first. "The code, AvR0la. What will I do?"

AvR0la pauses. "Find a way to quadrant 11H-R15-B800L.
The fallen carrier craft IpS1L. It is the last one left undisturbed,
but is close to the Andarran domain. If you set foot on their
property, you will breach the treaty, and I am not sure what
the outcome will be. And sir…" There is a stiffness in their
voice. "There is at least one tracker on your vehicle. It would
behoove you to gain some distance before disposing of it, although it would be best if you find alternate transportation."

"AvR0la," M0Rr1S cannot keep the worry from his voice,
even if the connection is in his mind. "IpS1L is a tomb. Do
we know if it still works?"

"No one has been aboard since the crash. Leadership is concerned about the Andarran presence. It is a risk you will have
to take. Would you like to know the probability—"

"No. Probability and odds will not help me, not now."

After a slight pause, AvR0la's voice returns almost heavy
with emotion. "It was a pleasure serving you, sir."

M0Rr1S keeps the surprise from his voice. "Thank you,
AvR0la. Thank you for everything. And if they question you…"

"I will be selective with the truth," AvR0la finishes.

"You should hide. They may come for you."

AvR0la hesitates. "We all have our role to play, sir. I will
do as you have asked. I will take care of these three humans
within my capabilities. What G00287 granteth…"

M0Rr1S does not recite the rest as he normally would. "Be safe."

AvR0la disconnects before M0Rr1S, leaving him in temporary silence. At least he was able to do something in his final moments of command, and he was fortunate to have them beside him. His shoulders sag before he hits his charge button. Seventeen percent left. *Conservation needed*, it flashes.

"I'm sorry, Ellie." M0Rr1S should drop his hand from her, but he cannot. She almost died because of him, and he promised that wouldn't happen.

She is quiet as she stares out the window. Only darkness surrounds this lone electric car.

"It isn't your fault." Her voice is small, and he wishes he could see her thoughts like AvR0la's. "Can you pull over?" The words come out choked and short.

He steers the car over to the side of the deserted highway. Ellie scrambles out of her seat and falls to her knees on the iced pavement. She rips the hat from her head, and thick black curls tumble across her back.

M0Rr1S bolts out of the car and runs to her. He falls beside her and holds her hair back as she vomits, her body wavering in the wind and cold. His hands graze the back of her neck as he brushes pieces of rope away.

"I thought I died. I mean—I thought I was going to die. It doesn't seem real."

"You're okay now. Shhh…you're okay. I promise." Ellie gazes at him, and he wonders if she is truly seeing him for who he is—what he is—or if she is really looking at him at all.

"Morris, my parents. My best friend is… I don't know where—"

"Safe. Hidden. They're okay. It's okay." He pats her shoulder again.

"Nothing's okay." She angles her head toward the smaller

hovercrafts marring the black sky above the city. He wants to comfort her, and the truth is all he can give her.

"My father told me if I didn't do well here, my execution would be broadcast across the colonies as an example of his discipline. After, he would punish my mother for my many faults. It is her material that lies within me, and therefore she will be held accountable." M0Rr1S drags a hand through his hair. "All my life, he told me that there was something wrong with me. Something defective. I feel, you see. Ilori aren't supposed to feel, and especially not express emotions. We are supposed to be strong, obedient and unwavering in our loyalty."

Ellie turns to him, her eyes wide.

"I knew when I was a child that I did not, and could not, fit or belong. When my father presented me with this ultimatum, I boarded a ship without hesitation. I could not bear the thought of my mother…" He can't finish the thought. "I told myself I would find a way to save her and please him. But then I found music. The music led me to you. And you understand it, this need." M0Rr1S inhales the cool air, his fingers entwining in the curls at the base of her neck.

"My people will arrest me if I don't provide an excuse for my behavior, and if they are suspicious they may pry into my mind, finding things I don't want found. Then they will kill me. But they will kill you first." He inhales sharply. "I promised you that I would keep you safe, and I will as long as my body survives. I did what I could for your family, and we may never know if it was enough. I am deeply sorry for everything, Ellie. I mean that."

Her mouth opens and shuts, but no sound comes forth.

"Ilori taketh and taketh all. They know no boundaries." He's rambling now, and he can't help it. "But I've come to realize this one truth—in the end, all Ilori feel. It is foolish to deny biology. They are greedy, righteous, vengeful and angry.

They have become too confident. And therein lies our— What is the word?" He searches through his vocabulary, still holding her shoulder and hair. He likes the way it feels; soft and bouncy, like the silky, coiled flowers that grow outside his palace back home. "Advantage. They will look for this car. They believe they know where I will go. But they do not know how determined I am, nor my capacity for discomfort."

"What do you want to do?" she asks through shaky breaths.

"We are going to make our way across this country to quadrant 11H-R15-B800L, to…" He thinks of the map and tries to recall the human name for it. "To California. I have a plan… I will take you with me, and if—"

She peers at him through the dark mists of night. "You want me to go with you?"

"Yes." Until he can find somewhere safe for her, until he knows that she will cease being hunted. His mission is too dangerous for a human to embark on, but he can't leave her here. "If you'll join me?"

She whips her hair over her shoulder, her body shivering in the cold. She doesn't ask why, perhaps she doesn't care. Or she's too tired. M0Rr1S takes off his jacket and wraps it around her.

"Can you still keep my family and Alice safe?"

He can't tell her everything now. The truth is too much. And if they are caught… "There may be a way."

She turns, her eyes lock on his. "I'll go if you promise."

M0Rr1S thinks of his pod, which he can no longer access because he saved a human girl from death. It's close to where they are, outside his quadrant. But it's also where they expect him to go. All the plans he has made, time spent researching relevant tidbits of human microbiology, everything he has worked toward, has been compromised by this split-second decision. And now he must rely on chance, something no Ilori would ever choose to do.

Yet, he cannot—*will not*—regret what he has done, even if it means he will have to accomplish the nearly impossible. It will take time, it will take energy he does not have, and it will require him to move undetected through the quadrants. He glances at Ellie. The safest place for her is with him, for now, and that is why he lies. "I promise."

Her lip quivers from the cold. "I'll go."

M0Rr1S wants to hug her. He has heard humans do this when they feel relief, but he doesn't want to make her uncomfortable. Instead, he settles with a quick statement of fact. "It brings me joy to have your company, Ellie."

"Morris." She takes a deep breath. "I'm tired and I haven't been outside the center walls in years, but I think if we drive to an abandoned house, we may be able to find some clothes and food."

"Let us go, then, while the night still hides us."

He stands and extends a hand to her. She takes it, and he pulls her up. He doesn't want to seem overjoyed, but the idea of spending time with Ellie makes him feel…good. Happy. Optimistic. Although he knows, someday soon, he'll have to leave her. Already the thought of saying goodbye makes his chest feel tight with some unknown emotion. Worry? Fear? Sadness?

Ellie collects her hat. "Ready." She takes one last peek at the sky. One of the last skyscrapers falls before her eyes and she cringes. She might never come back to this quadrant, and he wonders if she is saying goodbye. He promises to himself, at that moment, that another part of his mission will be to keep Ellie safe, and, if possible, happy.

And what a difference that is for M0Rr1S; to have someone beside him that he cares for. Until now, he's only ever been alone.

Oh, how his life is changing, he sighs to himself. In every possible way.

PART TWO

A WORLD IN DISARRAY

STARRY EYED AND BUSHY-TAILED!!

OMG! You know how I won that private concert and a meet and greet with the Starry Eyed back in March? Well it finally happened! I'll show you my outfit in the next post, promise. (I swear I'll be blogging about this for a year, sorry in advance!) Anyway, a few hours ago, I was standing in the Odyssey Auditorium after watching an amazing set from the Starry Eyed. They played their entire new album, *The Sound of Stars*, and I'm beyond obsessed with "Fairy-tale Girl" and "Everything." Honestly, though, every song is perfection.

Since this was a private show, it was really low-key and cool. There were maybe thirty of us altogether, the seats were comfy and there was a small buffet of snacks and drinks off to the side. Real comfort food, too, like bagels, chips and mini-doughnuts. Allister wasn't even in his usual concert uniform of spandex leggings and purple boa, AKA his Korean Freddie Mercury look. Instead, he was wearing some fitted jeans (which, wow), and a white button-down. His long hair was a shade of navy blue so dark that it almost looked like his natural black. He and the others—except Cecil, who was in red bell-bottoms and a sparkly matching cape—were all really laid-back.

As I waited for the greet part, I imagined Allister was going to be as tight-lipped as I've heard people call him online. Like maybe a hello and thanks for coming type of thing. But no, he chatted with everyone, snacked on cinnamon-glazed almonds (I know because the smell was incredible) and was just open. When he got to me, he offered his hand. I shook it, so smooth and firm, and he said, "Hey, how are you?" The words that left my mouth didn't make any sense and I totally panicked. He's just *that* beautiful, especially with his violet eyes and accent! I thought he'd slowly back away to the next person but he laughed. "You're the blogger, right?" I nodded slowly, my legs felt like melting sticks of butter. "Oh cool. I love reading your blog." I think I smiled and said something that made him chuckle again. We ended up sitting down next to the others, drinking hot chocolates (hotel staff brought us some since the auditorium was kinda cold) and talking about everything. When I told Allister the reason I love their music so much is that it got me through a dark time with my depression, his whole face lit up.

"That's one of the biggest reasons I love music. The world is a dark place, and bad things happen that we can't control. People we love can disappoint us, hurt us and finding forgiveness is hard…" He looked away at that, and I wasn't sure he'd continue. "But music is there. If it disappoints you, all you have to do is change the track. Sometimes we pick music

that speaks to the sadness within us, sometimes we play something that'll extinguish it for a little while. Maybe it'll make
the world brighter or maybe it'll understand you in a way that
no one else can. Music, stories, art…they're a bridge between
you and someone else…yeah, but also a bridge between the
person you are one moment to the person you are the next."

And with that guys, I can officially say, I LOVE Allister Daniels.

XOXO Gabby

CHAPTER 9

"He stepped down, trying not to look long at her, as if she were the sun, yet he saw her, like the sun, even without looking."

—Leo Tolstoy, *Anna Karenina*

JANELLE

That won't be my last time in New York, I tell myself. I'll find a way back to my parents. I'll find a way to see my family again. I inhale, clearing my thoughts.

The car smells like chemicals and something I can't put my finger on but reminds me of *them*. The Ilori. The beings that took this world from us and plan on doing the same with our bodies. I'll always hate them. But I suppose I've befriended one, too, and that's the most confusing thing ever.

"My family's safe?" I ask again. "Can I talk to them?"

"They are safe, I promise." Morris shoots me a glance before returning to the road we're speeding down at a pace I didn't think possible. "It's too dangerous to connect to Il-0CoM right now, though, I'm sorry."

"Is whatever number-sound you just made the thing you all communicate with in your minds? The Hive?"

Morris nods. "Yes. All Ilori have it, but I've had to disconnect mine." He's quiet for a moment. "My friend, Av—" He pauses, as if considering his next words, "Avrola is with your family. I trust Avrola. I hope you'll trust me."

I don't respond. Can I really trust him? What's the alternative? He did save my life. My gaze slides to him, the way he grips the steering wheel, the way he focuses on the dark road in front of him. Why would he save me *and* my family? Is he really that earnest about friendship? The thought almost makes me want to giggle in absurdity.

So an Ilori and I are going to be friends.

What do I do? How do I handle this nervous energy? I almost died, but here I am. My family is safe...maybe. My books are in the back seat.

My gaze flicks to the console. I could tell him that the car has a USB port and that we could, in fact, listen to music on it. That's friendly.

The car makes a little electrical hum. I have no idea what kind of car it is; the logos are gone and it's unfamiliar. It must have been formatted for them, too, since there's no gas pedal or brake. It probably doesn't even run on gas, just electricity. They want this planet in top shape, and it shows. Clearly, we should have cared more about global warming. But that's a useless line of thought.

I almost died.

The scene still flashes before my eyes. The rope, scratchy but strong. The North Star sparkling at me, as if welcoming me home. I wanted to believe that. And then the air, crisp as I fell forward, pushing at my cheeks. The ground drawing closer and closer. The abrupt certainty of knowing death is near.

But then there was Morris. And the rope falling in shreds around my neck. His foreign and strong arms. The ever-approaching pavement that threatened instant death. And the relief to be back on solid ground. Staring up into his eyes and knowing, in that moment, without a doubt, that I wanted to live.

Morris. He saved me. *Us.*

I turn in my seat and grab one of the dead iPhones I found in the center. I connect it to the USB port and hope it'll get some charge from the car. It would be lovely if it has the Starry Eyed. While I'm fiddling with the console, I turn up the heat one more bar. It's warm, but I'm not wearing enough for this winter.

Morris doesn't move. He seems lost in his head, at war with something.

After a minute or so, I see the familiar battery icon pop up on the iPhone screen, and soon the home screen appears. I tap the music icon and hit Shuffle. Sade's voice purrs out, and Morris's expression transforms into wonder and excitement.

"I've never heard music aloud before." His hands loosen on the wheel, and I sink back into my seat. "I like it."

"How do you normally listen?"

He tilts his head, exposing his panel. "I can plug any device cable into my panel, access the files and play an audio track in my mind."

"So your mind is like a computer, and you can play music inside it?"

"I suppose so, although I would like to believe it is a bit more advanced than your outdated technology."

My mind draws a blank on how to respond to the dig. I can barely keep my eyes from drooping as the heat travels up my feet and through my flimsy outfit, anyway. "Morris, how do you know where we're going?"

"The panel sends images to my eyes. I think where I want to go, and the directions appear."

My eyebrows lift. "You have a mental GPS?"

"I actually know what GPS is!" He chuckles. "And yes, a bit like that."

There's so much I want to say to him, but the conversation has done little to keep me from slipping into grogginess. He seems to notice.

"You should rest, if you need it. In a few more miles, we will search for a safe place to stop." His voice is soft and maybe a little wary. "Rest."

I should try to stay awake. I want to know where I am, but the combination of Sade's dulcet tones and the exhaustion of near-death helps my eyes close on their own. At first, it's nice—peaceful even—until the rope wraps around my neck once more, and the crowd below stares up at me. Their eyes are gone, but their tight smiles remain. When they open their mouths, blood pours out, and I scream.

I wake with Morris next to me, his fingers curled around my wrist. He whispers something soothing that doesn't really register but slows my racing heart. He's not as potent as anxiety meds but, thankfully, it works for now. I let out a sigh before I notice that we've stopped outside a house on a deserted street in the middle of nowhere. It's still dark outside and Sade is still singing about love, only a different song.

"I was about to wake you." His grasp on my arm is gentle yet strong. "We're here." He jerks his head toward the structure. It looks oddly well kept. I look around, my eyes adjusting. The street's mostly deserted, this is the only house that's not a patch of dirt. The windows aren't broken, and even the front door is intact and closed. Why is this still here? Where is here? Could we really be that far away from home in so short a time?

Morris hits the power button and the music dies. "We need to get this car out of sight."

"Did anyone see us? Follow us? Will the Ilori be here soon?"

"No," he replies quickly. "The Ilori lack numbers outside cities. I doubt anyone saw us over the last few hours. We are far enough away from our quadrant now. Pennsylvania, I believe you call it."

"Wow." I shake the sleep from my mind. "There's a garage there. Let's go inside and open it."

He reluctantly closes the car door, his shoulders hunched. "Are you okay?"

"I'm fine. I've just never been inside of a structure like this before. It seems very personal." He doesn't elaborate.

I choke back the urge to remind him that the Ilori invaded Earth, our home. That we're going into someone's home without invitation to take what we need without repaying them, and it's no different than what the Ilori did. But pointing that out doesn't change anything, and this is the world we live in now.

My teeth are chattering as I try to open the front door. It doesn't budge. Morris sighs, and the door swings open.

"I'm also tired," he admits. "My charge is low." I don't know what that means, but I'll ask him later.

We step inside, and I gag at the stale air. I nod my head to the hallway door that likely leads to the garage. He holds it open for me, and the moment it closes behind us, we're enveloped in darkness.

"Do you think the electricity works?" I adjust my glasses, although I can't see much anyway.

"I feel it," he answers, which I guess means yes. "I need to conserve my energy, maybe there's a switch somewhere?"

He moves to the other side as I thrust my arm against the

wall, keeping my back toward the open doorway. I'm not a fan of mysterious dark spaces and might bolt if there's something horrible waiting for a light to be shone on it.

My effort is rewarded with a plastic panel and a series of switches and buttons. We toy with them until the garage door screeches open, causing us both to cringe. It's dark outside, but there's enough light for me to see a flashlight on a workbench table. I grab it and wield it like a searchlight as I watch Morris run to the car. The cold wind nips at my cheeks, but I hope it's blending into the dull house air, making it more breathable inside.

Seconds later, Morris parks the car in the space. I head to the switch and lower the door, closing us in. He drops down on the floor beside the car.

"Morris, what are you doing?"

"Finding the tracker."

"Oh, okay…but wait, what? Does that mean they'll be here soon? Oh God." My free hand goes to my neck on instinct.

"Don't panic. We have time." He grunts a little and stands up. He sweeps his fingers around the tires, then inside the car. At the back of the bumper, he pulls his hand away to reveal a tiny silver chip.

"Oh," I say unhelpfully.

I click the flashlight off as I follow him outside. He brings his arm back and throws the tracker farther and faster than anything I've ever seen before. It has to be miles away now. My jaw falls, and once again, I realize how different Morris and I are. He has power and strength beyond human imagining.

"That should give us a day at most. Let us find you some clothes and food." He walks past me to the house, and I stand there a moment longer, still reeling from his display of power.

Back inside, my flashlight leads the way to the kitchen.

"Are we really leaving the car and walking the rest of the way?"

The smell of rotting food wafts toward me from the dead refrigerator. I cover my nose and mouth with my hand.

It doesn't seem to affect Morris as he begins scouring the cabinets. "There may be another tracker on the car, and I don't want to take risks. We'll walk until we find another source of transportation, if that's okay with you?" He looks at me, and I shrug. I should probably begin searching for food with him, but the stench makes my stomach squirm.

He pulls out an unopened jar of peanut butter and a can of French-cut green beans, and then opens the disgusting fridge and places two bottles of water on the counter. I pocket the water, and find some clean utensils. Together, we creep upstairs to find clothes and anything else that might be useful. Morris tells me he'll wait outside in the hallway.

I suck peanut butter from a spoon while I open a closet. The clothes are jumbled in a haphazard pile but I find some clean jeans and a thick off-white cable-knit sweater. I shimmy into the jeans, loathing for the millionth time the dramatic curves of my thighs and hips. The jeans are too long on my short frame. And a bit snug, but they'll loosen up eventually, I hope. Even though I haven't had access to excess food or sweets in months, I'm still soft, and thick, and my chest has too much padding. I'm lucky the sweater is a size too big, otherwise my chest would've turned it into a crop top.

I'm trying to find a jacket when Morris knocks. "Do you want to sleep here until dawn?"

"Is it safe?" I eye my hair in the mirror. I had no choice but to go natural after the invasion, and I like it, but not right now, not without products. My thick, coiled curls are matted, so I twist and hide them under my purple beanie as I've been doing. I take my glasses off and wipe them on the hem of my sweater.

"No...but you're tired." There's hesitation in his tone.

"We can walk until we find somewhere else to hide." I rub my eyes with the backs of my hands before replacing my glasses. I spot the edge of a coat peeking out of a container under the bed.

I pull off the lid, and the scent of fabric softener wafts into the room, and for a moment, all I can do is breathe it in. When I tug the peacoat on, I sigh deeply. It's warm, so warm. It's tight in the arms and across my chest, but I can button it. Thank God. Now the only thing I need is a pair of boots. My blue sneakers are thin, not made for this weather, and already have a hole in the sole.

There are more than a few pairs of shoes at the bottom of the closet. I rifle through them until I've got three pairs of boots in front of me. All two sizes too small. Damn it. I open the door and stride across the hall to another room. Morris is a silent presence behind me.

"I'm trying to find boots." The next closet is full of heels and other impractical footwear. "I have big feet."

Morris looks down. "Big feet cross greater distances." I imagine he says this in an attempt to sound reassuring. It strikes me how weird it is that an Ilori is trying to reassure me. But then, Morris isn't a normal Ilori.

I smile at him before continuing my task. We go through every room, and by the end, I've found nothing else that fits. We sit on a bed while I eat the green beans and eye a book perched on the windowsill. *A Wrinkle in Time.* Part of me considers taking it. If my family somehow end up vaccinated, I can travel with Morris until we find somewhere safe and deserted. I'll say goodbye and walk into the sunset with a bunch of books to fill my last days. The thought brings me some relief. And more sadness than I can bear.

"Humans lived well." Morris takes in the furniture and

closets, remnants of life before. He stretches before grabbing an empty backpack covered in a sheen of dust.

"Some of us did." The green beans are sweeter than I remember, and I drink the juice from the can, savoring the flavor and taste. I stick the half-empty jar of peanut butter in my coat pocket along with the spoon. I pick up the book and flip through the pages to see if there are any notes or highlights, maybe a dedication, but I find only a scribbled note in black marker blotting out the text. *If you can read this, head west to Kansas. We'll find you on the way.*

"Looks like the secret notes in books thing was true." I lift the book to show Morris. "I wonder if they made it."

Morris doesn't answer. It wasn't really a question.

I return the book where I found it. The owners aren't coming back, and I doubt anyone else will stumble upon it either. But maybe if, somehow, despite the odds, someone does, this will give them hope.

Morris and I go back to the garage. I rummage through the drawers on the workbench in search of extra batteries for the flashlight. A picture falls out and I pick it up, holding the glossy paper between two fingers so as not to smudge it.

A picture of a family. Two kids—one older girl, one small boy. They stand in front of this house, smiling. I notice a bow on the front door, behind them. This house probably meant the world to them and held a million memories. *They aren't coming back*, I tell myself again.

I turn to Morris as he shuts the car door, his face drawn and exhausted. "All of the books and music are in the bag now. But I'll need to recharge soon."

My jaw drops and I eye the now empty back seat that was once packed with our belongings. "How?"

"I am able to move things—inanimate objects mostly—with my mind, and I can also change the shape of them. However, it takes a lot of energy. More energy than I should be expending. If I overexert myself, I shut off. That's less than ideal."

"How do you recharge?" No one's ever mentioned Ilori recharging. I may be the first human to ask this.

Morris looks at me as if he is making a difficult decision. "Our panels have two outputs, one for a special cable that we can connect to a charger. We are also able to charge wirelessly through our connection to one another—the Hive, as you call it—but that's not always...feasible or ideal."

"Wow," is all I can think. "You didn't bring one with you? This cable thing?"

"I have the cable. What I lack is the adequate output and energy source. I'm used to buildings equipped for our use." He tries to smile. "Don't worry, Ellie, I will make sure you are safe."

"Is there any way to replicate the output? Like, can you just use a regular output?"

Morris considers my question. "Yes, maybe. But I'm afraid I don't know how. And the wrong energy could be lethal."

"I thought you all were geniuses?" I make a small sound. "I'll figure it out."

There's a ghost of a smile on his lips. "We should go. It's a long trip ahead of us."

"I'm ready."

Morris seems distant or nervous or...something. He drapes the backpack over his shoulders and winces.

"Is it heavy?"

"No, no. I just feel something I've never felt before."

We walk out of the front door and into the darkness. "What's that?"

"I believe I feel...uncertain."

CHAPTER 10

"The Times They Are A-Changin'"
—Bob Dylan

MORRIS

The sooner they get to California, the safer they'll be. But that means staying under the radar and his charge is already low.

He glances at her. He wants to tell her that he's afraid. That he has to avoid his own people to keep her safe, and he's worried he will fail. But he says nothing. He shifts the backpack. It's heavy, but it's not worth telling her that either. She's shouldered enough.

They crossed out of the former residential area an hour ago, and now they're making their way through some woods. This quadrant is colder than he expected, even though the sun is about to rise. There are patches of ice that blend into the ground, and the air is frigid. This is the first winter he has experienced outdoors, and it doesn't bring him joy. The sun will likely not provide warmth, but at least it will provide light, which will make it easier for Ellie to see where she's going. He had to tell her to leave that flashlight behind, because it would be too noticeable, and she's been on edge ever since.

Every once in a while, he catches her glaring at her shoes, and he wishes more than anything that they'd found her a new pair.

Cast aside your fear and fight for your future. Fight for freedom. His mother told him that as he boarded the carriership for Earth. But fear is blurring his vision now. Hours spent in silence. He has many thoughts to sift through, but the last thing he wants is for Ellie to feel he doesn't care for her or that she taxes him. It is true, she walks slow, and she can't see as well as he does, but these things don't matter to him.

"Where were you born?" he asks.

Ellie is quiet for a moment. He can tell he has caught her off guard. "Brooklyn. It's in New York City, but not. Kind of like a world of its own."

"Ahh, yes, close to where we met. I've not had the pleasure of seeing it. New York City was the first and only place I've been. I was in a ship above Earth until a few…days ago." M0Rr1S can't think of another thing to say. He knows he can't tell her what he was doing up there, or that while he was in isolation under constant observation from true Ilori, he was working on the vaccination. That he often felt immense guilt as the world below was stripped of humans and humanity and everything that made it Earth, to make way for Ilori colonization. And then, the words he did say slam to the forefront of his mind. "I did not mean pleasure. I did not mean to say that I—"

"Morris. I know." Ellie stumbles over a tree branch, smearing her shoes with mud. She grimaces but continues on.

He reaches out to her. "May I?"

She nods once before letting him hold her hand, and his heart beats a bit faster. "What about you? Where were you born?"

"A lab, in the capitol city of my origin planet, 40378BX-I. I'm sorry there's no English translation." When she's quiet, he answers the question she is either too shy or doesn't care enough to ask. "Some Ilori are not born in the traditional sense. We are made in labs."

Ellie uses her free hand to tug at the edges of her hat and bring it over the tips of her ears. "So, your parents...aren't your parents?"

"Mine are, but not entirely." M0Rr1S glances at their interlocked hands, considering how to tell his truth simply. "My parents already had a child and could not make another. I was a combination of genetic material—my mother's and a random donor's."

"Is that why you can throw things super far?" She tilts her head.

"Yes. It is why my panel holds a charge longer, as well." M0Rr1S doesn't feel anything in particular, knowing that he isn't made from his father, nor does he regret their decision to only use his mother's material. He is pleased to not share any similarities with that man. "I am a custom labmade Ilori. They made my generation to comprise the Acquisitions Force for Earth. It is why the Ilori you meet here can eat, breathe and survive in this atmosphere."

"Right..." She chews her lip, looking thoughtful. "You're a labmade, which is why you look human. And there are other kinds of Ilori?"

"Only one other kind. In the ships above the atmosphere, there are true Ilori. But they will not come here yet, as the atmosphere is too harsh for their physical bodies."

She is making a strange face as the trees give way to a clearing and the beginnings of dawn filter through the clouds above. "So labmade Ilori took over Earth. Why did you want it?"

M0Rr1S inhales the crisp air. "Not me. *Them*. The true Ilori. Labmade Ilori follow orders from our true Ilori masters. We are inferior to the true Ilori. We are expendable."

Her voice cuts through him. "Soldiers following orders *never* excuses the war. You know that, right?"

"I do know." He stops and meets her gaze. "I do. You may think us cowards, and you are right. To disobey the true Ilori is death, and they could just create more of us to follow. But sometimes, doing right means first doing wrong."

Her eyebrows knit together and she waits for a clarification that won't come. He can't say more. When she finally speaks, it's with resignation. "Why did your masters want us, then?"

He looks up at the first beams of light peeking through the clouds. "True Ilori live for centuries. They are endless. They have explored, conquered and exploited new worlds...but they have grown idle, surrounded by their technology and wealth. They decided to push their innovation. About 285 galactic rotations ago—that's about one hundred human years—they began an expedition around the universe, looking for new experiences, new places. Vacation destinations. They found many, including Earth." The cold seeps into his jacket, and he hopes they find shelter soon. "They began colonizing those worlds. Twenty years ago, they began creating us. The labmades sent to Earth were made to look and function like humans, to blend in. But we are stronger. We're here to fix your climate change, take orders and set up your world for their use."

She is quiet for a few minutes, considering his words. M0Rr1S brushes a wisp of black hair from his brow, waiting for her to keep their conversation alive. Silence with Ellie is better than silence alone, but speaking with her is better than speaking with anyone else.

When she does speak, her words are edged in anger. "A *vacation* destination? Humans died just so you could use our world for a vacation spot?"

"I told you, the death of humanity was never part of the objective. We had hoped to establish peaceful control. But peace became impossible when our ships were shot down without any attempt at communication. We were given a new directive—collect humans and kill any that do not conform or would strike us down. True Ilori command ordered us to kill humans for all sorts of infractions, not only to gain your obedience, but to establish your defeat and break your free will. And then...we were told of a new technology that could grow their empire, increasing their riches beyond measure. An out-of-body experience."

She yanks her hand from his. "An out-of-body experience...the vaccine, that's what it will do? You're going to use our bodies?"

He answers, knowing it will only further infuriate her. "The true Ilori will come here, choose a human body to inhabit, and vacation like a native. Their original form will await them in special spas—upgraded centers—once Earth's atmosphere is repaired. Labmades will facilitate their stays and accommodate their needs. And then we will market this destination throughout the galaxy to every world, every species looking for a new adventure."

She closes her eyes, fists clenching by her sides. "All of this death...all of it because a bunch of rich, immortal aliens got bored and wanted somewhere new to go? I—I...can't. I can't believe it." She scoffs, but it sounds like a sob. "So they can take our skin—our bodies—off and on at their pleasure, like we mean... Like we're nothing? You said you never wanted to kill a whole planet, but instead, you're enslaving one?"

M0Rr1S understands her hatred of the Ilori, both true and

labmade; it's not dissimilar to his own. "Their reasoning was that your world would have died anyway, from climate change. That, in essence, we were seizing an opportunity to save a world on the brink of destruction. Labmades tried to speak with human leadership—if we could fix the effects of global warming in exchange for the ability to share select human vessels—bodies—we could avoid war. Human leaders reacted violently without listening, a testament to the state of humans' political turmoil."

She narrows her eyes. "How did you know that? How did *they* know that Earth was in turmoil?"

The way she suddenly differentiates between true Ilori and labmades gives him hope that perhaps she realizes they're not the same. That despite the labmades taking their world, they had no choice. That maybe his words, however mysterious, showed her that he has a plan. He inhales the chilly air.

"Command monitors worlds and information." He shrugs. "The signs of your planet's demise were easy to determine. We were told the projected life expectancy was maybe another hundred years before complete annihilation by both nature and, we suspected, nuclear war."

"Yeah, well. That seems right." She huffs, but finally resumes her course. There's a sadness in her features now. He stays silent, knowing it is a lot of information to process at once. She rubs the palms of her hands together. "How old are you, Morris?"

"We do not celebrate or acknowledge the passing of time where I'm from, but I am considered young. I suppose I am the same age as you—seventeen years."

"You suppose?"

"I've been told that when a human is born, it is new. It must learn this world, the languages, the cultures, to eat and function. When we are created, we are fully conscious. We think, we learn and we grow just like you—from infant to adult. We know our food preferences before we have ever eaten." He remembers the way his mother would gaze at him with awe in her eyes when she was alone and unjudged. And the way his father would stare at him with disinterest.

"What are the real Ilori like? I mean the true ones or whatever you call them?"

The real Ilori... *What a distinction*, he thinks. "True Ilori are...where do I begin?" He kicks a pebble with the toe of one boot. "Physically, they have various body sizes and structures like humans, but they're not a solid mass, like you and me. They are energy. Their skin is laced with a sheen of violet, called a 'life energy shell.' The darker the sheen, the older and more powerful they are." He pictures them, although it has been days since he has seen one. "Like most aliens, their eyes are colored with hues outside the spectrum of Earth's nature.

"They need green atmospheres and natural electricity...like Earth had, before humans depleted the resources and changed the climate. Their abilities are strongest when surrounded by organic life, like trees and forests, oceans. This sustains and feeds them. Without it, they are weak. And unlike labmades, they do not need panels." He points to the panel alongside his jaw.

She nods, pursing her lips. "Are you the first labmade?"

"I was not the first. Every colony has labmades modeled after the dominant life force. I was made during the human production." He pauses to catch his breath in this chilly air. "Some of us, like me, were created as children for prominent families who struggled with fertility."

Ellie is silent, thoughtful, and he wishes she would ask him something else. He has never spoken to someone, or anyone like this before, and he feels relief from it.

She's quiet so long that he thinks she is done with their conversation. Then she surprises him. "How does the Hive work?"

M0Rr1S swallows. He expected her to ask him this, and he will answer, but he wonders if it will only reaffirm how alien he is—how different they are. "Il-0CoM is a network of minds connected through signals and sounds. True Ilori can use it at will, connecting to solo minds, having private conversations. Some labmades can also turn it on and off, but connecting to solo minds is difficult. I suppose it's like talking on a phone but not choosing who's on the other end of the line."

Her foot sinks into a small pile of snow, and she shudders as her mouth droops into a frown. "Were you happy on your home planet?"

He lets the question bounce around in his head. "I miss home. I miss my mother, and the food. But no, I wasn't happy."

"Because you're labmade?"

"My father hates me, my brother wishes to kill me, and yes, being labmade makes me reviled among my people." His voice falls as he remembers the stares and displeasure even his teachers wore when he was in their presence.

"Is that why you're different? Why you like music?"

M0Rr1S brightens, his steps feeling lighter. "True Ilori look down on emotions. Even though they feel them, they've found emotions cause chaos. The labmade were conditioned to not use our emotions, but some of us do. Some to serve our masters—to please them—but some use it to enjoy music and beautiful girls with purple hats." The last part is a risk, and he worries it will push her away, but he wanted to say it.

Ellie drops her head, and he sees it—just there—a blush of pink crosses her dark cheeks where there was none before. Her lips tug into a small smile, but she doesn't respond. He has embarrassed her. He should apologize. But he also wouldn't mean it. He decides instead to ask her questions as they continue through the woods.

"Before the invasion, what did you plan on doing with your life?"

The smile's gone now. "I wanted to become a librarian, like my dad. Or a cellist." She snorts as if she doesn't quite believe her own words.

"What is a cellist?"

"A musician who performs on an instrument called a cello. It makes classical music."

He doesn't know if he has heard classical music yet, but he would like to listen to her make it. "We must find a cello for you to play."

"Let's just find a shelter tonight, and we'll cross that bridge when we get to it." She sighs, and lifts her wet foot. "I'm so cold."

"What bridge? How far?" M0Rr1S stops and widens his eyes. The morning light helps him see what he couldn't before without using extra energy.

She smiles. "Sorry, just a saying that means we'll deal with that later."

M0Rr1S focuses into the distance, using a fraction of his abilities. There, less than a mile away, shrouded by trees in the middle of the forest, is a tiny house. It looks abandoned, intact and cold, but will supply adequate shelter.

"May I?" he asks Ellie, and she eyes him with confusion.

Ellie squints at him. "May you—?"

He places one arm around her back and scoops her legs into the other, holding her to his chest. "Carry you?"

She nods with raised eyebrows. He feels a stab of guilt for not waiting for her answer first. But the need to move at full speed and get out of this cold is too much to bear.

He runs through the forest, expending more precious energy as the wind whips at his face and the cold bites his cheeks. His back aches, and his body is exhausted. When they reach the cottage, he gently sets her on the porch and leans against the railing to catch his breath.

"I apologize for rushing, but I believe this shelter may be useful." He pants, trying to fill his lungs with oxygen and keep himself from falling over. He needs a rest or a charge. Soon. He pushes his charge display. Thirteen percent. Resting will give him a few bars of charge but nothing more.

Ellie crosses the threshold to the door and it squeals open. "Go inside. I'll collect something for a fire."

Inside, M0Rr1S sets the backpack on the floor beside the door. He lets out a relieved groan as his muscles relax.

Ellie returns with a bundle of chopped wood in her arms. "Whoever lived here must've stocked up on firewood before they left. There are loads of stacks behind the house." She dumps them into a little man-made cave behind a fence on the floor.

M0Rr1S sits down on a shredded couch. "Would you tell me a story? Maybe one from your books?"

Ellie fumbles with a little box in front of the wood. "What kind of story would you like?"

M0Rr1S stretches his legs in front of him. "A story about someone refusing to let their voice be silenced. Like the other book of yours I read."

Ellie grabs a dusty, holey blanket and drapes it around him. She sinks down beside him and lets her head fall against the back of the couch. He's aware of every place their bodies touch and the gentle breaths she takes as she concentrates.

"Well it's not all that similar, but in a very different future, there's a girl named Katniss, who would do anything to protect her sister..."

He tries to keep himself awake despite Ellie's soft and comforting voice. As his eyes close, he knows he's never been more at ease in his life.

Gunshots sound, not too far away.

M0Rr1S jerks awake as Ellie dives flat on her stomach on the floor. He bolts to the window to search for them. *Hunters.* The question is, are they Ilori or human? He shakes his head. That is a silly question. Ilori don't hunt, at least they didn't before Earth. And never with guns. Another shot rings out, but no howls or yelps sound. Whatever the humans are hunting or protecting themselves from, they missed.

Ellie's gaze is glued to his in fear. She crawls to the fire and grabs her shoes while he turns back to spot two burly humans pointing at the house. *The smoke.* They must have seen it and come to investigate They hold long weapons as if they mean to use them. M0Rr1S slows his breathing, picking up their voices outside as they discuss what to do. There's a large vehicle, a truck, he thinks it's called, parked in the clearing of trees. Yet the humans are somewhere just out of sight now.

M0Rr1S moves toward Ellie.

"We need to get out of here. The other way, okay?"

Together they tiptoe to the back door and out into the cold. He leads Ellie into the trees as darkness falls around them. He scans the area until his gaze falls on a vehicle in the clearing.

"They have a truck."

"What do you want to do?" Her whisper is harsh.

"Stay here. I'm going to get their keys."

She shakes her head. "How?"

He grins. The sleep makes him more confident, invincible even. At 15 percent charge, he almost feels normal. He leaves Ellie behind a tree and strides back into the house just as the humans come in the front door. They stumble back, letting out curse words as their eyes lock on his blue-lit panel. M0Rr1S lets them embrace their terror until they knowingly lower their weapons. They know he can do so many things to cause them pain, from attacking their minds to throwing them into walls. They don't know his charge is too low and he has no desire to harm them.

"I'm not going to hurt you." He enunciates the words in what he hopes is a soothing manner.

They are far older than he. They lower their weapons, but grip them tight. "We don't want no trouble, alien."

"Nor do I." M0Rr1S keeps his voice calm, hopefully reducing the tension. "I just need your keys."

"No," one of them says. "We ain't giving you our truck."

"You have a choice. I could kill you before you have a chance to escape." M0Rr1S takes a step closer, standing tall and, he hopes, menacing. "Or you could give me the keys and stay here. There's a pile of wood outside that should last you a long while before you move on. Most free humans have found refuge in the middle of the country. I'm sure you could find them."

They eye him with suspicion, their hearts pounding. "How do we know you won't kill us?"

"Because." M0Rr1S's gaze flicks in the direction of Ellie. "I have no desire to kill humans today. I want peace, friendship. Love." He shakes his head, clearing the thought from his mind. Did he say love? Has the music addled his mind?

The keys jingle in the second one's hand. "You look like one, but you don't talk like one."

"I've been told this before." M0Rr1S shifts. The exhaustion begins to creep in again, causing his next words to be short. "The keys or death?"

They exchange a glance before the second one tosses him the keys. M0Rr1S plucks them from the air, and his shoulders droop. He turns around and starts toward the back door.

"The middle of the country…where? It's a big-ass country."
He pauses and turns back around. The one with the thick,

furry cap steps back, as if they aren't sure if M0Rr1S will kill them but are also curious.

M0Rr1S thinks about the geography of the land, pulling up the map behind his left eye. "I believe you call it Nebraska. And the farther north you go, the better. My kind avoid the cold whenever possible."

"Why?" the second one asks, fingers gripping the zipper of their puffy vest. "Why did you alien scum come here? Why did you take our world?"

"Because we could." M0Rr1S steps outside again, ignoring the hatred rolling off the humans in waves. The humans follow him gingerly, standing on the porch as M0Rr1S finds Ellie still hidden in the trees. "Ready?"

"Hold up, what're you doing with that girl?" One of the humans picks up their weapon again. M0Rr1S tosses the gun a glance and with that small charge he received from rest, he moves the atoms in the metal, heating the gun until the human drops it. They groan, yet still won't back down. "Is he keeping you captive? Has he hurt you?"

"No." Ellie shakes her head as M0Rr1S takes her hand. "He saved me."

"Traitor." They spit on the ground. Ellie cringes, but she doesn't respond. She keeps her eyes trained on the humans and their fallen guns as she and M0Rr1S walk through the trees and around the cabin toward the big, black truck. He yanks the door open for her to slide in, and then quickly does the same.

Music purrs out of the center dash as M0Rr1S turns the key in the ignition.

Ellie raises an eyebrow at him. "Bob Dylan's 'The Times They Are A-Changin'.' Couldn't be a more suitable song." The corners of her lips quirk into a small, haunted smile.

His foot pushes down on the gas, and they peel away into the woods.

CHAPTER 11

—◦—✦—

"Anne hoped she had outlived the age of blushing; but the age of emotion she certainly had not."

—Jane Austen, *Persuasion*

JANELLE

I didn't mean to fall asleep with my head on his shoulder. Honestly, I feel pretty weird about it. I was just so cold, and my shoes were drying by the fire. And although I know Morris is an alien with abilities like a superhero, there's something comforting about him, as well.

I steal a glance at him. He's drumming his fingers against the wheel, and I can't help but warm a little. It's not because he called me pretty. *Okay*, it might be because he called me pretty. It's not like no one has ever called me pretty before. But I don't know… I just liked that Morris did. It's been so long since I could find even a little happiness out of something so small.

Besides, knowing his past, what brought him here and how he's treated by other Ilori…knowing all that changed things. The way he feels and sees and smiles, how he put his arms around me and held my hand back at the cottage… I felt safe. Feel safe. I still need to know more about him, why he thinks he must do something wrong in order to do something right, but we have time. I will figure him out. We're on two sides of this invasion, but he and I aren't enemies. To him, I'm a human, not just a black girl from Brooklyn trying to fit in where she never belonged. I'm his friend.

Traitor.

The insult clangs in my mind. Am I a traitor? No, but perhaps that's what I look like. That I prefer the company of an Ilori to humans. I shake my head. I'm not a traitor. I'm a survivor. And I'm going to save my family. I'm going to save Alice. I'll do anything for them.

"Ellie." His gaze stays on the snowy road in front of us. "I want to know everything about you. It may very well take more time than we have, but I like you, and perhaps telling me everything will make time pass more quickly."

I chuckle, unable to keep it to myself.

"That is the sweetest sound I've ever heard." Morris looks over and beams, and his smile is wobbly but so… *Morris*, as warm as a cinnamon bun from the oven. It's easy to be taken in by his earnestness.

"My full name is Janelle Quicia Baker, and…uh…you know, I don't know how to tell you everything." I laugh again.

"Tell me about the things you love."

"Besides my mom and dad, and Alice… I love books, of course, and music, especially the Starry Eyed. The words of their songs always felt like they spoke to me. Movies. Science. Puzzles. I'm a puzzle master. Oh, I also loved going to concerts. And doughnuts. It's been years since I've had one."

"What's a doughnut?"

"It's fried dough that's glazed in something sweet, like blueberry glaze, my mom's favorite—or regular glaze. Or my favorite, an oatmeal doughnut with sugared cinnamon oats on top. We used to get a dozen every Sunday morning." I smile, remembering hopping on the subway with Dad in search of new bakeries featured in *The New York Times* or *Eater*. "The doughnuts in Brooklyn were the best. So many different places, and all of them were amazing."

Morris grins. "What else? Tell me more."

"I saw Beyoncé in concert once and decided I wanted to learn all the dances to her music videos. It took forever, but I did it to prove to myself that I could. I've never showed anyone, though." I pause, not knowing how to go on.

"There has to be more than this." Morris tosses a look of disbelief my way, and I force down another chuckle.

"Well, my favorite food is ramen. Not the packaged kind, although I doubt you'd know there is a packaged kind." I shake my head. "I loved going out for ramen. It's essentially silky, flavorful broth with a soft-boiled egg and noodles. I think the biggest takeaway is that I love food. New York City has the best food. Had." I pick at my lip with my fingers, trying not to feel upset, but I do anyway.

"I enjoy food, as well." Morris cuts in, distracting me. "On my origin planet, most of our sustenance comes from within the tall trees that cover the surface and rise up into the sky. There are little animals filled with sap that are steamed in the fallen leaves that are the size of my head or even bigger. We also import food from different colonies all over the galaxy. One of my favorites is stardust. There are different types of it, like starberries or starcrusted loaves, but stardust alone is like eating... I suppose something that makes you feel connected to the universe. That's not a very good description, is it?"

"Not really." I sniff. "So, is it the actual dust of stars?"

"Yes." He smiles warmly. "I wish you could try it."

"Me, too, but I'm most likely going to die here without my family and friends, or my favorite foods, or anything I know. I'll never see space or eat stardust." The mood falls immediately.

"Ellie, may I?" he asks, and I never know what it is he plans to do.

I shrug.

"I'm sorry." He pats my knee.

Morris is one of the reasons my life is what it is, I haven't forgotten that. He may not have killed anyone, doesn't want to kill anyone; he's been forced into this life just as much as humans have, and that makes me want to forgive him. But I can't. Not yet. Not really. Not without knowledge. If I were in his place, I'd like to believe I wouldn't stand by and watch people die, but the truth is, humans have done that since the beginning of time. Being brave and righteous can get you killed. If they created him for this purpose and he died taking a stand, they could just create others to do it again. And he saved my life when he didn't have to. "It's not entirely your fault, though, is it?"

"But I knew. I wasn't down here on Earth, but I knew what was happening." He's quiet briefly, as if considering his words. "I am sorry, Ellie. I'm sorry for everything that has happened. I'm sorry for the role I've played in it."

I accept the apology but change the subject to something more pressing. "My parents and Alice. Do you think they're okay?"

"Avrola would have told me if something had happened."

"But they could be vaccinated?" I ask, a crack in my voice.

"Only if they had to be. If Avrola had to let them." His tone is strong but low, like he feels regret. "I don't believe so, Ellie."

A new song begins and, for a moment, we stay silent. I stare out at the snowy fields as they swirl past us. The general lack of people, buildings and noise is disquieting. I wonder where the rest of humanity is, where those guys came from with this truck.

But then I realize I don't really care.

I decide that it's too quiet and I can't bear it anymore, even if that means I have to make small talk. "So...are we going the right way?"

"My mental GPS, as you call it, tells me we are going west."

The reality of our situation makes me anxious. "If you could go anywhere in the universe, where would you go? Where have you been?" The idea of life and worlds out there is intriguing enough to distract me from wallowing in the destruction of Earth.

"I have been to..." He stops to think. "Many planets, and about seven Ilori colonies. Each was different and more beautiful than the last. But if I could go anywhere in the universe, I would go to 50-B-18-RT or PR2-57-lu-96. They are free colonies. You make your own future, and you live the way you choose. I find this fascinating."

"Why don't you go there?"

"I don't want to leave my mother behind."

Unlike me. I left my mother behind.

He seems to read my mind. "Not like that, Ellie. Your mother is—" He cuts off as we reach a main road and what seems to be a standoff between our species. The other side of the street is packed with vehicles, and there are figures on either side, weapons pointed at each other. The headlights on the trucks shine bright and threatening behind the humans, cutting through the dimness of twilight. The brilliant glow of the Ilori panels illuminate their group. There's an Ilori on the ground, not moving, stuck in the middle. Dead? I know they can die, but how?

Morris cuts the music off, and stops on the shoulder. "Ferk."

"Do you mean *fuck*?"

"Yes, that is exactly what I mean."

"It's quiet… It looks like no one knows what to do." I narrow my eyes. "They haven't seen us. Do we have to go in there? Can we get around them?" I touch the tips of my fingers to my neck, as if the rope is still tied around it, waiting for me to fall again as I regard them.

The humans look aggressive while the Ilori seem out of place, as if the humans stumbled upon them taking a leisurely walk or something. They have their hands up, and yet the humans don't withdraw their weapons.

Morris hesitates. "I prefer to stay out of conflicts."

"Me, too." I nod. "We don't know them, and it's none of our business."

"We will get around it." The Ilori stop and turn to stare at us. And then the humans do the same. "Well, we could have."

"Shit, what do we do?" I sink lower into the seat.

"I'm going to try to defuse the situation. It would be safest for you to stay here."

He gets out and crosses through the cars and over the road, which riles up the humans even more, as their shouts become frantic and one swings a weapon Morris's way.

The air leaves my lungs in one big exhale. My fists tighten by my sides. They're going to shoot, I know it. And right now, Morris is all I have. He says he can save my family. And I don't know them, my fellow humans…but I know they could just as well shoot me. I should let it be. If they die, it's not my problem. They mean nothing to me.

But there's a voice in the back of my head, loud and clear,

asking me if I can truly sit back and watch the humans die. I can't forgive Morris for doing that. Why should I do the same?

Traitor. A cowardly traitor stands aside and lets people die at the hands of the other.

I'm not a traitor.

I heave a sigh before I get out of the car and maneuver through the cars along the street until I stand in front of the line of humans. They're all dressed in plaid winter gear, shotguns balanced in their arms. None of them shake. Morris stands in front of the two Ilori, their bright blue panels lighting the concern and maybe fear in their features, as he puts his fist over his heart and bows. They return the gesture. My eyes flick to the Ilori on the ground before I peer back at the humans.

There's a tremor in my voice, but I try to stay cool. "What's this about?"

"You a human or one of them?" A large, bearded white man eyes me for a moment, then stares back at the Ilori. He seems like the leader of the group. The bright lights from the trucks behind him make it difficult for me to see every detail of his face, but I do notice that his lips are curled back in anger. He doesn't lower his gun.

"Human. My name's Janelle." Why did I do this again? There are so many characters from books that do this very thing and end up dead. Throwaway characters. I don't need to be a tragic hero.

"Janelle, you better run. We won't get taken by these fuckers. Already got one."

"What if you could just walk away? Just walk away, don't kill them. Killing them…they don't like that. And the one behind me, he's the strongest." I plead with them, waving my arms around as if that will help me make my point.

"Don't give a shit. Nothing'll survive a gunshot to the head."

From what I know of the Ilori, guns are useless scraps of metal that humans try to use against them before the humans die. But the unmoving Ilori behind me is proof enough that whatever these humans have for ammunition works. I turn toward Morris, but he is communicating in weird sounds with the others.

"Back off. Please. I don't want to see any more death. I can't." My voice cracks, surprising me, and I swat at sudden tears. How many bodies have I seen hung from our building? How many people stabbed in the halls, bleeding out on the floors while fights broke out? Moms missing, parents joining the Kill Squads… At the beginning of the invasion, the cities fell first. And we stayed in our building, looking out windows as people fought and died around us. But we didn't leave. We were safe, locked inside. When the Ilori came for us… Maybe I am a traitor, or at least a coward.

"Get out of here." He doesn't even hear me, doesn't care. But he huffs when I stand in front of his gun like a wannabe protagonist hero who hasn't yet realized that she's made a fatal error.

"Please."

"You think I won't kill you, too?" He looks me in the eyes. My anxiety should be peaking right now, but part of me doesn't believe that a fellow human, even at the end of his rope, will shoot me. He can't hate me; he doesn't know me.

A little voice in my head reminds me that this isn't true. This world has a history of hate. The names and events rise to the surface of my mind with my numbers.

Five, Tamir Rice, Heather Heyer, Emmett Till, Oscar Grant, Nia Wilson. *Four*, little church girls, Addie Mae Collins, Carol Denise McNair, Carole Robertson and Cynthia Wesley. *Three*, Tree of Life. Christchurch. Emanuel African Methodist Episcopal Church. *Two*, people out shopping, Mau-

rice Stallard and Vicki Lee Jones. *One*, so many—too many—
black transgender women to name.

And so many, many more, I'd have to count again and
again. That's not my situation, but I'm staring down the bar-
rel of a gun, held by a stranger who might take this opportunity to express his deep-seated hate.

To my relief, he lowers his weapon. I did it. We are in this
together. I made a change. I helped, maybe I even saved a
few lives tonight. A hand touches my shoulder, and I freeze.

"Lower your weapons." Morris stands against my back, his
voice reverberating through our shared contact. Goose bumps
creep up my spine. Suddenly, I'm aware that Morris is an in-
timidating alien to everyone but me… "The other Ilori are
leaving. We want no fight."

I tilt my head to see the Ilori disappear into the trees beside
the road, one carrying the fallen one. I glance back to the men.

"Fuck you, alien. You came here to fight. You took everything. We'll take our world back." The guy raises the gun with
me still in the crosshairs. Morris stiffens behind me, and then
the gun warps in front of my face, melting before my eyes.
The guy screams and jumps back. The others do the same,
dropping their guns.

"Go. Travel west, you may find refuge in the middle of
your country. You may battle for freedom there, but not now.
I have saved you, but you have threatened the life of my friend,
and this I cannot tolerate."

The men stare at me, differently this time. I'm an alien's
friend; and I can't tell if they're disgusted or enraged or confused or all three. At the moment, I don't care. Morris is my
friend. He saved my life, he kept his promise. He said that he
saved my family and Alice, and he's told me the truth since the
beginning. That's more than even my parents could do for me.

The humans jump into their SUVs and trucks. Tires screech

as they speed off, sending up pebbles that hit my legs in their wake. I cover my eyes, hoping no dust or dirt gets in. When they're gone, we're enveloped in blackness. I can't even see their trucks anymore, just the lights from our own truck.

I turn around to Morris. The Ilori he communicated with are long gone, even the fallen one. I can't see that well, but I know I'm looking up at him, because his breath tickles my face and his body warmth radiates onto me.

"How did you do it? With the Ilori? Aren't you like the Iloris'-Most-Wanted? Did one of them die?"

"She was fatally injured. The humans had electric ammo, and the Ilori scouts were on low charges." He ignored my question about being wanted by his masters. I guess he doesn't want to answer.

I exhale slowly, letting the fear go until my muscles lose their tension. "But how did you get them to spare the humans? Why was there a standoff to begin with? The Ilori are powerful, they could have killed them."

Morris's tone is soft. "Death defeats our purpose, Ellie. The labmades on the road weren't being commanded by the true Ilori, they were observing nature, geology, farm patterns for Habitation. They don't feel the urge—they weren't created to kill, and although we aren't supposed to feel, we do. We feel fear and loss and worry. We are like humans."

"Only less violent. Well, the labmades, I mean." My gaze lands on a dark puddle of blood in the middle of the street, lit by the moonlight. "I'm sorry. Is she…?"

"She was shot in her panel with electric ammunition. Instant death." His breath shakes. "There have been too many losses. Many of my race and yours have died…" He looks at the ground and then back at me, sorrow marring his beautiful features. "The other Ilori will give our fallen comrade a proper burial, for which I am grateful. To leave her body in the street, as if it did not matter, would have been dishonorable. It may not seem it, for there has been so much death by our hands, yet we labmades treasure life. Respect life."

I shake my head, remembering the news of dead black children shot in the streets, immigrant children locked in cages, murders, politics, white supremacy... The Ilori have more honor and respect for their people, even in death, than some humans. I glance up at him, and for a moment, I see an expression that's been etched into my own face, my dad's, my mom's. It's the look of a person who knows that, to someone else, their life doesn't matter. It's a side of Morris I haven't seen before. Vulnerable, scared, hopeless.

Morris steps closer into the beams from the headlights of our car. His brilliant eyes brighten and soften on me. He seems to struggle with something but says nothing as his hand swings by his side. He brushes a finger against the corner of my cheek. "They were going to kill you."

"Who?"

"The humans. They didn't care. They were burdened with such hatred that they do not care if they hurt others like them." His voice is small, raspy. "I know we deserve their hatred, but you don't."

My eyebrows lift. "I thought you said you couldn't read minds."

"I can't, but I could see it on their faces."

"So... I've escaped death twice now. I'm becoming The Boy Who Lived." I try to joke, but my heart's hammering, not only because my own species was about to kill me, but because Morris is running his fingers along my jawline.

"I've never... I've never touched a human like this," he whispers. "Do you mind?"

"No," I gulp. "Is it much different than touching an Ilori?"

"Yes. You are warmer, and I can feel the beat of your heart." He closes his eyes and sighs. "I'm sorry. I don't want to make you uncomfortable."

"You aren't." I surprise myself by the truth of it. I like Morris. Even though there are millions of reasons that I shouldn't. This friendship has no future. It's hard to hold hatred in your heart for long, so I close my eyes and let it go. I feel sadness for what my world was, and what it could have been if the Ilori hadn't come to claim it. I can't forgive them for all this, but I can let myself be free of the anger for a moment, if only because it's healthy.

"We should go." His fingers lace through mine.

"West?"

"To either doom or salvation."

I roll my eyes. "That's very dramatic, Morris."

We cross the road back to our car. The sound he makes is something between laughter and choking. "I'm working on it."

"You don't have to be human for me. Just be yourself." I slide into my seat and Morris closes the door.

Morris slides behind the steering wheel. "Be myself? I hardly know what that is. But I know whoever I am is very happy to have met you, Ellie."

"So am I, Morris." And I mean it. "Let's see what other songs are on here."

"Music would be great, but another story, perhaps, as well? I like your stories."

I chew my lower lip. "Once upon a time in England, during the Second World War, three siblings were transported to another world called the Woodlands. Evelyn, Jamie and Philippa—who my mom said I'm very much like, because she's strong, although I don't always see it that way—return home but still struggle to find where they belong…"

I tap on Morris's shoulder as I awake to the first rays of sun on the horizon. I remember finishing the story and drifting off to sleep. "Let me drive. You look tired."

Morris wearily scrubs at his forehead. His blue panel light

is dim. He looks exhausted, if that's even possible. "Do you know how to drive?"

I hesitate. "Well, no, not really. But, I mean, there's no one out here, and there isn't a whole lot I can get wrong, right?"

He gives a reluctant sigh but pulls over. "Ilori don't normally need sleep. But a few hours will restore 1 or 2 percent of my energy."

"Do you know how much charge you have left?"

He grimaces, hitting a button on his panel. "Seven percent. Melting the gun, running in the woods…it took a lot out of me."

I nod. "Don't worry, if anything serious happens, I'll wake you." I'm about to open the door when Morris puts a hand on my arm.

"There's snow on the ground, and it's very cold outside. I really don't like the cold. Please."

I cover my mouth, trying not to laugh. "I had no idea, Morris. I thought you were invincible."

"My home planet is warm. The cold makes me unhappy."

"Okay, I'll go up, you stay down and slide over. Got it?"

I scoot against the window while Morris slides over. For a brief second, I'm hovering over him and he's beneath me when our eyes lock. He draws his face closer to mine, but I pull back and turn around before plopping onto my seat. I feel a bit breathless but I don't know why.

"All right, so what do I do?" I look at Morris, but he's fallen asleep or powered down or whatever Ilori do.

I sigh and hit the gas. We shoot forward, and Morris startles awake. "Not too hard. Just a little touch till you figure it out."

"And where am I going?"

"Follow this road for the next three hours. I will wake before the path changes, if that is satisfactory to you?" He is already drifting to sleep, his breathing slow.

"Mmm-hmm." My nerves are all over the place, but if we're ever going to get anywhere, I need to learn to do this. I can't rely on others to always save me. My foot gingerly pushes down on the pedal, and we move forward. Simple. I take a deep breath. I can do this.

I give myself another mental pep talk and, by the time I finish, Morris is asleep, his chest rising and falling softly. I relax and settle in, hoping I won't have to brake or use that shift thing in the center again. But I hum along to the song—it's either John Denver or James Taylor, I can never tell the difference. I take a deep breath and daydream about an alternate version of me that didn't live through an invasion, where driving with a boy would be equally new, but in a very different way.

CHAPTER 12

"Why Don't We Fall in Love"
—Amerie

MORRIS

Ellie is singing. Her voice is beautiful, and it fills him with warmth and this weird feeling in the bottom of his stomach. It's the sort of feeling he gets when he hears a new song for the first time; an all-consuming desire to listen to it again and again and know every note—every lyric—until he can breathe the music. He pretends to be asleep while she continues to sing and counts in between verses to keep herself here and focused.

There are so many things he wants to tell her, things she won't want to know but are worth discussing. But he can't do that now. Not while she's singing and rocking her shoulders back and forth. Dancing—that's what the humans call it. Ilori don't dance; it serves no purpose. Yet, M0Rr1S wants to dance, just like that, and with her.

He'd almost kissed her. He didn't plan to. It was just…she was close, and since the beginning, he's been drawn to her. So much so that, in that moment where they swapped seats, he felt compelled to lean in. To feel his lips against hers… He wonders what that might be like. Ilori kiss, but never on the lips, not like humans. M0Rr1S has kissed for pleasure, for fun, because he was expected to. But humans? What does kissing mean to them?

Ellie sings louder, interrupting his thoughts. M0Rr1S catches himself smiling. "Oh, you're awake." Ellie doesn't take her eyes off the road. She's focused, and M0Rr1S finds his smile widening.

"Yes, just awakened. How long have I rested?"

"A few hours," she responds, skirting a car lying upside down on the side of the road. She grins. "Turns out, I'm a natural at driving."

"Is there anything you're not good at, Ellie?"

"I'm total crap at plenty of things."

"Such as?"

She huffs. "Such as I suck at writing, I have way too many ideas to focus on one." She pauses a moment before continuing. "I'm a horrible cook, have no clue about anything fashion. I'm also the worst at parties, socializing—I'm generally not good with people—and sports. All sports. It's like my body just can't do them. Oh, and paying attention is hard when I have a million daydreams and fantasies going on in my head. As one of my teachers said, I live in my own world…" She laughs a little. "And high heels. I can't walk in them."

M0Rr1S sits up. "I don't believe you."

"I have a lot of faults."

"Even if all of this is true, you counterbalance it with other talents." M0Rr1S nods with enthusiasm before sobering. "I also struggle with socializing, I find it very draining. Too many people talking at once, or trying to communicate something a certain way...it's difficult for me. I'm also afraid I might be bad at sex."

Ellie gasps, swerving the truck a little. "What?"

"I believe you call it sex, yes? When two people engage in intercourse?" He sounds confused.

Her eyebrows rise. "Yes."

"I am worried I am bad at it." His shame hangs heavy in the truck.

"Why?"

"Because my partner—her name was 0rsa—didn't seem satisfied." M0Rr1S remembers the way he sloppily tore off his clothes at the sight of her naked body, and his clumsy attempts to please her. 0rsa's face glazed over in boredom; not once did she smile. No Ilori do, really, but he had hoped... She reminded him of his labmade birth nothing short of three times before their first and last encounter. Afterward, she'd said it felt mechanical, and didn't elaborate further on why.

M0Rr1S can hear Ellie's heart racing, distracting him from the memory, which is most welcome. "Does it make you uncomfortable to discuss intercourse, Ellie?"

Her cheeks pink, but her gaze stays glued to the road. "Well, maybe a little. Humans don't normally discuss it. But... I don't mind discussing it with you."

"Was your first experience satisfactory?"

"Um...you know what? Let's just talk about you." Her voice is pitched higher than normal, and he worries she might be slightly ill. "How do you know she wasn't satisfied? Did she tell you that?"

"Well...no. But she didn't say it was exemplary either. I

believe she found some pleasure, but she never called upon me again."

"I think you're making too much of it. Was it your first time?"

"Yes, my first and only. I was very…"

"Nervous?" Ellie suggests.

"Yes," he admits. "I read a manual about it, but it didn't prepare me for the actual procedure." He shakes his head, trying to cast aside his embarrassment. He has never spoken to someone about this before, and it is freeing to do so now. Besides, he trusts Ellie.

"From what I've heard, everyone's first time is awkward. No one's just going to be a pro at it, you know?" The corners of her lips lift. "Alice told me a big part of the experience is failing and learning how to do it together. No one expects perfection."

"You haven't experienced it?"

She exhales slowly. "No."

M0Rr1S stays silent. What should he say? "0rsa is my betrothed. Our parents, my father, arranged my marriage before I left the lab."

"Oh." Her voice is small, and he wants to know if she feels anything about the news of his betrothal.

"I don't care for her. She's a labmade, like me, but she loathes our kind, especially me. I told my father as much." He blows out air between his teeth. "Our family is very well-known and powerful. My father believes that, when I return, I will be more amenable to my duty."

"Will you be?" She shifts in her seat.

"No." He's surprised by the conviction in his tone. "I will not try to please him. In fact, I don't think I can." He looks out the window. The sun is hidden by heavy clouds, but that allows him to see the stars and galaxies far away. None of which are home. It's even farther away. "Have you ever liked someone, in a romantic way, that you would date?" He remembers her words and definitions, and so many song lyrics come to mind.

"No. I don't—I… I don't know." Ellie huffs. "I'm weird."

"You don't have to talk about it, if you don't want to. I'm sorry if I made you feel pressured to disclose your personal sentiments regarding your private experiences."

Ellie begins to laugh, and M0Rr1S can't help staring at her in awe. "I'm sorry, that was just…you speak so well for an alien."

He tries to laugh like her, and this time it almost sounds right.

"Alice says I'm demi-ace, because I'm attracted to people, but I wouldn't want to date them or do anything else unless, until, I feel like I know them, and trust them. That we've bonded. That we're friends, you know? And I could be myself and not worry about being judged, and… Yeah, if I felt that, I would date. But right away? No. I'm just different about it. I know we're going through the end of the world—the end of humanity, too, I guess—but I still can't bring myself to…be with someone. Everyone says it's fun, but not for me. At this point, I don't even know if it'll happen. I mean how much time do I have left? I've never even been kissed. Romantically, anyway. It's not that I don't want to, I do, but I get in my own way, and I'm also nervous and awkward. I'm sorry, I'm rambling. I've never discussed this before. Does any of that make sense?"

"It makes sense," M0Rr1S doesn't hesitate to answer. "I think… I… It's very similar to how I feel."

"Really?" She glances at him, hope flashing through her eyes before she turns back to the road.

"I don't care for 0rsa, because I don't really know her. We

never had a bond. I know she hates who I am, and she hates herself." He runs a hand through his disheveled hair. "Anyway, I don't believe there is anything wrong with doing as you wish when you want to, and there is consent."

"Yeah, exactly. I envy people who can do that."

"I wished my first time was with someone I knew and I cared for. That would have made me feel...better about my failings."

"I doubt you failed."

M0Rr1S sits up. "Why do you say that?"

"Because it was your first time, and maybe it was hers, too." She shrugs her shoulders, releasing some tension. "Everyone has to learn who they are and how to be in that new kind of situation. So, don't beat yourself up over it, Morris. It's not a fault. It's a strength to know that you aren't perfect." She gives him a small smile. "If you'd said you're the best at sex, then I'd be worried." She laughs, her cheeks rosy.

"Ellie, I like you." He shifts in his seat.

The corner of her mouth rises, but she doesn't look at him. "I know."

His eyes lock on the way her hands grip the steering wheel firmer. "Do you like me?"

She bypasses the question. "I'm not ready to kiss you."

The rhythm of her heart fills his ears.

He lets out the breath he may have been holding in. "I will not kiss you until you want me to."

"Okay." There's relief in her laugh, and something else he can't pinpoint. "But you know, it'd be a little sad if we didn't kiss before the end of this trip."

M0Rr1S already dreads the moment when they will have to part. "Ellie, I will kiss you before the end or the beginning, whichever you like."

Her face flushes a shade that brings out the light in her brown eyes. "Look!" She gasps and slows the car as they cross a main street of a deserted town. "It's a public library. I meant to ask before, but why haven't they knocked down all the buildings?"

He likes the way her voice amplifies with excitement. "The Ilori will keep some structures and buildings as... I think you call it museums? History. There will always be traces of humans." Silence falls as she considers his words. "We should go to it."

"Can we? Should we?" Ellie glances at him before returning her focus to the road. "What if we get caught?"

"Most Ilori are surveilling human housing, working with Habitation to clear the surface, or fighting humans far away. We shouldn't stay anywhere long, but yes, we can go in." He relaxes into his seat once more, the talk of kissing done for now, even if he still cannot help sneaking glances at her lips. They don't really have time for a stop, but it will make her happy. "You can save more books and tell me what happens. Maybe a story about friends on a trip."

Ellie drives straight through the melted snow and wet grass toward the building. M0Rr1S is concerned that she won't brake and they'll hit the front doors, but she does, although the truck jolts forward and screeches on the pavement as they come to a halt.

She parks the car exactly between two lines. Then she twists the keys and gives M0Rr1S a lopsided grin before collecting her flashlight. "I'm learning."

"You're doing very well."

They step out of the car and she pauses to close her eyes as the sun beams down on her face. "Ah, haven't felt the sun in forever."

M0Rr1S doesn't want to stare at her—he doesn't want her to feel uncomfortable—but she is so beautiful that he cannot help it.

She sighs. "If we had a solar panel, maybe we could find a way to funnel it into usable energy for you?" She chuckles. "I'm overthinking it. In my defense, I haven't been able to think about scientific stuff in a long time." With a shake of her head, she squares her shoulders. "Of course, we can do that, we just need a stationary, heavy-duty solar panel. If we collect enough energy and we can connect your cable to the panel, it won't deliver the amount of energy you're probably used to…but it might work. Let's go find a book on sustainable energy so we can build it. I want to make sure we do this right."

M0Rr1S's mouth drops. Ellie Baker. Although his heart only serves as the center of circulation through his body and is incapable of feelings or thoughts, he begins to understand why humans like to believe otherwise. Ellie makes his heart flip and beat faster just with her presence.

"You are very intelligent, Ellie, and you seem to understand a great deal more than I about energy sources."

"I tried to tell you that, despite what you think, humans are smart. *I'm* smart." She opens her eyes to stare at the library. "I haven't been inside a library in forever either." Her lips move as she silently reads the dusty, chipped sign outside. "Illinois. Never been here before."

She takes his hand and pulls him up the stairs to the small, one-story building. The stones are gray, the steps are cracked, and the windows are too coated in dirt to look through. The door is locked, but M0Rr1S crushes that easily.

"It smells horrible in here." Ellie turns on her flashlight and gasps.

His eyes take in every detail: charred books litter the floor— they must have been used for a fire. There are knocked-over racks, smashed computers and overturned desks.

Ellie steps in farther, waving her flashlight around to see everything his eyesight already allowed.

"Stay here, it might not be safe." M0Rr1S squeezes her hand before striding into the mess, searching for life. The space is too small, though; it would be difficult for anyone to hide in here. "All clear."

Ellie pulls the collar of her shirt over her mouth and rushes to a shelf to begin picking through the books. She takes one and coughs, her fingers turning the pages. "This one's good." He's not sure if she tells this to him or is talking to herself. She continues sorting through them, traveling between the shelves, until she has four books.

"I wish you could have seen the New York Public Library at Bryant Park. I think you would've liked it," she says between shifting books. "This one's horrible."

"I would have loved to see that library with you. Maybe one day, you'll create your own library again."

Her eyes sparkle at him. "That's a nice dream." She pulls one more book. "Survival guide from 2016. Still relevant. Might have some useful information in it. Probably not any on how to survive an alien invasion, though." A few rats skitter by the shelves. "Time to go." She stumbles against the door. "This is what happens to the world without humans."

"This is what happens to a world when the Ilori take control." M0Rr1S looks up at the gray sky. The world is so very quiet, just as the Ilori like it. And so very wrong, just the way Ilori want it.

THE STARRY EYED: "THESE STARRY DREAMS"

The Sound of Stars
Written by: Cecil Wright, Allister Daniels, Rupert Montague,
Whisper Landsome

Ohhh
She stole my heart
And then she kissed my soul, yeah
She kissed my soul and told me we'll never part
And she, she's a star shining at the seams
These starry dreams

Ohhh
She's got glitter
Yeah, she sparkles and shines in my sky

I want to hold her close, to look her in the eyes
Shining so bright but I can't look away
Promise me
Promise this is more than it seems
These starry dreams

This world
It's bigger than the two of us
But it's really only them and us
And I want them all to know
My star, I'll never let her go

Ohhh
She's so strong
No, she don't need me, I knew that all along
But I need her, she lights the path for me to see
I never felt before, but oh the feelings she gives me
I love her, from the rooftops I'll scream
These starry dreams

This world
It's bigger than the two of us
But it's really only them and us
And I want them all to know
My star, I'll never let her go

I'll never let you go
No, I'll never let you go
Stars in my eyes just for you
I just want to be with you
Only you
My starry dreams

CHAPTER 13

"The best way out is always through."

—Robert Frost

JANELLE

I'm back in the passenger seat scanning the books for mold and information while Morris drives through the small town. My stomach gurgles. I'm hungry. So hungry. I drank the last bit of water on the road, and the peanut butter jar is in the back seat, empty and licked clean.

Morris must have heard it. "We have to find you food."

"Aren't you hungry?" I ask.

"I am, but I can survive without food and water for a long period of time, as long as I still have a charge." His voice is flat as he maneuvers the car around potholes. Soon, Habitation will have either smoothed them over or made them into patches of luscious grass.

"How long will it take to get to California?" My internal geography has never been on point, and in my mind, it could take a week or longer.

"A few more days with rests," Morris answers.

I scan the buildings in the wavering morning light. There are patches of gardens in between perfectly intact, lifeless structures. Glass litters the ground around where a window must have been smashed. My gaze catches on two buildings.

"Wait—Morris, there's a hardware store next to that grocery store. If we can get into those, we might have a chance at recharging you and finding food."

Morris turns off the road to the highway and parks the car in front of the stores. "We've been around this area too long. Let's be quick, okay?"

"There's no one here…it's a ghost town." I wonder if this was once a small idyllic community with mom-and-pop shops. One of those places where everyone knew each other's names, like in *Anne of Green Gables* or *Dumplin'*.

"There are spirits here?" Morris looks at me with complete seriousness in his eyes.

"Just a saying, meaning there's no one here." I almost ask him if there are such things as spirits in his culture, but I remind myself to stay on task. "I think I know what parts we need at the hardware store for a solar panel charger, so let's go there first and then the grocery store."

The hardware store is in a similar state of disarray as the library. It smells awful, and I spy a few rats. We dash through the aisles with my flashlight and his enhanced sight, scooping up a solar panel hidden underneath a fallen shelf. I grab wire cutters, a screwdriver and hammer—tools we might not even need.

But I still can't find batteries; that section of the store is bare and littered with empty plastic packaging. I groan, trying to snort the miscellaneous odors from my nostrils.

Morris makes a small noise, and I pause. "Are you okay?" He makes the noise again, and I realize he's clearing his throat. "Morris?"

"*This girl, named Ellie, she's just…the best person, She's something, something cool, and really…really smart… She's Ellie…*" Morris sings to the rhythm of Queen's "Crazy Little Thing Called Love" and my mouth drops open, a small laugh escaping.

"You know those are the wrong lyrics, right?"

His big eyes hold mine with the force of his earnestness. "Yes, I'm making these for you. Sing with me."

I shake my head before clearing my voice a little, ignoring the way the air leaves a bitter flavor in my mouth. I snap my fingers and sing the correct lyrics, eliciting a big smile from him. Part of me wants to dance, despite our setting, but singing without care is enough for now.

We are in this world, but this world doesn't define us. I may be scavenging, but I'm not a scavenger. I'm alive. And safe. Morris is here for me, he saved me and helped me. I'm allowed to be happy for a few moments. We both are.

Morris stands in front of me, swaying as we sing the song. His breath tickles my cheeks. I bend my head back, staring at his lips while he mouths the words. His eyes are on mine. My body shifts closer, and I swallow.

A kiss. Maybe? What would it be like? What if I hate it? Are we there yet? Am *I* there yet?

But something furry and soft touches the side of my bare leg between my shoes and pants, and I nearly jump out of my skin. The moment's over.

Guilt washes through me.

"We should go," I say, hoping I have everything I need to help Morris.

I find a small plastic bag and shove everything inside it. Then we head to the grocery store. Given the smells at the library, the hardware store and the first house we stopped at, I expect gag-worthiness. But it's mostly just empty and clean, like brand-new clean. We walk up and down the aisles, hoping to find something—anything—but everything's gone.

"Well there goes that idea." We walk back toward the exit. "I'm getting hungry. And really thirsty."

"We'll find something, don't worry. I'll—"

I turn to Morris just as his eyes widen and he drops to the ground, twitching and screaming. The world seems to slow and my heartbeat floods my ears. Ilori rush into the store. The noose feels like it's tightening around my neck again. I can't run. I can't hide. I won't survive. And I won't leave Morris. Not when he's given up everything for me. I fall to my knees beside him and drape an arm across his chest, trying to stay calm and be there for him like he was for me.

Five, Ilori in black coats. Four, a sky gray and cloudless. Three... three. Think of a three, Ellie! Three, Morris.

Through the pain that plagues him, he grabs my wrist. *Two,* his voice inside my head. *I'm sorry. Don't worry about me. Tell them I kept you a prisoner. We were never friends.* I shake my head. I would rather die by the side of a friend than throw him under the bus. *Compliance will save your life, Ellie.* He touches my face before the light in his eyes darkens and his twitching stops. He's asleep or dead. I wish I knew which.

"Morris? Morris! Wake up, Morris!" My voice is halfway between a scream and a whisper, shrill and terrified. "Morris, please." I peer up at the Ilori surrounding us, frozen like statues. "Is he dead? Did you kill him?"

One.

With Morris still in my arms, my vision goes black.

My last thought is that I'm gone and might never come back.

I wake up in a cell. A small jail cell, furnished with only an uncomfortable bench. The sun shines through a little window above me, the rays of light creating shadows on the gray cinder block walls.

Ilori.

My fingers twitch, and I rub them together until feeling comes back. How long have I been here? My stomach rumbles. As if on cue, a plate of crackers, ham and canned peaches slides under my barred cell door, thanks to an Ilori with pale blue eyes and long blond hair. It also rolls a bottle of water toward me. Then it disappears down a small hallway.

I run toward the food and shove dry crackers into my mouth.

Not too fast, you'll get sick, I tell myself.

I finish in what feels like seconds. I hope it won't come back up. If my anxiety kicks in like it always does, I might vomit.

Morris. Is he okay? Will he get into trouble for saving my life, for taking off like he did and protecting me?

Hours pass with me going through my numbers over and over again. Counting the same things. The bench. The blanket. My fingers. At one point, I sing "These Starry Dreams" by the Starry Eyed, the melody stuck in my head, keeping me from counting one more time.

I yell out for someone to let me go to the bathroom. Another hour goes by before an Ilori comes. There's no point in locking me in chains or securing my arms. I know they could kill me whenever they want. So I silently follow to the bathroom. I splash cold water on my face, and duck my head into the sink to drink from the tap. Although I don't know where we are, not really, or how good the water is out here, I trust that the Ilori would keep the water systems clean. After all, that's what Morris said: they like their nature.

When we left New York, it was almost flattened completely. Wherever permanent housing is, I'd bet it's isolated, in the middle of nowhere. Surrounded by the nature that's come back all over the Earth. They've been here for two years. This world is theirs now.

I follow my guard back to my cell. Another plate of food and water awaits me. It's amazing how fast you adjust to being a prisoner when you have shelter and sustenance. This time I eat slowly and save some water for later. If there is a later.

Cold seeps in through my jacket, and I'm shaking a bit when Morris suddenly appears in front of my cell. His eyes look brighter, his movement less sluggish. He's been recharged, and has changed into more formal attire with numbers and colors pinned across his jacket. His eyes shine as he takes me in. But he makes no move forward to unlock my cell or touch me.

"Human JQB-305-7-21. Are you well?" His voice is flat, disinterested. There's no recognition. Just like my dad.

"I'm fine, Morris." My own voice wobbles. Did they change him? Can they do that? "Did they reset you? Do you even remember me?" Panic sits in the center of my gut. I can't be forgotten again. What about my family? What does this mean?

"In the morning, you will be delivered to a nearby center for your vaccination. You needn't worry, this is for your own benefit. What G00287 granteth, Ilori taketh, but we shall not harm you."

"Morris—" I bolt forward, resting my fingers against the bars. I need a sign, even a small one that he's still in there. That he has a plan. He pulls away, a look of disgust flashing in his eyes. It hurts.

I warble out a bar of "Raspberry Beret" and he cringes.

Physically cringes. The air feels like it cools between us. This isn't the Morris I know. I want to scream and throw things and fall into a pit of despair.

"Human expression is a transgression, human. If you do that again, I will be forced to take punitive action."

I nod once before he strides down the hall, and for the first time in days, I feel all alone. I sit back on my bench and, this time, I let my tears fall.

I'm alone.

My mom. My dad. Even Alice. They could all be gone now. The grief that I've been denying since I got in that car with Morris washes through me. How long have I been holding it in?

Morris could be acting the way he is to protect me. But I've never felt so alone.

The tears are coming in full now, and I can't stop them. Sobs rack my chest. I don't care if the Ilori hear me. I've lost everything. It's all catching up to me now: how desperate I've been to be happy as the only world I know crumbles around me.

Night falls, and I can't sleep. I let myself remember my family, Alice, Mrs. Turner, even Erica Schulman.

I remember sitting on the Q train with Mom on our way back to our tiny one-bedroom apartment in Brooklyn. We lived on the wrong side of Flatbush, that's what Mom would say. I was nine, but I felt older. I looked out the window at the Brooklyn Bridge, in love with what I saw. Mom nudged me with her shoulder.

"You know we aren't always gonna live like this, right?"

I sank into my seat. I'd heard Mom's big plans before. Move into a bigger apartment, she and Dad would get jobs that paid more and I would go to a feeder school for an Ivy League or something. We'd live "the good life." She'd been saying it since I can remember.

"We'll have a nice apartment where you won't have to sleep in the living room and you won't have to worry about mice getting into the little food we have. And all this shit—" she pulled a face in apology for swearing "—all this *crap* we went through won't matter anymore. It'll balance out." She said this more to herself than to me.

"Mom, I'm happy, and I like it here." It was the truth. We'd lived there my entire life, and I had friends. Yeah, the mice raiding our kitchen sucked, but we were good. And there were plenty of mice in Manhattan, too.

"Baby, you live in the right place, you do well in the right schools, and you and your cello can go to Juilliard." She tucked one of my stray braids behind my ear, her warm brown eyes holding mine.

I made a face, my usual face, when she started talking about the future like that. Even my music teacher told me that music wouldn't pay the bills, and every other night my parents were complaining about bills. Juilliard was a dream. Not reality.

She harrumphed. "Stop worrying. You're too young to be worried all the damn time. You gotta loosen up. What's the worst that could happen?" She smiled at me with her eyebrows raised.

I nodded. "Okay, Mom." But I wasn't the loose type. My worries kept me safe, and my feet on the ground. When we finally moved, by chance, and started living "the good life," I was the only one who saw what was going on around us. All the overreaching, trying to get somewhere and be something we weren't, put us in the crosshairs of a new world filled with old hate. Dad was just trying to keep up, and Mom was just trying to fit in. And me? I was trying to make a home out of a place that didn't welcome us; a place that slowly tore us apart with its microaggressions and clutched pearls before it sent us crawling to wherever they thought we belonged. I was scared what would be left of us when that happened.

Now, lying in this cell, I'm still scared. There's no home anymore. Tears stain my cheeks and drop onto the stone bench beneath me.

I remember my dad, too. "You know, sweetie. I don't think humans are going to win this war," he told me, while turning the lights out in our apartment. Outside our window we saw a mob of humans with guns and bats surrounding just one Ilori. Our building was already occupied by then, but humans were being rounded up and pushed out of their hiding places. A tall Ilori put out a hand, and the attackers flew in the air, their bodies soon crunching against the pavement. Blood splattered and pooled in the pockets of the sidewalks. My blood ran cold. "If your mom and I don't make it—"

"Dad, I can't—"

"Ellie, listen, okay? I know it's not what you want to hear, but you need to hear it. Your mom and I, we might not make it through this. If we get separated and you have to choose between life and joining us, choose life, okay? Live. Live for us. Breathe for us. Survive for us. You are our greatest achievement. You are our dream come true."

"Daddy," I sobbed. "I can't."

"You have to, honey. Because they're going to take me and at some point, they will take your mama. And then it'll be only you. You're going to be alone. You're going to want to give up. Please, Ellie. Please don't. Even thinking about it—" My dad held my face in his hands and put his forehead against mine. His tears fell onto my cheeks, and soon I felt my own mix with them. We didn't sob or say how unfair all of this was. We held each other and cried.

A little over a week later, they gave him a form of the vaccine that didn't kill him, but stripped a big part of him away, lost, maybe forever. Not too long after, Mom started spiraling harder and faster.

Live for us. Breathe for us. Survive for us.

Sorry, Mom and Dad, but I made unwise decisions. I trusted an alien boy with cute eyes and a love of music. Now I'm surrounded by Ilori and making my last living memories in a jail cell. I'm not sure it's much better than getting the vaccine in the center, surrounded by people I used to know as we face oblivion together.

It's still dark when the door opens and Morris, accompanied by another alien, comes for me. I stand, my legs stiff and back sore, and follow the alien I don't know down the hall with Morris at the rear. They take me in a nondescript car like the first one we traveled in, and I'm loaded into the back seat beside the bag of books and music.

The alien says something to Morris in their language.

"No, it will remain quiet. Yes, human?" He says it to me in English, and my eyebrows furrow. He doesn't wait for an answer.

Maybe real Morris didn't betray me, but this one is different. He's pretending. He has to be. I'd like to believe that more than anything else. Or…maybe they changed him back to the way he is supposed to be through conditioning or… or the Hive.

I think about the stories I told him. I need to figure out if he's on my side or not. "Are you just volunteering for Prim, are you Katniss-ing?"

The alien turns to Morris and asks something; probably what or who is Prim. Morris responds in English. For my benefit?

"The human is questioning my loyalty and undoubtedly worries about the occupants of Center 11408-H. I gained the human's trust by stating I had saved its family."

The alien makes a small noise.

"I told the human I couldn't connect to Il-0CoM to give proof of their well-being because it was too dangerous." Morris sounds lifeless. "The center was completed. All viable husks were vaccinated. I've been traveling with this human to find an adequate solution for our current situation as discussed. It has aided me in gaining trust and finding hidden locations of their kind."

The other alien nods in approval, its clicking and beeping language hanging in the air like a tangible thing I can't grasp.

"Thank you for your praise." Morris settles back in his seat as I try to wrap my mind around what he is saying. None of this is real. He told me about the true Ilori, about the lab-mades and their panels. He shared with me. And he said he saved my family. I know him. He wouldn't betray me. He's lying. Am I supposed to play along?

I try to catch his attention through the reflections in the windowpane. I look for any sign he's trying to give me, to tell me that I need to sit back here and pretend, just like him. But he doesn't look my way.

Morris turns to the other Ilori. "This center we travel to, how many humans does it house? All primed for the vaccine?"

The Ilori responds.

"Yes, speaking English seems to keep the human quiet. I have noticed that they tend to be overwrought when they do not understand what is being said." He sniffs before continuing in a clipped tone. "Are there enough supplies in the center? When I produced the final formula, we were prepared for instant administration. It's important we move quickly."

I ignore the Ilori's response as my mind wraps around what Morris just said. He produced the formula? Morris...*he's* the mastermind behind the vaccine? "It was you? You created the vaccine?"

"Every Ilori contributes their gift," Morris answers, as if that's an acceptable response. "It was my purpose. I am a humble servant of my empire."

"You're lying," I whisper, a lump lodging in my throat.

"You are only *human*, JQB-305-7-21." He says *human* like it's a dirty, disgusting thing and it pains him to even speak the word. "I do not expect you to understand the complexities and dedication needed to serve a greater purpose. Nor the discomfort of emulating an inferior being to gain insight on how to manipulate your kind."

My blood runs cold. What if he's not lying? What if Morris was using me? How well do I really know him, and how do I know he wasn't just saying what I wanted to hear? I did help him find more humans... On the side of the road. What did he say to the other Ilori to get them to back down? There's no way they would have let those humans go after killing one of them. He's been keeping secrets the whole time.

I helped him.

He knows me. He knew my weaknesses, my books, my family, and he exploited them. He probably lied about the music just to forge a connection. And I'm an easy target. The girl sitting alone at the party, willing to do whatever it takes to save her books and family. He saved me, but maybe that was part of his manipulative plan.

I used to be smarter than this.

"I didn't know you at all." I want to punch the window and feel pain worse than what I feel now. I hate myself for being so naive.

The Ilori beeps.

"I remain unperturbed by it. I am certain it will stop being a nuisance as it finally comprehends the reality of its situation. I have been quite clear about my motivations. How much farther?" Morris doesn't even glance my way, as if my presence means nothing to him. I tighten my fists, my fingernails digging into the palms of my hands to keep myself from breaking into sobs or smashing the window open and jumping out.

The other Ilori answers, but I'm too enraged to listen. Morris created the vaccine. Morris killed Alice and my parents. Morris, the alien boy I held hands with, and I fell asleep on. The alien boy who I thought about kissing, hoped to kiss. I sang, I laughed. I planned on saving him, I told him stories. I found music for him. I gave him Mrs. Turner's personal belongings.

"I hate you." There is no shaking in my voice, no wavering. I mean every syllable when I say it to him.

Morris turns in his seat and regards me with curiosity. I flinch but maintain eye contact. I still don't understand why he did everything he did. Maybe I never will. My eyelids suddenly feel heavy, and my shoulders relax on their own.

The other alien chirps.

"Yes. I've been carrying the contraband with me, gaining the human's trust. I even suggested I found the contraband entertaining for her benefit. I do not wish to transfer it to another center. I will incinerate it now. Thank you for reminding me."

"No!" I shake my head. He can't do that. He won't.

Morris's gaze flicks to mine before it lands on the bag carrying all of my books, my memories, the only remnants of a life with my parents. It disintegrates into a small, gray pile of ash. There is no sound, no fire, nothing to mark the end of my world. My lips tremble until I let out an anguished sob, startling us all. Tears drip down my cheeks.

I hope Morris sees this look on my face. I hope he sees my hate. He's good at reading humans, right? I hope he reads that. Suddenly, under his gaze, my brain begins to shut down.

And then I'm gone again.

CHAPTER 14

"Don't Let the Sun Go Down on Me"
—Elton John

MORR1S

The full charge is tingling under his skin. Even using his abilities back there wasn't enough to take the edge off. He's jumpy now. Restless. He keeps looking back through the side-view mirror at Ellie while she sleeps. She hates him. The anger in her eyes was like nothing he's ever seen from her before. Janelle Baker—Ellie—hates him, yet still he feels this fluttery sensation in the pit of his stomach when she's near.

H1lbe pulls into a lot at the center, and security runs up to investigate.

"Identification and quadrant?"

"Commander M0Rr1S 1lv, I am male from quadrant

4H-R12-B800L1," M0Rr1S answers in his mother tongue. His thoughts flicker back to New York, his section of Earth, his responsibility. All gone now.

"Commander H1lbe A1lln, I am female from quadrant 5I-G763-Bl1R6," H1lbe replies. That's a location north of here, Nebraska, M0Rr1S believes.

"You are far from your quadrants." It is not an accusation, merely a statement of fact.

"My quadrant is complete. I am relieved of service. However, I have decided to aid in the current situation in this area. A decision that was implied before my abrupt, unorthodox departure." M0Rr1S tilts his head to Ellie in the back. "You may have been alerted."

"I have." Security nods before focusing on H1lbe.

H1lbe turns off the car. "I am here to check progress and to further assist."

Security remains inscrutable. "My name is Khun1, I am nonbinary. Please let me show you inside, commanders."

M0Rr1S nods and steps out of the car, eyeing Ellie. "I wish for this one to be delivered to my domicile. I believe it will aid me in streamlining the formula for larger distribution." He pockets a small rock on the bottom of the car floor while H1lbe sets off toward the building.

"Are you sure, sir? We can have it sent to live with other humans. Surely you do not wish for the human to cohabitate with you and contaminate your residence with its incessant shrillness?"

M0Rr1S exhales through his teeth. Contaminate his residence? This is the humans' world, everything has been touched by them. "You are in need of the formula, correct?"

"Yes, sir, but—"

"*But* I know this human. I have experimented with its blood. It will do. Thank you for your understanding, Khun1." M0Rr1S dismisses them.

"Yes, sir."

Two more guards arrive to pick up Ellie and deliver her
to his room, most likely on the highest floor. Ilori, especially
those with titles, are always given rooms at the top of buildings. He pictures home, the mansion atop the clouds, with
glass floors and open ceilings. The air is pure, and the skies
are variations of blue, even as the sun sets and the two moons
shine down through the branches and leaves.

He reminds himself again, for the hundredth time, he will
never go back.

They walk into the tall center. There is a wide area undoubtedly used for emergency vehicles, and the walls inside
are sterile, emitting a citrusy odor. Whichever commander
operates this location is particular. There's an organization to
the white walls and individual rooms that suggests this was
once a medical center; a hospital, humans called it.

The bright lights comfort him as they bounce off the gleam-
ing white surfaces. White, everything is white and clean.

M0Rr1S stops, gaze caught on glass windows with small
rooms behind them. Humans languish there, the rooms furnished only with toilets and cots. They avert their eyes as he
and the other Ilori pass by. *Fear.* He can smell it even behind
their walls and windows. This center is run much differently
than he ran his. With no sense of humanity, no kindness or
compassion. His lip curls, fiery anger blurring his vision. There
is nothing he can do to stop this.

At the end of the hall, there's a face he'd hoped never to
see again. Instead of fire, M0Rr1S suddenly feels frozen. He
sets his jaw and resists the urge to bite the inside of his cheek.

0rsa tilts her head back and forth. She is a vision of ice.
Black hair falls straight down past her shoulders, covering
her blue panel. Her pale skin seems almost a shade lighter
than the walls, and her radiant blue eyes sparkle in the fluo-

rescents. Why is she here? If he had known this center was within her quadrant…

"Commander M0Rr1S." It is stated with an inflection of surprise. "I am pleased you were so easily forgiven for your transgressions."

"Commander 0rsa." His voice is cold, distant, just the way she likes it. "I was able to justify my actions within Il-0CoM. I believe they were deemed satisfactory."

"You saved a human from execution." She says it matter-of-factly, but there's a snide edge to her words.

He instinctively stands straighter. "I saved a human to use it as a remedy for our current situation in the middle of the country."

"And yet, there have been zero reports of you making contact while traveling." She leans forward as if she'll catch him in a falsehood with her bare hands.

"I daresay you are behind on reports, 0rsa. I met with a group on the road during a confrontation. My guidance led to the capture of several humans, and an opening of human defense in the midquadrant." M0Rr1S tilts his head to the side. Lying to 0rsa, especially when he suspects she has Il-0CoM recording, would be dangerous. Thus, he tells the truth, though not completely. When he and Ellie interrupted the standoff on the road, the Ilori were able to track and capture the humans that killed their comrade. But it was merely out of safety for future labmades, not a coordinated plan. "Although they were confounded by my initial actions, true Ilori leadership praised my efforts as innovative. I do hope that is acceptable to you."

0rsa adjusts her posture, lips quirking as if she could smile. "Nevertheless, it is a pleasure to have you in my quadrant. It was a sudden decision for me to come down here to Earth, and I had not expected to see you. But I am…satisfied to have you share your expertise about the vaccine. As you know, we've had…difficulties with humans bombing distribution centers. Not in your quadrant, of course, but out here." She doesn't wait for him to respond. "It is good you can resume your duties."

Her black garb stretches across her form, fitted and tailored for her. She is beautiful, but she makes him nervous in a way Ellie does not. When he sees her, there is no fluttering inside him, only a physical need to sweat and avoid her gaze. He cannot bear to stand close to her. It isn't just that she is a reminder of his failing, but that she is difficult to please in all things. Her family is only one step below his, but she is more respected in the empire than he.

"I did not expect to see you on Earth either, Orsa." *Careful*, he tells himself, *there may be priers near*. "I would have thought you would come over with the emperor for the demonstration ceremony."

"A fortunate development arose." That is the only answer she provides.

The guards carrying Ellie glide past them, and Orsa merely glances at her.

"You care for this human?"

"How could any Ilori care for a human?" M0Rr1S answers, afraid the walls will close in on him and leave him trapped with Orsa. He has to believe his own lie. Orsa was not trained to read or pry into minds, but she is observant. She could be his undoing.

Orsa doesn't answer. "Please, let me give you a tour of our facilities." Her body is rigid, even as it moves aside to make space for him to join her. They ascend the first set of stairs together and emerge in another hall of glass and white.

M0Rr1S finds himself pausing in front of a pair of rooms. A woman in a white gown rocks back and forth on a small blue mattress attached to the wall. In the second room, a short man scratches at the sides of his head, mumbling under his breath. They wear flawless white gowns.

Suffering. The humans here are suffering, cowering from the Ilori that experiment on them. 0rsa doesn't look at them as if they are alive, but dirty and in need of organization and refinement.

"Why," he can't keep himself from asking, "do you keep the humans like…this, behind glass walls?"

0rsa stares at him oddly. "While I don't mind executions, it is easier to operate with fewer guards when the humans are locked up and surveilled. Their bodies are useful to us, nothing else."

"They are living beings." M0Rr1S keeps the anger from his tone. "They deserve their dignity and fair treatment. We have taken everything from them. We have—"

"Careful, Commander M0Rr1S 1lv." She taps the side of her panel. "That could sound like treason. I would find it disconcerting for you to face severe punishment for needless sentiments," she threatens.

M0Rr1S nods, tamping down the desire to argue further. His fist curls at his side. 0rsa turns as if she has won, knowing that Command would believe her before him. That she holds power over him.

As they continue down the hall, M0Rr1S's gaze only registers the occupants behind the windows. Up and over, up and over they walk the halls. 0rsa is silent and M0Rr1S doesn't intend to change that.

"Will you join me in my chambers tonight? I admit, it is unconventional, but I do esteem you in your uniform and rank. And as you said, true Ilori leadership found your actions innovative. Perhaps you will be more innovative in other areas."

It is amazing that, even in Ilori, a dispassionate language, her voice causes dread deep in his gut.

"I will be quite busy with replicating the formula for mass usage. Perhaps another night." It is a confident decline she can admire.

"Yes. Another night." She leans in close. "I am…pleased that you will join me."

He steps back. "Thank you, 0rsa. It pleases me, as well."

"We appreciate your aid." She spins on her heels and ascends one floor higher to her own chambers. She has deliberately disrespected his name and rank, and yet he will do nothing but take his room on the lower floor.

M0Rr1S exhales and opens the door to his assigned lodgings. It's sparsely furnished with basic but functional items designed for Ilori. Ellie is lying on the floor in the corner, like a discarded suitcase.

He stops himself from adjusting her. There are two cameras that hum in little pockets of his room. He must be careful; someone is watching. Darkness continues to fall outside his windows as he crosses the room and places a cushion in front of a camera on the desk. He takes off his jacket and throws it over the closet door in front of the second camera attached to the white metal. And then he allows himself to pick Ellie up and set her down on the bed. She doesn't wake.

He takes the smooth, black rock from his pocket and sets it on the kitchen counter. A slow, deep breath steadies his energy while he focuses. It took 30 percent of his full charge to condense the atoms together, it'll take the same amount to expand them. He pulls at the edges of the molecules with meticulous care until the backpack sits in front of him, every item inside just as he and Ellie left them.

M0Rr1S sighs as the tip of his finger pushes down on his charge status. He was at 100 percent before the drive. Creating an illusion, burning that illusion, shutting Ellie down and then shifting energy again has cost him 70 percent of his charge. He leans the bag against the leg of the couch, out of sight, and takes a fresh, standard uniform that should fit from the closet.

He attends to his hygiene in the bathroom with a long and hot shower equipped with a power hub built into the wall that he can use to wirelessly charge. He scrubs away the dirt of the past few days. By the time he finishes, his energy is replenished, and he feels stronger.

When he steps back into the bedroom, Ellie is awake and sitting up in the bed. He wears nothing but underclothing but feels no desire to dress himself in his stiff uniform just yet.

"Where are we?" Her voice sounds dry, and she refuses to look at him. "Why am I here with you? Why haven't you vaccinated me?"

He runs a second towel through his hair and sets it down on a chair before crossing the room and pouring a glass of calef juice. The glass shakes a little in his grasp as he extends it toward Ellie.

"Drink."

She takes it but eyes it with suspicion.

"It's highly concentrated vitamin juice."

"How do I know it's not a new form of the vaccine or something to put me back to sleep?"

"If I wanted to put you to sleep again, I would not need juice, only a charge." He keeps his voice cold and distant.

Ellie places it on the side table next to her. "I don't trust you."

M0Rr1S huffs and goes back to the kitchen, grabs the bottle of juice and returns to the room. He captures her attention and drinks from the bottle until it's all gone. Her expression changes from dislike to something softer as she regards his bare chest and legs, but still she frowns.

"That proves nothing except that you can drink it without a shirt on."

M0Rr1S fights the urge to smile. "Drink, Ellie."

"Don't call me that," she spits out in anger. "Call me whatever my human number is. We aren't friends." But she takes a small sip from the drink anyway. Her eyes widen as energy streams into her before she quickly chugs the rest.

The glow comes back to her skin, hair and eyes. For the first time since they left the house, he takes in her ripped pants, which are rolled up at the ends and a bit tight across her broad hips, her coat with a bulging button over her breasts and the sorry state of her shoes. He must find her something else to wear.

"What are you looking at?" she snaps, and he is brought back to the moment.

His fingers long to run across the skin of her jaw, and his lips long to feel hers. She is so alluring and warm, but angry. Justifiably. "Clothes, you need clothes and shoes."

"What does it matter anymore? You're going to vaccinate me, right?"

M0Rr1S doesn't answer. He opens a new bottle of juice, refills her glass and hands her a protein bar imported from his home.

Ellie takes them both and finishes in big gulps. "Where am I?"

"A center in Oklahoma." He doesn't dwell on further details. Someone could be listening.

"How long do I have until you give me the vaccine?"

Again, he doesn't answer. There is no answer.

"Why? I want to know why you befriended me. Why you saved my life. Took me with you and offered me your protection. Why you talked to me. Pretended to want to—"

M0Rr1S holds a finger to his lips, eyes rounding for Ellie's benefit. She must know the danger they're in. *"Shhh."*

She shakes her head angrily. "Just tell me why."

"There is no answer that will seem adequate to you." It hurts him to say this, because he wants to answer her questions and tell her a million other things until she trusts and believes him again.

"I don't understand." This time it is less angry, more disappointed, which is worse for him to bear.

He takes a seat next to her on the bed. She flinches away from him.

"You will."

"I'll never forgive you," her voice cracks.

You will, he wishes to say, but doesn't. He can only hope she will.

Ellie is silent for the next hour until she falls asleep. During that time, M0Rr1S re-creates the formula exactly as before on a program set up within his mind. He recalculates the atoms used and their placement, so that he can upload it to Distribution Services—labmade Ilori trained specifically to use their charges, their abilities, to form physical copies of the vaccine expediently. They wait with the same ingredient list M0Rr1S gave them the first time, in centers across the world, ready to create. M0Rr1S shifts on the kitchen stool to steal a quick glance at Ellie while she rests.

He serves a purpose, as all Ilori do. To create the vaccine. But he serves another purpose, too; to implant the chips and write a code, his masterpiece, that will trigger a shift in the consciousness when it's broadcast across Earth through the Il-0CoM frequency. Plans upon plans that required an incredible level of evasiveness, especially inside Il-0CoM.

Glind, M0Rr1S's mother, not only trained and prepared him to read his fellow Ilori minds, but to avoid detection. It takes focus and a level of energy that, if used for too long, can drain his entire charge. Until recently, he played his role without arousing suspicion, never needing to mask his actions. He created the vaccines under surveillance. He did everything required of him. He was the picture of loyalty and compliance... until he landed in New York and then saved Ellie. Now he has a chance to rectify a problem that occurred the moment he left his quadrant.

The vaccines he created were not the ones being distributed to centers across the world. He was not aware that the doctor in New York had changed his formula until they took him to the police station two days ago.

There, M0Rr1S learned that, after he'd left, the Ilori doctor had fixed one minor glitch for all outgoing distributions of the vaccine from the center. He had asked whether the consciousness of the human was still in there. His slip had made things difficult. He'd *known* it was a mistake as soon as he'd asked, but he'd hoped it had been overlooked. It was naive of him to believe it could have been. Optimism had no place in his plans.

The humans already vaccinated still carried the glitch, but the new vaccines were...a problem. So, M0Rr1S had to lie about why he saved Ellie. Why he did not take his pod to the carriership above as planned. He had to guard himself through surface prying, through four separate interrogations, through fatigue and cold. He made himself believe his own lies. And when they cleared him, he connected on a private channel with AvR0la, one Glind had helped him create to avoid detection from true Ilori and Il-0CoM.

M0Rr1S very briefly checked in on Ellie's family, all fine and hidden in permanent housing, then had AvR0la contact cohorts to destroy distribution centers, making it appear as if the human resistance was fighting back. The plan worked. The doctor was incapable and did not have the clearance to re-create the formula, not without M0Rr1S, the lead of Human Services. AvR0la had also managed to invalidate the doctor's work by suggesting that the humans were having negative responses.

Getting captured had inadvertently allowed M0Rr1s to fix his error. It also helped that Brixton had baited him within Il-0CoM to go west and solve the human problem. That one action by Brixton had saved him and his mission. As had those Ilori on the road, allies who'd vouched for him. The true Ilori believed his actions were honorable.

Crisis narrowly averted.

His panel pings, and an invitation to connect to the private channel springs up over his left eye.

AvR0la.

We must be quick, AvR0la's tone is choppy. *I'm taking the humans west. Despite your reinstatement, Inquisition has contacted me regarding a full debriefing in six rotations. I need to disappear by then. And you will have to disable your own connection to Il-0CoM.*

Understood, Avi. M0Rr1S puffs out air as he leans back in his chair. *Are they still safe?*

The humans are fine. The father's part of the half-solutions program and unreachable until the enhancement leaves his system, although he may require reprogramming. The mother experiences mental illness that I may be able to resolve with time and medication. The girl is chatty, and I find myself amused by her. But the real concern is you. You must break into IpS1L. The ship is not safe, and you will have to upload your code and time it for the best possible moment. Our cohorts will be on the lookout for you, guiding your way should you need it. I cannot say if and when I will be in contact again, sir.

You don't have to call me sir, Avi.

Old habits. There's a hint of humor in their voice.

I will do my best. Thank you for everything. I am most grateful for your companionship and support.

Be safe, M0Rr1S. Avoid 0rsa. From the chatter I've received, she is suspicious. Priers lurk to sniff out disloyalty as distribution centers have been attacked by…humans. You are too important.

So are you. We will talk again, I believe that.

After they disconnect, M0Rr1S heads to the labs to give the new formula to the head doctor. "Follow it precisely, and we will not have any issues with production or endangerment to the physical bodies of the humans as the doctor in New York experienced." The lie slips easily from his lips.

Such arduous work. But when it's perfect, it will be worth it.

"Yes, sir."

M0Rr1S pauses in the doorway. "Once you've tested a human, please share your results with me via Il-0CoM."

"Yes, Commander."

"Thank you, Doctor."

M0Rr1S finds the linen closets where clean clothes from the humans are held for further use, namely for the future when Ilori will inhabit the humans and wish to wear something "local." He picks through until he finds a flowery sheath that looks to be Ellie's size, a jean jacket, black leggings, and a pair of boots that should work, although he cannot attest to their comfort. She might hate them, but based on his measurements, these are the only items in good condition that will fit her.

When he arrives in his room, she's still asleep. He opens the windows, letting in light, and prepares a breakfast of toast with vegetable spread, apples, more calef juice and two hard-boiled eggs taken from the farms outside of nearby permanent housing. AvR0la told him once that many Ilori enjoy operating land and farms, as opposed to the centers. They especially enjoy delivering eggs and milk to the humans in the mornings, as a way of apology. M0Rr1S found that fascinating then, but now…he imagines it is a coping mechanism, like Ellie's counting.

He takes off his jacket and balls it up, then tosses it on the couch. The weight of his medals is heavy, and he enjoys the light synthetic shirt he wears underneath that leaves his arms bare.

Ellie awakens with a small yawn and stretches her arms behind her head. He wanted to remove her coat during the night, but she didn't give him permission to touch her, and that would have made her more uncomfortable. But now she's covered in sweat, and her hair sticks to her face. He waits until she sits up before approaching her.

"I have new clothes for you." He places the folded clothes in a pile at the foot of the bed.

"I have clothes." She motions to her current outfit.

"Yes, but your pants are ripped, and the bottom of your shoes are open."

She sets her jaw and turns away.

"The bathroom is just there for showering, and there is breakfast for you in the kitchen." M0Rr1S doesn't wait for her to answer before heading to the couch, where the bag hides. He pulls out a vinyl record, then drops down on the cushion. He closes his eyes while holding the record up by the tops of his fingers, focusing his energy, and lets his fingertips trail across the grooves. The vibrations make the music, although it's very soft, so soft that it's nearly inaudible. It's poetry, rhythm and rhyme, and it's like nothing he's ever heard before. The beat makes him want to move around, and the words are deep and interesting. He likes it.

He is halfway through the third song when Ellie emerges from the bathroom, enveloped in steam with a white towel wrapped around her deep brown skin. Her hair frames her face in a fluffy cloud of corkscrews. She peers at him through her long eyelashes before grabbing the pile of clothes from the bed and disappearing back into the steam.

M0Rr1S smiles to himself. She is so very beautiful.

When Ellie next comes out, she is wearing the leggings,

her old white sweater over the flowery dress and the boots M0Rr1S scrounged up earlier. He admires the way the leggings stick to her form. And her hair—he's only ever seen it briefly without the hat. He likes seeing it down. It makes her look so alive, and young, and…breathtaking.

M0Rr1S steals glimpses of her as she eats. She notices but doesn't say anything. She hates him right now, and he understands. That's the way it's supposed to be.

There's a knock on his door and they both jump. He throws her a worried glance as she takes a sip of the juice.

"Coming!" he says stiffly in Ilori. He stuffs the vinyl under a couch cushion and doesn't bother covering up with his jacket when he opens the door.

"M0Rr1S."

"0rsa."

He senses Ellie shift in her chair.

"The human is here?" 0rsa strides in without invitation. She eyes Ellie with distaste before settling on the dirty breakfast plate on the counter. "Are you feeding it? You are aware that we provide sustenance specifically for their kind?"

M0Rr1S will not rise to her bait. "I am permitted to do as I like. This human has aided me in developing the formula."

"How?"

"Its mother was the first I vaccinated." *Lies.* "The father was part of the half-solutions program." *Unfortunate truth.*

0rsa's eyebrow knit together. "But *how* did it help you?"

"Its bloodwork from the center was used to create and re-create the current vaccine."

0rsa steps closer to Ellie and hovers over her. Ellie's shoulders hunch, but she doesn't turn around to regard 0rsa. Ellie doesn't cower or falter. If she was an Ilori like them, she would be warier of 0rsa. She'd know that 0rsa requires respect, and that her purpose is pain. M0Rr1S reroutes 0rsa's attention, hoping for an adequate distraction.

"Please, leave it be. When it gets hysterical, it no longer serves a purpose and I do need it. In case there are further issues with the vaccine." M0Rr1S keeps his voice light to conceal his worry.

"As you like, Commander." She steps back from Ellie, who holds her head high but her eyes cast downward. "Is it intelligent?" 0rsa switches to English, just to see Ellie's response.

"No," M0Rr1S lies in Ilori. "No humans truly are."

0rsa closes the distance between them and runs her hands down his arms, leaving goose bumps in her wake. "We can make our own entertainment, if it pleases you?"

"0rsa—"

"Are you worried your human will watch?" Her English is effective, and Ellie continues to look away. "We can go up to my chambers?"

"I have provided the formula and await the testing. When the results come back, I will be able to begin the journey home. We will continue our betrothal there."

"I desire your services now." She doesn't pout. Her tone is no different than it is when she's giving orders to the directors of this building, but the words are wrought with demand. He is expected to please her. They're betrothed, and though they are the same, they are not equal. Her labmade generation is older, better received than his.

"We will go upstairs, then." M0Rr1S holds her gaze, establishing a sense of confidence. "I am at your command, 0rsa."

He grabs his jacket and follows her out of the room, leaving Ellie alone.

CHAPTER 15

"Doubt thou the stars are fire;
Doubt that the sun doth move;
Doubt truth to be a liar;
But never doubt I love."

—William Shakespeare, *Hamlet*

JANELLE

Morris left with her. Morris is going to sleep with that monster. Why do I even care? He's a liar, and a monster in his own right. He burned everything I had left. My books. The music. Poor Mrs. Turner's collection.

But why did he make me breakfast? Why did he find me clothes?

I pace around the tiny kitchen, my mind stumbling through this situation. If I had to guess, I'd say these apartments used to be hospital rooms because there are outputs and markings in the walls where I'm guessing large screens and equipment used to be, while the floor gives off the tiny wafts of disinfectant.

The tile floors are covered in white rugs, and the one room has a white couch, a massive potted plant and a chair. The large, open windows reveal the plains and most of the leveled city below. Oklahoma, Morris said. It looks like he was honest about that, at least.

I search the refrigerator for more of that weird juice that makes me feel invincible and chug it from the bottle like Morris did. How long has he been gone? Twenty minutes maybe? Morris will come back, and then what? I stay and get the vaccine?

No. I've waited too long.

The door isn't locked. I could just walk out and pray not to get caught. What do I have to lose? I dash across the room just as the door swings open. Morris steps inside, regarding me with raised eyebrows as he gently shuts the door behind him. "Thinking of leaving?"

I take an uncertain step back. He doesn't wait for an answer.

"Are you ready to go? Because now would be a good time. The vaccines are made. They are being distributed exactly the way I planned, and Orsa is preoccupied." His gaze darts around the room, as if he's figuring something out. "A car is waiting for us downstairs. We have to go."

"I don't want to go anywhere with you!"

Morris doesn't respond. He crosses the room and stoops beside the couch, his eyes glazing over. And then he picks up something off the floor before grabbing his jacket from the closet. He sets the jacket on the counter and stuffs it with packaged foods, fruit and juice. He pulls the edges together and carries it like a makeshift bag.

"Right now, you *should* leave here with me. We'll get out of this city, out of this state, and then you can go wherever you want. Please trust me, just one more time, and come with me."

I blow out a long breath. *Trust.* Do I trust him? I know that if I stay here, Whatever-Her-Name-Is will kill me. The way she looked at me earlier still sends shivers down my spine.

I make a snap decision, stuff my pockets with the protein bars from the cupboard and leave my tattered, too-thin coat behind. I grab my purple hat, which I left drying in the bathroom, and pull it over my head. I feel eerily calm as I return to Morris. "Is it safe?"

"Yes…but momentarily. We need distance."

I don't try to understand, but I'll never turn down freedom.

I follow him down the hall and the fourteen flights of stairs to the bottom. We quicken our pace through the first floor until I notice what we're passing by. I stop and stare at the humans locked behind glass windows and doors, like fish in bowls. I told myself that none of them matter anymore, because I can't do anything for anyone. Just the ones who love me, my patrons. But these people are innocent. Helpless. Not everyone is like the people we lived with back home. These people behind glass don't share my history tainted with hate and judgment in New York. They've done nothing to me.

A little girl with big eyes and skin as dark as mine hides beneath her bed. Feelings rush through me. Everything I shut off, everything that closed up inside me and reminded me I can't change this world cracks open. She can't make her own happy ending, she's not a character in a book. I have to help her.

"She's just a child." My heart sinks. "Can we save them?"

"We will, just not now." He goes to grab my hand, but I pull away.

"Morris, just because you gave me food and clothes and you're keeping me alive doesn't mean I trust you. These humans are trapped. If I leave them, I'm killing them. I'm a traitor. We have to do something."

"Ellie. I'm asking a lot of you, I know this. But please, please believe me. I am saving them. I cannot explain more, not now, but you must—" Morris glances over his shoulder and drops his extended hand. "Orsa."

"You left without saying goodbye." Orsa's clothes are disheveled, and her hair is tangled around her shoulders. She speaks English because she wants me to understand. Why though? I have no idea.

All I know of Orsa is what Morris told me, and how she acted upstairs. She was Morris's first lover—and second, it would appear. And she's not a fan of humans. It's that last part that makes me hate her, although if I'm honest, it's probably all those things. Which is ridiculous, because he's a liar and an Ilori.

I'm going to translate. I'm sorry to not ask your consent first, but I want you to know what we are saying. Morris's voice whispers into my mind, while he speaks Ilori aloud. "AvR0la commed. I'm needed at another center."

"Oh." She walks down the hall and stands before us. "You are taking the human?"

"Yes."

She eyes me with disdain. "I don't understand."

"It will be husked soon. There is little to understand." To me he adds, *It's not true, Ellie. Don't do or say anything, I am violating your privacy, I know, but please stay quiet.*

Orsa leans into Morris. "Humans kiss, did you know this? They press the flesh of their lips together, and it means affection." She looks at his lips. "I personally find humans abhorrent—" she drags the syllable out just for me "—and their world nonsensical. But I am curious to try it. Shall we?"

Morris winces, but I doubt Orsa notices. She wets her lips

with the tip of her tongue and brings her head inches from his. And I should let it go, really. This has nothing to do with me. But I can't.

"Can't you see he doesn't want to?" I blurt.

Orsa pulls back and regards me with a ghost of a smirk. "I told you this human has feelings for you. It's dim-witted and pays no mind to natural order. Is it really worth keeping alive?" She steps closer to me, expecting me to shrink back. I don't. "You should kill it. Now. If you can't, I will."

"Neither of us will kill her. She has helped me, and I will vaccinate her personally." He tosses me a quick glance. *Please, Ellie, don't say anything else. I do not know what she is capable of.*

Orsa narrows her eyes and tilts her head. "Why?" Her tone is flat. But I can read the expression on her face like a book. "Why keep it alive? Why do you travel with it? Let it share your room? Do you know how this looks? For you...for me?"

Morris straightens his posture. Now he responds in English, an edge creeping into his voice. "Orsa, do I answer to you?"

Chills creep up my arms. I instinctively hunch my shoulders. This is not the Morris I've come to know over the past week. Not the Morris I've come to...

Come to what?

I force the thought out of my head, to be reexamined later. Or never.

Orsa clears her throat. "You answer to the Ilori Empire."

"When they question me, I will answer. But for now—" Morris steps between me and Orsa "—I'm leaving. You may check the records before I go to see that it is done, but you may not question my methods. Or you may have someone question yours. There are children in those cells. Children and elders. Already, I've notified Command to remove any that are not primed for the vaccine, clarifying their presence here was a mistake. Imagine if I said it was not?" He stands tall.

"You wouldn't." This time she says it in their language, and Morris translates.

He tugs my hand, and together we walk down the hall. But we aren't free of Orsa just yet.

"They gave you a new assignment and a passcode for a new pod, correct?" She doesn't wait for him to answer. "Since we won't leave together, I wish for you to tie up this human and leave it against the hatch of my pod. It's beside yours, future husband. Her body belongs to us."

"Of course, Orsa," Morris replies without hesitation in Ilori. My mouth nearly flaps open as I stare back at her, but she can't know I understood. She smiles and, for a second, I see flashes of anger, hatred and jealousy in her eyes. Not directed at me—all of this has nothing to do with me—but at him. No matter how much she tries to keep herself from showing it, her feelings have gotten the best of her.

She continues staring as we leave, the glass doors shutting behind us. The air is crisp outside, and I'm grateful to leave that terrible place, though I wish I could have taken the humans with me. Their faces will haunt me for the rest of my life.

Morris leads me to the same nondescript car as before. I jump inside, hoping to quiet my thundering heart before Morris can hear it.

Neither of us says anything. My hands remain in tense fists on my lap. I count anything I can see in my mind, as many times as I can, as hours pass. On my last round, I try to find new things outside my window, even though the landscape is bare and my anxiety is at its peak.

Five, a car. *Four*, an Ilori. *Three…three…focus, Ellie! Three*, the moon. *Two.* I rock back and forth in my seat a little, panting in air. I feel dizzy and hot. *Two. Rein it in. Don't let it win. Two. Deep breaths. In and out. Relax. Sense.*

What do you see? I can hear my therapist's soothing voice

in my mind. I always hear her, never my own voice. *Two*, my boots that squelch on the car mat. *One*, the stars, sparkly and bright. *Zero*, I count because I need it, the dirt-smeared Welcome to Texas sign. We've left Oklahoma.

"Let me out," I demand.

Morris doesn't hesitate. He pulls over the car and turns to me. "Please don't leave. Please, Ellie. Please, you have to believe me…"

"I don't have to do anything." I open my car door and step into the dry heat and early threads of dusk. I have nothing, I am no one and out here I can die by myself. Morris lied—there's no way to save anyone or anything. He gets out of the car and follows me. "I wish I could have my books back. I wish I could have them all back. And Mrs. Turner's vinyl records and her player. I promised her. And you burned them. I wasn't a traitor. You've made me a traitor."

Without a word, he jogs back to the car and pulls a bag—*the* bag—out of the back seat. My mouth opens.

He drops beside me before emptying it. I see little black chips and tiny boxes, but within seconds, they shift and change into their true form. I fall to my knees to hold the books in my hands. He didn't burn them. He didn't destroy them. Why did he lie?

I need them more than anything right now. They are my hopes and dreams and knowledge, my life.

Nearly fifty books surround me. Morris hovers above them. "Janelle—"

"Leave."

"Please, Ellie. I don't want the sun to set on us. If you let me explain—"

"I said leave!" My voice echoes through the dirt and darkness. "I never want to see you again." Bile climbs up my throat, but as I lean over, nothing comes out.

Morris staggers back. His gaze holds mine before he retreats and climbs back into the car. But the car doesn't start. It—and he—lingers on the outside of my periphery and I turn my back, pretending they don't exist. If they do, it means this pain raging through me is real.

Tears finally come as I sit surrounded by my scattered books and a smattering of records. I cry for my mom, my dad, Alice, Earth. Everything. Once it starts, it won't stop. I scream louder than I ever have.

I scream again and again. And then panic sets in—no, not panic—anxiety. An attack this time. My heart is beating uncontrollably. I try to calm my breathing, to focus, but I'm lost in books and darkness. There's a ringing in my ears as the world swirls before my eyes.

Alone.

I'm going to die alone. Far away from my parents. From everything I've ever known. It was always going to end this way, Ilori invasion or not. Every day a struggle to fit in, to be normal, to be this…this *thing* that didn't have anger oozing from its heart, or rage within its soul for every misdeed, every snide comment, every inequality and injustice. For having to work harder, be smarter without letting on how smart I really am, to speak softer, and never, ever be aggressive. And now I'm alone.

There's a wild panic spreading through me as the world around me narrows and darkens at the edges. The numbers don't rise to my lips. They've abandoned me, too. Humanity trapped behind glass walls. Everyone will be gone. The world will forget we once ruled it. I never wanted to care. I made myself believe I couldn't anymore. That caring only sets you up for disappointment. But I do care, and there is nothing I can do to change that.

Time. It fades in and out. *Darkness. Alone.*

And then Morris is beside me.

"Breathe." His voice is steady despite my storm. His hand falls gently onto the middle of my back, spread-out. Fingers. Five. Four. Three. Two. One. Tapping with slight pressure, one after the other. Over and over again. The numbers. He knows. My brain picks them up, focuses on them. *Fivefourthreetwoone...fivefourthreetwoone...*

"I can't breathe," I cry out, gasping. My vision blurs.

"Yes, you can. In and out. Feel it, Ellie." His hand presses harder, steadying the shakes that make my shoulders heave.

I clutch my books against my chest, and still the tears fall. *In and out. Yes.* My lungs fill, but I swear my heart is beating in my throat. "I can't do this anymore."

"Just keep breathing." Morris doesn't let go, doesn't move. I don't want him to either.

His touch reminds me of a time when Alice found me after the mother and daughter were taken outside our building. She found me lying there and held me in her arms, her fingers on my back like Morris's are now. "*Five*, you have me and I smell like Chanel. Don't glare at me, you know you love it," she laughed. "*Four*, these tacky tennis shoes, all scuffed and flimsy. God, I hate them. *Three*, the air coming through the crack in the door, it sounds like a windstorm in a tunnel, right? I know that's weird, I'm learning. *Two*, my warm hand on your back. I'm here for you.

"*One*, you, Ellie. You are the best person. Even when you're judgy and you like literally no one else, and the way you hate it when I say *literally* too much. Your heart is so big and beautiful. You're my best friend."

I close my eyes and remember her, that moment. She was my lifeline, and in this moment, so is Morris. For better or worse.

"I'm sorry, Ellie. I'm sorry for not telling you how much

I loved the way you sang 'Raspberry Beret' to me," he says gently near my ear. "You make me feel, and I couldn't show anyone. I couldn't let them see."

He's quiet for another pause. "You're music to me. You're 'Yellow' by Coldplay, and 'As' from *Songs in the Key of Life* by Stevie Wonder—what a great name."

I look over at him through shaky breaths.

"These are all the songs that make me think of you, that I want to sing to you. All the songs that would be on the record if we were an album. And there are more. So many more. I just don't know them yet." His hazel eyes glance my way. How are they so bright even in the darkness? "I don't know why you count things when you're upset, but I know why you cry. I know you hate me right now. But if I don't tell you the truth, the music will stop and never play again. And your stories… I need your stories."

My head falls forward, and I close my eyes and breathe. *In and out. In and out.* "Tell me."

"I engineered the vaccine."

I groan in anger.

"I had to." His voice rises over mine in desperate need to get the words out. "Even as we speak, the vaccines will cross over this country and be administered all over Earth."

Disgust threads through my stomach and I feel sick again. "Why?"

"You need to know, Ellie." He takes a deep breath. "I made them imperfect."

My head shoots up. "What?"

"The vaccine is supposed to shut off the brain, stop the electricity but keep the body alive. It's like…" He pauses. "If the human brain is a book, the vaccine hides the words, leaving blank pages. On a brain scan, it will look like there is no activity, no residual fragments of memory. That the human is shut down and prepared for implantation.

"But the words, the story...is still there. Inside each inoculation, there's a chip. Three millimeters big. This chip includes the frequency upload for Il-0CoM. The true Ilori share energy and live forever through Il-0CoM. That is how true Ilori will transfer their consciousness into the humans."

I furrow my brows, trying to follow, but I'm not sure I understand, and my brain's not used to having to think too hard anymore.

"Once a human is injected, their essence, personality, thoughts, memories flock to the empty chip and sink into a chamber I've left inside. I've given them the perfect vaccine with desired results. Doctors have no reason to believe it will not work as expected. No reason to suspect. The chips were always part of the plan."

My mouth falls open and shut twice before I can respond. "What does that mean? Really mean?"

"The humans...they're asleep. They don't have control, but they're still in there. Waiting to be reactivated by a code."

I think I feel sick. "How do you know it'll work?"

"It's been tested before." He glances at the clouds roving across the sky. "Glind, my mother, experimented with it on me when I was a child. I was the only labmade with the right anatomy whom she could trust then. She wanted me to be human. She encouraged it, for this purpose. That is why I did not need live experimentation. I already had half the formula."

A strangled sound escapes my lips. I don't know what to do with that information. Where to begin. His own mother... "How are you going to...activate the code?"

He exhales slowly and glances up at the sky. "In California, there's a ship, IpS1L. When humans struck at us, that ship, along with two others, crashed to the ground. It has been abandoned as a tomb as it lies close to Andarran land. Ilori aren't allowed near Andarran land—there's a treaty that, if broken, could be grounds for war. But the systems may still be intact. They could connect to Ilori command, to the center hub and the physical Il-0CoM.

"You see, all Ilori, both true and labmade, have Il-0CoM. We can share energy, we communicate. But like human computers, like your 'cloud,' we need servers to back up information, to hold large quantities of data.

"IpS1L is the only way I can upload my song into the Ilori servers to broadcast it around the world. Once it's uploaded, set to a timer and broadcasts, it will activate the humans. Any Ilori transplanted inside a human body will die."

The world seems to spin around us. Die? Activate? Morris did this, all of this. And he's been keeping this secret for two years. How?

My mouth feels dry and chalky, but breathing becomes easier. "Why?"

"It was the only way for all of us to get what we want." His tone is soft but determined. So very Morris. "We—some labmades and an underground resistance of true Ilori dissenters—have come to realize we're all trapped in Il-0CoM. Freedom means revolution. We will need the humans, we will need anyone we can find, to destroy the Ilori Empire."

I shake my head, my back straightening as realization sinks in. "You want a war, like a *Star Wars* kind of war." I picture the ships, great battles and alien races. The death. And then I remind myself that *Star Wars* is an epic story with a happy ending. This is real life. There are no Jedi, only me and Morris, humans and Ilori. Nothing is guaranteed.

Morris drags a hand across his forehead, and suddenly I can see how tired he is, how keeping this to himself has taken a toll on him. "Earth was never going to be spared. Either they were going to kill humans or use you until you were no longer useful. Like the labmades…like me. Rebellion was a plan before I was even created. But with Earth, the leaders of the resistance, including my mother, saw an opportunity and decided now was the time. To save Earth and humanity, we would first have to let the true Ilori believe they had won, that they were in control. Lives would be, and still will be, lost in pursuit of freedom for both our kinds. But those lives… they were nothing to how much more would have been lost if we didn't try.

"I was born into this life, it was never my choice. Duplicity was always to be my role, but it was never who I am."

"What's the plan?"

He turns to me, the corner of his mouth lifting. "Acquisitions goes home once all of the humans are captured and vaccinated, which will be anytime now. Habitation and building continues, but they're nearly complete. Within days, Earth will be completely formatted for true Ilori. The New York we left just days ago is already gone. Cities and continents across the world are ready for their arrival. I can already smell the shift in the air, in the atmosphere.

"Everything will be compliant with Ilori systems, the centers will transition to spas, where Ilori can leave their shells behind and upload into human hosts. First there will be a test, a demonstration among the lower-ranked true Ilori. When satisfied, the emperor and leadership will transfer their consciousness into human husks. When they do, my song will broadcast into their systems, on the Il-0CoM frequency. I'll be killing the Ilori emperor, leadership, and the first of the 1lv line. My family."

There's a sadness to him now. Guilt.

"But I will save you, Ellie, and your parents, Alice…all

of them. All of us labmades. I will do whatever I can while I can."

I try to root out the one detail that hasn't been said. "What'll happen to you if you succeed?"

"True Ilori leadership, my brother most likely, will take me to my father, and he will end my life. But it will all have been worth it. Allies from other Ilori colonies will come to Earth, and the labmades will stay to stand beside the humans. To fight for freedom. I will have played my role."

I gasp, my hand covering my mouth. Success means he'll die?

"If I fail, we all fail. My mother's life, my fellow labmades, humans, you...depend on my code, my song. That's why I must succeed." He gives me a bittersweet smile. "I made my own music, Ellie. Music to destroy. It was my way of show- ing the true Ilori, my father, who I am. That they might have created me, but they cannot control me. And when my mis- sion is complete, they *will* capture me."

The edge of his hand touches mine, but he doesn't grasp it. "I can't take you with me all the way to the ship. It's too dangerous. I..." He scrubs his chin. "I am sorry for every- thing. For taking you this far, for Orsa. For the vaccine. For everything I made you feel. The distrust. I am truly sorry."

There's still ringing in my ears and I shake my head to clear it. "You did all of this?"

"Not all, no, but some. I'm not that smart and I'm not a natural leader. Communication is limited, so I don't know most of who work against our empire. It's best I don't. All I know is that I'm the only labmade that could create the code and upload it to our systems. The other rebels will make sure it's broadcast at the right time if I cannot."

I try to wrap my mind around everything he's just told me. "You vaccinated humans to save them. You didn't want to kill us. You had a plan." The truth is a beautiful, dangerous thing, but part of me is grateful to know it. To know that the end is not as near as I thought.

"I couldn't stop the deaths. I'm sorry, Ellie. I tried. But I can do something for those still living and in captivity. It is my gift to share. My mother created me for this purpose. She made me understand my emotions, let me experience them. I think... Part of me imagines she did this so that my father would hate me, and that would lead me to coming here, to rebel against him. I was never going to earn the 1lv name, never going to be a proper Ilori." He sniffs. "Knowing I'll change the universe is how I cope with my guilt for what I've done. For humans, labmades, your mother, Alice, your father. Your center. This world."

I stare at him, my cheeks wet with tears. "Why didn't you tell me before?"

"If we got caught, they could hurt you to get the truth. I didn't want you to experience that. And I never wanted to upset you. When we were captured outside of that store... the only thought I had was to protect you. I tried, Ellie. I've been carrying this with me, alone, for too long. It is time for the truth.

"We were brought to that center because I made a mistake in New York. I asked a question I shouldn't have. I was rattled and nervous. The doctor compromised my vaccine, and I needed to cover my error and continue with production and distribution. I had my part to play, and now I'm nearly done. I'm nearly free."

I let that sink in for a moment. "Did you know Whatever-Her-Name-Is would be there?"

"Orsa?" He shakes his head. "No. She caught me by surprise."

"Did you...?" I look up at him through my eyelashes.

"Did I have intercourse with her?" Morris asks with raised eyebrows. "Does it matter to you?"

I gulp in air, rubbing the palms of my hands against my knees. "I just—I want to know."

His eyes follow my movements. "No. But I violated her privacy to make her think we were going to. I may not be able to read or implant thoughts into human minds, but I can to other Ilori."

I frown in confusion.

Morris shoves his hands into his pockets and shrugs. "When she realizes that I implanted images into her mind, I will face a new set of problems. That's illegal."

"Why did you do it then? Why didn't you just have fun with her?"

"Because I have a heart, and it belongs to you. And I have a body that wishes only to be near yours."

Butterflies swarm around my stomach and my heart flips. *Calm down.* "You don't know me that well."

"I feel like I do." He moves closer to me with an earnestness in his eyes. "But I wish to know you more. In whatever time we have left. I feel like we…we have a bond. You and I."

"You've known me a week."

"It's been nine days, Janelle."

"This isn't like the stories I've told you, Morris. Where people fall in love in one day and everything works out. Those aren't real. They're just stories. You're an Ilori and I'm human, we're going two different ways," I point out.

"I didn't mention love or falling in love. I mentioned my heart."

"It was implied," I huff despite the butterflies in my stomach. "I'm still mad at you."

"I know. But I still like you."

I snort.

"Do you still like me?" Morris's eyes glow through the falling darkness, and in them there's both hope and despair.

"What does it matter? You're going to California to save Earth and humanity. I can go home and wait." I shrug.

"No, Ellie." Morris runs his fingers through the tall grass beside us. "You will die if you travel home now. Orsa will look for you, she will hunt you. Your existence plagues her. If you somehow defy the odds, you will get vaccinated. Do you want that?"

I exhale. "No." That sort of lack of control, I wouldn't choose that. And if I die, never seeing my parents again... "But where else can I go?"

"Come with me, and along the way, we'll find somewhere safe. When the humans come back, when they are free, you can help them. You can tell them what the future will bring. This is your chance to change everything."

"I don't know." I let the breath whoosh out of me. It's time to admit my truth, too. "I don't know if I'm the right person for that. Up until the hospital back there, I didn't even think most humans were worth saving. I want to save my family. I want to save that little girl behind the glass. But part of me worries that if everyone and everything goes back to the way it was, we'll just destroy each other again. I know that's horrible."

His eyebrows knit together, but he doesn't ask me to explain. "It's not horrible, Ellie. To think and feel and experience and doubt means you are alive. And it is your decision to make." We fall into a heavy silence that seems to last forever until his fingers touch the edges of mine. "Do you still like me?"

I stamp down the feelings floating around inside of me. "I don't know."

He smiles, lifting the mood. "If you had said no, it would have hurt."

"'I don't know' could mean either."

"I believe, Janelle Baker, human and collector of books, that you will like me again."

I sigh and stack my books by my sides. Anger wears me out, and I've spent the last day and a half angrier than words. Morris isn't my enemy. His people are, and while he could have told me the truth sooner, I understand why he didn't. If our roles were reversed, I would have done the same. But I'm not completely over it. Not yet.

"Are there other things you're not telling me?" I ask.

Morris helps me gather my books. "Oh, there is plenty I haven't told you, but not because I'm withholding it. There isn't enough time. And nothing that changes your world quite like this."

"Have you listened to the Starry Eyed yet?" I ask. He shakes his head. "There's an old phone in your bag. We should listen to one of their albums and eat."

"Really?" His eyes are round and brilliant in the moonlight.

"Really."

"That sounds like a good idea. And Ellie?" He holds my gaze. "I've never liked anyone as much as I like you. I don't want to… I don't know the right words, sometimes. Give me a moment." He runs a hand through his hair. "I don't want anything to come between us again. I'm sorry."

I bite my lower lip, trying not to smile or let my heart loose. His words make me happy, but I'm not ready for that. "Just get the car and let's drive. This is the farthest west I've ever been. I doubt my parents ever saw Texas. I always sorta wrongly thought of it as a super patriotic, weird kind of place. But the sky is brighter here. The stars…" I'm rambling. My emotions are a jumble, and my heart settles one moment only to race the next.

The truth of what he's told me finally clicks into place, and I understand now more than I did before. The situation is all sorts of fucked-up. To save everyone, he has to temporarily erase them. The "what-ifs" rattle around my mind as Morris picks up the books and races with them back to the car.

Morris is trying to save humanity. He will sacrifice everything, including his life, to free us all. Morris, this beautiful alien boy who loves music and who says his heart belongs to me. Morris, who puts me at war with myself and tangles my emotions more than ever.

"May I?" he asks, holding an arm out for me to take.

"May you what?"

"Carry you across this world while I can?"

I never know the right answer with him. He wears his emotions on his sleeve, and I don't want to be the one to tell him to hide them again. He's free with his words, he feels no shame in them—maybe because he could never own them before.

"You may," I answer, before he takes my arm and pulls me closer. His eyes lock on to mine, and he scoops my legs from under me.

"I like you so much, but you humans move so slow." And then he takes off with me in his arms. The world around us blurs, and I feel weightless. He's so fast that I'm not sure his feet ever touch the ground.

He sets me down in the passenger seat, and I've barely adjusted to sitting up when he's already in the other side and speeding through the open plains.

"Let's find the best view."

PART THREE

THE WORLD IS OURS

THE GOOD MORNING SHOW

Transcript of the interview with hosts Mel Kendell "M.K." and Tracy Summer "T.S." Rae

Guests: Cecil Wright, Allister Daniels, Whisper Landsome, Rupert Montague

ANNOUNCER: *The Good Morning Show* comes to you live from New York City's Time Square. Special guests include the band the Starry Eyed, who will be performing from their new album *The Sound of Stars*. Here now are hosts Mel Kendell and Tracy Summer Rae.

Gratuitous audience applause

M.K.: Good morning, America! Today, we're here with the Starry Eyed. Guys, we're honored to have you on here to talk about your new album. But first things first—where do you get your costumes? These are gorgeous, and glittery. And Allister, your cape is art.

Allister Daniels: *(laughs)* Thank you! It's important that we pay homage to our culture, which celebrates colors and individuality.

T.S.: That's so important and we've always wanted to know, where do you all call home?

Rupert Montague: Earth, of course.

Audience laughter and applause

Cecil Wright: Rupert's just being cheeky! It doesn't really matter where we come from…we met when we were young and mashed our cultures together, and we chose how we wanted to represent that.

M.K.: All this time, people have been speculating on your accents and looks and…

Allister Daniels: Time, I think, better spent just enjoying our music.

Whisper Landsome: What really is time, anyway? *(laughs)*

T.S.: It's funny you should ask that. When you debuted, you were teenagers, what, fourteen and fifteen? Now, a few years later, we've seen you grow up before the world. Young, talented, smart and lacking major scandals. Role models. Your music is often compared to Coldplay, and M83 as your sound evolved into more dreamlike, more beautiful, less pop—

Rupert Montague: It's dream pop. And we'll certainly take the comparisons to M83 and Coldplay, both bands are definitely our inspirations.

Allister: Speak for yourself, Rupert!

Whisper Landsome: We've grown up in front of cameras. Instead of losing ourselves to fame, we stayed focused on our…work, on each other as a family, and our music matured with us.

Cecil Wright: We're lucky we can make music together, and we'll keep doing it while we can.

Allister: Absolutely. We know our purpose, and we've stuck to that.

M.K.: And what's that? What's your purpose?

Allister: To save the world with music and love, obviously.

CHAPTER 16

"Just Like Heaven"
—The Cure

MORRIS

They're sitting on the hood of the car when his hand brushes against hers. She opens her fingers to let his in, and they stay like that for what seems like eternity. The stars shimmer above them in the clear sky, illuminating the crumbs from the impromptu picnic scattered between them. They should be on the road, finding a place for her to stay while he embarks on the dangerous road to IpS1L. But one glance at Ellie, and he's not ready for that. Not yet. What if he'll never be?

"Are you the first aliens to come to Earth?"

"No." He tries to keep from smiling at her expression. "There are others. More peaceful races that inhabit small corners of this world. We have treaties with them, allowing them to stay here."

"Really?" She props herself on her elbows with her mouth open. "Who are they? Where are they? How many? What do they look like? What if I know them?"

"No, now it's my turn to ask a question." M0Rr1S lets his back sink deeper into the roof of the car. "What happened to you that made you ready to give up humanity? I know this is a personal question. But it startled me, and I must know how this world has hurt you."

Suddenly she looks tired. "Years before all of this——" she waves her hand at the nothingness surrounding them "——my mom, dad and I lived in Brooklyn. We didn't have much, but I liked my school, I liked my library, I liked my life. I remember our apartment in Flatbush, and the roti with red beans around the corner. We were happy. *I* was happy. But then Mom's aunt died and left us this apartment. Dad quit his job to work closer to our new home."

"At the center?" M0Rr1S asks.

"Yeah. And for a while, everything was okay. My mom finished school at Columbia. I got to play the cello at a performing arts school across town. Dad started working down the street at a prestigious academy. We had more money than ever. But somehow, it seemed overnight, we weren't happy anymore. Mom started drinking, at first just a little with dinner. Dad got angrier. He never said why, but I think students and their parents complained about him and his 'otherness.' Mom took a job as a professor, but she seemed... I don't know, exhausted." Her shoulders slump. Sadness spreads through her eyes. "We would watch the news, and it was all terrible. Black kids like me, gunned down or missing. One after another. And it seemed like no one cared. There was no justice.

There was this…this mixture of defeat and anger." Her expression slackens.

"Politics became shameful. Soon it was like everyone felt free to do something about all the irrational hate they had inside of them. I went to the grocery store one day after school, and this man pushed me out of line and called me an animal, said I didn't belong where I was. All of these people stared at me. But no one said or did a thing. And it happened again and again. Not just to me…to everyone who was different.

"My mom lost her job from the drinking. My dad took a pay cut. Money became tight. Mr. Hughes—that was one of the other people living at the center—had the board of directors threaten us with eviction. I was the smartest in my class, but my grades were falling. Nobody wanted me there, and I couldn't concentrate. The news told us—people like me— that we didn't matter anymore. When I asked why, no one could tell me…that's when we became afraid. People in the government agreed with the hatred. We were scared to walk around the Upper East Side." She shakes her head. "Everyone said they were on our side, but even after everything my mom and dad did for the community, when it started to get worse, they disappeared. The nationalists felt empowered, creeping out of the most liberal cities in America. There'd been attacks and police brutality. They could do whatever they wanted, and with politicians behind them, there was nothing anyone could do to stop them. Everyone was scared, upset, shocked. But no one stuck up for us—us, who were being picked off one by one. Outside of our building, it was chaos, there was nowhere to go anymore for anyone who is—*was*—different. Nowhere safe. And our neighbors wanted us out. They seemed to hate us." Her breath catches. "I'll never understand why. We didn't do anything. We just lived. They took our security and our peace of mind. But it wasn't enough. I—" Her voice cracks, as if her truth is lodged somewhere within her.

M0Rr1S grips her hand tighter. "I'm sorry, Ellie. When I look at you, I don't see someone who is lesser, or who doesn't matter. You matter. And you are strong."

"You don't see it because you aren't like them." She turns to him. "Before this week, humanity as a whole didn't seem like it deserved saving. I had to stop caring about others outside of my life, others like me, because it was easier that way. I was too powerless to change the world. But now…those humans in the cells. That little girl. I wanted to save her. I wanted to save them all." She's quiet for a few beats before continuing, "We were always so divided, and never learned how to unite, even when you, the Ilori, came. I wonder now if we can. Like you and the labmades."

He brings the back of her hand to his lips and kisses it, but lets a silence span between them before responding. "The Ilori are just as divided. How you are born and who you are born from matter. Labmades were created to be inferior. We were made to serve. I may carry a prominent last name, but if I did not, I would not be a commander. I would not have created the vaccine, played my intricate role, or be here with you right now. My last name is the only thing saving me from instant death. From what I know of true Ilori, they are not worth saving. But the labmades are. We did not choose this life. The true Ilori will make more of us, use us to acquire everything, take our energy and then, when we stop being useful, they'll destroy us."

M0Rr1S inhales the salty night air. "Sometimes when things are too broken to fix, we replace them. Our worlds have changed and are ever-changing. But we have power, you and I…we have our books and music. It's what brought us together. Your book gave me strength—imagine what it could do for other labmades…

"If we can do this impossible thing, perhaps together, we can do many impossible things. We can make this world, any world, what we want it to be. Me with my song, you with your knowledge and determination to not let things go back to what they were."

She purses her lips. "I want to go with you to California. You said it yourself—there is nowhere safe anymore for humans. And you're right, together, we can do impossible things. We can upload your song, broadcast it at the right time. I can help you. Like that time on the road when the two of us stepped between the Ilori and the humans."

"You almost died, Ellie."

"But I didn't, because you were there. And you didn't die because I distracted them. I might not have powers and abilities like you, but I'll look out for you. I can help. You can't do everything alone. If we fail, at least we'll be together, at least we won't die alone. No one dies alone." She gazes at him. "I want to see my family, but I want them to come back, to be human again. They deserve to live in a world where they don't have to be afraid anymore, not of aliens or…or other humans. Where everyone is equal. Where everyone has the same chances." Her breath comes in pants, and her heart races. "So, I'm going with you, to the end."

"If you die, Ellie…"

"Then I will have died free. And with my friend."

"Ellie," he mutters, uncertain what to say.

"Don't think I'm not afraid. I'm terrified. But I won't sit back and let someone else decide my future. I want to be a part of that. Okay?"

The corner of his mouth lifts as if a smile wishes to break free but remains unsure. He doesn't know what to say. The fear of losing her grips his heart, but there is nowhere safe for her anymore. Which is better? To lose her on his mission meant to save her and her people, or to leave her somewhere and lose her anyway?

"I want you to see your family again, Ellie. And there is still time to decide if you want to change the world. You always have a choice." He clears his throat. "You asked me a question before, about how many aliens there are in this universe. There are many races and planets in the universe, but to tell you everything would take a very long time." And time is something they are constantly short of.

She settles back on the hood of the car. "Well, then I get another question. How many planets are there?"

M0Rr1S cuts Ellie a sideways glance. "More than anyone can count, and new ones form and old ones perish too often to keep track."

"Tell me about the prettiest world." Her voice is breathy in the fresh Texas air.

"There is a world—" he opens his eyes, seeing through space and the darkness of nothing "—seven systems away that has five moons. When night falls, each moon glows a different color like a rainbow. In Ilori, we call it PR2-57-lu-96, but the chosen name is Andarra. There is no concept of time there—no future or past. All is known. And the people—the Andarrans—are the kindest people I've ever met in my life. The Andarrans live by a philosophy—whatever makes you different makes you powerful. I like that.

"The grass is a shade of green that I don't believe exists anywhere else, and you can travel by boat through little rivers all over their world. Below the crystal clear waters, there are fish that chase your boat and kiss your fingers when you let them. They are called the Jadu, and are considered sacred in the Andarran culture. They are so big and your first instinct when you see them is to be scared, but they won't hurt you. Their kisses mean something like destiny. It's beautiful."

She turns her head to his. "Did a Jadu kiss your fingers?"

"Yes. It was…remarkable. More than remarkable. I can't even describe it."

Ellie's gaze travels back to the stars. "Will you go back

there, if you succeed?" There's a wistfulness in her now that he enjoys.

"If we succeed, will you go there with me?" He raises his hand and gently runs his fingers down her jaw. He loves the way she feels like contradictions. Strong but soft, smooth but hardened by a life of adversity. When he first met her, he thought she was stone. She had to have been, to risk her life for a library. But now she lets him see her, truly see her. There is pain, suffering and sadness simmering beneath her surface, but there's also something else…something maybe she sees within him every time her eyes land on his.

She doesn't answer. Just angles her head back. "You've seen so many places."

"Yes, but never for fun." M0Rr1S snuggles closer.

Her voice is quiet, measured. "If I went with you one day, despite every obstacle in our path, would it ever be safe for us?"

"I will make it safe."

She's quiet again, and he wishes that he could read her mind. He wants to tell her not to worry so much. That everything is going to be okay one day. Yet, those are lies. "Tell me about the ugliest planet you've ever been to."

"There is one that is always dark. It has no sun or water. The beings that thrive there are monstrous. It is dangerous and terrifying. And cold." He shivers thinking of it. "I won't go back there."

"Tell me about the coolest place in the universe."

He shakes in silent amusement, and ponders what will seem most interesting to someone who knows only Earth. "There is a realm formed between three planets where there is an opposing gravitational pull. Thus, depending on which planet you enter the realm from, you will see people walking perpendicular to you on two sides like a triangle. You can buy fruit from a market across the realm that must be weighted for delivery.

It's hard to explain, but it's amazing. There's nothing else like it in the universe."

"Tell me—"

"You have asked many, many questions. And I will not tell you about any more places, because you will travel there with me, and we will see these worlds together. I will not spoil this for you." He's resolute. He likes the dream of them together, Earth saved, her parents happy and healthy, and the two of them traveling the universe, even if they remain only friends.

"Morris—"

"Ellie."

She huffs. "All right, then tell me about why sex with Orsa was horrible."

"Janelle," he groans.

Ellie cocks her head. "Oh, too touchy a topic? Hmm, want to go back to discussing the universe?"

"Actually, I'd like to discuss the Starry Eyed, if you don't mind." The corners of her lips rise, scrunching her nose. He won this battle. "That song that you said was your favorite, what was it called?"

"'Lost With You.' Although, 'Everything' is beautiful as well, so they're tied in first place."

He recalls the words. *"I never wanted to see you cry out in pain. The fault is mine, I'm covered in shame… I know it hurts, but I can explain. I shout, you weep, I lie, you speak… The truth,"* he sings. "It's very relevant to our situation."

She turns her head toward his again with a small giggle. "You think?"

"Well, it's about the singer breaking another's heart, and trying to gain their love's trust again, right?" His eyebrows rise, and he studies her face.

Ellie's eyes sparkle. "It starts off with their dirty boots because they're burying secrets. I always took that to mean that whatever the heartbreaker did, they are both trying to get over it. And so the singer—the heartbreaker—is telling their love that they will never do it again. That it killed them inside to hurt them, and that they mean everything."

"Yes, see? That's us! We've listened to that whole album, and every song was about us." M0Rr1S lets his head fall back against the windshield close to Ellie's.

"I guess, in a way, parts of it could be applied to our weird relationship. Maybe. But these things are also universal, I bet," she admits.

"Universal," he laughs. How true is that? He rolls to his side and asks the most important question that has been on his mind for as long as he can remember. "Love is in every story and in every song. In theory, I know what it is, but what does it feel like?"

She purses her lips. "Love is…it feels like, hmm." Her fingers pick at a strand of unraveled thread from her sweater. "It's affection and wanting to be with someone… I think I read somewhere that love is the connection of two hearts."

M0Rr1S is quiet for a moment. "But hearts cannot feel or connect, no matter how we wish they could."

"Well, don't take it quite so literally," she says, with the corner of her mouth raised. "I'd imagine it's the connection of two minds, too. That seems more plausible anyway, since you're right, hearts only function."

He considers it. "When I'm connected to Il-0CoM, there are so many minds connected to mine. And that's not love."

Ellie's lips scrunch together. "It's really weird," she says, bemused. "But Allister Daniels—he's the lead singer of the Starry Eyed, said that love feels transformative. If music is a story, it comes alive with love. The more love it has, the more likely the story will never end."

"See? Further proof that this band and their music is for us." He smiles. "Love transforms. I like this."

Her eyes flick to his and he feels a warmth spread through him. "Don't you have love where you're from?"

"Love is an abstract concept that's never discussed. True Ilori get married, share energy and, if they should choose, they take strands of their genetic material to create a new being. There is no love. Only respect and compatible programming."

She lets out a chuckle. "That sounds so…alien. What about labmades? What were you supposed to do with Orsa?"

"Orsa and I would have gotten married, shared energy, lived our lives and died. We can have intercourse, but we cannot make new beings organically. Labmades are traditionally made to serve and expire when we no longer can."

She stiffens beside him. "You'll die when you can't serve?"

M0Rr1S shakes his head. "My life was created to be similar to a human life, to yours. I am made of electrical currents, organs, blood, emotions… I can feel pain. I can dream when I sleep, although, with proper charge, I don't require sleep. I was born, I have grown, I will age and then I will die."

"I'm sorry."

"Don't be. I'm Ilori and, sometimes, it feels like I'm human, too. I'm of two worlds."

She gives him a small smile as silence falls between them. Has he made her uncomfortable? The need to hear her voice overwhelms him. That can't be it. He reaches over and touches the edge of her purple hat, warming as her heart rate picks up at the sudden contact.

"Have you always worn this?"

The moon shines in her eyes. "It's my purple crown," she laughs. "A few months before the invasion, my dad bought it for me at this little booth under the Brooklyn Bridge. I sorta fell in love with it and haven't stopped wearing it since. It reminds me of the Starry Eyed's 'Fairy-tale Girl.' It's about a girl who wears this purple crown and has to keep her stories hidden—at least I think that's what it's about. Anyway, I know that's weird, but this hat is like my security net. It makes me feel safe, and… It's hard to explain."

"It's so…vibrant. Like you." He slides off the hood and extends an arm to her. *"She's got glitter. Yeahhhh, she sparkles and shines in my sky. I want to hold her close, I want to look her in the eyes… Shining so bright but I can't look away."* His voice wobbles and the notes are short, but she beams up at him through her eyelashes.

"We've only listened to it once. How do you remember all the lyrics?" Ellie props herself on one elbow, color flooding her cheeks.

He shrugs, inviting her again. She glances at his hand once more before she takes it.

They stand close together. M0Rr1S is briefly unsure what he should do or can do. But then he pulls her into a hug and dances with her. *"Promise this is more than it seems. My starry dreammmmmms."*

"This world… It's bigger than the two of us, but it's really only them and us…and I want them all to know my star, I'll never let her go." This is the moment. A big moment. Her heart is slow and steady, and he appreciates that. It means she's comfortable, maybe she even trusts him again.

"Janelle Baker."

"Don't tell me you like me again," she says quietly, the corners of her lips quirking upward.

"But why not?"

"Because it makes me nervous." She exhales. "And before you ask me again if I like you, the answer is yes. It was always yes, even though I tried not to."

His own heart races, suddenly. She likes him. *Him.*

He feels like he's walking on clouds and holding a star in his arms.

She likes him, even if she didn't want to. He understands. Would he not feel the same way if he were human and she, an Ilori, destroyed his world? He is asking her for too much—yet he can't stop himself.

"I never imagined someone like you would exist, or that I would find you." He pauses, trying to contain the truth, but it bursts through anyway. "I've listened to a thousand songs, and those—they made me feel something. *You* make me feel something. I don't want to live in a world without you in it. I *can't* live in a world without you in it."

"You're ridiculous. You know that, right?" Her voice is small but her eyes are big, and beautiful.

"If someone meant everything to you, would you waste time pretending they didn't?"

"I don't know, Morris." She pulls back, but not away.

"I know," he replies, his own heart pounding. "But I have this feeling deep in my chest that is both warm and cold at the same time. It makes me feel like I could jump over walls and swim in the ocean, although I don't know how to swim. It makes me feel like I could do things beyond imagining." The slight breeze cools his face. "Hope."

The stars are in her eyes that crinkle at the edges.

"I have hope, Ellie." He takes her hand in his and lifts his head to the sky. "Hope doesn't rid me of the fear, but it changes it, and so I must say that despite our circumstances, the danger and the terror I feel taking you with me when it may very well be the last thing either of us do, anything can happen."

"Morris, I—" she starts but doesn't finish. "What do we do now?"

"We go to California. And we continue to hope."

"Oh, is that all?" She laughs, her chest heaving.

"No one is looking for me, yet." *They will soon.*

"So, it's safe for now?"

"For now," he answers. As long as he doesn't enter Il-0CoM and AvR0la stays under the radar.

"I've never been to California." It's dark and he doubts she can see much, but she looks west as if she can.

"We have to go. Time doesn't stand still, even for us." M0Rr1S doesn't drop her hand and instead turns to her. "Janelle, may I?"

"May you what?"

"Kiss you?"

She hesitates. "No. Not yet. I'm too…nervous." She shakes her head. "I can't…not right now."

"Ellie, I will wait to kiss you until the end of our time together if you ask it."

"I—" She looks away, her cheeks pink despite her dark pigment. "I don't think I could wait *that* long."

"Good, because I'm not sure we have that much time either." He opens the car door for her. "You can sleep, as reaching our destination will still take a while."

"I'm not tired yet." She shrugs before sliding into the car. He walks around and gets in the other side.

"Would you tell me another story?" M0Rr1S's eyebrows lift in anticipation, but he tries not to show too much excitement.

The sun is in her smile and the stars still in her eyes. "Would love to. What kind of story?"

"Any story read by you will be my favorite."

"You're a bit of a hopeless romantic, Morris." She twists in her seat, getting comfortable.

He presses the ignition button, and the car purrs to life. A smile spreads across his cheeks. He understands why humans show their happiness instead of saying it now. Because she beams back at him. "No, Ellie. I just told you, I have hope."

CHAPTER 17

"Freedom (feat. Kendrick Lamar)"
—Beyoncé

MORR1S

Ellie tells him a story about two teenage boys falling in love through emails—he thinks that's what they're called—before she drifts off to sleep. Her breaths come slow and steady now, and M0Rr1S wonders how the rest of the story goes. She awoke earlier, screaming out once and scratching at the door of the car, but he calmed her and urged her back to sleep. Since then, her face has been tilted toward him and he can't help but snatch glimpses. For hours, the scenery has been consistent; fields of flaxy tan waving grass, and the sun beating down on the pavement beneath them.

M0Rr1S takes a deep breath before hitting the small third

button on his panel. Charge 93 percent. He doesn't regret spending too much time talking and dancing with Ellie, but they can't afford many more delays. 0rsa will check in on him, try to figure out where he went and what he is doing. He needs to finish this mission.

He shouldn't do it, but he flips the switch for Il-0CoM, telling himself that he'll just check in.

Status on the vaccine?

A labmade general crackles only seconds later. *Commander M0Rr1S. We are pleased to hear from you.*

Commander M0Rr1S, a true Ilori who has nothing else better to attend to states with little inflection. *0rsa D3ihl stated you haven't arrived at your pod location in her quadrant for a debriefing and memory installation. We are concerned you are not following protocol. Again.*

I am still finding active solutions to our humanity problem west, as my familial code, he stresses that part, *suggested. I will arrive at my pod soon. Is there a status on the vaccine?*

Yes, the general cuts in again. *Distribution was able to re-create your formula and begin new production. We expect the supplies to reach every center within a rotation.*

Tonight? M0Rr1S almost gasps.

The timeline has shifted. Your familial code, Our Esteemed Leader, Emperor 1lv, has discussed his imperial visit within Il-0CoM, which you have missed from your constant absence. The true Ilori's tone is biting, and M0Rr1S understands how thin a line he walks. *He wishes to explore the facilities before we offer Earth to tourism. A demonstration for upper command. Acquisitions battles in only seven quadrants now, as opposed to twelve yesterday. Rehabilitation, Agricultural Services and Habitation, while working slowly over the course of occupation, are now at full speed, and expect to be done within eight rotations. We are ahead of schedule.*

Three days. That's very soon. Too soon. *And when does Our Esteemed Emperor wish to arrive?*

Thirty-three rotations.

Eleven days. *I see. Then it is most prudent that I offer my guidance to those battling humans.* At any point, someone could call him on his lies. If there was a prier, he would already be collected and under arrest. Thankfully, he doesn't feel any slight nudges into his mind.

Follow protocol, Commander. We do not wish—

No, Brixton interrupts. *Any guidance you can supply, I'm sure, would be appreciated, Commander M0Rr1S. However, if no results are produced, we may have to further inquire into your mental well-being.* There's a pause. *Your methods have impressed leadership, but they are unpredictable.*

Thank you, Captain. I assure you, I am in control and work only to serve the Ilori Empire. A chill travels down his spine. Brixton being nice can't be good.

Very well. When you are ready for extraction, you need only ask.

M0Rr1S wants to get off Il-0CoM as soon as he can. *Thank you. And may I—*

0rsa D3ihl stated you are traveling with a human. That you found companionship with a human. Another true Ilori remarks before Morris can end the conversation.

Brixton's tone holds a slight edge to it. *My brother would not embarrass himself or the 1lv line by finding kinship with his inferiors. Would you, Commander?*

Before M0Rr1S can deny the accusation, tell them he is loyal to his race and to their new colony, his gaze flicks to Ellie. It's warm. She shrugged off her sweater at some point, but there are beads of sweat on her hairline and the wispy curls are stuck to the sides of her face. He should lie. Lying isn't hard. Yet, they will pry regardless now that the accusation's been made. 0rsa made sure there is no way to avoid suspicion.

No, she is... She is bait? She is everything to him? She is music and a story that has come alive? *Permission to sign off?*

Permission n—

He flicks the switch on Il-0CoM anyway, the voices disappearing all at once. By not answering, he exposes himself to their derision, but they can't charge him. They don't know his location. No one can pry. He can still get out and complete his mission without becoming a fugitive. AvR0la was right, he should never have gone on there.

But now he knows he has eleven days to download his song into Il-0CoM. Eleven days to kill his grandfather and free his race. All of this to save humans, labmades and Ellie. Especially Ellie.

And he'd do it again.

He casts the thoughts aside as he turns on the air conditioner for Ellie's comfort, noticing the car is a bit low on fuel and electricity. Perhaps draining it last night for a few hours was a bad idea, but it was also one of the best nights of his life. He huffs to himself. No need to worry. There's a backup battery in the trunk, they won't get stranded.

M0Rr1S wonders if it's the Starry Eyed that is keeping him calm. They've listened to the same album four times. The band's music plays to his emotions, and it speaks to his experiences here on Earth. Like it was written for them. He smiles, the Il-0CoM incident already pushed to the background of his resounding emotions.

"Why are you smiling?" Ellie blinks her eyes slowly as the corners of her mouth lift into a yawn.

"Just thinking about music." *And you.*

Ellie stretches in her seat. "What was the first song you heard when you got here?"

M0Rr1S doesn't have to think long. That first song was a gateway into a new world. "'Across the Universe,' by The

Beatles. I loved it. It reminded me of home and the universe and the colors. Although I didn't understand the song entirely, it was beautiful."

She nods. "It's a good song."

"What was your first book? The first book you read that made you fall in love with reading?"

"When I was little, my dad would read me *Corduroy* by Don Freeman. It's a story about a little bear who feels alone in a big department store, and loses a button. In the end someone buys him and loves him. I cherished that book." She exhales slowly. "It's in your bag now. But what book made me fall in love?" Her eyes glaze over in thought. "*The Witches* by Roald Dahl. I was looking for a book at the library, I was maybe nine years old, and I wanted something scary. This was when my dad worked in a small school library in Brooklyn, and they didn't have any new kids' books. But there this was, and I loved it. I love stories about witches. I think for a while after I wanted to be one. Oh, and *The Perks of Being a Wallflower* by Stephen Chbosky. That book opened up another world to me."

"I feel the same way about music."

"Yeah. Music and books, they transport you. They make you feel in ways you didn't know you could. I listened to Taylor Swift and Adele so much, even though I'd never had a boyfriend, but she made me understand heartbreak. And Beyoncé. I listen to her and feel strong, powerful, unapologetically black and like a queen."

Little flutters of warmth spread through his stomach as she laughs. It's happiness. That's what Ellie does to him; she makes him feel weightless and happy. No one has ever done that to him before.

Pebbles from the road pelt the sides of the car, startling them both. The car slows down, like all of the energy is suddenly drained, until it comes to a stop.

"What's happening?" Ellie asks, a tinge of fear in her voice.

"I have to switch the battery and add gasoline to the tank, don't worry."

"Oh, okay. That's okay… I have to go to the bathroom anyway." Ellie gets out of the car at the same time as him, but she runs in the opposite direction, into the field. He looks away, opening the trunk and taking the battery out.

He spots a palm-sized black chip that's stuck to the hood. He yanks it off with a huff, and feels tiny pulses of electricity. What is this? Then he feels it spread like poison through his system. He attempts to drop it, but it's magnetized to him, to his energy. It's draining him. He shakes his hand. *Get off, get off, get off.* A red flash appears over his left eye. *Warning! Energy source compromised.*

He pulls with everything he has left, wishing he had used his abilities as soon as it stuck to him. He finally severs the strings connecting him to the chip. It falls from his grasp, and he bends over at his knees.

His finger searches for the button to tell him how much charge he has left. It can't be much. But then Ellie screams somewhere in the distance.

M0Rr1S doesn't think, he only runs to the sound of her voice.

That's when the field starts to move. No, not the field. Humans. Hidden in the fields of long flaxen grass. This is his fault. He should have been paying attention.

Now, because of him, they have Ellie.

He runs toward her, halting when seven different guns point at him.

"Why's a human traveling with an Ilori?" He can't see the speaker through the camouflage makeup and clothing. He's distracted by the way their hand shakes holding the gun.

Another human holds Ellie's hands behind her back. She's trembling. "He's my friend."

"Is she one of them?" Another with a mask over half their face asks. They eye Ellie.

"Nah, she doesn't have that light-up screen thing."

"But what if they've adapted? How would we know?"

"Kill 'em or take 'em in?"

Ellie's gaze locks on M0Rr1S, her eyes big and fearful. The human shifts the gun to Ellie. "I say we kill 'em."

"Let me radio Oz," the other one says, unclasping something from their belt and speaking into it. M0Rr1S doesn't listen. If he had enough charge, he could connect to their frequency and remove the energy or stop it momentarily. But he can already feel the lethargy spreading through him. His charge is too low. There is only one way to avoid these humans. Connect to AvR0la in Il-0CoM. It's risky, but AvR0la can patch through some energy, if only a little.

If he isn't careful, he'll be exposed to all of Il-0CoM. The way he left things only minutes before…they'll read him, find him, see what he sees and 0rsa will be the first to do so if he's not fast enough. She's probably waiting for any reason to ruin him.

"Oz says—"

M0Rr1S can't sit and wait. He flicks the switch and jumps into—and through—Il-0CoM to AvR0la.

AvR0la, M0Rr1S begs.

Sir? AvR0la's voice is quiet.

My charge is low. I need you to accept the connection and give me energy. Please.

Sir, I am currently detained. My own charge is low and I don't have much time. I'll do what I can.

AvR0la accepts the connection and they link. They see what M0Rr1S sees.

I will freeze the electrical energy in their minds. It will not last long. AvR0la sloppily connects to the human minds, pulling at synapses too gently to be of use.

Stronger, AvR0la, M0Rr1S commands.

AvR0la, with hesitation, pulls just enough to suspend the humans, rendering them at a standstill. M0Rr1S seizes the moment and reaches for Ellie, just as 0rsa enters the connection. He's not fast enough.

It's still alive?

Not now, he answers.

M0Rr1S, why are you traveling with a human? Voices echo in his mind, but he still reaches for Ellie as she reaches for him. Their fingers clasp together in the middle of the circle of guns and humans. Terror bubbles inside of M0Rr1S while Il-0CoM burrows deep into him, searching for answers. He needs this connection. He cannot let the others find them.

Commander.

Why?

Brixton. Coming. His father's voice. *Labmade.* They are only fragments from so far away, but he understands the gist.

M0Rr1S tugs on Ellie's arm. "Run."

They dart through the fields, the dirt hard beneath their feet. Fighting Il-0CoM, and carrying Ellie would be too much, even for him. They are slow. His own charge hovers at 4 percent. When his charge is gone, he'll go to sleep and won't wake up until energy wakes him.

Secrets, many secrets. Too guarded to pry. A voice whispers in his mind.

M0Rr1S, you are wanted for inquisition.

His mind does not open for me.

Must employ other methods. A general cuts through all of the unrecognizable voices in his head.

Can we shut him down?

From here?

Too strong. Familial Code: 1lv.

But a Labmade.

M0Rr1S, you are to report to Inquisition now.

"M0Rr1S, what is happening?" Ellie shoots him a look with her brow raised, her chest heaving.

He can't do it anymore. Too much prying will jiggle the truth loose. No. He shuts down Il-0CoM, disconnecting from AvR0la. He pulls Ellie into the grass with him. Her breathing is heavy, and she tightens her grip on his hand.

He puts a finger to his lips. "Shhh."

Shouts ring out across the field. "There are mines here. You're lucky to be alive."

"Come out."

"Morris," Ellie whispers.

His stares at her deep, brown eyes and smooth, radiant skin. Frizzy, humidity-riddled hair pokes out of her hat and by her ears. She has a small black dot—a mole—on her nose, and her lips are parted slightly as she pants in hot, sticky air.

"We've got your car," one of the humans yells. "There's no way out."

"Morris." Ellie's hand is clammy in his, and her lower lip quivers.

"Come with us. We won't kill you." The voice is closer.

M0Rr1S has to decide what to do. He won't leave Ellie here, but there is no way they can run and avoid bullets. His charge is too low now, and fighting could kill them both. "Do you trust me?" he whispers.

She gulps before nodding.

He pulls her up with him and together they stand. "Kill me. Not her. She's a human, like you."

The humans whisper among themselves. He listens, his eyes drooping from using too much energy too quickly. His request will go unmet. Their leader wants them both alive. "Take 'em in."

Ellie raises her arms before them, her gaze cast down. She is silent, but her heart pounds in her chest and in his ears. Why is she so afraid? She's a human among other humans. They surround them, closer and closer.

"Sorry about this," a younger human hits the back of Ellie's head with a gun, and she crumples to the ground.

M0Rr1S lashes out. He strikes them, sending them flying through the field. Another percent gone. He rushes to Ellie. She lays unconscious, a small smattering of blood leaking from a cut on the back of her head. They crowd around him.

"Stand down, Ilori."

"She'll be fine."

"I said, stand down."

Their voices…their species…none of it matter. "She's human, why did you do this?"

"Only way we take you back is knocked out. Your turn," one says. They shakily unzip the satchel by their side.

"You'll have to hit me a lot harder." M0Rr1S looks up at them, holding Ellie on his lap. He reaches for her glasses and shoves them into his coat pocket quickly.

"We will." They step closer. He can feel their fear as if it's a tangible thing. He barely turns in time before something connects with his head hard. At first it does nothing and M0Rr1S rolls his eyes. But then, slowly, he falls on his back beside Ellie.

THE STARRY EYED: "EVERYTHING"

The Sound of Stars
Written by: Cecil Wright, Allister Daniels, Rupert Montague,
Whisper Landsome

The dirt clings to our boots
We bury the secrets in the cold, dead Earth
Our world is tilted askew
I laugh, you cry, I whisper, you scream
I broke your heart
But still you give it to me

Don't say, don't say you don't love me
Don't say, don't say you don't feel it
Because I can't bear it
You are everything

You are everything

I never wanted to see you in pain
The fault is mine, I'm covered in shame
I know it hurts, but I can explain
I shout, you weep, I lie, you speak
The truth, always the truth
I hold your heart in my hands
I broke it once, but never again

Don't say, don't say you don't love me
Don't say, don't say you don't feel it
Because I can't bear it
You are everything

You are everything

You are
You are
You are
everything

CHAPTER 18

"We are what we believe we are."

—C.S. Lewis

JANELLE

My head is killing me. I open my eyes to blurry stars in my vision, and not the pretty kind. I lie on a damp, earthy floor in a room without windows. Light filters in from the hall outside. My fingers touch my sides, then my face. Damn it, my glasses are gone.

I turn, the pain intense. There's a body propped up against a gray stone wall. Morris? I sit up, groaning, and size up the bars sunk into the dirt ground. Where are we? Another prison? Although it reminds me more of a storage locker, but at least I'm not in chains. I rub the back of my head.

The memory hits me like the butt of the gun did. *Humans.*

Humans have us now. This should be an easy solution: I'm one of them, after all. I'll call out, ask for help. This has to be some misunderstanding. But first, I need to check on the figure.

I crawl toward him and touch the tips of my fingers under where I think his neck is—it's hard to see without glasses—and feel for a pulse. If they were created to be like us, then he has to have one, right? My fingers shake. His pulse is there but soft. I let air sail through my teeth. He's cool to touch, but his chest hitches. I trace the edge of my glasses in his coat pocket, and I'm relieved to put them back on, the world coming into focus around us.

"Morris, wake up," I whisper. I nudge him again and again.

Color blooms in his face and his eyes slowly blink open. His body rises as if to get up, but promptly falters.

"Ellie?" His voice is raspy, and his eyes are dazed.

"Are you okay, Morris?"

"Ellie." He moves forward, bringing his hands to the sides of my face as his stupor subsides. "Are you okay? Are you in pain?" His fingers search for something on the back of my head. The sting makes me gasp.

"Ow!"

"Sorry… I'm sorry." His voice wobbles.

I kneel in front of him, with my hands still pressed against his chest. For some reason, I can't move them. I'm glued to him, half out of comfort, half out of desire. "What happened back there?"

"Il-0CoM." He doesn't elaborate.

"You said it was dangerous. Are they coming for you?"

His hands fall from my face and land on mine. "Yes."

"Do you know where you are?" *Are they coming to kill me?*

His closes his eyes but he doesn't let my hands go. "No." He sighs. "But they will. I wasn't fast enough. They may know where I'm going."

I gulp. "Do they know about the vaccine?"

"No." There's confidence in his answer, but he also looks weaker than I've ever seen him.

"Morris, tell me how you're feeling." I shift and fall back against the wall next to him, breaking our embrace. I leave one hand under his, not ready to end contact.

"I am… I was supposed to protect you and I failed. I was supposed to leave you, to not get attached, to let you be free from the Ilori and from me, and I failed. I failed before I even tried. And now, the one thing left for me to do, get to California, save humanity… I failed. I keep failing."

I squeeze his hand. "That kind of thinking places a lot of responsibility on you and doesn't hold anyone else accountable. You can't control everything, Morris. And you haven't failed. *We* haven't failed. We've only encountered a new obstacle. Well, a few new obstacles."

He raises my hand to his lips and kisses it, and I feel a blush coming on. "I will get us out of here. I'm just a little weak."

"How'd they overpower you?"

"They hit me with something that set off an emergency shutdown and reboot. Nearly all my charge is gone."

I shake my head. "*I'll* get us out of here. I'm human, they're human, we have that in common. I don't see why they should hold us here."

He exhales. "I don't think any of that matters, not when you're with me, Ellie." He closes his eyes, swallowing. "You could stay with them. You could run with them…"

"I'm not leaving you, Morris. I said I'm coming with you, that's my choice." I slowly stand and press myself against the bars. I clear my throat. "Let us out! We just want to go somewhere else. We don't know you. We won't hurt you! I'm human. He's my friend. Let us out!"

I continue screaming this for a long while until a tall, bald man with beady eyes strides down the hall. He's escorted by five armed, camouflaged soldiers.

"You vaccinated?" His voice is higher than I would have imagined, and because of it, the fear isn't too much to bear. But I am afraid. Everyone who has come down that hallway is white, and I'm still black. Now, we're supposed to be past these things, but…hate isn't sensible. And my mind travels there regardless.

"Which vaccine are you talking about? Measles, mumps and rubella? Chicken pox? Hepatitis or the flu?" I cock an eyebrow before wanting to kick myself. My dad's defiance and distrust in authority must have slipped out through the cut in the back of my head. It really hurts. "You can look at my arms—no marks, no shots. I'm human."

The guy regards me as if trying to figure me out while taking a drag from his cigarette. He ignores my snark. "Why do you travel with it?"

I let my voice drop, so I don't seem aggressive. Now's not the time to piss these folks off, even if my head is pounding. "He's not like them. He's sabotaging his own kind to save us."

"Yeah, how?"

I turn back to Morris as he shakes his head, even though he's not looking at me. *Don't tell them.* I know that's what he's thinking.

"He saved a center of humans and set us free. He stopped Ilori from killing humans in the street. He's—"

"Little girl, I don't care what you *say* he did. There's no proof. Why are you here? Traveling through here?"

"We're going to California," I answer.

"The Ilori took the coasts, and made their way in. We're the last of the humans out here."

"There are others. North. We know that. There's a big fight happening right now in—"

"Your people are dying," Morris cuts in. "You may be the last free humans. And her." Morris doesn't stand, nor does he look at them.

"Big savior he is," a soldier grumbles.

I shoot him a dirty look. "Why would I lie?"

"How do we know you aren't one of them half-solutions weirdos?" the man in charge demands.

"I—I don't know. I'm—" Panic rises in my throat. It's striking now of all times? Can't my brain give me a break? *Breathe in, breathe out. Relax.* They aren't going to free me. They think I'm working for the Ilori. They're right to be suspicious. I could be. But there'd be something off about me? Like my dad. He looks like us but acts like them. I mean, is there any way to act more human? Should I cry? Should I sing or dance?

"Where'd you come from?"

I jump on the change of subject. Counting things around the room in my head while I answer. "New York. New York City."

He looks me up and down. "That'd explain the accent. Where are your parents?"

"Gone." They might very well be vaccinated at this point. Which causes another round of numbers to rattle in my mind.

He considers my words before blowing smoke through the bars. "You can come out. We've got a doctor here. Can look at your head, and check to see if you're one of them." He spits it out, looking at Morris. "But it stays here."

"He won't hurt anyone. He's different…and the Ilori are coming for him."

"We'll see about that." He nods to the soldiers. "Let her out. Escort her to Doc."

He eyes Morris. "Move and we'll kill you. Maybe even her, if she means so much to you."

Morris opens his eyes and stares at the man. For the first

time, I see hatred in them. "Hurt her, and your death will follow."

The timbre of his voice sends goose bumps down my arms. The man's eyes flash briefly.

The gate swings open. Two soldiers pull me out and press my arms behind my back. Morris still doesn't move. I stare at him in the darkness, although the light is brighter in the hallway, blinding me a bit. "I'll come back for you, Morris. I won't leave you here."

Morris looks at me, and my breath catches. There are rings around his eyes, and his black hair clings to the sides of his face. His skin is sallow, and even his movements are slow. They've drained him. He can't save us now.

But he's still beautiful. The kind of beauty that almost doesn't feel real and therefore can't be anything but alien to this world. That's how they'll look at him. An alien. An outsider. A monster. What he really is, though... My heart thumps in my chest as the realization sinks in. He's my friend. He's my... We have this...thing, this bond between us. I didn't feel it till now. But there it is. I know him. I feel comfortable with him. I care about him.

"Ellie, I trust you." His gaze holds mine.

The other humans push me forward, breaking our eye contact and I stumble on the tiled floor. I'm led down a windowed hall and up a flight of stone stairs. We were—Morris is—on the bottom floor in the middle of a desert. I store that thought away. Every time I try to take in my surroundings, I'm shoved onward. At first it seems like we're in a strip mall, but then I realize we're in an actual mall. We walk by a Victoria's Secret that's in shambles, a Gymboree and an Orange Julius. The surroundings remind me of a dystopian novel, and I imagine the characters who live within these walls. Who are fighting a system. The idea entertains me on the long walk to wherever I'm going.

I end up in a nurse's office of some sort, like at school. It's a small white room with an examination table and medical-looking things on a tray. There's a bored looking woman with brown hair in a ponytail and cutoff jeans, wielding a stethoscope around her neck. She looks at me briefly before returning to her patient. She's got to be in her late twenties tops, but she's hardened and weary, covered in dirt, as she assesses a little girl's leg.

"Stay off it, feels like a fracture. And tell Jilly to stop playing so rough, okay?"

"Yes, ma'am." The little girl's accent is strong Texan, and it's adorable.

The doc tilts her head, and a soldier sets the little girl in a wheelchair. They push her away, leaving me and the others standing there waiting.

"You're the girl who travels with an Ilori?" Her eyebrows rise, but she's unimpressed.

"He's my friend. He's saved my—"

"Don't care. Sit up on the table." She turns her back to me and I do as she says. There's no paper lining, and she doesn't wear a lab coat. It's an odd experience.

She comes over with an instrument and the tool-laden tray. One is a black dot, a circular device that could fit into the palm of my hand. First, she shines the light in my eyes and then she checks my ears, my mouth and nose. She attends to the cut on the back of my head, then tests my reflexes.

"Hypo and anxiety, yeah?"

I gape at her. "How did you know?"

"Your hands are shaking and your body language is tense. Your heart is racing and you've been counting under your breath throughout the examination. There could be a lot of reasons, but I've seen this before. Used to be a psych student," she answers, matter-of-fact. "Did you take meds before they came?"

"Yes, and after."

"What did you take?"

"Synthetic hormone treatment for the hypothyroidism, around thirty micrograms, and a small dosage antianxiety med, ten milligrams. Can't remember which one now."

"Well, good news? You're not an Ilori or one of those mood-enhanced humans." She snorts. "Bad news? We ran outta antianxiety meds maybe two months ago, and I don't have any thyroid meds here with me. They're upstairs. But I think if I give you twenty mil packages of the synthetic, and load a bag with it, you'll be set for a long time. As long as any of us have anyway."

"Really, you have meds?" Through my surprise, I'm hopeful. I knew I wouldn't find something for the anxiety. People needed those pills the most when the Ilori came, and if I had hypo pills and got my vitamins in, the anxiety was manageable using coping mechanisms. But it's plagued me for so long, I forgot what it's like to have help dealing with it. The way my mind reels while I'm sleeping, the way books and my hat are the only comfort that takes away the jitters and worries. Help. I could have help. And then I remember the end of our world is nigh. "What's the point when who knows how much time we have?"

"The people here, they think they're gonna survive here forever. They take their meds, water their gardens and continue believing in this fantasy world they've made for themselves. We don't wanna tell them the truth—the Ilori will come for us any day now. There's nowhere safe anymore to just exist." She hands me a slip of paper. "And I do have the meds."

"There's permanent housing. It's not bad." I accept her offer and close it in my fist. "Too bad about the antianxiety meds."

She pats my shoulder. "I know what it's like. I do. You need the hypo medicine, even if you get captured, it'll help your energy. I can see that in your fingernails, and you look tired. But anxiety? We've lost a war with aliens, kid. No amount of meds will make you feel all right with that. What matters is that you've found a way to cope. A lot of 'em upstairs haven't."

I take a long, deep breath and let it out slowly before nodding.

"Look, normally, they wouldn't even let me give out the synthetic hormone to an outsider but…give this to the guy upstairs." She sighs before leaning closer. "What's up with you and the Ilori?" Her voice is low, and she glances at the guards by the door. They can't hear us, at least I don't think so.

"He saved my life and I think…he doesn't want me to tell you the rest."

"You don't have to trust me. But…they're not going to let you go with him. They'll kill him or ask me to dissect him. He's not leaving here alive. As for you? I don't know what they'll do. Maybe they'll keep you for a while as long as you're useful. You need to know what you're getting into here. This is one of the last shelters in this state. It's big. Leaders rise, leaders fall. None of them will be sympathetic."

"Why can't I just take Morris and leave? We don't want anything. We aren't going to tell anybody—"

"There's a strong sentiment here—if you aren't with us, you're with them. I mean, we know the vaccine is happening, right?"

"It happened," I admit.

"How soon will it be before there are humans walking among us, coming here, acting like us but aren't us?"

I shake my head. "If you let them take you to housing, you'll be the safest."

"If they take us, we'll be vaccinated. And if taking the vaccine makes you safe, why haven't you taken it?"

I bite my lip. How do I tell her I don't want to? That I'm going with Morris on possibly a suicide mission to upload a frequency-code-song-thing that will restore the humans *if* the ship we go to isn't completely wrecked. Then, if we don't get captured or die, I'll see my parents and Alice again. I'll fight for Earth. And if we somehow, miraculously, win that, we'll settle in here before we fly off into the universe exploring new worlds. That sounds unrealistic…she'd never believe me. I don't believe me. "I can't tell you," is all I end up saying.

"You keep your secrets, but don't be surprised if you die with them."

"What is that?" I point to the black dot on the tray.

She sighs. "Tech. We call 'em buzzkillers. When the invasion happened, the remaining army, you know the ones not killed during the strikes, found out that these things were built to run on electricity. The buzzkillers stick to electrical products and drain them. Got a million boxes of them around here. The manufacturer's a few miles away. Well, they were, anyway."

I slide off the table, about to walk toward the guards as if I've been dismissed. The doctor stops me with a hand on my arm.

"They'll take you upstairs. I don't know how long they'll keep him alive."

I raise my head. "Then I'd better find a way out before they kill him. He's the only chance humanity has."

"If that's the truth, then you need my help."

"Are you going to give it to me?"

"Maybe." This time she walks away, and I really have been dismissed.

The guards escort me upstairs, up a broken escalator, no less. I'm brought into an old Macy's that's been gutted but still has the sign hanging above the awning. There are children playing with blocks and toys, people sitting at makeshift tables, some crying, some mixing food or cutting vegetables. My eyes can only take in so much. This is humanity with freedom, or something closer to freedom.

I'm led through it all. I earn a few glances, but not one word. I expected curiosity, but all I see are tired, worn-down people trying to survive despite the odds. The last thing they want or need is another mouth to feed, or body to take up space. This great mall is theirs, and suddenly, I realize I might be in one of the biggest human sanctuaries on Earth. How long can this place last?

An office door opens and I'm shoved inside, reality slamming back to me.

"Sit."

It's an order from a man who stands with his back to me while rummaging through a pile of... I can't make it out. I sit in a cushioned red chair that's been slashed down the center. Still comfortable, though. A yawn escapes through my teeth, and he turns back to me.

"Why are you traveling with an Ilori?" His Texan accent is thick. His salt-and-pepper hair's cropped close to his scalp, and he looks like he used to fight in the army before—maybe even during—the invasion.

"He saved my life and helped me escape two centers." *Also, I sorta like him. Like, a lot.*

"Is he carrying the vaccine?"

I shake my head. *But he created it.*

He huffs. "What are his plans?"

"To change Earth." *And save it.* I hold my head high.

He rubs his chin. "How old are you?"

"Seventeen." But I feel so much older.

"Why are your hands shaking?"

I look down and realize the paper the medic handed me is crumpled in my shaking hands. I place it on the desk in front of me. He scans it. "All right."

He turns once more and sorts through a file cabinet until he produces a small box.

"Thyroid meds?" He holds out the box. I reach for it, but he pulls back. "Tell me why you're traveling with an Ilori. Tell me everything you know, tell me everything about it. And you get the meds. I bet they'd make you feel a lot better, right?"

I lean back in my seat. "Do you know that it'd take about one month, maybe two for those meds to kick in?"

He sneers. "Do you want them?"

I could lie. "I do."

"Tell me everything."

"No."

"Fine, you can go back into a cell." I shrug. I'd rather be with Morris anyway. "I'm not putting you next to your alien friend either. You can go sit with the wolves. We'll see how you feel then."

"Wolves?"

"Part of that half-solutions vaccine mess. Escaped from whatever centers they lived in after the vaccine addled their mind. Made them weird. They call themselves the wolves. Enjoy."

I'm lifted from my seat by a guard behind me and nearly dragged out of the office. They don't take me back through the people. *Five,* the long white hallway with flickering fluorescents above. *Four,* a set of double doors. I squint as we move from the brightness of the hallway into the darkness of this new area. But I catch sight of, *three*, an oversize dog crate in the center of the room as the minimal light beams off the metal bars. The rest of the room is cast in impenetrable darkness. They lead me in, stopping in front of the cage. *Two...*

"Get on your knees."

I do as I'm told before there's a soft pop of the door swinging off its hinges.

"Get inside." I crawl in, holding back the tears and anger and horror. The door closes, and then they leave me there, enveloped in the pitch-black. Am I alone?

I blink repeatedly. My vision's starting to adjust when someone calls out to me. *Two*, whoever's in here with me.

"Little girl, what have you done?" And then there is a collective howling, like wolves, but so distinctly human. The sound of metal chains clinking against the floor has my heart hammering. "Ever hear the story of the little girl eaten by a wolf?"

One...

"You mean Little Red Riding Hood?" I counter through shaky breaths. "She lives in the end."

"In this one, she won't."

Fingers drag across the cage, rattling me. *One*, a breath that warms my cheek. I may be locked in this crate, but I am not safe, and I don't know how many of them there are.

I scream but that only makes them laugh harder.

CHAPTER 19

"Bohemian Rhapsody"
—Queen

MORRIS

The stone walls feel like they're caving in on him, and the dirt floor lacks comfort. It's been hours since Ellie was taken away, and he doesn't know if they hurt her, or if she'll come back. She said she would, but who knows what forces will stand in her way?

His charge is at 1 percent. Enough to sit here, to breathe, but even movement is tough now. Resting will help, but then what will he do? He could try to dislodge the bars of his prison. He could try to walk out of there, but they have Ellie. And they have those eerily effective weapons. Another hit with one of those will wipe him out. He will not leave without Ellie, not when he doesn't trust the humans to take care of her. Even if death is certain should he remain, he would rather face it than a life without her. Besides, if he doesn't get out of here soon, Brixton will find him. Maybe even 0rsa will come. They might kill the humans.

They might pry into his mind.

M0Rr1S finds himself thinking of his mother, Glind. She showed him love when his father and his brother showed him only hatred. She would never kill innocent creatures simply because she could. Because they possessed something she wanted. Why couldn't all true Ilori be like her?

His mother commissioned his creation, and she loved him before he even existed. Glind is the head of a secret government within the empire, and has worked tirelessly to overthrow both the emperor and Father, the heir. To expose their plan now would mean exposing her, and he cannot do that either. She created him to enact this plan on Earth. She hopes it will be the first of many failures for the Ilori Empire, and although she may forgive M0Rr1S for his mistakes, he will not forgive himself if anything happens to her. Or Ellie.

Or AvR0la.

Or any of the millions of humans and labmades working within these structures to impact change.

A song comes to his mind. He closes his eyes as he hums it, the highs and the lows fitting perfectly to this moment. It's his fault that he and Ellie are here. He pulled over without checking the area, he let the humans capture them.

He allows himself to indulge in a daydream, imagining a moment where everything is okay.

Ellie is there behind his eyes, waiting for him in front of the car. The moon beams down on them as she sings, holding her hand out to him. "Bohemian Rhapsody" by Queen swirls around, the melody in and out of time. Her brown skin is luminous, as if she has painted herself with stardust, and his breath hitches. He pulls her close, his hands twitching with nerves. And then the instrument solo—he doesn't know what makes that noise—is amazing and full of life. He and Ellie dance, close but never close enough. He misses her. He imagines her eyes on his, her mouth parted with small breaths escaping between her lips, as they lean toward each other. A kiss. Finally, yes, a kiss.

"Didn't know aliens liked music." A small voice comes from the hallway, startling M0Rr1S out of his fantasy. It's quiet once more, and he begins to wonder if the voice was real.

But his question is answered when a child stops in front of his cell.

"Is it true? You're one of them?" They run their fingers down the sides of the bars, and squeak when a bit of grime sticks.

M0Rr1S gives a small nod.

The little kid shakes their head and twitches their lips. "I thought you hated music? I thought you can't feel stuff?"

"Not all of us are like that." His throat is dry and he wishes he could have a large sip of the calef juice that's stored inside his bag back in the car.

"My name's Josef." Their little voice sounds like a song.

"My name is… Morris." The Ilori way of saying his name is too difficult for any human, and only affirms his otherness.

"Morris…that's a cool name."

"So is Josef." M0Rr1S gives them a small smile. Josef comes closer, but does not touch the bars again. "Are you a girl, boy, nonbinary?"

"I'm a boy." He laughs as if the question is weird.

"Me, too."

The little boy's brows furrow. "How come you're here? How come you took our planet?"

M0Rr1S hates this; hates his excuse that he was just doing his job. What does it matter to the child? What does it matter at all? All Josef knows is war, and evil aliens coming to take his land, and his body. So he doesn't answer, and Josef deflates a little.

"Do you know any music, Josef?"

Josef puffs up again. "I can sing 'If You're Happy and You Know It.'"

The lids of M0Rr1S's eyes feel heavy again. "Will you sing it?"

Josef starts to sing, and then he claps his hands. He looks at M0Rr1S with eager eyes to do the same and M0Rr1S obliges. He couldn't say no to that face, even with his minimal energy. Human children are much cuter and far more innocent than Ilori. A child back home is no child at all.

The song is a series of instructions, and he is pleased to follow along. And then they stomp their feet, and shout hooray! They giggle and do all three, and Josef is about to sing another rousing song when someone shrieks. They run down the hall, pulling Josef into a hug.

"I told you never to leave my side. You could have been… Do you know how unsafe this is? Josef, do you? Look at me!" They pull back as tears slip down their cheeks. "Tell me you won't run off again. Tell me!"

"I promise, Mama," Josef intones, his lower lip quivering. "We were just singing."

"Singing?" She looks at M0Rr1S, a black scarf covering her hair and neck. Her eyebrows are raised as she takes him in.

Josef tugs on the woman's patterned dress. "He's a good singer, Mama."

She shakes her head. "Ilori don't sing."

His voice is earnest. "This one does."

"What's your name?" She holds eye contact with M0Rr1S.

"Morris," the boy answers for him. "We're friends now, right, Morris?"

M0Rr1S laughs. "Yes, Josef. But your mother is right, my kind is dangerous. You should go."

"You don't seem bad to me," he says, his little lips frowning as his mother pulls him.

"I think," M0Rr1S says carefully, "that we don't know much about each other and sometimes that makes everyone afraid."

The mother regards M0Rr1S suspiciously before taking Josef away.

"See you later!" Josef calls before he disappears from view.

M0Rr1S sighs and stretches against the wall. He should tell them that if they surrender, no one will die. But he can't trust the humans with his secrets, not when so many are at risk.

Time passes. He doesn't know how much. He needs to conserve his energy, and that will require rest. Maybe a manual shutdown. But what if something happens? What if Ellie needs him?

Footsteps echo down the hall. A tall human with an escort of armed guards stops in front of his cage. Their weapons are aimed at him, but he has no desire to engage. He closes his eyes.

The voice is raspy with an edge of authority. "Let's get this out of the way, alien. I know you like labels, so here they are. I'm male and I'm the boss. Why have you come here?"

"I didn't come here, I was brought here." M0Rr1S doesn't want to quibble, but facts are facts. "Where is Ellie? Is she well?"

The man's tone changes in intensity. "What is your reason for traveling through this area?"

"I have been relieved, so I'm now ready to depart this planet." M0Rr1S shifts against the wall, trying to find comfort.

There is a rustling by the bars. The man steps closer, his feet kicking the dirt through between the metal. "Why do you travel with the human girl?"

M0Rr1S doesn't hide his frustration. "She's my friend, and I deserve to know if she's okay."

"Don't lie to me." His voice is direct and sharp, laced with anger.

"I'm not lying to you. Janelle Baker is my friend. She tells me stories and we sing together. Where is she?"

The man huffs. "I should kill you. That's what your people do to us."

"There are two kinds of Ilori. The ones that kill and the ones that preserve. I am the latter. I have never killed a human. But I might if you don't tell me where Ellie is."

"No. You probably just don't see the vaccination as genocide, right?" Now his anger is outright.

"The vaccine serves many purposes," M0Rr1S admits. "It also preserves."

"Lies." The man spits.

"If I wanted to, I could send messages over and over to your mind until your thoughts scramble. I could make you believe me. I could stop the electricity in your body. I could melt these bars that keep me here… Tell me, have you ever kept an Ilori in a cell?"

The man doesn't answer.

M0Rr1S opens his eyes and glares. "I have not left because I do not want to threaten you," he lies. "Nor do I want to kill you. I want Ellie, and then we will leave. I have no interest in anything else."

The man considers his words and relents. "Tell us about the vaccine we've heard about. What does it do?"

Soft and unaggressive. "Where's Ellie?"

There is hatred in his voice. "I'll tell you when you speak the truth."

M0Rr1S draws an uneasy breath and sets his attention on the man emitting his rage.

The man looks away. "Your friend is upstairs. She's safe... for now."

"How do I know you aren't lying?"

The man smirks. "Why would we kill another human?"

M0Rr1S doesn't trust him. The corner of the man's mouth twitches in a way that suggests half lies or obfuscated truths. But questioning him will do nothing. "The vaccine hollows the human until it is a blank space for an Ilori to inhabit."

"Shit." He rubs his mouth with the palm of his hand. "How will we know if they're humans or Ilori?"

"Physically they will look the same. However, their speech will be different, and they will not be as expressive or understanding of the human experience. It won't be hard to differentiate between a human and a human with an Ilori consciousness."

The man leans closer, his head almost touching the bars. "Is it done? Are they coming for us?"

"Yes. If you want my advice, here it is—turn yourself in. They will house you, take care of you. Only some get the vaccine."

There is spittle by the corner of the man's mouth. "I'd rather die."

"If you die, how will you stop them? *Us?*" M0Rr1S remembers that he is, in fact, one of them, and telling the human otherwise is not safe for anyone.

"I'm not letting you out of here." The man sniffs. "You'll tell them where we are."

M0Rr1S shakes his head. "I could have already."

He snorts. "Don't fuck with me. You have no idea where you are."

"You're going to kill me anyway." M0Rr1S lets his head fall back against the wall.

The man steps away from the bars. "Damn right."

"I only ask to see my friend before you do." M0Rr1S needs rest. Simple movements drain him now.

"Depends."

"On?" M0Rr1S is desperate to know, desperate to see Ellie again, but his speech is slow.

"Her behavior."

M0Rr1S doesn't respond and instead slumps to conserve his energy. If it's fully depleted, he'll be of no use to Ellie, to his mission. He hums "Bohemian Rhapsody" once more until the man leaves in agitation. He doesn't mind. All he can think about is Ellie. Where is she? Is she okay? What are they doing to her?

Are you dreaming, M0Rr1S? Where are you? Brixton's voice burrows deep into his mind despite his disconnection from Il-0CoM. *You cannot escape me. You know this. I'm your familial code. I am stronger than you. I have energy to spare, unlike you.*

M0Rr1S cannot stop the dream of him and Ellie dancing in a field of grass while the Starry Eyed provide the soundtrack. He's dreaming. *Dreaming.* His charge is too low to control or protect himself now.

Familial code can penetrate his dreams when his mind is at its weakest. He's not safe here. Not from Brixton, and he's too exhausted to fight him off.

Ellie twirls in the starlight. Glossy pearls dot her curls along the edge of her hat while the rest of her sparkles. "Morris. Are we infinite?"

He doesn't know the answer, for he doesn't understand the question.

Brixton's voice cuts through the beautiful dream like dark smoke, obscuring the happiness and Ellie. *Is this the human, M0Rr1S? How fascinating.*

M0Rr1S tries to push Brixton out, but it's like trying to uproot a tree. Brixton is powerful, and the hatred he has for M0Rr1S is unparalleled. *You don't belong here.*

You think you can fight me off? I don't need a strong charge to linger here, only a strong will. Chills creep along M0Rr1S's spine and prickle at the edges of his mind. The dream fades away around him, and he catches Ellie's purple hat before it disappears into nothingness. *M0Rr1S. I'm coming to you. I can give you energy, we need to—*

No, he needs to shut down. That's the only way. A complete shutdown. If they kill him, he will feel nothing. If Ellie comes... Maybe M0Rr1S will have time. Maybe he can upload the code into her mind somehow. Maybe the ship will still be usable. Maybe, maybe, maybe. He cannot expose his secrets to Brixton any longer, not while he is like this.

His fingers flick to the panel beside his ear, and he scratches at it frantically until he hits the power button. He will restart in eight hours. Either he'll wake up in the cell, or the humans will kill him. He hopes it's the former. Death would rob him of Ellie.

She's his last thought before shutdown.

CHAPTER 20

"Beware; for I am fearless, and therefore powerful."
— Mary Wollstonecraft Shelley

JANELLE

'm curled in a ball in the middle of my crate. No more tears; I have no more left. My throat is hoarse and my body shakes. I feel like I've aged ten years over the course of a few hours. Fear will do that. Memories I'd love to delete forever play on repeat.

The woman and daughter outside the basement hatch. Their screams. My weakness and how I couldn't save them. I blink back tears. Where is that little girl now? Is she dead? Did the man kill her? Did he kill them both, or did the Ilori?

I've used that memory to tell myself that my library was worth all the risks. But now I can't deny the other side to that story just because it hurts too much. The anger, hatred, rage. I'd hated that man, whoever he was, but I'd also hated the way I'd felt. Completely helpless. Part of me believed that lending out books was enough, that it was a simple way of rebelling. But I stood by for the executions. I stood by when Dad was taken and never really came home. I stood by while Mom drank herself into oblivion. When Alice was dragged away... Maybe I couldn't have done anything.

I can now.

And I won't leave M0Rr1S behind that door.

I push up onto my knees, my back grazing the metal bars above. The wolves howl and laugh and taunt me. Because I'm more human than they are now.

That man who sent me here wanted me to cower, to beg him to take me out. Not today.

I take a deep breath and run my hands down my waist, wiping away the sweat and shakes. They won't help me now. But the anxiety keeps me alert. Narrows my focus.

I have no weapon on me but my wits and fists. Strong girls, characters from my favorite books, pop into my mind. None of them would wait around for someone to save her. Most of them would bounce out of here, in worse shape than me, and they'd fight. They'd fight through broken hearts and ruined dreams. I'm alive, and I'm strong. My heart isn't broken, and I hold my dreams close to me. And I've already lived in a cage for years; I won't stay in one anymore. Not when I can save and change the world. And my family.

Morris needs me.

I feel around the outside of my bars. Quick, before the wolves catch me. I can't see, but I know how these things work. I cat-sat once in Brooklyn, this cage has to be just a bigger version of that. Right?

I thrust my hand out and find the latch, but it's stuck. My

nail snaps, and I grind my teeth to keep from crying out. Almost there. I can't afford to mess up now. *Breathe in, breathe out. Focus. Sense.* There's a small *pop*, and I shift it up with the tips of my fingers. I use my shoulder to ram it open before I land on the floor. The wolves circle. Their chains clink against the floor. They're just as trapped as I am.

"Little girl torn to bits."

"They say they bleed red but this one's skin is black."

"They all bleed red."

"Traitor. Prefers them to us. Broken little girl."

One's nose sniffs my neck as I stumble to my feet. "Smells good."

And that's when my fists flex by my sides. No fictional character pops into my mind now. Only Morris. What would Morris do? Would he fight, would he run? I know the answer, because I know Morris.

In my mind, I belt out the Starry Eyed. The first song that comes to mind. *"Fairy-tale girl, don't give up now... The story's not over yet, you can't take your bow."* I slam my body into one man, and he falls unceremoniously to the ground.

"Don't!" I swing out my fist and connect to another's jaw. *"No, don't!"* I scream and kick one more, and jump over the fallen one. I pull back the door, I pull, and I pull. *"Don't ever!"* But the knob won't turn. *Keep trying*, I tell myself over my pounding heart and the adrenaline rushing through my veins. I jam it up and twist. *"You can never give up!"*

Bright light shines into the room, and onto my harassers known as the wolves. They howl in pain, running for the darkness in the corners. There are five of them; older men with no weapons. Chained there and treated like animals.

I stand tall in the doorway. They wanted to break my spirit, to make me afraid and give up Morris, and so, I broke them a little.

And now I'm going to break everything I can to get back to Morris.

I bolt out and slam the door shut behind me. I run for the office, praying that the man who sent me to the wolves isn't there. The medicine is probably on the table where he left it. I hope. Do I need it? I want to seem normal again, have the option at least. But it probably isn't worth it anyway. Either I'll die, get vaccinated, or go with Morris, and then die. And Morris accepts me the way I am. Counting and panicking, gray days and exhausted.

I hear an unfamiliar voice from inside the room as I draw closer.

"We have to kill the thing. Our people know it's in there. They don't want it anywhere near them or their children."

"What were you thinking bringing it here? For fuck's sake, even if we kill it now, it could be communicating in the Hive. And what if there's more to their electronic panels? A homing device or some shit?"

"If there was, they'd already be here, Bill." His voice is authoritative. It's the man from before, with the cigarette. Something about him scares me, and I know his voice will haunt my dreams for a long time to come. "Did anyone check on the girl? You know those Ilori rejects love to scare kids shitless."

"Think she'll give us any info?"

"Maybe. Check on her."

"I was just about to—"

There's no more time to listen now. Forget the medicine, I've got to save Morris. My feet hurt when I burst through another door and accidentally hit a guard with the backside of it, knocking him hard enough to drop his gun. It skitters to the tip of my toes. There's a long moment where we both look at each other in surprise and then he rushes forward just as I snatch it up.

I point it at him even though this thing makes me really uncomfortable. It feels both heavy and light, at constant odds with itself in my hand. Nothing good has ever come from these. In fact, if we'd been a more peaceful world, we wouldn't be in our predicament. Maybe we would have tried to communicate first, instead of bombing and shooting and annihilating. What would that world look like? Where would we be now?

"Stay back," I shout at him.

He puts his hands up. I realize he's young, probably not much older than me. "Don't do this."

"I'm just going to leave." I try to stop my hand from shaking. "I just want to leave. Okay?"

He exhales. "Do you even know how to fire one of those?"

I don't answer. I keep backing up until my back hits another door. I reach behind me and yank it open. I don't need to turn my head to know I'm in the main room where hundreds of people and children loiter. There are screams and children crying within seconds. I feel like a criminal. I don't want that judgment, but if they stand between me and my freedom, my survival and Morris… I'll play that part. I don't know them and I don't owe them anything.

The sun shines through the windows on both sides, setting a heavenly glow around the humans. I keep my gun trained on the guard.

No one stops me. If this were the center in New York, someone would have stopped me already. And none of them would be frightened either; what was the worst I could do? Kill them? They were already dying. Kill myself? Who would that hurt? Freedom has made them fearful. Maybe they're more human than me now.

"Don't hurt us."

"Please, there are kids."

The way they look at me like I'm a monster…it hurts.

"Look, you don't know me," my voice wobbles as I project it to be heard. I wish I were like Alice, that I'd say the right thing the right way. "But I've come from New York City. They moved some of us into housing. You're safe there. Turn yourselves in. Even if they give you the vaccine, it won't work the way they think. Save your kids. Save humanity. And this guy—" I shout as two more guards lunge for me. The man from the office steps into a patch of sunlight. "He found us, me and my Ilori rebel friend. He locked us up and refuses to let us leave. We don't want to be here. My Ilori can save us all, and I'm gonna help him. Just…let us leave. Please."

A woman with a stick in her hand and a little boy with beautiful round eyes cowering behind her hesitantly steps beside me. She hands me the stick. "Take this and put it through the handles of the doors. We'll buy you some time."

I take it, staring.

She sniffs and backs away. "I met him…the Ilori. He sang to us. To Josef. He said his name's Morris and he's not like what we thought. I… I believe her. Let's give them a chance to save the world."

At first the crowd mutters, but the woman lifts her head and her voice grows louder, stronger. "We were never going to last here. You all know this. They'll be here any day, any moment. But this girl and that alien might save us. Shouldn't we at least let them try? Shouldn't we believe that it's possible? Otherwise, what's the point of living?"

"That's not your call to make, Mira," the man says to her with his eyes boring into mine, his guards spreading out behind him. "I am in charge here. I'm the leader."

"Well, then…" Mira's eyes flick around as the crowd comes to stand behind her. Her son holds her hand and juts his chin. "I think it's time for new leadership."

The crowd cheers, and I take that time to whip around and

run through the room and past the two heavy doors. When they close behind me, I shove the stick through them just as she said and make my way down the escalator, where the doctor stands in my way.

"Here." She holds out a few boxes of medicine. "They'll help with the hypo. You need that." I promptly shove them into my bra without shame. "Your car is about seven miles east. Good luck."

"Tell them to surrender. Force them," I advise. "And… and thank you."

She nods and stares over my shoulder. "You better get going."

For a moment, sheer awe of all the support and kindness threatens to pull me under. I want to cry and hug people. I want them to live and survive. To be happy. I was knocking on that basement hatch, and that mom, Mira, let me in. She did what I couldn't.

I want to give her and her son everything I can. Maybe some books. Maybe my copy of *Corduroy*. But I can't. The world relies on me right now.

As I sprint down the hallway, I vow that somehow, I'll pay this forward. That I'll somehow step up and do the same if I ever find myself in a similar situation.

I don't look back. Finding the right hallway to Morris is tricky. It's dark and there are no other cages or cells or prisons down here in this makeshift prison maze built within mall storage.

"Morris," I call out. "Morris!"

No one answers.

"Please, Morris."

I stumble through the walls and the halls. The pounding of feet behind me on the dirty pavement tells me at least one of the guards made it out. I turn back: there are two, maybe three, of them. I stop counting and twist around. They are more than a few paces behind me, not running, but cornering me.

"Morris."

I turn another corner in the maze. Until there it is, the dirt-packed cell, with Morris inside.

"You caused a lot of trouble for us." The man from the office that threw me in with the wolves stands at the opposite end of the hall. He slumps a bit, his face downcast.

"I'm not sorry." I brush the tears from my eyes, seeing the way fear pinches the edges of his lips, and how tired he looks around his brows, as if he has aged years in hours.

"He's a fucking alien." His voice echoes down the hall and reverberates in my ears. "All this, for an alien who stole our world and wants to steal our bodies."

"He's my friend," I say between pants. "He doesn't know where we are. Neither do I. The longer you keep him here, the sooner they'll come for him. You're endangering them." I point up to the main room. "Let me take him. Please."

He eyes me with distaste. "My people demand we let you go. Said if anything happened to you, I'm out. These two here—" he points to his two guards "—are to make sure I do. But I won't make it easy for you."

"Just unlock the cell. I'll carry him." I pray that my strength holds up under his weight.

"Don't come back, or we'll kill you both." His voice rattles my confidence, but I nod once anyway.

A guard steps closer to me. I point my gun at him, even though he keeps his hands in the air until he unlocks the cell.

"You're gonna die. You know that, right?" The man shakes his head like I'm out of my mind.

"I'd rather die with a friend than with strangers who locked me up in a cage."

"We were never going to hurt you."

"Could've fooled me." I try to keep my gun trained on him as I crouch beside Morris. I pull Morris's arm but quickly realize I'll need both hands for this. With the gun tucked into my waistband, I try to swing him onto my shoulder. He's too heavy and falls back on the floor with a thud.

They snicker. I swipe at the sweat pouring off my face.

Think, Ellie, think. I shrug off the jean jacket and wrap it around Morris's chest. I hope I don't hurt him. "How do I get out of here?"

"They'll escort you out." He stalks off, leaving me with two guards. They eye me, but neither unlatches his gun.

I touch my gun. What should I do with it? Should I carry it or leave it where it is? My leggings are soaked in sweat and plastered to my skin around the gun. I take both of Morris's arms and drag him out of the cell, hoping the jean jacket will cut down the friction for him.

One of the guards leads the way out. The other stays behind me as I pull Morris through the parking lot of the massive complex.

"The field we caught you in is over there," a guard says, pointing. Then they turn their backs on me and walk away.

I exhale and twist Morris around, taking his legs under my arms and dragging him through the field. Sweat rolls off my back under the oppressive sun. So far, I'm not a fan of the West. And whose idea was it to put a massive mall in the middle of nowhere?

According to a book I read, you can tell which direction you're going by the position of the sun. I squint up at it, but no other knowledge wiggles free from my mind, so I have no idea where we are.

With another breath, another shrug, and a good roll of my shoulders, I continue through the field. The complex is far off in the distance now, and my adrenaline is waning. The field is soft beneath my boots but I look down at Morris and become concerned that his head may get scratched or worse. I set him down and unbuckle my boots. I take my leggings off, slide the gun under my underwear band by my right hip, and wrap them around his head. And then I giggle, because he looks ridiculous and I don't know what I'm doing. I'm hysterical.

How long can I keep this up? I haven't eaten in a while and I'm so, so tired. And what if he never wakes up?

No. We've come this far, and I won't abandon hope now.

If he dies, who will upload the song? Who will broadcast it? Who will save the humans? My dad? I know he said there were others, many others, but what if he alone is the key to our salvation?

A million thoughts run through my mind. He looks so innocent while he rests, which is exactly how I think of him when he's awake, too. I know he's attractive; I know if he were human, if he'd been here before everything happened, he'd have been on the soccer team or something, and have some sort of cheerleader-type girlfriend. He's beautiful, and his smile, even though he's still learning, is warm and lights up his face, and maybe even mine.

I do like him. More than like, if I'm honest.

It doesn't make any sense. It takes forever for me to like anyone; in fact, this is the first time that a person I've liked feels the same. And his people killed and are imprisoning mine. Sure, he's fighting it; now that I know him, I can't imagine Morris going along with that, but still.

I pick up his legs again and drag him through the field. "Everything" by the Starry Eyed pops into my mind.

"Don't say, don't say you don't love me. Don't say, don't say you don't feel it. Because I can't bear it. You are everything." I'm singing quietly to distract myself from the pain and the exhaustion, and although my singing is okay, it's not as good as Morris's. I

sing anyway, because my arms hurt, and my face burns. The sun never relents. My dress is torn, my thighs are rubbing together, the medicine boxes are cutting into my breasts, the gun is poking my hip, and my feet are drenched, slipping inside my boots. But I won't stop or leave him. I'll pull him all the way to California if I have to. It's not only humanity that relies on him, but me. And I can't lose him. I've lost everyone already.

Thinking about him makes butterflies flutter chaotically around my stomach. The thought of kissing him doesn't seem so weird anymore, or all that scary, after fighting those wolves and handling that gun. A kiss doesn't seem like it'll end me.

Although, glancing at his lips, my heart races. I imagine his lips on mine, and it might just be the end of *my* world.

Figures the first person I fall for would be a rebellious alien with a penchant for David Bowie. I sure do know how to pick 'em.

The sun begins to let up, and I bring a hand to my forehead to assess the horizon. The sun will set soon. Thank God, because I need relief.

Another deep exhale, and I continue forward into the vast unknown. I sing, but my lips are chapped and my throat's dry. By the time night falls, I'm still in the middle of tall grasses, and the car is nowhere in sight. I know I'm slow, but at this pace, I might die of dehydration before Morris wakes or I find the car.

My body shakes and aches, and my vision blurs. I can't go on. I need to stop. My breath comes in short puffs. I set Morris down and reluctantly curl up beside him in the grass, weeds and a million insects I'd rather not think about. And snakes.

Oh God, there are probably so many snakes.

I close my eyes and fall into the sleep of someone who's too tired to be afraid.

E! NEWS

Allister Daniels, the lead singer of the Starry Eyed, is in some legal trouble after a wild night of celebrating his eighteenth birthday at the infamous LA club, Debauchery. Not only was there underage drinking, it's been said that Allister made some real estate moves; winning the last three properties surrounding his current mansion in a game of poker. When asked, the orphan heartthrob responded via social media:

We had fun, we got drunk and I won some property. I assure you no one got hurt, no one got cheated, it was all about love. Don't you all have much better things to talk about like…idk, the current administration, climate change or the constant degradation of humanity?

But that wasn't the last we'd heard of the party. Possible flame and supermodel Tandi Larson left with tears in her eyes, telling our reporters that Allister's acting as if the world is ending.

He's not in his right mind. He keeps talking about "after they come" and needing to be prepared for something. When I told him he wasn't making any sense, that our president is a nice guy who cares deeply about immigrants, no matter where they're from, despite the media's lies, his band kicked me out. I still can't believe it!

Tandi was just the last of several rumored relationships the singer has had in the past months. We reached out to his other paramours to see if they shared Tandi's concern, but none commented. So what do you think? Is Allister Daniels in trouble for a night of questionable illegal activities, or is he in mental peril? You tell us.

CHAPTER 21

"You Send Me"
—Aretha Franklin

MORR1S

Power returns to M0Rr1S's body. Three percent flashes before his left eye, but he looks beyond it to the stars above him. Sleeping boosted his energy only 2 percent. Air sends wisps of dirt skittering across his cheeks. He's outside? Something shifts beside him and drapes a leg across his. *Ellie*. In the moonlight, he can see that she's pale, her lips are chapped, possibly dehydrated. And then he realizes that turning his head feels weird. He brings his hands up and touches material wrapped around his head. He unties it, trying not to disturb Ellie, and realizes it's her pants. He sets them aside.

He likes the way she feels tangled up with him, how her

breaths send warm air across his cheeks, her heart beats both steady and softly. He could lie like this forever, but they don't have forever. Also, there are some pointy boxes coming from her chest that are poking him through her dress, and something metallic at her waist that feels heavy and strange.

How did she get him out? He tilts his head to look upside down, in the direction he thinks they came from, and he can see that she dragged him through the grass. And probably quite far. Janelle Baker, strong and determined. She saved his life. He sits up and gently lifts her head onto his lap.

Now that his head is above the grassline, he looks around to assess the situation. His mental GPS is a little off, but he can see their car is about five or six kilometers east from here. He takes a deep breath. His head is quiet, which means Brixton has decided on another path to find him. That's troubling, but a concern for later.

M0Rr1S scoops Ellie into his arms and stands. A few small reptiles, snakes he thinks they're called, hiss in the surrounding grass, but he ignores them. He's the real predator.

His energy is low, but he is willing to go on reserves just to get out of here.

Shutting down helped him conserve his energy, but clearly depleted Ellie's. He has no idea how she got him free, how they got away. She must have been terrified. Exhausted. But she didn't leave him.

He brushes his lips against her hat before running to the car at full speed. His feet feel like they barely touch the ground. When he opens the car door, the air is stale and stifling. He sets Ellie inside, then grabs two bottles of juice from the back seat. Energy pours back into him with each gulp as he drains one. It doesn't energize him like a charge would, but it makes his body stronger, lessens his aches, which he needs if he wants to not shut down again too soon.

He tucks the bottle under his arm, then gently nudges Ellie. When she doesn't move, he begins to worry that she's ill. He keeps a hand on her shoulder, feeling her pulse beneath his fingers as he shakes her.

She blearily opens her eyes. "Morris?" Her voice is raspy, and she licks her dry lips.

"Ellie." His voice hitches as he holds the juice to her mouth.

She's in a daze as she takes a slow sip. She sits there for a moment, silent, as she wakes. "Morris. I—"

"Shhh, just drink. Okay?" M0Rr1S holds the bottle for her until the juice is gone. Color returns to her face, and her eyes open once again.

"Still thirsty."

"Don't drink it all at once. Hold on." He pulls out some crackers from the backpack and hands them to her.

She takes them and a bottle of water. "Thanks."

He hovers over her. "Ellie, you saved my life. It's I who should be thanking you." There are stalks of grass poking from her hair and hat. Her face is streaked with sweat and dirt. But still she shimmers.

"Well, you saved my life, too." The corners of her mouth lift.

"Perhaps we're even then." He gazes out at the fields they laid in. It is not like home at all. Everything there is so tall and populated, but here...there's nothing and no one. Only nature. Nature is engineered on his planet. Perhaps that's why the emperor views Earth as a prize—a perfect destination.

Ellie nibbles on the cracker, distracting him. "Morris, I wouldn't leave without you. I couldn't..."

He turns back to her and plucks some grass from her hair. "Janelle Baker, you like me." He strides around to the driver's door and slides inside. He's still got a smile on his face when he presses the ignition button, but the car sputters. "The battery. I forgot." He slumps.

"Actually, you need energy, right?" Ellie tosses him a sideways glance.

"Yes. But there isn't an energy source for me out here in this nothingness."

"There's a spare battery, though. We can connect you to the battery. All electrical energy is compatible, so it has to work."

M0Rr1S perks up. "I know there's energy in the battery, but I don't know how to transfer it. How do we plug the battery into my panel?"

Ellie gives him a crooked smile. "Wires. Let's grab the battery and your charger. And don't worry about safety from the humans. I've got a gun."

M0Rr1S glances at her. "You do?"

Her head droops a little. "I'll tell you that story when we're far away. But right now, I want to get out of here, and I want to get you charged before you pass out again." She opens the door, and pauses. "Look away."

He nods before doing as she asks. The sound of small boxes hitting the floor makes him want to turn his head, but he respects her wishes.

"The doctor gave me medicine to take, and I stuck it in my underwear."

He keeps his eyes on the road outside. "That's an odd place to keep it."

She chuckles. "I didn't know where else to put it."

He doesn't comment, only looks up at the stars through the windshield. The stars shine brighter back home. Usually thoughts of home make him long to go back. But here, with Ellie, he can't imagine being anywhere else.

"You can turn back now." Ellie opens the compartment in front of the passenger seat and gingerly places the gun inside. And then he follows her as she gets out. Together, they lift the battery from the ground where M0Rr1S left it before the capture, and set it on top of the car's engine. M0Rr1S takes the empty battery out, while Ellie rifles through the contents of the trunk.

"Hey look, a full container thing of gas. And... Aha!" she

exclaims, coming back with two cables, one red, one black. She clamps the red cable to the battery where it shows a plus sign, and the black to the minus. Then she hands the ends to M0Rr1S. "You need to connect these to your panel. I don't have scissors, so if you use your amazing power, you can strip down the rubber to the metal."

"If this doesn't work… I will shut down and stay asleep until charged." Ellie nods as he concentrates on the wires, stripping away the layers piece by piece. It's agonizingly slow, draining and precise. He slumps, the flashing over his eye saying he's on reserved energy now.

Ellie turns him and pushes him back till he's sitting against the edge of the car. She stands between his legs. "Okay, now twist these together."

His movements and breathing are slow, but he does as she says.

"Now—" she takes his head into her hands and softly tilts his head "—give me your hand."

She takes his hand in hers and pushes the cords into his USB port. Nothing happens.

M0Rr1S brushes his fingers against her arm. "You know, it was only a matter of time before you fell in love with me, Ellie."

"Oh yeah?" She puts a hand on her hip, her head cocked to the side.

"Yes. I believe the universe has a way of bringing two people together. Two people who are just… What is the saying?"

"Meant to be?"

M0Rr1S nods. "Exactly."

She scoffs, sounding unconvinced, and guides the wires into his panel, holding them gingerly. "Who said I'm in love with you? I told you I liked you. And up until a little while ago, you didn't even know what love is, let alone what falling in love means."

And then it happens. Small at first, but growing. Energy

courses through him, his advanced technology pulling the electrical charge fast.

"Is it working?"

He gulps. The air suddenly smells sweeter, and her warmth starts to seep into him. He notices everything at once, from lines of concern on her face underneath the sheen of dirt, to the way her breath catches. "Oh, Ellie, your pupils are dilated, your heart races when I'm near, and you blink a lot. You also angle your body toward me often. And I did just wake up to you lying on me. You saved my life, and you're saving me now. These are facts. And the facts imply that you and I are... We are music and stories brought to life...by love."

She's quiet as her eyes lock with his.

M0Rr1S pulls the wires from his panel, and they both let them fall to the ground. Her hand hovers by his jaw. He pushes down to see his charge status flicker in his left eye. Eighty-two percent. Enough to be useful, not enough to be inundated with senses. He moves until the palm of her hand rests against his jaw, and he looks up at her. "But as you probably know, I'm very much in love with you, too."

"You're ridiculous, you know that?"

"Perhaps humans dither around with their feelings, but I want to be honest and direct. I will not waste time and I will not say that which I do not mean. Janelle Baker, I love you. I don't care if it doesn't make sense, if it's fast, if this is a star about to explode into oblivion. It means more to me to tell you this, this truth of mine, than to hold it in. I don't wish to have regrets. Not about you."

Her lips purse. "I just... I don't know."

M0Rr1S feels wounded. "You don't believe me?"

She puts her free hand on his shoulder. "I do. It's just...everyone knows that a love like this, love that's sudden...it can't be real. Every story I've read where someone says they love you after a week is ridiculous. It's a cheesy trope. Or infatuation."

"Before the Ilori came, did you believe that aliens were real? Aliens powered by electricity, who can charge from a car battery? Who can mentally communicate with each other? Who have seen worlds you can only begin to imagine?"

"No. No one did."

"Did you think any of what has happened was possible before now? Or likely?"

She shakes her head.

"If you didn't know we were real, what we could do, then perhaps you humans have a limited perception of reality." He puts his hand on hers. "I'm not like you. You have always been free to feel. I've had to hide emotions deep inside of me, telling myself that they were false, unnecessary, shameful. I had to believe my own lies. Now, I'm here." He looks up at the cloudless sky, before letting his gaze fall back on her. "I can own these feelings. I may not always understand them…but when I know something, I'm confident. And I cannot and will not lie to you or to myself. What I feel for you is love. I feel alive with affection, and wanting to be with you. When you were gone, and I was in that cell, I thought only of you. You were in my dreams. You've set me free in a way even music couldn't. I've never been more myself, since I met you."

The corners of her lips quirk. He moves into the limited space between them. She lets her head lean back slightly, gazing into his eyes. Her cheeks bloom a rosy pink and her teeth graze her lower lip. "May I?"

He stares down at her. She's asking him. She has to know his answer.

M0Rr1S wants to take her in his arms and kiss her until the moon fades and the sun rises. But he decides to take this slow. He wraps one hand around her waist, her fiery warmth permeating her dress into his hand. The other hand brushes against the smooth skin of her jaw before he tilts her chin higher. He bends toward her to breathe her in, her mouth only centimeters from his own. "Yes."

His lips touch hers, soft and perfect, and there's an explosion of feelings and colors and lights and notes of songs that could perfectly capture this moment swimming around them. It's everything. Her heart pounds against his chest, her mouth parts to let him explore her. They are clunky. It isn't experienced, but it's right. Her eyes close.

He, M0Rr1S 1lv, is kissing Janelle Baker, the human girl who controls his body, his heart and soul, if he has one. And nothing else matters.

She gasps and smiles against his mouth as his fingers pull her closer to him. He wants to know every corner of her, but he pulls away. "You like me?"

Her face is heated, and her eyes are round. "I like you. That other *L* word's going to have to wait."

"It can. *I* can." He kisses her again before resting his forehead against hers. "We have to go."

She sighs. "I know."

"My starry dreams," he sings softly.

She looks up at him with the stars reflecting in her eyes. "You *would* sing at this moment."

He should be embarrassed, he knows now, at this display of vulnerability. But never with her. "I love to sing. Especially to you."

She giggles. "I do *love* when you sing."

He imagines there's a thing such as fate and destiny, like the Andarrans believe. "That is why the universe brought us together."

Her cheeks widen into a smile that makes his heart beat faster, if that's possible, before she steps away from him.

Time. So little time. He sinks the battery into place and removes the cables, while she stops and plucks something from the ground. From the open trunk, he takes the container of gasoline from inside and fills the tank quickly.

"What is that?" he asks as he sets the empty container back in the car and closes the hood.

"A buzzkiller." She scrutinizes it. "We might need it."

He eyes the little black device that can deplete his energy in a matter of seconds, but he doesn't question her.

She opens the car door, and then the glove compartment. She gingerly takes the gun into her hands. "I can't keep this. I hate guns." Her arm stretches back before she hurls it into the night. It goes a considerable distance, given she's a human, and plonks onto the ground.

With a happy sigh, she slides inside and shuts the door. Before he does the same, he tilts his head to the sky and smiles up at the stars. That kiss was everything he expected and more. With another deep breath, he slides in beside Ellie.

"Not much longer now."

She twists in her seat and grabs another cracker. "So about the story... I can't remember, where did we leave off?"

"He's in love."

"What happened back there, in the field, when we got caught?" Ellie takes a sip from her water after a short nap.

"I was low on energy and I connected to Il-0CoM."

She shifts in her seat. "But you connected to the humans in the field, too...?"

"I didn't, AvR0la did. But in doing so, I opened my mind to Il-0CoM." He doesn't want to scare Ellie, but he must tell her the truth. "0rsa, my brother, Brixton, and my father were able to communicate with me. I learned that 0rsa wants you dead, Brixton wants me dead and my father is disappointed, which means he would also be pleased if I were dead. And Brixton is coming. 0rsa... I don't know what she plans to do."

"Ilori," is all she says, shaking her head. For once, he can't read her expression.

"All of my life I've looked up to them—I was meant to look up to them. They were perfect and I was their lesser." He scoffs.

"The farther away I've gone, the more I realize they are weak. To understand and appreciate your emotions is strength."

"Why does your brother hate you?"

The pain hitches his breath. "Because I exist."

She huffs. "I'm sorry. He sounds horrible. Maybe he just... he doesn't know how to be a brother, or...or you know, he's used to following orders. Maybe he's afraid of being compassionate."

"Remember that when Brixton stops us at IpS1L, surrounded by a bunch of his Ilori soldier friends. And then when he tells you that I can't possibly love you, because I'm a lab monster, and nothing I feel is real."

Ellie looks over at him. "You think he would?"

"I know he will. The question is, when we get there, will he let me go?"

She turns her head toward the window. "We should plan, Morris. Stop and plan. How far away are we?"

"A few more hours and we'll be close to Los Angeles. We'll stop outside the city and figure how to get to the ship from there. It's close to the coast, so we'll have to run through the city undetected."

She makes a dramatic huff. "You mean you're going to have to run and carry me? Morris, it's too much. I'm chunky, you know?"

Now it's his turn to look at her. "What's chunky?"

"You know... I'm sorta fluffy? Thick? Fat?" She does some weird gesturing with her hands to infer that she is large.

He furrows his brows, staring at her incredulously. "You—you are the most beautiful being I've ever encountered."

"Most people think I'm unattractive. Too heavy to carry." Her voice is strange, embarrassed.

"I love everything about you. I desire every part of you... immensely. And I *will* carry you across this world, and worlds beyond this one, Ellie. You are never too much for me." He shakes his head, hoping she understands that any statement that implies she's anything less than perfect is absurd. Her cheeks pink, and her heart is racing in his ears. His fingers reach out to trace the edge of her jaw quickly before dropping back on the wheel. He doesn't want to make her more uncomfortable, so he decides to change the subject. "We'll plan when we get closer to the city. Let's enjoy the last few hours together."

"Actually..." She smiles a little. "If you don't mind, could we pull over somewhere?"

"Yes, but this time, I check around first, okay? It seems that every time we leave a car, someone attacks us. I find this troubling."

"You're right." She chuckles before tapping on the window. "Hey, look at that old-timey diner. Surprised it's still intact."

"How do you always see these places, but you couldn't see the snakes around us in the middle of the field?"

"There were snakes?" Her mouth drops open.

M0Rr1S bursts out laughing. "Let's go there. Maybe you should leave that human device though? Having it close may harm me."

"I will. I don't even know how to use it."

"I think it acts like a magnet to our electricity and depletes it. Simple yet effective." M0Rr1S steers the car across freeway lanes. Gravel swirls into the air as they pull into the empty parking lot outside of the diner.

There are all sorts of colorful signs posted around the small building. It looks untouched by invasion. Another building the Ilori must have planned on keeping as a remnant of its human past.

"It says it has the best burgers in California, and features live music on Tuesday nights. But neither of those things are true anymore." There's a dull edge in Ellie's voice that he wishes he could take away. "It was probably a busy trucker stop."

"Stay here. I will look inside. And please stay here this time." He steps out of the car and looks around. He can't sense any movement or life. He's halfway toward the diner when he turns to find Ellie at his side.

"I asked you to stay in the car."

"But what if there are Ilori and they shut you down again? You need me."

He doesn't comment, only reaches for her hand. Sometimes he wants to sing that song about wanting to hold her hand by The Beatles. But what if she grows bored or annoyed with his singing? Is it too much?

Yet, as Ellie's fingers lace through his, she hums the song, eliciting a chuckle from him. "I was just going to sing that."

"I was waiting for you to." She smiles at him and pulls him up the sidewalk with her.

"Wait," he says, taking the doorknob with his free hand. He can't see through walls, but he can sense movement in his mind. But there's nothing inside, not even a rustling of air from an open window. "Okay."

They walk inside, and she hits the light switch by the side of the door. "Worth a shot." But the lights flicker on, and her eyes widen. "Oh my."

Colorful orbs light up the black-and-white checkered flooring. Red booths line the walls, and flimsy furniture and chairs crowd the center. She navigates the forest of furniture to a bare platform. She stops next to a microphone but her gaze zeroes in on a machine in the corner. She skips over to it with a small gasp. M0Rr1S follows behind her, curious.

"This is a jukebox," she chirps. "You're going to love this, assuming we find some spare quarters."

"It takes money?" M0Rr1S eyes the machine, noting the

words on the screen and the records inside. There are little buttons and knobs, and a space to insert coins. He glances at the side of the machine; there's a little compartment toward the back with a lock. Stooping down, he uses his power to manipulate it. The pieces of metal vibrate until they pop open, spilling coins onto the floor. His fingers graze the silver pieces before he hands them to Ellie. "These?"

"Yes; exactly." Ellie takes them from his hands and pushes one through a small slot. She hits a button, and music streams forth. "It's Aretha Franklin. I've heard her a million times, and I'll never grow tired of her."

It's loud, but the jukebox machine has this old and muffled sound to it that makes it atmospheric. He closes his eyes and sways with the beat for a second before glancing over at Ellie.

"Do you want to dance with me?" Ellie holds out her hands.

He is hit with a sudden case of nerves. "I am…uncertain about my level of proficiency."

"Don't get shy now. We've danced before and it's easy. Just hold me close, and I'll show you how." He treads toward her and into her arms. "Put your arms around my waist, and I'll put my arms around your shoulders and neck, like this."

Her waist feels electric under his fingers, like she could be all the charge he needs to make his body run. He never wants to let go. Or maybe he wants to hold her closer until every part of him heats in her presence. He can't decide. She moves with him, and her smile widens. The song is by a woman, Aretha, with a deep, lovely voice. She sings about a love that has finally come into her life.

"My mom and dad loved this song. It's called 'You Send Me,' and it's about love. All these oldies are about love." Ellie rests her head on his shoulder. "Is this okay?"

"I like this." His voice cracks a little with nerves.

They stay like that until the song ends. "All right, pick out another one—just hit a random combination. I'll be right back."

She runs off toward the bathroom, and he goes over to the machine. There are numbers and letters. He finds it confusing but sorts through them until he ends up hitting something. The music starts back up just as Ellie returns. Her purple hat is peeking from her left pocket, and her hair is free around her shoulders.

She catches him staring. "My hat was dirty." A big, crooked grin splashes across her face as she begins to move around to the rhythm. "This song."

His eyes are stuck to every angle of the way her body moves. "What is it?"

"Beyoncé's 'Single Ladies.' Of all the songs... Come on, I'll show you." Ellie waves him closer to her. An invitation. He readily agrees to forget the world around them and dance for a little while.

Fear worms its way into his mind as he realizes that this may be the last joy they have together. But he chooses to ignore it for now. Ellie wants to show him her dance, and he will not ruin this moment.

He settles in beside her as she throws her hands up just like the song commands, and he follows. Then her movements come faster, and more difficult to copy. Yet, his heart is thumping in his chest, and it feels good to try. And Ellie hasn't stopped grinning at his efforts.

His gaze roams over her, and he forgets to imitate her as her hands flex at her waist; she dips, and twists around. And then she... M0Rr1S's breath catches. She shimmies to the floor, and if that is not the most attractive thing he's ever seen...

He stands there in awe of her. "Ellie. I want you to dance this dance every day for the rest of our days."

She giggles, pulling him closer, but M0Rr1S is too dis-

tracted, too powerless to dance beside her. He is utterly mes-
merized. Humans use their emotions to create emotions in
others. M0Rr1S follows every step Ellie makes. He can't take
his eyes off her. If anything happens to her on the rest of their
journey, his guilt will consume him. He couldn't live with
himself. But if she departs from his life now, it would be as if
the sun could never shine on him again.

The universe has planted him here at this time at the right
place. This was fate. The fate Andarrans believe in and he
scoffed at when their sacred fish kissed his fingers and promised him a destiny. This must be it. He was meant to find
Janelle. Meant to find her book. To engage in a series of weird
and dangerous events so that he could stand here, at this moment, enjoying her dance and realizing every plan he's ever
made means nothing if Ellie isn't there with him.

She keeps pointing to her finger throughout the dance, and
singing something about a ring. His body aches to respond
to her, to dance with her, be close to her in a new, exciting
way. But it's not the right time, and neither of them are ready.

Still, he yearns.

The song ends and she smiles through shallow breaths.
"What'd you think? I've never done that in front of anyone
before."

"That was the most amazing thing I've ever seen in my
entire existence." He can't keep the awe from his voice, nor
the desire.

"Morris, you're blushing." So is she. Her eyes lock on his.
"Do you want to dance one more time?"

"Yes."

PART FOUR

THE WORLD IS THEIRS NOW

THE STARRY EYED:
"LOST WITH YOU"

The Sound of Stars
Written by: Cecil Wright, Allister Daniels, Rupert Montague,
Whisper Landsome

Lost in the cosmos, stuck in the colonies
Worlds upon worlds in the galaxies
The spectrum as far as our eyes can see
Honey, do you trust me?

Past the sun, on the other side of the moon
I know you're scared, we'll be there soon
You read me the book, I'll sing you the tune
I make you laugh, you make me swoon

If we're lost, my dear, I don't care
I found you

If we're together, it doesn't matter where
I want you

Places in the universe we're going to explore
I'll break the lock, you push open the door
With you by my side, I'll never ask for more
You make my soul smile, I make your heart soar

If we're lost, my love, I don't care
I found you
If we're together, it doesn't matter where
I need you

I'll show you everywhere and anywhere my dear
I'll take you places, I'll always hold you near
I know you're scared, but there's nothing to fear
One shot into space, right through the atmosphere

If we're lost, I just don't care
I promise you
If we're together, it really doesn't matter where
I live for you
They say we're in space, but please stay close to me
I revolve around you, you're my gravity
They say we're too different, that it can't last
That you're a star, shooting too fast
But you put your hand in mine, taking me with you
I love you
I love you

CHAPTER 22

"To be fond of dancing was a certain step toward falling in love."

—Jane Austen, *Pride and Prejudice*

JANELLE

My mind keeps traveling back to that kiss. The way his lips felt against mine.

Then my mind travels to Alice, and her kiss. My first kiss. I liked Alice, loved her as a friend. She was my first crush. If we'd had time and our circumstances were different, maybe we would have dated. But now that I've had the best kiss of my life, there's no one else I want to kiss. My cheeks heat, and I distract myself by peering out the window at the shifting landscape.

I wonder if that's how Wylan felt when he finally kissed Jesper, or Dimple and Rishi's first—no, second—kiss, or when Camille finally got to kiss Lazare, or Jack when he gets to kiss Kate the first of many first times, or Elizabeth and Darcy... although they never do kiss in the book. I imagine it would be a lot like ours.

We pass a sign welcoming us to California, The Golden State. Another version of me would have held my phone out, taken a picture of it and posted it online. But this version of me doesn't have a phone, or anyone to share with.

My mind travels to my parents, possibly unconscious in their own bodies by now. I wonder what they would think about me traveling across the country with an Ilori boy who I've kissed and might be falling in love with.

My mom would have been weirded out but happy. She was always trying to goad me into making more friends and finding a significant other. Probably neither of us imagined I would.

Now I'm sitting next to an Ilori boy. An Ilori boy who I might sorta love? I guess in a way it all makes sense. It all comes together. The only person I'd fall in love with is an alien. But how can I love Morris when our future is so uncertain?

Morris is lost in thought as he drives. If he's scared, he hasn't said.

It's the middle of the night, and I wonder if now would be a good time to pop one of my newly acquired pills. I guess I'm expecting to live longer in this body, so I'll need this medicine to last longer than a few days. Then I wonder, if I get vaccinated, will the Ilori inhabiting my body have the same hypothyroidism with a generous dose of anxiety? Will they take the medicine, or will they have some magical cure?

I bend forward and pick up one of the small boxes of medicine. I forgot how delicate the cardboard is, and am careful not to crush it.

Morris looks over as I open the flap to release a flimsy metal sheet dotted with tiny pills. "What is that?"

"Medicine for my... I have a thyroid condition." I don't really want to talk about it, though. I told all my friends; it was hard not to when I had to keep canceling plans because I felt like there was fire in my veins, and I analyzed everything a million times. Alice and I talked about it often. She did wellness checks and knew how to talk me through an attack. But right now, I want to enjoy the last few hours we have left, not thinking about my illness or the medicine I'll take that won't actually work for weeks.

Morris seems to understand and doesn't ask more about it. I appreciate that. The pill sits on the tip of my tongue till I wash it down.

"Want me to tell you the rest of the story?" We're almost to the end of it, and Morris has loved it so far.

"No, although I want to know how it ends and I really want them to get together. But if they don't, and that is the last story I hear in this world, in your voice, then I don't want to imagine any story where love doesn't find a way in the end."

I sigh. "Oh, Morris."

"I know." And I know he does. He's afraid that our love story might not have a happy ending.

He pulls the car over and turns it off. "We'll be in Los Angeles in a few hours if we keep at this pace. But unfortunately, the closer we get to the city, the more the Ilori control, and then we must also be careful to avoid the Andarran lands. IpS1L is on the coast, along the beaches. I wish I had a map to show you."

"Andarrans? As in other aliens?"

Morris nods, and I open my mouth, but nothing comes out. I decide not to ask as much as I can about it. "It doesn't matter. You know where you're going, and I'll follow you."

I stretch in my seat and give him a half shrug that I hope encourages him to continue.

He clears his throat. "We will have to leave the car somewhere before Los Angeles. Otherwise, we would attract unwanted attention and more danger than necessary." He takes a deep breath. "We'll have to walk the rest of the way. Are you okay with this?"

I twist my hair up before pulling the hat down over it. "We've already made it this far. What's a few more miles on foot?"

"Your optimism is both surprising and delightful."

"No one has ever described me that way," I joke.

"Oh, really? Does anyone truly know you, I wonder?" He turns his beautiful, round eyes on mine.

"I'm difficult to know," I admit.

"I think I do. Know you, that is."

"We've known each other—what—eleven or twelve days?" I bite the inside of my cheek to tamp down my heart.

"And that is all it took." His gaze drops to my lips.

I lean forward to kiss him. Never in my life did I imagine that, in a series of eleven or twelve days, I, Janelle Baker, would be kissed three times. But now it's happened, and I have to say, I really enjoy it. Alice's kiss was sad but filled with platonic love. Morris's kiss is…filled with desire and a very different sort of love. The kind of love that makes your stomach warm, and your heart flip in your chest like it just doesn't know what to do.

The seconds turn to minutes, and the softness turns to passion. Next thing I know, I've straddled his lap, and the steering wheel is poking into my back, but I pay it no mind. I'm lost in Morris, and he's just as lost in me. Every place our bodies touch feels like fire—deliciously warm fire—when all I've known is the cold.

His hands are firm around my waist, and the world falls

away around us. Heat blasts through every dark and distant thought that warns me that time is running out. That we don't belong together. That this thing is too wild to be tamed. Right now, all I want is to live; to be truly alive and human, with an Ilori boy who inspired love in me.

I pull my lips back from his. "I don't know what I'm doing."

His gaze falls. "Do you regret this?"

"No, I'm sorry, I don't mean that. I mean, I don't know how to do this...you know? Um, intimacy? I don't know."

His tongue darts out to lick his lips, and my breath hitches. "Neither do I."

"But you've done it before."

"But I've never felt like *this* before."

"So what do we do?"

"We..." He sighs. "If we were going to...make love, I don't wish for it to be in a car. Nor do I want our fates to remain unknown, or you to worry, or—"

"If we wait for perfection, we might never experience anything." I shift in his lap, aware of how my actions affect him. Part of me, a big part, knows he's right.

"This is true, but I'm nervous and I want it to be perfect. Do you think that would be okay?"

I nod in agreement, before kissing him quickly on the lips. I'm rushing it, because I never felt this way, never wanted to feel this way, and I'm afraid my life will be over soon. "We'll wait."

"Are you disappointed?"

"No." I slide off him and sit back in the passenger seat. "Never."

"Can you tell me the rest of the story?"

"I'd love to." I adjust myself, letting the coolness of his absence wash over me. "And we still haven't listened to the first Starry Eyed album."

"Well we should listen now, before we lose the chance."

I twist in my seat and search for my other phone through the hard drives and books. I find it underneath my copy of *The Hate U Give*, the book that started it all. I yank the old phone out and push the new one in. A moment passes before the familiar voice of Allister Daniels fills the car. I lean back in my seat. "Where did we leave off?"

We finish the story when we slow to a stop in West Covina. I hand Morris the USB stick from the console so that he can rearrange his bag, then step out and stretch my legs. I yawn. I wish we hadn't left my leggings in a field somewhere in Arizona, because the more my thighs rub together, the more they'll become an intolerable, painful, fiery hell.

I can't help but cringe as I remember this happening to me while walking the Brooklyn Bridge after stopping for ice cream. I'd been tempted to drop it between my legs for relief.

Maybe we'll stop somewhere and I'll miraculously find some pants that fit me. But the invasion started in eight places: São Paulo, Lagos, DC, Moscow, Paris, Tokyo, Sydney and Los Angeles. I'd be surprised if there's any clothing or supplies left out here.

"Are you ready?" He stuffs the medicine into his bag as I collect the buzzkiller from the glove compartment.

We start walking down a deserted street on broken pavement that eventually melts into dirt and grass. There are a few immaculate buildings standing—only a few traces of humans—interspersed with gardens that have all sorts of dangling fruits and vegetables I don't recognize hanging from tall trees.

"Wow. This is another world."

Morris squeezes my hand. "This is how most of your world will look in just a few days. Forest, gardens, green spaces and wildlife. Flowers. Pure enough for the Ilori. This atmosphere might even be clean enough for them now."

My eyebrows lift while dread sits in the bottom of my gut. The Ilori may be better for Earth, but I think humanity can still change. That humanity deserves to reclaim our planet and be better to it.

"You told me that your dad will kill you and then punish your mom if you fail here. Why would he do that?"

Morris plucks a shimmery purple fruit from a garden as we pass. "Because I didn't want to marry Orsa. Because my mother gave me her genetic material, making me one of the strongest labmade Ilori. And because he didn't want me. I guess I should say, he didn't want a labmade son. My mother couldn't have more children." He takes a bite and sighs. "Would you like one? They're called starberries."

I shrug and take it from him. My teeth sink into the soft flesh, and I think I make a little sound. The fruit is sweet, like eating ripe strawberries, but has the sharp tartness of a plump clementine. It's the most delicious thing I've ever eaten. Morris looks at me, a blush creeping onto his olive cheeks. "Sorry, you were saying?"

Morris nods, looking a bit distracted. "When I was in the labs, my father spoke to me. He explained the rules of our home, of our people...he described the palace. I am not certain why he did this, whether my mother forced him to—but as his visits became more frequent, I became more attached to him. I liked hearing his voice and his thoughts. But I do admit, I was not listening as carefully as I should have. I was too in awe. When I was born, I mistook his interest in me as love. And I remember the look he gave me when I made that mistake. I didn't know it then, but I know it now as disgust. And therein began our complicated relationship. I'm too feeling, too impure for him. I will never be a true Ilori. From the beginning, I've felt deeply, only with shame." Morris's mouth wobbles. "I've been carrying this burden longer than I can remember."

His head droops a little. "When my grandfather dies, my father will become emperor. He can forbid any communication between my mother and me."

I pat his arm, but the news surprises me. "I'm so sorry. Is that why you're rebelling against him?"

Morris stops and looks at me. "In a way, yes. But also for my mother. She loved me...she helped me, groomed me for this purpose regardless of my inferiority, to become the seed of rebellion against my own father. How long she's been standing beside him while plotting against him, I don't know. She gave me this mission, and that is why I have always been careful in Il-0CoM."

We begin walking again as he catches his breath. "I'm telling you this because I trust you. I kept the truth from you before because I was trying to protect you, but I was also pushing you away. I won't do that again."

I take his hand as we continue through the forest. "Thank you for trusting me, Morris."

"Thank you for...everything, Ellie."

I keep my head down as a grin spreads across my face. I hope we don't run into any Ilori, and I really hope that I keep Morris's secret with me forever. He and his mother seem to have a close bond, as close as I had to my parents. I don't want to be the human girl who destroys that.

"How long a walk is this going to be?" I find myself wishing for the flimsy blue sneakers we lost in Oklahoma. My feet are sweaty in the boots without socks.

"Around nine hours without using my abilities. Six with." Morris shoots me a look of concern. "Are you okay?"

"I'm just a little worried. Every time I take a trip I worry."

"What are you worried about?"

Honestly? What aren't I worried about is a better question. My legs, my feet, my hair, his brother and, of course, making the decision to go with him or stay here, be killed by his betrothed or vaccinated. What if that ship, the only chance he has at uploading and broadcasting his song, doesn't work? The other aliens. And death. I'm probably going to die today. Oddly, that doesn't scare me as much as all the other things.

"Nothing important," I answer.

"Ellie, if you're scared, we can find somewhere for you to hide. I don't want anything to happen to you. This was a bad idea…"

"Morris, I want to go, and there's nowhere else anymore. I doubt we could hide me in permanent housing, wherever that even is, it's probably guarded, right?" Morris nods once. "I bet that mall we left behind is already under siege." I let that sink in before adding, "Whatever happens, we'll do this together."

"I never wanted to see you cry out in pain. It hurts me, oh it hurts me, it was me who did it… I shout, you weep, I lie, you speak…the truth, always the truth, I hold your heart in my hands. I broke it once, but never again…" His voice has strengthened so much now that he could actually be a pop star if the world was different.

My heart leaps every second his voice fills the air around us. It's beyond corny, but he's so unabashedly adorable. He's fearless and unafraid that I'll hurt him. I want to promise him and myself that I won't, but I know better than to make a promise I can't keep, especially right now.

"You are! You are! You are everything." He draws out the last syllables in a jumbled mess of notes. I purse my lips, trying not to laugh. My worries melt in the western sun, and I give in to feeling in love as we walk through the surreal landscape.

I think of my favorite books and decide on one. "Do you want to hear another story?"

"Always."

CHAPTER 23

"By Your Side"
—Sade

M0RR1S

Hours have passed, and M0Rr1S worries that not only will they not make it to the ship without getting caught, but that Ellie's legs are hurting. He points at a lone building with clothing displayed in its window. It's the only building they've seen for miles as they reach the outskirts of LA, as Ellie calls it. "Perhaps there is something in there for you?"

She eyes the building wearily. "Everything else has been torn down. We've seen at least thirty or forty gardens, and lakes I'm sure never existed before. And yet they kept this store? How do we know it's not a trap?"

"Habitation will keep unique structures that offer a glimpse into humanity. Besides, they like clothes." M0Rr1S cuts a glance at Ellie. "There's no one inside. I sense no movement. Do you want to go?"

"Yeah." Ellie exhales. "I need relief from this hell."

They enter the store gingerly, and the scent of florals hits him first. Both human and Ilori, like the gardens they passed on the way here. And it's clean, so very clean. The carpeting is an immaculate dark green, like the forest floor, and fake tree branches climb the walls, congregating on the ceiling with shards of crystals dangling. Light dances around the space. Suddenly, M0Rr1S understands why they kept this. It is unique, but also familiar. Like his home.

Ellie rummages through racks of well-kept garments, squealing in delight at one point. She takes a pile of mixed, colorful fabrics and goes into a small chamber behind a wooden door made from tree bark. He can glimpse only her hat as she undresses. M0Rr1S stands next to the room, crossing his arms, cautious.

Minutes pass, but he's unperturbed by the delay. He needs some rest as well, this time not because his charge is low, but because there is worry in the pit of his stomach.

What if he fails?

Ellie comes out in a black T-shirt with a spaceship and words that don't mean much to him. Patches of her legs are exposed in a pair of jeans with holes around the knees.

"These are so comfortable. And look at this vintage *Star Wars* T-shirt! I can't believe we found a store with clothes my size! After an alien invasion!" She poses for him, makes pouty lips that he longs to kiss. "Now shoes…"

The shoe area is a neat pile of boxes across the store that reach up to his chest. Ellie sorts through them, causing an avalanche of boxes, tissue paper and various footwear. M0Rr1S peers around, hoping the noise doesn't attract any attention.

She hums softly as she admires the multicolored shoes on her feet. "*Vans*. The most comfortable shoes I've worn in years." She groans in pleasure. "All right, I'm ready. Let's go."

M0Rr1S wraps his arms around her shoulders, and, for the first time since he met her, she seems at her most energetic. "You are my favorite person."

"I know." She grasps his hand. "I still don't know what we're going to do. But you..." She takes a deep breath. "You see me. All of me. You accept me. You don't look at me like some weird black girl who keeps books as friends. You understand."

M0Rr1S feels like his heart might burst upon hearing her words. "And you don't see me as an evil Ilori who has destroyed your world." He smiles. "I think, Ellie, we were meant to find and understand each other."

She pecks him on the lips and slides her hand through his. "I don't know about that, but I'm glad we found each other."

"So, let me tell you a story inspired by this shirt I'm wearing." She points to a picture of a man wearing a strange black suit, a woman in a white gown holding a gun of some sort and another man holding a sword made of light. It is very odd, but also fascinating. "Once upon a time, in a galaxy probably not far away from yours, there was a girl named Ciena, and a boy named Thane..."

The labmade Ilori become more and more visible as they enter the former city. M0Rr1S and Ellie hide behind trees that climb into the sky, imported from home, and within the high grass. They've had some close calls. M0Rr1S picked up Ellie twice and ran around harvesting farms to avoid capture. But moving that fast too often takes a toll on him. He sets Ellie down inside a subway station that dips beneath the grass. He clings to the vines as he calms his own breathing.

"*Five*, the sun. *Four...four*, my hat... *Three*, my soft new shoes. *Two*." Her voice steadies, and her shoulders droop. "*Two...*" She closes her eyes and exhales slowly. "*Two*, the smell of gardens and earth and hope. *One*—" she glances at him, a small smile tugging at her lips "—Morris."

Their eyes lock, and everything around them fades from view. A melody drifts through his mind, something he's never heard before accompanied by their two hearts beating in near unison.

How has he ever lived without her?

And that distraction, beautiful and monumental, is all it takes for him to be surprised by an Ilori guard on the opposite side of the tunnel. The guard stops in their tracks.

The color drains from Ellie's face as her hands travel to her neck. M0Rr1S wants to run to her, tell her everything will be okay, but the Ilori stands before him. They take in M0Rr1S's jacket, the lack of identification. Their gaze slides to Ellie quickly before snapping back to M0Rr1S.

M0Rr1S prepares to battle with the other Ilori, a battle that could result in death. He has never killed before. But he must keep Ellie safe even if it means doing something he would regret for the rest of his days. He rises onto the balls of his feet, and lets air sail between his teeth. He's unprepared for this.

"I—"

"Stay off the main road," the Ilori states in accented English, surprising them. "Bl0n, male, this is my quadrant." He flicks a button on his panel, motioning to M0Rr1S to do the same. "I have uploaded the patrols to your panel."

"Thank you." The words tumble from M0Rr1S's lips unexpectedly. "The vaccine—"

"Has been administered globally. There are no more human rebels. All have surrendered, with limited loss of life. True Ilori command will begin the descent in five rotations."

Before he can ask why and how, Bl0n steps back.

"May the road lead you to success, M0Rr1S 1lv. What G00287 granteth, the labmades taketh," the Ilori says, putting his fist over his heart and bowing once, before turning and jogging off.

M0Rr1S runs to Ellie's side as she hunches over, gasping for air. Her fingers circle her neck as if she is bound by that rope on the rooftop in New York City once again.

"You're safe. They won't hurt you." M0Rr1S wraps a steady arm around her. "I'm here."

Minutes pass as her breathing slows and her back straightens. Her hands shake by his side. "I'm sorry. Panic thing. I'm fine. Are you…are you okay?" Ellie pushes sweaty strands of hair from his eyes.

"Perfectly fine," he lies, but she sees right through him.

"Is there anything I can do to help?"

"Just stay by me. And if I say run, please run." She nods and touches the tips of her fingers to his cheek. The sensation of her electrifies his body, and it takes so much for him not to touch her back. To tell her that perhaps, they only have now.

But instead, he uses the scanner to determine the location of the patrols. None register. Their safest option is to linger here awhile.

Ellie slumps against the wall and slides down. "How long will it take to get to the water?"

M0Rr1S sits beside her. "Maybe four hours."

"Are we going to make it?" She lowers her voice to a whisper.

"Yes, but we should wait until night falls. Reduced visibility will help us move through the landscape."

Her eyes keep darting to the shadows. "Are you hungry? Do you need juice? We have to do something…"

He takes her shaking hands in his, hoping their closeness

will settle her down, make her calm. "We'll both have something to drink, okay?"

Ellie lifts the supply bag beside her and grunts. "Wow, this is heavy. You didn't tell me."

He cocks a smile at her. "Too important to leave behind."

She sorts through it, shifting things aside until she produces the last bottle of juice. She twists the top off and hands it to him. The first few drops feel like electricity on his tongue.

"Your turn," he holds it out to her.

"I feel fine."

Yet he knows she needs it just as much as he does. "When is the last time you drank?"

"Okay, okay." She rolls her eyes before taking a sip. "This stuff is so good. What's calef juice made of anyway?"

M0Rr1S chuckles to himself. "You might not want to know."

Ellie scrunches her nose. "Is it something gross?"

"There's an animal in Ilori colony V3-77-1011 called the calef. It's a little larger than your Earth elephant. They roam the colony freely and bathe in the large pools of water, turning the water orange." Ellie's face drops in disgust. "No one knows who decided to test the water, or what led them to drink it. But from then on, Ilori from all over the universe drink it. It's high in vitamins and minerals. It offers more energy than pills or injections."

A warm memory hits him.

"I remember asking my mother why it tastes so good, and she told me because it tastes like freedom."

Ellie regards him with some emotion flickering across her expression. "Have you always felt like you were imprisoned in your world? By your dad? Your brother? Your circumstances?"

"Yes." He answers without hesitation. "But never when I'm

with you. You don't expect me to be anything, and you… I know you care about me."

She bites her lower lip, and her head bobs in a little dance. "Are we going to survive this, Morris?"

"I don't want to lie to you, Ellie. We're in danger. But this is the only way to undo everything that has happened. To change our worlds. It's not too late to stay behind, to wait for the song to broadcast. You don't have to come…" He doesn't want to beg her, or put pressure on her, but the truth is, he's not ready to say goodbye. Part of him needs her there with him, despite how selfish it is. "When this is done, you can go back to your parents, to Alice. I promised you I would save them, and I will keep that promise, Ellie. It's your choice. Always your choice."

Darkness falls, and Ellie's gaze lingers on it. "I know I'm supposed to feel terrified. But, right now, I feel nothing. I don't know how long ago I lost this part of me that can't grasp what's happened, and the shock. Nothing and no one was spared. We're all the same here."

M0Rr1S tilts his head. "Were you ever not the same?"

Ellie doesn't hesitate. "No. We were never the same. We all wanted to be. We took to the streets. We put on two faces—one for them, one for us. But no, we weren't the same. Some people were always valued, and some people never were. Didn't matter how much you tried, how hard you worked, or that you did everything right. We asked for equality and they thought we were asking for more." She laughs bitterly. "Humans weren't perfect. Neither are the Ilori. But I'm not as angry anymore. It's easy to sugarcoat the memories, but the truth is—was—we were already killing each other before you came."

M0Rr1S, in a way, understands. Nothing in this universe is perfect.

"I could stay somewhere, hope to survive all of this. But I've done that for two years at the center and I can't go back now. Not when you've given me the chance to do more. To be more. To change everything." She turns to him. "If I die trying, it's better than just watching humanity fade into nothing. To feel myself slipping away into nothing."

The conversation dies as they both stare out into the silent world.

"Whatever happens, I'm glad to have met you," she whispers, still holding his hand.

"You are the highlight of my existence, Ellie."

Tumbling Rocks
Music Entertainment
Magazine

Review of *The Sound of Stars* by the Starry Eyed
By Chris Vogel

When the Starry Eyed announced their release of *The Sound of Stars* a week before it dropped, there was a collective gasp. It's often remarked, by both casual observers and fans, that the band likes to quietly release albums without warning. Either you're Beyoncé, who gives us a sparkly new album one day, or you're Taylor Swift, getting our interest a month in advance by dangling juicy singles for our consumption. Both scenarios work for big-name artists. Both scenarios worked for the first two Starry Eyed installments. Yet, a week before their newest album was gifted to the world, the Starry Eyed was everywhere. Promoting this album on every big stage they could.

I don't think you could change a channel without seeing their faces or hearing tidbits of their new songs. They promised this work was different, their best, and needed an audience.

Some of us in the music industry rolled our eyes and groaned into the void, myself included. Every band on the verge of mediocrity says that to bolster appearances, make money, save face.

However, the Starry Eyed did give us their absolute best here. And this one *is* different.

You can tell after mere minutes that these lyrics and sounds are important to the band, more so than any music they've made before. Let me be clear, it doesn't deviate from their brand of beautifully constructed work; you've got a dreamy, gentle orchestra drifting through each track, intricate guitar work—further proof that both Cecil Wright and Rupert Montague are masters of their mediums—and the drums… Whisper Landsome shows us how far she's come in a little under two years. She's truly in her element here, and I'd say she's the real star on this album. Unexpectedly and quite refreshingly, Allister Daniels isn't up to his usual showboating, breathy performance. His vocals are an integral piece of the art, moving and transitioning fluidly with a sense of both hope and melancholy. From "Fairy-tale Girl" to the finale of "Lost With You," listeners will be invested in this story. And it is very much a story the band is trying to convey—a tale of love that feels open to interpretation, and another that doesn't feel entirely meant for us.

The lyrics make it seem as if the girl in "Fairy-tale Girl" is real, and the Starry Eyed need her and this mysterious other to take note. There's an urgency to the pacing, as if the world depends on our two lovers to save us all. I could wax poetic about it longer than it takes to listen from beginning to end—that's what this album does so well. It speaks to our very human desire to explore our feelings and find a connection to our lives through the music. Every note demands your attention, every word pulls at your heart. With that in mind, I can't imagine how they'll top this.

CHAPTER 24

"He's more myself than I am. Whatever our souls are made of, his and mine are the same."

—Emily Brontë, *Wuthering Heights*

JANELLE

The miles stretch into hours. Despite the heat, I hold on to Morris the entire way, navigating a dark LA. We've been lucky; we haven't run into any other Ilori or humans. And my new jeans are saving my life. I almost feel like a bit of me has come back. It's silly, but good clothes make a world of difference.

We're both struggling. Sometimes Morris will hum something that'll settle us both momentarily, but I can tell he's worried. Everything's about to change. It all ends here.

"Do you want to hear another story?" I ask, and he squeezes my hand.

"Yes, please."

I smile. "Once upon a time, there was a girl named Amari whose brother, Quintin, was missing..."

Morris is quiet, enthralled by the story, and it's not long before I think I hear waves crashing.

"We're close now, aren't we?"

He nods, but aside from the moonlight reflecting in his eyes, I can't see much. I'm stumbling in the dark with him as my guide. I don't mind, but Ellie from two weeks ago would've freaked out. Ellie from two weeks ago didn't like relying on anyone and didn't trust most people. *That* Ellie thought nothing was really worth saving. This new me is okay with Morris showing me the way. If it were anyone else? I would have chewed them out and stalked off by now.

But this new me thinks about the woman in the mall with her small son who helped me escape. She didn't know me, but still she trusted me to do something that wouldn't harm her or others. She believed in us and hoped we would succeed. Same with that Ilori in the subway.

I remember the woman with her child trying to break through the door of our building in New York. I was too late to save her. Never again. The world still has a chance. What would it do with a second chance? What would *I* do? The answer surprises me. I'd fight for my own happiness, while fighting for change, too.

The sound of waves grows louder and louder, and I resist the urge to run to them. I love the water. I've missed it. I remember standing in Brooklyn Bridge Park, gazing out at the East River as I waited for my turn on Jane's Carousel. And sitting on the crowded beach during our day trips to Coney Island. But this will be different. I've never been on a beach at night, nor have I seen the Pacific. There's a whole lot of firsts happening for me.

And lasts, too.

"The ship." Morris's eyes are wide as they focus on something in the distance. "It's this way. The map tells me we need to tread carefully to avoid Andarran land. We're not alone."

"Your brother?"

His exhale whistles through his teeth. "I think so."

"What will happen?"

He squeezes my hand tighter. "I don't know. I have to get aboard, and you have to stay safe. Maybe you should—"

I squeeze back. "There's only one way to do this."

Morris turns to me and holds my face in his hands. "I will protect you. But if I can't—"

I don't let him finish. "If you can't, I might die. But I might have died a few times already. I want to be here. I want to save Earth. I want to be with you."

Morris gives me a quick kiss, but there's fear in his expression. I moan a little, as his body wraps around mine. *"Honey, do you trust me?"* he sings, and I let out a small, nervous laugh. He pulls away. "I love your laugh, Ellie."

I can feel the heat rising to my cheeks, but I don't break the contact. "I know, Morris."

"If we're lost, my dear, I don't care… I found you. If we're together, it doesn't matter where… I want you." Even at the end or the beginning, Morris sings to me, and my heart dips with a familiar happiness only he can inspire.

"We either lose, or we win. But we can't do either if we stand here." I look up at him through my eyelashes. "I hope we win."

"Me, too."

Together we take the long walk to the beach. I don't need him as a guide anymore; the moon lights up the sky and reflects off the ocean. Water splashes over the chrome spaceship embedded in the sand, shimmering in the moonbeams. My eyes widen as I pause to glare at the ship, gulping air into my suddenly empty lungs. It's far bigger than I expected, stretching more than a mile along the coast as far as I can see. I have no idea where it ends as it dips beneath the Pacific.

Then there are the other, smaller ships to the right, inland from the gargantuan one the military shot down. They remind me of smart cars only way smarter.

"Pods," Morris says as if reading my mind. "For leadership to come and go as necessary."

There has to be forty or fifty of them studded along the beach in neat, tight rows.

And, yet, what surprises me most of all is how deserted it is; how, once we enter this beach, it's just us on the edge of this continent. I want to run my fingers over the chrome ships to feel the foreign, smooth metal. I want to hit the pause button to grasp the enormity of spaceships, but I hold Morris, following him, until he stops suddenly. My stomach twists into knots as he whirls, narrowing his gaze into the distance. I whip my head around, but it's too dark to see much beyond a shape in the shadows.

It moves into the starlight, and my heart races. A blue form, not quite solid in structure, with a layer of purple hovering around their skin, stands beside a pod. Their outfit, more like a uniform, is black like Morris's, but decorated with brightly lit buttons. Morris pulls me closer.

"Brixton," Morris says aloud in English before entering my mind. *I am sorry to invade your mind without permission again, Ellie, but it is important you understand what is being said. I will do this as long as I can.*

"M0Rr1S." The words sound like robotic clicks. Brixton, the first alien I've seen that truly looks like an alien from a *Marvel* movie, glances my way with curt interest. His expression, mouth, nose and eyes, are similar to mine. I squint a bit, trying to make sense of what I'm seeing. He's like a human, only instead of being comprised mostly of water like us, he's made of pure, vibrant energy, and it streams through his veins, alighting beneath his skin.

He looks away, returning his attention to Morris. They don't resemble each other. He's far taller than Morris. Yet he walks slowly and takes shallow, short breaths, like he's not quite comfortable breathing this air. There's no panel marking him as labmade, but his rigid posture and the way he takes in Morris, unblinking, is alien.

"The atmosphere is clean but still I taste the pollution on my tongue," he says more to himself than to us. "I traveled all this way, to this—" he looks beyond the pods at the nothingness that probably used to be million-dollar beach houses "—wasteland, because Father wants me to kill you. Call it an accident. You've made it easy with your insubordination."

"What do you wish to do?" Morris's voice is soft, calm.

"I have not yet decided. Give you time. Do what you came to do."

Anxiety churns in the pit of my stomach, and my numbers escape me right now. Morris's mouth draws into a scowl as he turns away, clutching my arm tighter. We walk slowly toward the massive ship, and as if it senses our presence, a solid metal ramp emerges from within and soundlessly plops into the sand before our feet. I gasp, and Morris squeezes my hand. The metal glimmers bright, and I have to wait for my sight to adjust.

"Are you sure?" he asks softly.

I nod once. I'm going to be a part of saving my world with him. We tread up the ramp, my breaths coming faster with each step. I toss glances at Brixton, who makes no move to thwart us but instead kicks sand with the toe of his boot.

The ship. All we need— Morris's voice cuts off as he punches some keys with strange symbols on a holographic panel that slides out from the wall. The dark metal door whooshes open, and we rush forward only to stop dead in our tracks.

Orsa saunters toward us into the light of the moon, followed by four blank-stared guards. We stumble back down the ramp toward the sand and, for a moment, Morris is quiet. His head oscillates between Orsa and Brixton, but his wild look softens as he meets my gaze. This is it. We've come this far for nothing. Desperation tugs at my heart just as it pales on his face. If we don't get aboard, there's no saving this world. My parents. My life. And what will happen to Morris? The possibilities stream through my mind, each worse than the last. We can't fight four guards, Orsa and Brixton.

We retreat until we're stuck between two enemies.

Orsa's face is impassive, but her words are cut like ice. "You've kept the human alive. I'd hoped you might." She takes small steps toward us until she's facing me and Morris. "Do you know why I'm here?"

"I don't possess that knowledge, Orsa." Morris's tone comes off as civil, but I catch the anger simmering beneath. His gaze sweeps past her to the guards, as does mine. There are more behind her, ready to end us both.

"I know it came to you as a…surprise to see me here on this world. You were not happy."

I shift from foot to foot, my head swiveling to focus on something, anything that will give me control. That I can count till my breaths become easy, till my heart stops thundering in my ears. Orsa glares at me.

Morris lifts his chin, authority seeping into his voice. "Orsa. You will not harm Ellie."

Orsa drops her head to examine her nails in detached interest. "You are one of the newer generations of labmade, so you wouldn't understand my motivations. They taught your generation that you are subpar from the beginning, built to resemble the creatures of another, inferior world. But the earlier models like me, we were raised to be like true Ilori. We were not created as a disposable army. We were created to broaden our Ilori Empire. My parents always treated me as if I were one of them. Our empire regards me as true." Orsa takes a deep, steady breath. "But when it came time to choose my suitor, they picked you. See? I'm only fit to wed another labmade. You." She balls her fists. "I desire so much more."

"Orsa—"

"I will make a deal with the human and see what it decides." Orsa regards me with distaste before her expression dulls once more. She speaks English, causing Morris's translation to retreat from my mind. "Human JQB-305-7-21. I have something for you."

Orsa juts her chin toward the ship, and her eyes glaze over. Communicating in Il-0CoM. The ground shakes, thunder rippling over metal as three more guards march down the ramp, dragging something behind them.

Unease seeps into the pit of my stomach just as the scent of rot wafts from the ship, filling my nose. I gag, but I can't look away. The dread deepens as I realize it's not something, but someone. More than one.

Morris grits his teeth. "Hostages outside of regulated centers, Orsa? This is illegal. Inhumane."

"Breaking the law was never my plan, but you gave me the idea. I suppose it's funny how the implanted memories of our intercourse were better than reality. I could have you shut down for that." Orsa sneers.

I squint, trying to see the prisoners behind the guards. I gasp, my heart pounding, as light lands upon them. My mom and dad. An Ilori I don't know—Avrola? And Alice. I sink my feet into the sand to keep myself from running to them.

Alice wipes at tears spilling onto her pale cheeks and my mom—despite the rings beneath her eyes and disheveled hair—smiles. She *smiles*. "Mom?"

"Honey." My mom tries to step toward me but she's quickly yanked back, letting out a yelp. My dad stands beside her but remains rigid; the same version of him I left behind.

I'll do anything to set them free. My parents begged me to live for them, but how can I live for them if I'm not able to die for them? How can I live with myself?

Smoke begins to billow from the ship, flooding into the night sky. For a second, I don't understand what's happening.

"What have you done, 0rsa?" M0Rr1S's voice cracks as he cranes his head back to gape at the rubble.

"This ship. I glimpsed it in your mind. Well no…not me. I was not trained to be a soldier, but I employ personal priers. I never leave home without one." Her lips tighten and curve at the corners before her face goes slack. "You should have been more careful, M0Rr1S. While you were implanting images of us together in my mind, you left yourself open. I admit, I almost respected you when my strongest prier struggled to invade your mind, but eventually, you gave her an image of this ship. I knew it must mean something to you. Perhaps you needed it. I do not suffer curiosity for long, and so, I decided to burn it down from the inside out. Careful not to scar the Andarran land. We wouldn't want a war, now would we?"

My gaze locks on my family. My mom mumbles under her breath while Alice stares back. They've been through so much, and now I've dragged them into this. If they die here, it'll be because of me.

Orsa clears her throat to get my attention. "Now that you've seen your family, you understand what's at stake. I've taken the courtesy of bringing AvR0la for you, M0Rr1S. They are most reluctant to speak against their commander. But I do believe with the current situation, we may all come to a solution. So, I offer you this, human. Die, and they all can live. I can make our home, our emperor, believe that you corrupted M0Rr1S. And I've saved my inferior betrothed dutifully."

Morris can't hide the hurt and anger in his voice as he asks what I can't. "All of this. Why, 0rsa?"

"You think this is jealousy? I'm Ilori, regardless of the matter of my birth. I feel no jealousy. Only desire. A marriage into your family is all I ask. But not to you, M0Rr1S. To Brixton. Our alliances were more recon than actual fun. I'm sure you noticed." She raises her eyebrows at Morris, waiting for an argument that will not come, before settling on his brother. "I will not kill M0Rr1S. I will cover up his misdoings and your name will remain untarnished." An ugly smile graces her pallid face.

"You think I care if you kill my brother, 0rsa? That's why I'm here." Brixton glances at me as he speaks, giving me the impression he knows Morris is translating his words.

"No, perhaps not. But I do believe your mother will. I've heard she cares a great deal about her labmade son. And I am certain your father does not wish to call attention, especially negative attention, to your family before he—someday soon, I think—becomes emperor."

Brixton considers her words. "You told me to meet you here. That you had a plan. This is not what I expected."

The smell of chemical smoke replaces the rot. It travels down my throat, sticks to my lips and nostrils. My mom coughs at the same time as me, and for a second, we lock eyes. I mouth *I'm sorry* through the wheezes that seize my chest. We failed. The one thing getting me through this was the idea that I could save my family. But here they are. Brought all the way to California and dropped into the center of the mess that started as a journey of freedom for all.

Suddenly, the guilt is too much; my parents are going to watch their only child die. The child they asked to live for them.

For the first time, I'm grateful they'll be vaccinated. My mom is still in there behind the trauma, but this will break her completely. At least the vaccine will take it all away. She won't be in pain anymore. And my father will never come back, never know that he watched me die and did nothing.

It feels different. Knowing I'm about to die. I wasn't prepared before, but I am now.

"Your lack of a decision leads me to believe you find it amenable." Orsa stands taller as she whirls toward me. "What do you say, human? Do we have a deal? Your life for the ones you love."

"Janelle, don't," my mom calls, before her eyes flick back and forth, and she's lost inside her illness once more. "A sip, a sip…"

"Ellie." Alice shakes her head wearily. "I'm ready to die. I've always been ready. Don't die for me."

"Put them to sleep," Orsa orders. A guard steps forward, their eyes trained on my mom and Alice. They slump to the ground, and a gasp escapes through my teeth before I clamp my mouth shut.

My father stands there still as a statue, unseeing, uncaring. I wish, more than anything, that what I'm about to agree to will bring him back.

Don't do this. Don't forfeit your life. We can still walk away. We can still save them. We came so far.

Morris's voice lingers in my head, but I ignore it. "We have a deal," I say through shaky breaths. The universe gave me a gift, just like Morris said. It showed me love and music in my last few days of life. But it also allowed me to save my family. And Morris. I can't watch Morris suffer either. I want to remember him. His eyes. His beauty.

It will be the last thing I see.

I let his hand drop from mine. "I'm sorry, Morris."

His eyes glisten as he reaches for me once more. "Ellie, please...there's another way."

"I'm doing the right thing. I believe that." I walk away from him for the last time since we've met. My heart breaks, knowing how much this will hurt him, but he understands. I know if he were in my place, he'd do the same. We share a connection, a bond. We are music and stories come alive with love.

The walk toward Orsa is long. My heart beats in my ears and my mind feels blurry. I will die here tonight. My new shoes dampen from the wet sand, and salt lingers on my lips from the ocean air.

"You will make your family proud. And I promise you, your death will be quick and clean." She sighs like this is a necessary task she must perform. "All I ask is that you bend before me."

I drop to my knees.

I could have died on our rooftop in New York. I could have died or been captured like that family who kept hope alive by resisting and leaving a note in a book for someone like me to find. I could have screamed myself hoarse behind glass walls in the hospital in Oklahoma, or wandered aimlessly till the end with the humans in Texas. But none of those fates would have given me a final glimpse of my family.

My books and Morris have kept me company till this moment. And this moment was always going to come. I believe that.

Orsa shows me a countenance full of false comfort as she slowly lifts her arms and extends them toward the sides of my face.

"I'm going to record this for—" she begins.

"Orsa, I've changed my mind." Brixton's back straightens

and he narrows his eyes at her. "I'd rather tarnish my family name than marry you."

"What?" Orsa's head whips toward him. I take that moment to swipe the buzzkiller from my back pocket. "What do you want?"

I'm pretty sure she's asking Brixton, but I respond anyway, trying to sound confident, strong and powerful. None of which I feel at the moment. "Free my family, my friends and his, and I won't hurt you. We can all walk away." It's a ridiculous request; she can kill me just with her mind, and she probably has no idea what the buzzkiller is, yet a few extra seconds of distraction is all we need.

From the corner of my eye, Morris blurs as he captures one guard with his hand and lifts him. The guard falls over in a pile by his feet. Another guard charges at Morris, but my attention sweeps back to Orsa and Brixton. Morris still manages to translate what Brixton says.

"Enough. Orsa, leave here, and we won't speak of this again." Brixton steps forward. "You will not have me, or my brother. And you will not kill these humans."

Morris is in the process of getting rid of a second guard when he stops. A line of six labmade guards stand behind Orsa, in front of my family, as he backs down. Confusion spreads across his features as he regards his brother.

Venom drips in Orsa's tone. "I never suspected you were working for the rebellion."

Brixton's response is threatening. "What are you going to do about it?"

"I will tell your grandfather. This will cancel your father's ascension. Every plan you've made—"

Brixton lunges and I toss the buzzkiller at Orsa. She catches it in one hand. "What is this?" And then her eyes widen as it starts to drain her energy on contact. She tries to shake it from her hand, howling in frustration when it sticks to her like a magnet. Her gaze flicks to mine. I can barely gulp in surprise when she backhands me hard with her free arm. Her Ilori strength sends me flying in the air, the wind whistling in my ears, until my back hits the side of the ship.

Something inside of me, something big, snaps.

I crumple to the ground. The air flees my lungs before I can scream.

The pain is instant and everywhere and radiating from my spine, I think, to the tips of my toes to my lips. Something wet drips onto my lips, and I wonder vaguely if it's water or blood.

My heart pounds in my ears…or is that a ringing? I can't tell. I attempt to move… I can't. Nothing works. I have no control. Breaths come in short pants, as if my body can't take in or let out anymore, and my vision blackens at the edges. I'm alive. Not for much longer, I suspect.

I don't want to die alone. No one dies alone.

The world moves around me. My gaze drifts over to the melee, my body stuck to the sand that softened my fall. Orsa finally detaches the buzzkiller, but her movements are slow. Brixton grabs for her. I see flashes of hair and limbs, but they're too fast.

Where is Morris? Where is my family?

A howl pierces the air as Morris faces off against three Ilori. His voice flickers in and out of my head.

I'm coming, Ellie. Wait for me. You're going to be okay.

And then he's on the move. He whips an opponent in the air like he's tossing a ball. Sand flies up, and screams bounce off the ship. Panic envelops me. Not only am I going to die, but so will Morris. He can't win. There are too many.

As his movements slow and a crowd forms around him, my heart sinks further in my chest. Please no. *Please.*

Morris, I try to shout, to prove I'm still here with him. But his name stays locked in my throat.

I squeeze my eyes shut, refusing to see him fall. Metal screeches, prickling my eardrums. The smoke drifts into my nostrils and I cough, the movement bringing a fresh wave of pain to my failing body.

Don't give up, Ellie. Never give up. I'm coming.

I'm trying, but sounds and thoughts are drifting away.

A memory passes through my mind, and, briefly, it feels more real than everything that's happened over the past few days and years. As if the center and executions were just a nightmare conjured from a book I read.

I'm thirteen again. The sun blinks down at me in front of the steps of the central library in Brooklyn. There's a jazz band playing for Summerfest, while my mother dances within the crowd and the air fills with laughter and music. I turn, catching the MTA Flatbush line driving past as my dad plops his heavy hands on my shoulders, startling me, nearly knocking a stack of books from my arms.

"Got you your favorite." He hands me a cheddar scone from Four & Twenty Blackbirds.

"Oh, thanks, Dad." I take it from him and sniff the salty deliciousness just as Mom curls a finger at him from across the crowd. "You better dance with her."

He kisses my cheek and vanishes into the sea of people. I twirl in my favorite white dress that makes my skin shimmer. I feel good. I feel happy. Alive. Beauty and light surround me. Thirteen-year-old me takes a mental photograph, promising that if I ever feel out of control, I can come back to this moment, and all will be right again.

But then it floats away, and I'm back in darkness, lying in the sand, wishing I could go back in time, away from the present where everyone I love is losing.

Morris floods into my narrow view as he picks up my head and holds me. I want to hug him close, to yell at him, to ask him how he managed to break away, but I can't.

He stares down at me with so much sorrow that my heart breaks alongside the rest of me. "Where are you hurt?"

I cough, feeling something warm and sticky on my lips. Blood. Bleeding from your mouth is never a good thing. Pain radiates all over my body, but it's beginning to numb. This is it, isn't it? I'd always wondered if you felt pain up until your very last moments.

More blood dribbles out of my mouth with each cough.

"You are going to be okay." His voice shakes. And then I think about my family, Alice, Avrola, the ship, but I can't get the words out. He seems to read my mind, though. Because he knows this is the end. "They are fine. Everyone is fine. AvR0la is trying to wake your mom now." He draws my head closer to his as he crouches beside me. "Ellie, please don't leave me. Please."

There are so many things to tell him, but I'm dying. I know that now. I'm not invincible. One strike from an Ilori, and my body is broken. My chest feels caved in, and my mind is overcome with thoughts and memories and words. I expected it to hurt more.

His fingers graze the edge of my face, and there are tears in his eyes. One plops onto my cheek, and he gasps, bringing his hands to his face. "I've never... Hearts must feel, for mine is breaking."

I want to tell him that he has inadvertently quoted *The Wizard of Oz.* Even while dying, I am reminded of stories. I blink up at Morris, concern and hurt and pain all mingling in his expression.

More tears stream from his eyes and fall onto my cheeks. "I love you, Janelle Baker. I love you."

I wheeze, trying to say the words back to him. I want him to know that I love him, too. It's the only thing I can do.

"I know, I know," he says, bringing his lips to my forehead. "I can't read your beautiful mind. But I know you." He brushes tears away. "I know you love me. This will not be the end. It can't be. What can I do?"

I think about him singing to me. His voice. How I love to hear him sing. He looks down at me with a small, sad smile. He knows.

"This world… It's bigger than the two of us. But it's really only them and us, and I want them all to know. My star, I'll never let her go."

I remember our first kiss. The way he looked up at the sky as if thankful afterward. I was thankful, too.

"Please stay close to me… I revolve around you, you're my gravity. They say we're too different, that it can't last, that you're a star, shooting too fast. You hold your hand out, pulling me with you… I love you."

One last time. Just one more try. One word.

"Love."

And it's all I can say before my eyes close on their own, but I can still hear him breathing and singing. I can still feel his hands holding me, my body draped across him. The world is fading to black.

I hope my mom finds peace. I hope my father finds himself. I hope Alice finds love that will shine brighter than the darkest of her memories. And for Morris—I hope that he finds happiness and that, when he thinks of me, I'll bring a smile to his mind and a song to his lips.

Even as I die, the love in my heart is profound.

CHAPTER 25

"Swallowed in the Sea"
—Coldplay

MORR1S

M0Rr1S has never cried before, but then he's never felt sorrow like this before either. He promised to save Janelle. He promised to protect her. But he also let her come with him, even when the chances of success were slim. Now she's dying in his arms, and there's nothing he can do about it. Everything is his fault.

Through the tears he sings "Swallowed in the Sea," expressing everything he feels, everything he wishes he could have said to her. *Please come back to me. Please.*

"I told you I heard someone singing, Rupert!" a human with long, dark blue hair announces. They are dressed in fitted, tight jeans, and a white dress shirt with a feathery red cape attached that billows gently in the wind. M0Rr1S's jaw drops as this person crouches on the other side of Ellie.

"Coldplay," another voice responds. "We can never seem to escape them. Remember when they tried to steal our look for their last album? Humans are so unoriginal."

Humans?

M0Rr1S is at a loss for words. Has the onset of devastation addled his mind?

The being beside Ellie touches her face. "Janelle. Oh dear. Rupert, do you have the kit?"

"Of course I have the bloody kit, Allister! Is this not the reason we left?"

"Cecil, do make yourself useful for once and hand me the jars. Our girl's life is hanging in the balance, for Jadu's sakes!"

"You're so dramatic," Cecil responds before handing Allister a small container of bottles. "We already know the story's ending."

"You're Andarrans," M0Rr1S mutters, sounding odd to his own ears. "I'm sorry to breach your property, please don't—"

"This is only the beginning," Allister responds. "And yes, I'm male and Andarran. All of us are males and Andarran." He sinks deeper into the sand and takes out five dark glass bottles with various liquids inside. He uncorks one and holds it before Ellie. "We aren't going to kill you. The treaty is fine. Just, shush, okay?"

M0Rr1S will not shush. "What is that?"

"Right, M0Rr1S—goodness it's such a weird name, yeah? I'll call you Morris, like she does. Yes, all of you Ilori broke the treaty by coming here, but that was all part of the plan, wasn't it?" Allister rolls his eyes. "I'm going to save her life, if you'll let me."

M0Rr1S rescinds his hand, unsure. Andarrans are kind.

Healers. But very strict about their treaties. And old, so old they don't have to adhere to time like Ilori or humans. They look so much like humans; there are very few traces of their otherness, unlike the Ilori labmade.

Allister drips a few drops of liquid into Ellie's mouth. M0Rr1S waits—hopes—impatiently for her to somehow spring back to life, but an explosion floods his eyes and screeches in his ears. Sand shoots into the air as the Earth shakes beneath them. The ship is destroyed, and with it, the hope of saving humanity.

The remaining shell of IpS1L slowly descends into the ocean. Beside it, he catches whirs of 0rsa and Brixton clashing. 0rsa cannot keep up with his brother; M0Rr1S doesn't know how long she held on to the human weapon, but she looks close to depletion, moving slow. She's strong, so strong, yet not strong enough to defeat a true Ilori.

The guards rise from the sand. Prepared to fight again. He sets his jaw. Didn't he overpower them? But then, they're 0rsa's security tech. Either he'll have to use blunt force or sneak behind their code without triggering further alarms.

They turn simultaneously to regard him, causing him to push his thoughts aside.

The waves crash around them, as if they must match the battle raging. And then M0Rr1S remembers. Ellie's parents, Alice and AvR0la are there. He needs to get them out.

Ferk.

"Go," Allister insists, as if he can read M0Rr1S's mind. Andarrans don't have that talent. Do they? "I've got her."

M0Rr1S snatches a reluctant glance at them before running off. He catches the footfalls of the other men behind but pays them no mind.

"Love a bit of action," Cecil says in a singsong voice

M0Rr1S finds familiar, but he can't quite place. "So far Earth has been dangerously entertaining."

"Oh, do shut up," Allister yells from where he's still stooped over Ellie.

The labmade guards run at M0Rr1S all at once, but Cecil intercedes, landing a quick yet powerful jab to one of their panels. The guard clutches their neck before falling forward and gasping for air. Blunt force works.

M0Rr1S barely has time to register when hands wrap around his neck. He pants before swinging his head back into soft flesh. A groan is all the reward he gets before there's a visitor in his mind, searching for his shutdown tab. He pulls at the presence, latching on to it as he boots it from his system. Easy. Sneaking into human minds requires less power than entering Ilori minds.

Precious milliseconds pass as he streams through the Ilori's channels, shoving miscellaneous data aside until finding the shutdown switch buried behind code. He slams his energy at it, and a guard drops a few feet away. How many more left?

The Andarrans—Rupert and Cecil, he recalls—gracefully sweep through their remaining opponents, much to his surprise. M0Rr1S had no idea Andarrans could be violent, but the thought is fleeting as he moves around the chaos to AvR0la.

He drops down before them. "Are you okay? Can you help me?"

AvR0la holds up their cuffed wrists. M0Rr1S has only heard rumors of these before. Poisoned. They block neural transmitters and movements. AvR0la winces.

"I don't know how to break these." M0Rr1S inspects them, taking care not to touch their silver surface. A touch could very well poison him, too.

"Oh, we might," Rupert intones behind him. "We'll take care of it."

Beside AvR0la lies Ellie's mother, facedown in the sand. M0Rr1S doesn't waste any more time and picks her up. He runs toward an empty car that the Andarrans must have arrived in and sets her inside before running back to find Ellie's father. But he's gone.

M0Rr1S whips his head around to scan the shore. He can't see anything through the smoke and the haze that has started to creep through the field of pods.

Just as he prepares to bolt in search of Ellie's father, 0rsa flies past him and lands in the sand at his feet. Her body is bent and broken. There's black blood leaking from a cut above her eyebrow and a weariness in her that M0Rr1S has not seen before. That must be the difference between the first models and the second. Still, it would be an easy fix for a healer.

"Please...stop Brixton." She drags in a breath.

M0Rr1S considers letting them battle it out. 0rsa is no match for Brixton, and her death would settle many of his issues. But even if he denies it, he is a labmade, and killing another labmade is wrong. And 0rsa...even if she hates who she is, she is like him.

His knees sink into the sand beside her. She looks up at him with resigned anger. "Don't."

"I'm shutting you down, 0rsa. For your safety."

"No." Her nostrils flare.

"Let me in, 0rsa," M0Rr1S demands. "I'll save you, but you need to help me, too."

"I will crush you and your family." Her eyes flash with hatred.

"I have no doubt." M0Rr1S sighs. "I never knew you were so ambitious. I apologize for denying you that which you've desired most. If I had known—"

"0rsa! I will end you for your treachery." Brixton calls from the distance. M0Rr1S only holds 0rsa's gaze as she flinches at Brixton's words.

"I am Ilori, I do not feel," she whimpers.

He doesn't respond.

"I'm true," she says it more to herself than to him. "I'm not like you. I'm not."

"No, you're better than me, 0rsa. You are the perfect Ilori."

Footsteps approach them, and 0rsa sinks lower into the sand.

"Allow me in. Let me shut you down. I can end your pain. I can get you home. Continue to struggle and you will die." M0Rr1S is not lying. 0rsa's only chance at life right now, out here, is to shut down and wait for healing. There are no healers here. Ilori, especially labmade, are not invincible.

"I hate you," 0rsa spits out.

"I know," M0Rr1S says quietly. He wants to pity her, and in her weak state, he almost could. Being subjected to his inferiority meant she had to question hers. Made her desperate to hurt anyone who stood in the path of her ambitions.

She looks beyond him to the sky. He wonders if she is looking for home and imagining another life, where she is true Ilori and respected. Her voice is soft, relenting. "Take it away."

M0Rr1S closes his eyes and enters her mind. He pushes at the pain until is dissipates. A sigh of relief shudders through her, relief she doesn't deserve. And then he presses forward, shutting 0rsa down, overriding her systems. She is strong, and it drains him to battle her mind for control. His knees are soaked from the moisture of the sand before she loses the fight. She shuts down, the life in her eyes dulling until it is gone completely. Asleep, but for how long? Sleep is eight hours for him, but 0rsa is older than him, so it could be shorter.

M0Rr1S shuts her eyelids just as Brixton approaches. "Brixton, stop."

"She was going to expose us. Expose our—" Brixton comes

closer, his voice dropping to a whisper so small, only meant for him. "We should kill her, M0Rr1S. Step aside."

"I have every reason to, but I will not." M0Rr1S will fight his brother if he must. He does not feel anything for 0rsa; she might have killed Ellie, and her punishment should be death. But he can't kill her. It's wrong to take a life, and so many lives have been lost already.

"You would expose Mother for this? Do you know what her penalty will be?" Brixton casts M0Rr1S a dark look.

"You—you knew? *You?*" M0Rr1S stares at Brixton as the world burns around them. There is nothing he can do. Each time he thinks he can grasp the events of this night...

"Not as long as you." Air rasps through Brixton's teeth. "We all play a role."

"Is that why you killed the humans in my quadrant? A role?" The anger is quick and unrelenting.

"Father did, to torture you. He knew it would expose your feelings." He rubs his hands together, awkwardly. "I tried to save as many humans as I could for you, M0Rr1S."

M0Rr1S does not know how to feel about that, what to say. "Brixton—"

"Keeping 0rsa alive may cost us all."

"I know. But to kill her is... We are better than this. I didn't know that you—"

"Don't. It is my purpose and role to antagonize you for all the plans to work. *He* has to feel like at least one of us is on his side. You know that." Brixton speaks rapidly, as if he has too much to say and not enough time to say it. "When it happens, when you let the humans reclaim this world and kill our grandfather, only I can stop the wrath that will consume him before he kills our mother."

Brixton shakes his head at the thought. "You think you've

failed, M0Rr1S. But you haven't. Never me, and not her. I've been with you the entire way…"

"You *have*?" M0Rr1S gulps at the salty air as if the breath in his lungs has fled. "How?"

"I was there when she extracted her material for you. I watched her leave, exhausted but hopeful. And then I extracted some of mine, too. Not much, I was too young." His voice falls softly, and he wipes away a tear that trails the side of his cheek. It's silver and unexpected. "I think I may have wanted a brother more than Mother wanted a soldier."

"Brixton." It's all M0Rr1S can say.

"We were always connected because of that little piece of myself I shared with you. I couldn't hear you…unless you let me, and sometimes you did, but I could feel you. Always." He sniffs, looking away. "Your despair with the vaccine. Your guilt, endless guilt, M0Rr1S. Your joy, whenever you listened to music, I think. And then…your determination when you read that book. *That's* why art and expression were banned. Not just for the humans, but for the labmades. Feelings are powerful, I learned that from you." Brixton's brilliant green eyes lock on M0Rr1S. "They can't be controlled by true Ilori minds. You think we're almighty. But we need Il-0CoM to assert authority. We are connected to you…the connection goes both ways. If the labmades knew what they are capable of…"

M0Rr1S brushes away his own tears, watery, and so very human. "I wanted a brother. I needed you."

"Would you have left if you knew the truth?" Brixton steps toward him, tentatively, and then kneels before M0Rr1S in the sand. "May I?"

M0Rr1S nods, although he doesn't know what Brixton asks for…until he wraps his arms around M0Rr1S's shoulders, and lets out a deep breath.

"Humans do this, yes?"

"Yes," M0Rr1S whispers as his body collapses against his brother's.

"One day," Brixton says, "we will be free." The moment is over too soon. Brixton rises, standing straighter as he does. "Take your... Ellie. There's nothing here now, nothing you can break into to upload the code. There's a bounty on your head, colony-wide. You step foot onto an Ilori ship as of now, and they will capture you. 0rsa has seen to that." He huffs. "Find a way off this planet. You need Ilori systems and soon there won't be any on the ground. You have maybe, at most, twenty-one rotations. One Earth week. I'll stall them however I can."

"How can I do any of that if I can't get on an Ilori ship?" The exhaustion tugs at M0Rr1S, yet he doesn't want to see his brother leave without at least knowing what he's expected to do next.

"The Andarrans may have a solution to that. I have to go." His voice cracks with regret as he glances at the sky. "Mother will reach you soon. When you come back here, be prepared. Find a way to convince the rest of the labmades to join this fight. Father will be unhinged."

He steps toward 0rsa. "I'll wipe her memory and take her home, but it's a temporary solution. When she remembers, a war like nothing we've seen before will come. Our mother's life, the labmades, this world and colonies beyond depend on what you do next. Do not fail."

M0Rr1S chuckles mirthlessly, but dread sinks into the bottom of his stomach, not just of the future, but for Ellie.

"I'll be with you. Always." Brixton strides past M0Rr1S, the display of emotions gone as he swings 0rsa over his shoulder and strides over to an unscathed pod a few feet away.

"Brixton." M0Rr1S turns to his brother as the pod's hatch opens. "Thank you."

Brixton merely nods, but his bottom lip wobbles. He zooms past the smoke into the night until he disappears from view. Seconds later, the pod shoots into the sky.

The wind whips the billowing smoke through his hair. M0Rr1S closes his eyes before falling face forward into the sand.

"Come. Let's get you out of here, then." Hands wrap around his sides as he shuts down into oblivion.

M0Rr1S awakes in a sunlit room. A bedroom, he realizes as he shifts to observe his surroundings. He's on an oversize bed with translucent white curtains around the posts. There's a man—Allister, he remembers—silently sitting next to him, staring out the window. The man's eyes look haunted, tired, old. He hums something M0Rr1S has heard before.

M0Rr1S bolts up. "Ellie! Where is she? Did she—? Please, no." The hysterics are uncontrollable. He feels a tension all over his body as he throws his legs over the edge of the bed and staggers toward the door. But he's unsure where to go. His eyes water again, and he doesn't know where he is. He needs to see her.

He can't bear to think of her out of his reach.

"Morris. Morris." Allister calls his name over and over in a soothing tone. "Don't fear. Janelle is fine. She's resting in another room."

M0Rr1S rounds on him. "Is her family… Are they okay?"

"Her mother's with her. I was able to find her father, but I can't fix him. He'll need special help." He stands and crosses the room, holding his hands in front of M0Rr1S as if blocking him from leaving. "You need a charge. I have one."

"You're Andarran. Why are you helping us? I've trespassed. I am at your mercy."

"Oh, you know, destiny and all that." Allister waves a hand dismissively. "It's a long story."

"I have time." M0Rr1S grinds his feet into a pink, furry rug.

"You know, in your future, you're not quite as moody." Allister cocks a smile. "I mean, I still find it attractive, mind you, but it's hard to talk to you when you're like this."

M0Rr1S digs his feet in deeper. "Who *are* you?"

Allister clears his throat. *"I never felt before, but oh the feelings she gives me."* His voice sounds exactly the same as on the albums.

Suddenly M0Rr1S panics. The bag; the music, the books…

"Your belongings are fine," Allister says soothingly.

"You—you, you're the Starry Eyed?" M0Rr1S's voice cracks as he runs a hand through his hair. "You can read minds?"

"Well, not me singularly, no. There are four of us, but yes. I'm the lead singer. Central to the band, obviously." He grins. "I can't read minds, just emotions. For an Ilori, yours are easy to read."

"And you're Andarran," M0Rr1S scoffs.

"Well we can't all be humans or Ilori, can we?" Allister motions for M0Rr1S to return to the bed.

But M0Rr1S rubs his arm, unsure. His movements are slow now, and it's hard to keep his eyes open. Yet, he would travel the world at this moment to find Ellie; to see her.

"Soon, Janelle will wake up. Better than new. But you need a charge. Would you like it? If so, stop destroying my rug and come here."

M0Rr1S reluctantly nods and trudges toward the bed. He's uncomfortable how this Andarran seems to read his mind, it makes him feel a loss of privacy. Maybe that's how humans felt around him.

"Sit, and I'll hook it up."

M0Rr1S complies with a huff before sinking back onto the edge of the mattress.

"This will be quick. Just relax. Think of fountains of electricity or calefs roaming in a field of grass or whatever your kind finds calming." Allister opens a drawer in the bedside table and pulls out a cable.

M0Rr1S yawns, waiting. He lets his head fall to one shoulder, exposing his panel, but instead, Allister pulls M0Rr1S's hand toward him, takes one finger and places it between two prongs. M0Rr1S looks up at him. "What's this?"

Allister flips a switch on the cable. The charge is so strong and powerful that M0Rr1S's teeth chatter and his body twitches. Seconds pass. M0Rr1S's mind drifts to Ellie, and then to his failed mission. To his brother and their hug. To what he must do next. He snaps out of his heavy thoughts when Allister removes the charger from his finger and shoves it back into the drawer.

"Easy, yeah? I know you Ilori enjoy tedious things that teach you patience and increase your suffering, but Andarrans don't waste time on unfun things." Allister pushes a strand of dark blue hair behind his ear. "You've been there, haven't you?"

"To Andarra?" M0Rr1S gapes at him briefly. "Yes, with my mother."

"I remember you. A child holding Glind's hand, walking through the arch of my origin planet. I was on the same boat as you when you let your fingers dance in the water."

M0Rr1S could sort through the memories he has stored away in his mental files, but he doesn't care enough about it now. His mind is elsewhere. Too many thoughts, most about Ellie.

Allister continues. "The Jadu picked you. Destiny. Not everyone has one. But you do. So do I. My destiny is to secure hers…and yours by extension."

"Ellie's? Your destiny is to save Ellie?"

"She hasn't been picked by the Jadu, but she will be. We all play a role. Isn't that what you Ilori say? What you think your purpose is?"

M0Rr1S has a million questions, but the first one that pops to his mind rushes out. "You know my mother?"

"Every Andarran does. She's a hero, a mother of heroes."

M0Rr1S shakes his head. "You don't adhere to time. That is why you know me, and Ellie, and everything." A statement of fact. He should have known.

"That's what happens when the Jadu choose us. Time becomes...nothing and everything at once. We can't travel it, mind you, but we can know it like memories. It's both an intense burden and an exciting gift." He smiles, but there's no joy in it. "It's why we came here. Arrived a bit early, though. Thought it might be good fun to become famous pop stars. We read Janelle's book—her chronicles of the Great War for Earth. Don't tell her I told you, but she's not as bad of a writer as she believes." This time there's humor in his laugh. "Anyway, she wrote about that night you were sitting on the hood of a car in the desert falling in love. You both had stars in your eyes. I remember that line. It's my favorite.

"We called ourselves the Starry Eyed after that." Allister crosses to the window, staring out once more. "The future changes, yeah, but the path you're on now...you'll face destruction, trials, but the future as I know it now tells me you'll survive it. And this world...it will heal. Just like Janelle."

"But the future is not yet set?" M0Rr1S wonders.

"Any small change now can ripple the future I've seen. It's best not to think about that."

M0Rr1S decides Allister's right. Thinking about that can addle a mind. So he thinks, instead, about the fact that Ellie's favorite band are Andarrans. "All of the songs you wrote... they were for her? For us?"

Allister beams. "Of course. You provided good material. Plus, I thought if you really listened to the lyrics, you'd take instructions through them on your journey—saving you both from heartaches. I worried that you both are too literal, too practical-minded, to make sense of such meaningful poetry."

M0Rr1S shakes his head again, ignoring the barb. He can't wait to tell Ellie. "I knew it. I knew it! I told her that these songs seemed like they were made for us."

Allister throws his head back and chuckles. "Janelle Baker, as I recall, does not like being wrong."

"You know her well?" M0Rr1S sobers, and experiences what can only be a spike of jealousy.

"We all do. She's...she's wonderful. I needn't tell you, of course. Your love is legendary. It's what we all hope for. Or wish to experience again."

M0Rr1S doesn't know what to say. That flicker of jealousy, thinking that Ellie might not be with him in the future, and that Allister, the lead singer of her favorite band, knows her—thinks she's wonderful—subside into joy. There is a future, and legendary love. He is about to ask another question when another being from last night, Cecil, knocks on the door before striding inside.

"Oh good, he's awake. I need him to—"

"This is Cecil. He's the absolute worst," Allister proclaims. "Cecil, why is it always you? I literally like everyone else more than you."

Cecil narrows his gaze on Allister. "Are you having another of your tantrums? Come, Morris, he is unbearable when he has one of these. And anyway, I need your help. And also, no offense, but later you should bathe, you smell a bit too Earthy for an alien." Cecil tosses his raven-black hair from his deep, brown eyes. He's clad in only a pair of jeans and covered in tattoos of roses of every color. They're beautiful and odd, much like Cecil.

"I have to see Ellie—" M0Rr1S stands again. He feels better than he's felt in weeks, so much so that if he wanted to, he could burst through walls to find Ellie. He owes the Starry Eyed for saving them all. *All?* "AvR0la, Alice, they are okay?"

Cecil steps closer to him, and coyly bats his eyelashes. "Yes, yes, everyone is fine. Whisper's quite taken with Alice already. And AvR0la—Avi—is still in chains, unfortunately. Couldn't figure out how those contraptions work. You'll want to attend to that before your make out session with Ellie, believe me."

Allister frowns. "Cecil, you are ridiculous."

"Allister, I'm ignoring your venom today. One day you love me, the next, you can't bear to look at me. I deserve better than this, you know?" Cecil raises his head with a deep, dramatic sigh.

"Go, Morris. With the help of *Rupert*—" Allister stares at Cecil, who gasps theatrically "—you'll undoubtedly break Avi's cuffs. And then you can run to Ellie."

M0Rr1S keeps his mouth shut. Whatever is going on between them is not his business, and whatever they choose to call AvR0la is not his decision either.

"You'll have to forgive me someday, you know." Cecil sniffs, before turning on his heel and stalking off.

"Don't mind him," Allister sighs, "he's a performer. You'll find Andarrans make up for Ilori rigidity by embracing every tiny emotion and expressing it without shame. It is difficult to see the future and the past during the present. We're always grasping at understanding. Although Cecil really is a bit too much." M0Rr1S feels a bubbling of laughter in his chest but pushes it down. So far, they both seem a bit much. "If you need anything, don't hesitate to ask."

"Thank you, Allister." M0Rr1S bows slightly before following Cecil down a grand, checkered hallway that echoes
with their footsteps. The walls are adorned with gold-and
platinum-crusted albums and tiny ornamentations that must
have taken ages for humans to build. Cecil waits at the top of
the stairs, leaning against a dark, wooden banister.

"Don't mind him. He's still angry about me changing the
lyrics to one of our songs. It was ages ago, but he just…he's impossible. I told him you and Ellie wouldn't understand that the
songs were about you and your journey, and that it wouldn't
have stopped you from making the same, bad decisions. He
didn't listen. I had to remind him that everything happens for
a reason, you know?"

M0Rr1S does know but doesn't reply.

Cecil leads him down the stairs into a grand foyer filled
with flowers and shimmering lights. M0Rr1S can barely take
in the details before he's whisked down another hallway only
to stop when they reach the kitchen.

It's the grandest house M0Rr1S has ever seen, with long
hallways dotted with doors and tables with blue vases burst-
ing with flowers. There are myriad colors everywhere, and
distant threads of music. The kitchen is immaculate, with all
sorts of gadgets and equipment made of expensive chrome,
humming with electricity. It's most unlike the kitchens he'd
seen in the centers. And there, perched on a stool, is AvR0la.
Their face is slack, but M0Rr1S can imagine how uncomfortable they must be.

He wants to take AvR0la's hands in his own, but it isn't
safe. "I will get you out of these." He cannot touch the metal
without being poisoned himself, so he steps back. "It requires
energy to work. Cecil—"

"I think I have the solution." Another man walks in. Rupert, M0Rr1S recalls. He's dressed in a black tuxedo with his

silver hair pulled back from his face. He can't be much older than Ellie or M0Rr1S. His skin is the same shade as M0Rr1S's, and his eyes are a surprising amber.

"Oh, Rupert, thank goodness. Don't tell Allister it was you who came up with the solution. He's been especially foul to me today."

"It's fine, dear." Rupert kisses Cecil on the cheek before examining AvR0la's cuffs. "Yes, M0Rr1S, I do believe only you can attend to this. You will need to charge and use your abilities in tandem to break the chains. Can you do this?"

M0Rr1S nods, although he's not entirely sure. He's never done anything like this before.

"It will be dangerous. If you charge too long, you may combust. For which, I offer my deepest apologies." Rupert tosses a look full of sincere sympathy. M0Rr1S is beginning to believe that all Andarrans are strange.

"Combustion would be less than ideal," M0Rr1S agrees. He hasn't even seen Ellie yet. He can't combust without seeing her. But he also owes his life to AvR0la.

"Cecil, darling, would you get the spare charger?" Rupert turns to M0Rr1S. "We keep them on hand for our solopads. Lucky coincidence they work on labmade Ilori."

M0Rr1S has no idea what a solopad is, but imagines it's Andarran tech. He'd ask about it, but Rupert continues talking.

"I hope you haven't had the displeasure of witnessing the coldness between Cecil and Allister? If so, please don't mind them. They've been at odds for three years now. All will eventually be forgiven until the next argument. I suspect you Ilori wouldn't understand." Rupert turns AvR0la's wrists over, examining the metal.

M0Rr1S laughs. "You'd think we wouldn't understand, but we have our own feuds and emotional yearnings." He thinks of 0rsa and his father, his brother and mother. "We feel just as much as the humans. Just maybe not as much as all of you."

"Everyone knows that your masters feel. How else would your empire have amassed such a long list of colonies and territories? There must be desire for these things. It's not practical to own more than you need. Only greed compels this." Rupert casts M0Rr1S a quick glance with raised eyebrows.

"Greed but also fear," M0Rr1S states. "My grandfather, Emperor 1lv, is calculating and cunning. His desires mean doom for everyone else."

Rupert straightens. "It is good, then, that you plan on killing him."

"Well. I don't know how I can yet. We have no—"

Cecil returns with a black cord draped over his shoulder. He plugs it into an outlet on the shiny counter behind AvR0la, then places M0Rr1S's finger between the two prongs once more. "Go fast now."

The electricity streams into M0Rr1S. He's already full from before, but now he feels like he has enough electricity to light up the world. He focuses his mind on breaking the cuffs, but he feels fire in his veins. *Focus.* The cuffs slowly begin to melt, and M0Rr1S pulls back as much as he can not to burn Avi's skin. His hair lifts off his head and the panel streams colors into his eyes; bright yellow, blue, green… *Focus.*

The cuffs clunk to the floor. M0Rr1S screams as he rips the cord off his finger. He takes a step back, catching his breath as AvR0la throws their arms around him. "Thank you, sir."

"Avi, please call me Morris."

AvR0la tries to smile. "Thank you, Morris."

"AvR0la, I—"

"Disable Il-0CoM permanently first. It's very loud and accusatory in here, and any minute now…"

"I can't. That would require me to sign in and establish a secret…" He pauses. "I know what to do."

Brixton. M0Rr1S has never used their familial connection before, but then, he didn't know it went both ways. There's a long silence in his mind, and he worries that it's not real, after all. Maybe Brixton said that to make him feel less alone. Yet, there's a crackle and then a clear line of communication unlike one he's ever had before.

That didn't take long. There's a hint of amusement and maybe a little affection in Brixton's voice.

Can you disable Il-0CoM for AvR0la?

I will.

Thank you.

Family doesn't need to say thank you.

The line goes cold. Cecil and AvR0la eye him with raised brows.

"It's a long story." M0Rr1S laughs a little, disbelief and happiness at war within him.

"I do love a story, especially a long one. Make it twisty, though." Cecil pours himself and AvR0la a cup of steaming liquid. Tea, maybe.

M0Rr1S turns to the exit. "I'll tell you both when I come back. And, AvR0la, I want to know everything. But, I've got to see Ellie."

"Of course, Morris." This time AvR0la's lips quirk expertly and they exchange a knowing glance with Cecil.

M0Rr1S eyes them both before bolting out of the kitchen and up the stairs.

CHAPTER 26

"So come with me, where dreams are born, and time is never planned. Just think of happy things, and your heart will fly on wings, forever, in Never Never Land!"

—J.M. Barrie

JANELLE

I hear singing in another language when I wake. My eyes are blurry, and my hand grasps the soft comforter beneath me. Sun streams through the open windows. I turn my head, and my eyes squint at the figure standing there. My eyesight's not great, but I can make out blue hair. I shake my shoulders, jostling the glasses beside me. Through pain, I reach for them. In my grasp, it's slow going, but I slide them onto my face before turning back to the figure at the window. I slowly blink, adjusting to my improved eyesight.

The lead singer of the Starry Eyed, Allister Daniels, stands there singing. Lost in his own world. My heart pounds; his voice is angelic. He wears almost normal clothes with the exception of a glittery purple cape. His blue hair falls around his shoulders, and his bright violet eyes brighten even more in the sunlight.

Is this a dream? I'd pinch myself, but I've already had enough pain.

"Um…" I clear my throat.

"Janelle." Allister abruptly stops singing, and glides across the room to my side. "Hello, darling."

I mean, it's nice to wake up in a gorgeous bedroom, serenaded by a mega popstar and teen heartthrob, but it's also super confusing to be called darling. I don't know him like that. I'm sure my face says as much because he pulls back from me and smiles.

"Right, sorry. I'm the lead singer of the Starry Eyed but I'm also an alien like Morris, only I come from Andarra. A land far, far away in space and time. Like *Star Wars*. Only real." He gestures with his hands. "We'll know each other soon. We're best friends, though never when you were this young. But the future has changed, and so have we."

I can't make sense of what he's saying as there's a ringing in my ears and I'm not sure I'm completely conscious. He's a Korean superstar. Now he's an alien from a land far, far away in space and time? I want to understand what he just told me; it seems important, but I feel like I'm already forgetting it as I come out of a mental haze.

Mom. Dad. Alice. Morris's Ilori friend. The pod. The books. *Oh no.*

"Everyone and everything is safe. Your books are downstairs on a table in our library. We've been collecting everything for you, for humanity. Art. Books. Music. We even connected with the cloud and downloaded as much as we could before the Ilori took over. Not all is lost, I promise."

"You read minds?"

"You and Morris." He shakes his head. "No, you're both just predictable."

I want to cry, and hug him, and maybe dance. I don't even know. But my family...they aren't fine, I know it. "Mom." My throat is so dry and crackly, and the words come out with a rasp.

He angles his head to the other side of the room, where my mom is sleeping on a couch in a corner. She looks more peaceful than I've seen her in years. Her chest gently rises and falls, and the usual lines creasing her forehead are smooth. She looks younger.

"Is she okay?"

Allister holds my gaze. "She's better, but she's not herself yet. The trauma's deep. Rupert will help her and your father."

I rub my head. "I'm so confused."

"Morris will tell you everything." Allister strolls back to the window. "He loves you. There's this look in his eyes when he thinks about you or when someone mentions your name. Sometimes love needs only a moment to blossom, and it lingers forever." He sighs. "I should write that down. Would make a great line, right? Oh, how I love love."

I don't know why I ask it, because there are so many thoughts running through my mind. But there's something tragic in his expression. "Are you, do you...have someone?" I remember from magazines that he's dated supermodels and actors; and how quickly each relationship ended.

"I did, but she's...gone." He doesn't elaborate, and I don't push.

I sit up in my bed, my body feeling stiff with dull pain. But I'm alive. Small victories. "How am I still...here?"

"We got the good meds where I'm from." He laughs. "It's sort of our thing—healing and music. Probably why we have four platinum albums and thirteen Grammys." Allister doesn't look away from the window. Though I've only ever seen pictures of him, and he's apparently only a few years older than me, there's something serious—ancient, maybe—in his expression. But with one smile, he's as beautiful as his massive fan club suggests, and there's something sparkly about him that draws you in. I bet his glittery violet eyes aren't contacts at all, probably just an alien feature, like Morris told me once.

His dark blue hair glints in the beams of light. I've read that he dyes his hair for each new album. The latest album came out two years ago, but still his hair is a vibrant blue.

"This is really weird."

Allister chuckles. "I wanted us to have a proper meeting, you know? And you'd think, given my grasp of time, that I could have managed that. But the Ilori made it difficult to get to the beach, and I—" He pauses, swiveling toward the door. "Morris is coming. I think I'll go work on a new song. When you're ready to discuss what you'd like to do, come find me. Or, most likely, I'll find you."

I nod at him, and all the words I want to say finally break free. "Thank you, Allister Daniels. For everything. Thank you. I don't know what else to say."

His face lights up. "You're my idol, I would do anything for you."

"Me?" I snort in disbelief. "Your idol? You're a celebrity rock god. And an alien!"

He grins. "But I'm no hero. Not like you."

My brows furrow. "I'm not a hero."

Morris bursts through the door, startling my mom awake. She screams before falling on the floor, and Allister runs to her. "Mrs. Baker."

I bolt up, the pain aching along my sides, my head throbbing.

"Ellie." She pushes herself up and scrambles toward me. "Sweetie, baby." Her hands are warm on my face, and her eyes are wide. "Oh goodness."

Morris glances between us, hesitates, then follows Allister out of the room.

"Mom..." I have so many things that need to be said, that threaten to burst forth and linger in the air between us until she takes over, and I can be her child. I want to sob on her shoulder, while she pats my back and tells me not to worry. She's here now. But there's a big chance she can't do that. "Are you okay?"

She kisses me on both cheeks with dry lips and hugs me close to her. Tears fall from her eyes, while her matted hair tickles my cheeks. There's a frenzy in her actions that I'm used to, that I love and recognize. "No, honey, I'm not okay. I'm not— I don't feel quite right. Not yet. But I'm just so happy you're safe. And why are you traveling *alone* with an Ilori boy?"

"Mom, can we not talk about that now?" Seriously, after all this, she wants to discuss my love life? But she ignores that as she squeezes the life out of me, and my ribs still hurt, making breathing extremely difficult.

"Janelle Quicia Baker," she starts, stern, and then stops. "I don't care what you've done or whatever your connection to that Ilori is. You're alive. That's all that counts."

"Mom." My shoulders sag in relief. She hasn't been this lucid in months, and tears blur my vision. "Mama." I hug her as tight as she hugged me and begin to sob. When she pulls away, her gaze flicks back and forth, as if darting around to ward off invisible assailants.

"They're coming, baby. Did you hide my bottle? I need a sip, honey. I'm scared. Just a sip. Don't tell your father, okay?"

Her voice becomes shrill, falling into her familiar loop. "Don't tell him. We can't trust him anymore."

The moment's over, and the pain and anger at the unfairness of it all rushes back into me. I want to smash everything and scream until I'm hoarse, until my parents come back and everything's as it's supposed to be. The numbers tug at my lips just as there's a knock on the door. My mom jumps and throws an unsteady arm around me.

"They're coming."

Five, Allister slips in before wrapping his hands around my mom's shoulders, shushing her, and effectively calming her. He escorts her outside, where she asks him for a sip, something to help with the pain and worry. I don't hear his response.

Four, my blood-soaked shoes, no longer pretty.

Three, a window overlooking, undoubtedly, the Starry Eyed's massive estate.

Two, the Starry Eyed. *The* Starry Eyed.

My breathing slows... *One*, I run my hand through my frizzy Afro sticking straight up... *One*...

Morris pops his head in the doorway. "Are you okay?"

"Morris, please..."

He steps inside and closes the door behind him. He crosses the room and I shakily stand up to greet him beside the bed. I don't care that my jeans are cut or that I look like a mess and I haven't showered in what feels like forever. My worries dissolve into mush when he's in my orbit. He cups my face, then he leans down to kiss my forehead.

I bring my fingers to his cheeks to wipe away the tears there. "We failed."

"It doesn't matter, not right now. You're here, and I thought I lost you. Oh, Ellie. I promised you, I promised..." Morris chokes out the words and I pull him into a hug. "Can you ever forgive me? I can spend the rest of my days trying to earn it. I can—"

"Morris, I love you." My voice is low, and I'm both nervous and ecstatic to release the words I've been holding close to me, too afraid to let go. But I'm not afraid anymore. Anxious, yes, but I've been through a lot these past weeks and I refuse to cower anymore.

"I love you," he mouths into my hair. "I love you. And I'm sorry. So sorry."

We hold each other for the longest time, and I let the sadness out that I've been ignoring for so long. My mom and dad lost themselves, and I lost them. I sob into Morris's shoulder as he rubs my back.

I sniff. "What now?"

Morris pulls away to answer my question but doesn't let go. "I don't know. I have so much to tell you, Ellie. So much I've learned from Brixton." There's a hopelessness to his voice that I've never heard before as he exhales. "I can still broadcast my song. If I manage to get aboard an Ilori ship and upload it within a week. Which I can't... I have to find a way off Earth, which I won't. And I don't know how to fight for Earth and the freedom for both of our people. Ellie, it's impossible." He leans his forehead against mine.

"Nothing we have done has worked out in our favor. But I'm happy that you have your parents here, that you can stay and be safe among the Andarrans. It will be hard saying goodbye, but—"

"Then don't," I say. "Yes, I have my parents, but they're not okay. I have Alice, and this place, it's safe. But I can do more than just survive and hope and wait, Morris. My parents asked me to live for them, not just exist."

"It's too dangerous." His voice falls into a whisper. "I thought I lost you."

"Has your brilliant alien mind ever considered that I don't want to lose you either? That it's too much for one person to save the world? That you need me?" I cock an eyebrow at him, reminding myself of Alice, back when the missing book was my biggest worry.

"I can't ask that of you."

"You didn't ask, *I'm* asking. Do you want me to come with you, Morris?"

He smiles into my cheek, his forehead still pressed against mine. "You are better at people than me. You express yourself so well...and you're smart. I would follow you into a war. I would follow you anywhere, and I don't want to say goodbye." He doesn't meet my eyes.

I could both laugh and cry. Me? Better at people? "Then it's settled." I don't wait for an answer—I'm going anyway. Until I became a librarian, I didn't know I was a rebel. But I became someone who would risk their life every day to bring words and stories to my fellow prisoners. Even though I'm far away, this rebellious part of me still lingers. It demands I fight back against those who would take our humanity, our bodies, our land, our art, without caring or knowing who and what we were. *What we are.*

And I can do more than give books now. I can save humanity. Yeah, there are some shitty humans in this world; I knew more than a few of them. But I won't let humanity die because of them. I have to believe that we can change this world, and maybe even society in the process. Books taught me that anything can happen when you fight for it, and somehow, I missed that message until I was standing in that hospital hallway, staring at those humans behind glass walls.

"So, what's the plan? We find a new ship, encourage others to fight for Earth and labmades with us, because that's legit the only way we could win a war, and then broadcast your song?

And then, assuming we can do all of that in a week without getting killed, we come back and fight?"

Morris lights up our personal bubble with his brightness. "Impossible, right?"

"We've already done some impossible things. This almost sounds easy." I laugh, pecking him on the cheek. "Besides, you need me. Who else will you sing to? Who else can entertain you with Beyoncé dance moves? And most important, who will tell you amazing stories? I have so many more. We still haven't finished Amari's story either."

He lifts me in his arms and brings his lips to mine. "I want to hear them all, Ellie. And about the dance moves," he murmurs. "When we finally have some time alone and no pressing worries…"

"I would like that." I bite my lower lip and still, I'm not afraid. If there was ever someone I'd trust enough, that I'd be free enough, bonded enough to enjoy that with, it's Morris. I let myself live in that fantasy for a moment before pulling back.

"I have to see Alice, and we have to make a plan. Go into space."

Morris's eyes sparkle. "You know, we don't really call it space. We just call it…" I narrow my eyes at him. He chuckles. "We'll just call it space."

My lips quirk. "So, the Starry Eyed, huh?"

He takes my hand in his and leads me to the door. "They're the strangest beings in the universe. The arguments between Cecil and Allister—"

"They always fight! I remember reading that in an interview." We walk down the stairs together, and although my legs ache, I want to go and see Alice. Maybe even my dad, if I can bear it. Maybe my mom, too. They are a painful reminder of the center, but I love them with all my heart. And they *will* come back.

"I think they're genuinely nice beings, though. They saved us. They brought us to their home. If they were Ilori, they would have left us to die." Morris closes his eyes as we step into a hallway. "She's somewhere down here."

"Alice?" I call out. "Alice?" No one answers. There are four different doors down this hallway, and the lighting's low. The hallway is checkered red and purple—the band's signature colors—and has mildly luminescent sconces between the doors.

We hear a voice call from inside a locked room farthest down the hall. "Let me out of here." My father's voice calls from inside. "I have a purpose. I must serve them."

I cringe. "Will he ever be...himself again?"

"Yes. The half-solutions program requires a monthly injection. Without it, he should revert back to himself in time." Sadness threads through his voice.

"How long?"

"I don't know, Ellie. However long it takes to work out of his system. I'm sorry I cannot guarantee when that will be."

Another door swings open. Colorful lights dance across the marble floors and walls as Alice steps out. Her eyes are bright and wide, and she's wearing a long yellow dress that makes her shimmer like a beam of sunlight. Her thick hair is swept over her shoulders.

"Ellie. Oh God." She throws herself into my arms. I hug her, ignoring my father in the other room as I've ignored him for many months now. I know that he wouldn't want me to agonize over something I can't change. But I will save him. *I will.*

Another member of the Starry Eyed leans against the doorway. Her name is Whisper, Whisper Landsome. She wears a bright blue gown, same style as Alice's, that sparkles like shards of crystal. Her expertly cut black bob swings on the sides of her face as she turns toward me. Shimmery, gray-black

eyes flick to mine. Also not contacts. How did no one realize they're aliens? We all just assumed their brand was colorful eyes, questionable costumes and strange accents no one
could quite place.

"How are you?" Whisper asks, a polite smile on her face.

"Wow. You're even more beautiful in real life," I blurt,
and immediately wish I could take it back. Embarrassment
flares up inside of me and I step away from Alice and closer
to Morris, my safe zone.

"Thank you." She smiles widely, even though she must be
used to hearing the compliments.

I look back at Alice. "Are you okay?"

"I'm fine. Avi was supposed to give me the vaccine. Instead, they kept me hidden in an apartment upstairs with your
mom. I'm sure the reason I'm here is because of you, right?"
Her eyebrows raise.

"I told Morris to save you."

"Well, thank you, Morris." She peers behind me at him.
"Anyway, we lived like that until everyone was vaccinated.
They took my mom and baby sis somewhere, but Avi said
that they're safe and we'll get them out. I won't lie, the first
few days were hard, but then Avi brought us upstate. It was
quiet. Everything's gone up there...except a weird little cottage
outside Albany, I think? I was getting some firewood when a
bunch of Ilori guards came. They collected us all... And Ellie?
Your mom...she's not well. And your father... I didn't know
he wasn't lucid anymore. Why didn't you tell me?"

I wish I could say that I was afraid that if I told someone
else, it would make it real, but I don't want to admit that to
her, not now. I have to be like stone for whatever lies ahead.

She continues with her story. "Those guards—they were
working for some commander, somewhere. They took us in

this weird plane type thing across the country and brought us here. And you know the rest."

I touch her arm, bringing her back to the moment. "I'm so happy you're okay. I was worried about you."

There's a sadness etched onto her features. "I'm happy you're okay. I thought you died. I had no idea." She hugs me again and then laughs; it's just as loud and vivacious as I remember. "Wait till Jackson Hughes finds out that I've been hanging with the Starry Eyed. Bet he'd feel bad then."

I shake my head. Still Alice.

There are footsteps down the hall that shake us out of our moment. We turn just as Allister appears. "Come on. Let's meet in the den before you leave."

"Leave?" I ask, but Allister is already gone.

Whisper cocks her eyebrow at Alice. "We'd better do what he says. He's been insufferable since he lost Sidra." Her eyes flick to another locked door down the hallway. "No one wants one of his tantrums."

"According to two separate sources, he has many tantrums," Morris whispers in my ear. I would expect nothing less from Allister Daniels, the genius musician. He's everything I thought he would be.

We follow Whisper and Alice into a den in the opposite wing of the house. I want to stop and stare at all the details, the beauty and richness. But I know that there are more important matters at stake than admiring the architecture.

Alice and Whisper lounge on a couch beside each other, and I swear they share shy glances. But it's the platters of food sitting on a table near the far wall that catch my attention. I make a beeline toward them and start shoving random pastries—where did they even get these—and cold cuts into my mouth. I'm chugging my second glass of water when Cecil and Avrola enter the room.

Morris hovers over the food table beside me, glancing my way between bites of an apple and sips of orange juice. I guess neither of us realized how hungry we were. But he's happy. All in all, we failed, but there's hope that we can still do this, we can still save humanity. We won't give up.

Allister enters through another door, a cello between his arms. I gaze at its beauty with longing. It's been forever since I played one; since I lost myself in the music and notes, the strings and bow. It used to be a sort of medicine for me.

Allister sets the cello down against the empty wooden chair.

My stomach flips as Cecil takes a seat and pulls a guitar into his lap, while Rupert—he's the stoic one—grabs the other. Whisper languidly gets up from the couch and positions herself behind the drums. Are they going to play music for us? I sink down next to Morris on the love seat and I tap my leg on the floor in excitement.

Avrola slides into the empty seat beside Alice. I lean over to them.

"Avrola, I just... I just want to thank you for saving my family. For saving Alice. I can't thank you enough."

Avrola's head tilts and their lips quirk. "You just did."

I smile with a small shrug. I take in the rest of the room. We're a weird group, and it's a beautiful picture. I wish I could actually take one to savor for later when my self-doubt creeps in and tells me none of this was real.

"Thank you all for joining us." Allister's voice booms like a thespian. "Before we play some music for you—and Ellie, you'll be joining us—we want to discuss what will happen next." My mouth flaps open as he crosses his legs and looks at Morris. "IpS1L was destroyed. And you guys need to find a way to get away from Earth, right?"

We both dip our chins. How does he seem to know so much?

Allister's voice cuts through my thoughts. "We know your mission, and we've agreed to help you."

"What?" I ask at the same time Morris asks, "How?" We exchange a look before focusing on Allister.

"We have two Andarran ships here, below our feet. You and Ellie can take one as soon as you're ready. I would suggest sooner rather than later." He chews his bottom lip, his eyes slightly glazed as if he's lost in thought. "You need time. And you need allies. Your mother has found some, but they won't be enough. Go to my home, go to Andarra. You will find many sympathetic to your cause, especially with Ellie by your side."

"How did you know I'd go?" I ask, and Alice pats my arm.

"I sing and know things, Janelle Baker." He winks at me. "I know you aren't the type to leave the fate of your world in someone else's hands. You're stubborn, determined, smart and, above all else, hopeful even when the odds aren't on your side. Morris needs you."

Morris glances at me for confirmation, but I have no words. How does he know me that well? How?

And then it strikes me. It's happening now. Our adventure, our mission, our purpose. My nerves fray a bit. But I push them aside to listen to Allister.

"Janelle, your parents need to stay with us. We can help them, but your father…he's dangerous the way he is right now, hopefully it'll only last a few more weeks." He tosses a glance Morris's way before continuing. "We will always be safe on Earth, and this place is a fortress. The Ilori know better than to attack us, or our ships. We have a peace accord, after all." Allister's lips lift.

"Alice, and Avi, if you want to stay, you are more than welcome. We could use your help. We're already run off our feet with the humans living all over the compound."

"I want to stay," Alice says, her eyes flicking toward Whisper's.

She's literally known Whisper a few hours and already she's in love. I shake my head. Alice lives and loves better than anyone I know.

"I'll be able to provide help with the deprogramming of Janelle Baker's father, and can assist in training humans in combat," Avrola announces.

"Really?" I gasp. "You can do that?"

Avrola casts me a look of confusion. "I just said I could."

Rupert strums his guitar. "We're delighted to have you both."

Cecil leans forward, catching my attention. "Janelle, your parents, your friend Alice—they'll be safe here while they wait for your return. We promise to protect them."

My eyes fill, and I have to look away while I swallow the lump in my throat.

"You can do this," Allister claims, pointing to his head oddly. "I know it."

I look up at him through the tears. "I'll do my best."

Morris nudges me with his shoulder.

"Ellie, you'll do fabulously," Cecil says warmly.

Allister rolls his eyes. "Anyway, Ellie, we are going to play the song 'Lost With You.' I know you know it. It's your favorite, right?"

I nod, too nervous for words.

"If you would be so kind." He gestures to the cello leaning against the chair.

"Do we have time for this?" I squeak. The fate of our world depends on Morris and me. Already, my stomach flips with worry that we'll fail again.

"You need this," Allister answers. "We Andarrans believe

there's always time for a little fun. Breaks up the monotony of peril, don't you think?"

I laugh once. Yeah, I might need this. "I'm a little rusty."

Morris squeezes my hand before I stand up and arrange myself on the chair. I brace the cello between my legs.

I pick up the bow and run a scale. The sensation of it; the way it instantly trickles back to me and into my muscles that have been waiting for this one use, makes my fingers move of their own accord. It feels like home.

The world is broken, but right now, it doesn't matter. I have my cello and a story in my mind. And love, so much love.

I take a deep breath and remember the chords and notes and sounds from memory. Allister sits in his chair, humming a bit, while Cecil plucks at the bass and Rupert strums his guitar. And Alice sits there, waiting, staring at Whisper while she twirls her drumsticks. I fiddle with my bow, and I can't help but look at Morris. His nose twitches as the corner of his mouth lifts.

And then Allister begins to count off, and I realize I'm playing with the Starry Eyed. I want to scream and run away. Laugh at the ridiculousness.

A few weeks ago, I was imprisoned in a center. Surviving but not really living. Now I'm here, playing with the Starry Eyed. I've never been more alive than in this moment, which is funny, because soon I'll be in space. Where I could die. It hasn't been easy, but it's been an adventure straight out of a book.

I run my bow across the cello, opening the song, and playing what I can from memory. It's not perfect, but it helps to calm my shaking soul.

Allister begins to sing. Goose bumps rise on my arms. *"Lost in the cosmos, stuck in the colonies. Worlds upon worlds in the galaxies. The spectrum as far as our eyes can see… Honey, do you trust me? Past the sun, on the other side of the moon, I know you're scared, we'll be there soon. You read me the book, I'll sing you the tune. I make you laugh, you make me swoon."*

Morris mouths the words, probably too nervous to sing along with Allister. It's the cheesiest thing, but I love every second of it. I *need* every second of it, like it's sloughing off all the fear and death of the past few weeks and months and years. I'm a teenager again. So is Alice, as she stands and sways to the beat like a wild child. Cecil, Whisper, Allister and Rupert give it all they've got, and I pluck at strings, sliding my bow by rote. Right now, we're friends, family, musicians. We're alive. And this music is life.

My eyes flit to Morris, who catches my gaze. He beams like the sun; the Ilori boy who was shamed for his feelings before coming to Earth is singing a love song, just to me. *"You put your hand in mine, taking me with you... I love you."*

The way he looks at me, like I'm the only person in the room, heats my cheeks and melts my heart.

"I love you... I love you."

CHAPTER 27

"It's no use going back to yesterday, because I was a different person then."

—Lewis Carroll

JANELLE

The ship's in the basement below the atrium. We'll have to drive it out, and then blast off into space—I can't even believe that's the phrase I'm going with. Thankfully, Morris knows how to operate it to reach Andarra. In space, so I've been told, there are bridges called *Linx* between planets and patches of the universe that make it quick to navigate. I wish there was a book I could read about traveling the galaxy, but I'll take the aliens' word for it.

Once on Andarra, we'll contact his mother, and find out

how to upload his song. In the meantime, we'll have to persuade people to join our war, all within a week.

Honestly, I'm not sure I'm the best person for the job, given my lack of conversational skills with anyone but Morris, yet through everything, I've learned I'm capable of fighting and caring.

The road ahead is long, but there's hope.

I've changed my clothes once more into a loose white blouse that looks amazing when tucked into my new stretchy black pants. Allister had a closet of strange clothes and shoes, several in my size. He practically forced my feet into black boots to match the pants, and although they're the most expensive thing I've worn, I can't say I hate them. I did forgo the glittery black cape he offered, though...there's a time and place for a cape.

I showered and Cecil did my hair into two French braids that dangle down my back under my purple hat: my purple crown. It's a bit more frayed now, and loose, but it's a reminder that my dad is still with me, and that I'm loved. I will come back to them. I will save them.

Allister assured me, and Morris did as well, that I don't need a space suit for traveling into the universe. While humans lacked proper technology, Andarrans don't. But still I was nervous, so Allister gave me two items; a tiny chip that sank into my ear painlessly and will provide translation for any alien language, and a drink he called traveling serum. It tasted sweet, like a candy bar, and since drinking it, my body feels oddly lighter, and I've been able to take longer breaths. I don't think there's a way to feel prepared, but I'm ready to go.

After, we said our goodbyes.

We hugged.

We shed more tears than any of us have probably shed before. We made promises to be back soon. I kissed my mom even though she was asleep, and went to see my father, although he didn't really know who I was. Both goodbyes nearly broke my heart, but I'm fighting for them. I have hope they'll fight, too.

We're almost ready when Allister pulls me aside.

"Janelle, there is no limit to love, nor is there a limit to potential."

I don't know what he means by that, but I nod anyway.

Whisper leans against the wall with Alice wrapped in her arms. "The pod you're taking once transported Allister and Cecil here from Andarra. You'll notice the seats have scratch marks because, even then, Cecil grated on his nerves."

"I heard that!" Cecil responds. He's standing beside Rupert, who's inspecting the outer rim of the open hatch.

I stifle a giggle. "You know, for two people who argue a lot, I sense a lot of love between you. Sometimes people don't know how to express their feelings quite well..." I glance at Morris. "Sometimes they argue and blame others, or they hide everything inside, unsure and afraid to—to admit. But you two, you make music together." I think of our stories and songs. Of Alice and her newest love. Avrola and their undying loyalty to Morris. My mom and dad. "You're lucky to have each other."

Allister shoots me a look full of so many conflicting emotions that I can't quite place one. He swings his arms for a few beats. "Come here, Cecil. I'm sorry I'm such a scamp to you." Allister and Cecil hug, and everyone freezes as if moving while it's happening will result in another feud. "Let's try to be better to each other. If you start each day with an apology for what you did—"

Cecil huffs and shakes his head. My heart feels lighter for their levity. I'm scared, maybe even stalling.

"Janelle..." Allister's eyes glisten. "You're my favorite. And

Morris…" He turns to Morris who leans in the doorway of the ship. "Never stop telling her you love her."

"Never." Morris doesn't hesitate.

I step closer to Morris and the hatch. "You know we'll be back, right?"

Allister glances up at something beyond my sight. "We'll be waiting."

Rupert's voice carries across the atrium. "There's music in there. Listen to it. It's from Andarra."

Cecil swipes a tear from his cheek. "When you get there, catalog every memory you make so that you can tell me later. Help me remember my home."

"*Our* home," Allister chokes, throwing an arm around Cecil's shoulders.

I don't miss home. New York City stopped feeling like home and more like a prison before the Ilori came. I push down a laugh. I'll have explored the sky before stepping foot in my city again. It hardly feels real.

We wave one more time and close the hatch.

The ship is small, one room and one bathroom, and colorful. It's like being in a modern club on the Lower East Side. But cleaner and definitely more beautiful, artistic. The colors on the paneled walls change as we step farther inside. From midnight blue to a soothing lavender. I touch the panel beside me, and a brilliant purple seeps from my fingers until it surrounds us.

"What do you think that means?"

Morris does the same, and it turns a rich, dark green. "Something to do with emotions and auras…one never knows with Andarrans."

He tosses me a smile as he sets the supply pack by our feet. It's got all the necessities—medicine, my books and music. There's more music in it than before, but it's much lighter now. Allister gave Morris a hard drive with the best music in the human experience, so he said. Morris left a lot of vinyl records behind, including the ones we borrowed from poor Mrs. Turner. I promised to give those back, and I will. *We* will.

We strap in beside each other in the two seats across from the ship's console. My hand grips Morris's as he steers us forward into the sprawling back gardens of the mansion. It's beautiful, and though it's dark out here, I can see green grass—oh how I've missed the sight—and flowers and an elaborate water fountain. I wish we'd seen more of it before now.

"We'll be back," Morris says as if reading my mind.

I shake with nervous energy, and I begin counting everything I see in my vicinity. *Five*, Morris, who's currently humming David Bowie's "Space Oddity" to the rhythm of my counts. I laugh, but I also can't stop counting.

Four, the console on a ship that'll take us somewhere beyond the only world I know.

Three, the sky that's bright and terrifying and mysterious.

Two, me. Janelle Baker. Explorer and Possible Savior of Humanity.

One, I add, chuckling at my own nonsense, the shakes rolling off my shoulders. *One*…a love, new and welcome.

Morris hits a few buttons, and the panels light up. It's really happening. "Are you ready?"

I feel like speaking will allow my heart to jump out of my chest and the air to leave my lungs. So I don't answer, and rest my head on his shoulder.

I have to count again. It's too much.

Five, my heart pounding in my chest. *Four*, the paneled walls that are a light pink. *Three*, my books. *Two*, the music. *One*. I breathe. I don't need one. *Breathe in, breathe out. Relax. Sense.* I squeeze Morris's hand for dear life. I'm going to be okay. Slow and steady. *I'm going to be okay.* We're going to be okay.

"Hold on, my love."

I grip him tighter as we shoot through the night sky. My stomach plummets as we thread higher and higher and higher and the world below becomes smaller and smaller. And then we're past the sky. The sky is not a limit. I want to laugh. I want to scream. Earth is below us, and it's like every picture and movie and book and song I've read, seen and sung. It feels familiar. I know it. The rest is unknown, like stories I've not yet read.

"I'm scared," I say shakily.

Morris hums "Across the Universe," reminding me of the first time we met, when he calmed me in the storage closet. I add the words to it as minutes and Ilori ships pass, our Andarran ship keeping us safe, and planets I've seen only on posters or in planetariums come into view. They are wild, spectacular colors. Different than what I knew. Larger than I could ever have expected. I feel so small. Insignificant. Nothing could have prepared me for all of this. I gasp but keep singing. It's beautiful, this universe. So beautiful. My eyes widen, my horizons broaden. There's so much we didn't know, so much more than our world. And I'm going to see it all.

I look over at Morris. He presses his lips to mine and whispers, "You've got stars in your eyes."

I shake my head and kiss him one more time, the realization hitting. Legendary love. Stars in our eyes... *Stars in my eyes just for you, I just want to be with you.* Andarra has no time. *I know many things, Janelle Baker. Oh, how I love a love story.* Idol. Hero. *You read me the book, I'll sing you the tune.*

It was about us all along.

"How long have you known?" I ask, his lips centimeters from mine. His hazel eyes sparkle while he holds me close. The universe is right outside the window.

"Not much longer than you," he answers. "But I did tell

you—" I narrow my eyes at him, discouraging him from that line of thought. "Does it scare you? Does it weigh heavy on you? The knowledge of us?"

"No. *No*," I say with an ease I didn't have before. "It's freeing. It doesn't just give me hope…it gives me so much to look forward to." I can't help the smile that creeps along my face and the way my heart flips. "You and me."

We are alive. A story and a song. Neither of those things can die.

"Always." Morris leans in and kisses me again. "And Ellie?"

"Yes?"

"Before it…before you met Brixton, and the ship exploded, and you…died, you began to tell me a story about Amari and a world of magic. We have a while to go before we reach the outer worlds and I can establish a connection with my mother, so…in the meantime, would you tell me what happens?"

"It would be my pleasure."

Morris tinkers with the control panel and the music that streams forth is unlike any either of us have heard before. It's both enchanting and fitting as we navigate through space.

I take a deep breath, settling into the seat. "So…where did we leave off?"

★ ★ ★ ★ ★

ACKNOWLEDGMENTS

I would like to say a gigantic THANK YOU to:

The reader holding this book, thank you, first and foremost. You are the stars sparkling above on the darkest of nights.

My mom, who is undoubtedly in some heavenly universe right now, beating Prince at *Scattergories* and adding backup vocals for Aretha Franklin. I miss you.

My dad, for encouraging me to write, and for providing me with the most ridiculous stories. You are the definition of endurance.

My editor, Natashya Wilson, whose love of *The Greatest Showman* introduced me to new music and whose enthusiasm kept me smiling as we worked together to make this the absolute best book it could be. It is such a privilege and pleasure to work with you.

Dr. Uwe Stender. You not only believed in this book, you believed in me. You were with me on the sidelines, and you gave me confidence when I needed it most. I'm so happy to have had you championing my work. We stayed the course.

Everyone at Inkyard Press! Anne-Marie Rutella, whose copyedits made this book shiny and clean; Bess Brasswell; Linette Kim; Brittany Mitchell; Gina Macdonald; Connolly Bottom; Gabby Vicedomini—who fought for this book (I can't wait to see pictures of your wedding!); and Laura Gianino. Thank you so, so much for choosing Ellie and M0Rr1S.

Hillary Jacobson, who helped me shape this book; Amanda Farbanish, whose excitement encouraged me; sensitivity readers, whose insights made the story stronger; and Natalie Lakosil, who I'm beyond lucky to have in my corner. Natalie, thank you for choosing me.

Tracy Badua, Kendell Penington, T.S. Bazelli and Rachel Somer: I cannot thank you enough for your kindness, for letting me whine incessantly, for sending out Target boxes filled with Raisinets (Tracy), for sharing your talent, time and friendship. You all deserve a million boxes of German chocolate. I couldn't have done any of this without you.

Mel Howard, Maria Houssain, Kate Talbot, Jessica James, Kat Enright, Ayana Gray, J. Elle, Gail Villanueva, Faridah Àbíké-Íyímídé and the Inkyard Squad (Mara Rutherford, Laura Namey, Hannah Capin and Eric Smith): you all got me through every patch of self-doubt and kept me on track. Thank you a million times.

Justina Ireland for selecting me as a Writing in the Margins mentee. Those months changed my entire world, as did my mentor and friend, Tamara Mataya. I'm inhaling art and exhaling words because of you.

The B-Street 6 crew: Cass Francis, Tori Bovalino, Mara Rutherford, Adiba Jaigirdar and Rose Deniz. Meeting up with you all was one of the best moments of my life abroad. Your friendship and laughter sticks with me when I'm feeling isolated. I wonder where we'll go next.

Adrienne, thank you for supporting me, for being excited with me, for being a cheerleader. Amani, Amya and Pudge (we really should call you Christopher, huh?), you all have massively big hearts and you are so, so intelligent. I can't wait to see what the future holds for you and I'm always here, cheering you on.

My sisterpants, Nicole Redd-McIntosh. You are incredibly talented, and you light up the world with your creations. I'll always be awed and inspired by you. And I'm so glad to call you my family.

My guardian angel, Kristin Olsen. I'll miss you forever.

Darrah, you read my first (terrible) book in college, and you liked it. You have no idea that your encouragement was what got me to write again and again. You believed in me, and you made me believe in myself. Grams is always smiling down on you, I know it.

RAPID ROUND. Saundra Mitchell, Laura Weymouth, Erin Hahn, Joelle Charbonneau, Ashley Poston, Amie Kaufman, MK England, Dhonielle Clayton, Kayla Ancrum, Claudia Gray, Angie Thomas, Justin A. Reynolds, Julie Murphy, David Levithan, Gita Trelease, Suzanne Collins, Leigh Bardugo, Sandhya Menon, Becky Albertalli, Stephenie Meyer, Star Wars, for being Ellie's favorite stories that she both reads and shares with Morris, and for your incredible blurbs. Also, Brooklyn Public Library, Milford Town Library (especially Kathie Kirchner) and West Warwick Public Library. You were home to me. Beyoncé, David Bowie, Prince, Stevie Wonder, Coldplay, Elton John and "All the Stars" by Kendrick Lamar feat. SZA. I'm still listening. And to the Class of 2k20 and *The Sound of Stars* street team: you have no idea how much I appreciate you and the work you do to help me succeed. You all are the absolute best.

The Hirt family: Stephanie, Ingeborg, Markus, Manfred and baby Erik. Thank you all for accepting me, for your support, for reading this in English and for all the delicious *semmelknödel*.

Christoph, thank you for reading this book when it was only half an idea and coming along with me on this adventure. Your stubborn belief in me keeps me going (and drives me mad). I love you, my hubular spectacular.

Liv. Nothing in the world could have prepared me for how much I'd love you. You're so sassy, outspoken, smart and bold and I wouldn't have you any other way. Please know I'm proud of you, forever and always.

To all the librarians, media specialists, teachers, booksellers, book bloggers, vloggers, bookstagrammers and the online book community: you are superstars, and so much of this community relies on you. Thank you for everything you do.

To the teens who found this book while meandering through the bookstore or skimming the library shelves and decided to give it a chance, I wrote this for you.

Thank you for reading The Sound of Stars!
Turn the page for a sneak peek at
Alechia Dow's next intergalactic novel,
The Kindred!

The Inkara Royal Palace of Maru
For Immediate Release

PRINCESS LATANYA QADIN AND HER KINDRED, JOHANN KAO, TO WED

Her Royal Highness, Princess LaTanya, and her Kindred, Johann Kao, from Beyla-Monchuri, are officially set to wed in the coming week.

King Jevor, The Duke of Estrella, and the Queen Mother are delighted with the news.

Before their impending nuptials, the royal family will tour the Monchuri system to celebrate with their subjects and to schedule interviews with each planetary leader to discuss what this news will bring for the future of the Qadin Kingdom.

Thank you for welcoming Johann to our family.

chapter one

———

FELIX

Looking this pretty takes time.

The clothes must be expensive but not gaudy, complex but not as if I put in all my effort. My hair must look styled but like I've walked through a gentle, aimless breeze, and I cannot be sweaty, which, on a planet known for having three suns, is rather difficult.

Parties that start early are the worst anyway. Everyone should be thanking me, not giving me the stink eye, which they are. For some reason, they expect me to actually show up on time.

"Look who decided to join us," the drummer from The Monchoos mutters as I step into the dimly lit hallway. We're from the same planet, Maru-Monchuri, but there's no comradery between us. Who could be friends with a pompous, spoiled duke like me, right? I could be better, could be the person I'm expected to be, but why waste the effort?

I give him a quick wink as I look around. This coveted, hard-to-get gig's on Outpost 32: a man-made station between XiGra and Hali-Monchuri—Joy's homeworld. XiGra's a rich planet that's not a part of our Qadin Kingdom (yet), and Hali *is* a part of the Qadin Kingdom, but also extremely poor. Thankfully, this outpost is the perfect mashup of the two: international enough to be popular among wealthy travelers, cool and gritty enough to reflect the rock 'n' roll aesthetic.

The black stone walls are plastered with band posters, grime, and beneath it all, the touch of musicians that would either make it or break it on stage. I wonder which one we'll be tonight.

Joy *humphs* in my brain, but doesn't elaborate.

She said she wouldn't watch me choke, couldn't be a part of another concert experience that sets off her anxiety. And yet, she can't stay out of my head.

Of course, I'd be paired with the most judgmental Kindred in the system.

A coordinator peeks out from the curtain, a detached comm-ball hovering around their blue tentacled head. Dosani. They're music geniuses, and probably the friendliest species in the universe. They speak Dosan into the comm, and then it flies over to us, translating.

"You're late. Get on stage." The voice doesn't sound all that friendly. Weird.

My bandmates stalk behind the curtain, leaving me there in the deserted hallway for just a second. My nerves begin to spiral in the pit of my stomach, and I reach out to her, because she's there, she's always there—well, usually there—and she knows what I need.

Joy, I say through our connection. We've been together since birth. I'm exactly three minutes older than her, and I had to wait for our chips to sync for those solid three minutes. Not that I can remember. Still, that's the longest I've been without her in my life.

The Kindred Program was created decades ago, after The Second Chaos, aka "The Revolution." Apparently, the poor rose up, feeling like their voices weren't heard by the rich, powerful rulers, and so the lower classes threatened a reckoning. Maru's top scientists offered a solution: the citizens of the Monchuri system could be paired, one from the upper class, one from the lower. Establishing this would allow everyone to have a voice that could be heard, blah-blah-blah, and no more revolution. How could anyone ignore a mind pairing?

Given that I'm a duke and cousin to the Qadin royals, I was supposed to be paired with someone a little closer in economic class, because not just anyone should have a voice with the royals. Yet, I got paired with Joy.

Joy, who is dreadfully poor, living on the most impoverished planet in our system. Joy, who is my best friend, my moral compass, my judge, jury, and sometimes executioner. She's not always my biggest fan, but she supports me in whatever I choose to do. Which isn't much. I like traveling, adventuring to new worlds as long as my amenities are acceptable, and playing in a band. We both love music. She loves listening in as I practice, hearing new melodies outside of her Halin hymns. She thinks music has the power to transform you and make you feel anything and everything. She believes in it, just like she believes in me.

Which is why I need her right now.

Because as much as I love music—and I do, with all of my small black heart—my stage fright keeps me from making it. Already, the nausea creeps up my throat and my breaths come too fast to let oxygen into my lungs.

Joy, I say again with some urgency.

Yes, Felix…? Her question whispers through our connection. She's there inside my mind like a perfectly clear radio channel, the only one on my brain's frequency. She can read my thoughts, converse with me, feel my emotions. She can see what I see. She's the one consistency in my world, and I can't live without her. Even if our worlds seem hell-bent on keeping us apart... Nah, I don't need to be thinking about *that* now.

Tell me I can do it. I run a hand through my hair and blow air between my teeth. My feet bounce on the dirty tiles. *Tell me it's not a big deal. Easy.*

You're the most talented person I know. You can do this. And I swear, if you make me sick again, Felix, I will murder you.

I chuckle. *It's not my fault you get sympathy pains.*

The stronger we accept the bond in our minds, the stronger the feelings, including negative ones. Pain, illness, anxiety, sadness, anger... It can be so intense in such bonds that if one Kindred were to die, the other might follow shortly after. It occurs in maybe one in a thousand pairings, but it happens. Until recently, I would have thought Joy and I would be one of those pairs. But she's been pulling away more and more.

Go get on stage! They've been waiting hours for you and your beautiful voice. She laughs, shifting her body on the couch in her apartment, nearly toppling her sketch pad off her lap. *Get up there*, she commands again, and then she's gone. She's turned the volume down to a whisper and tuned me out.

I hate that she does that. I also don't know *how* she does that. Why can't we just always stay connected? Who needs space? Not me.

With that thought, I take another deep breath and strut down the hall. I tug on the velvet red curtain and step through onto the sticky levitating stage. We lift a few feet off the ground, but thankfully, unlike in most of the more modern venues, the floor doesn't spin. Thank the *Gods*.

My bandmates stare at me, wide-eyed as the crowd goes

wild. The excitement in the room is palpable, like a glittery haze that coats my limbs and makes me want to sing and dance and be alive. My chest rises and falls in sync with their cheers and stomps.

I both love it and hate it up here.

The band's set up and the microphone's hot. The lights are low, the room's packed, and I'm going to sing, even if my stomach churns and threatens to upchuck my dinner of steamed hopfal leaves packed with gooey black rice.

I swagger up to that mic, my legs wobbling like jelly. "Hello. I'm—"

"I love you, Felix!" someone in the audience shouts, though who it is, I can't see. They're all shadows and faceless bodies from up here. Just the way I like them.

The light beats down on me, and sweat prickles at the edge of my scalp.

"I love you, too." I laugh into the mic, which earns a few grumbles from my bandmates. "Now I want to..." I trail off as a shadowed body comes into view. Their eyes bore into mine. The face is one I'd know anywhere. A face that shouldn't be here.

My throat dries up as he stalks through the crowd waiting for me to finish. I step back, almost stumbling over my own feet. With a fleeting glance at my bandmates, I trip offstage and toward him.

The crowd boos. My brain's short-circuiting. He's not supposed to be in this part of my life. He's part of the Duke's life, the one I shrug off and leave at home whenever the opportunity arises. His being here can only be bad for me. It can only mean trouble.

My feet are on autopilot as he nods his head over to a private booth reserved just for us. I can feel my bandmates' glares, but they begin strumming on their guitars as if I was never really a part of their group anyway—which I wasn't. The drums pick up and the audience forgets all about me and my promises of a good time as they dance.

My visitor wears a long black tunic embroidered with crimson thread and matching pants. His golden hair's slicked back and his vibrant golden eyes flash as I slide into the booth first. He takes the seat opposite me, flips on the privacy switch in the center of the table, and then folds his hands on the table as a translucent wall falls around the perimeter of the booth.

We sit in silence for only a moment but it feels like a lifetime as my heart hammers unsteadily in my chest.

"Do you know why I'm here, Duke Hamdi?" he asks finally, his head tilting to the side.

I suck my teeth. "My parents think I'm at some interplanetary summit for the children of dignitaries on Kippilu and they found out I was lying?"

"I don't work for your parents." Arren huffs, leaning back. "I work for the Qadins. You may remember them as the royals that pay for the pricey state-of-the-art ships you use to jump planets and slum in music halls—" he waves his arm at the room "—your flashy clothes and instruments that you seemingly never play on stage, and the countless opportunities that have been provided to you over the course of your short life." There's a bitter edge to his words that has me sitting taller. "You are a disappointment to their name."

Arren's a royal advisor—*the* royal advisor, and he has done enough over the years to earn my fear and respect. But there has to come a time when I crack.

Tonight, I was going to finally get over my stage fright and make a name for myself that had nothing to do with my actual name. All of my hard work, practicing until late at night, and pushing myself to new limits both artistically and mentally would have paid off. Instead, I'm here, missing my chance, being scolded for chasing my dreams by the royal advisor that threatened my Kindred's life.

I will not forget, and I will not forgive.

"Do you think by doing all the Qadins' dirty work, it'll make you one of them? Do you think they consider you their equal?" I try to twist my lips at the corners, even if dread sinks into the bottom of my stomach. "What'll happen if I go into politics like they so desire and come for your job?" I'm balancing on the tip of a sword, and at any second, I'll get cut.

"You're a fool." Arren chuckles, though there's no humor in it. "I do not wish to be a Qadin. I am not their equal. And you…" He trails off suddenly to look at the carefree dancers and the band that went on without me. "You have responsibilities that come with your title."

"There are other dukes, other cousins." My nostrils flare as I watch him. "Why do they hold me to such high standards when the others are free to do what they want?"

"Because you are meant to be much more than you are. Soon, you'll need to step in and step up." He holds my gaze now, and in it, I see a flicker of something that's not frustration. It's a thoughtful, plotting look. Arren's got plans, and he wants me to follow them. "Soon your Kindred will marry and move on with her life. But where will *you* be? Failing on the stages of dingy bars—because at some point the good ones will stop booking you no matter your title—and burning through your trust fund? Do you know how many people would kill for the opportunities you have?"

Something about that question furthers my unease. Who would kill for opportunities? The Kindred Program makes sure that people are heard and happy. Murder doesn't happen anymore. Citizens are content with their roles in life.

"Don't you have other things to do, like I don't know, figure out the Ilori conflict or something? Aren't they trying to colonize us? The Qadins should be putting their energy into that, not whatever this is. What could they possibly want with me? I have no power or ambitions in politics."

"The Qadins didn't send me, so I don't rightly know." He stands, running his hands down his spotless tunic as I digest that news. If they didn't send him, why is he here? "*I* came because I am looking out for *your* best interests. King Qadin would have no issue ignoring your existence, but I know you have a great destiny. One day, you may have power, and you could create change. Stop this music nonsense and join me, join my side. Together, we can pave our own paths in this kingdom. You could find your voice, since you can't seem to find it on stage, and finally reach your potential. I believe in you—can you say that about anyone else?"

I barely keep the anger from my voice as I shuffle my legs beneath the table. "Is that why you threatened my Kindred?" I remember the way he had guards surround her without her noticing, pointing their weapons at her as he made me promise to never see her. Never allow her into my heart. "Was that your way of believing in me?"

"I was following orders. I work for the Qadins, but I am not one of them, and with Princess LaTanya's impending nuptials with her Kindred, Johann Kao, I never will be." He shakes his head, as if he didn't mean to say that. Admittedly, it was a weird thing to say, but then I do know from the tabloids that he's enamored with LaTanya… Still, that thought flees my mind as he continues, "They were right to make sure you keep your distance from your Kindred. There is only one person you can rely on, Duke Hamdi, and I believe, in time, you'll come to see that. Someday soon, you will need my help. And I won't hesitate to give it." He slips a card onto the table and with that, he strides off, disappearing into the dancing fray.

My fingers edge the tip of the card. It's solid black. It's an upload, something I'd need to stick into a holo-frame monitor to access. It probably has Arren's private info encrypted for me, so that I can learn to live up to my potential and what—overthrow the Qadins and stage a coup with him? Why would I do that? What makes him think I want any responsibility that big? Despite what he says, I learned early that my name gets me in doors, gets me a seat at the table, but that's it. I don't matter. No one cares about my opinions or thoughts, so why should I have them anymore?

I shove it deep in my pocket and punch the button in the center of the table for service.

He chose this night, this moment, on purpose. He probably even had Outpost 32 book this gig for me just so he could ruin it. So I would be miserable and malleable to whatever he's plotting. But he underestimated my indifference.

At least I'm here where I can get drunk enough to drown my sorrow as the crowd dances and the music thrums through them, and me.

At least his newest power move will keep me from thinking about Joy.

Copyright © 2022 by Alechia Dow